GOD'S ACRE

GOD'S ACRE

*The flowers and
animals of the parish churchyard*

Francesca Greenoak

Illustrations by
Clare Roberts

Foreword by
Richard Mabey

E.P. DUTTON · NEW YORK

First published, 1985, in the United States
by E.P. Dutton.

Published in the United States by E.P. Dutton,
2 Park Avenue, New York, N.Y. 10016

Library of Congress Catalog Card Number: 85-70847

ISBN: 0-525-24315-1

Produced by WI Books Ltd., 39 Eccleston Street, London SW1W 9NT
Managing editor: Sue Parish
Designer: David Goodman
Editors: Flax Green Associates
Filmsetting: Tradespools Limited, Frome, Somerset
Colour reproduction: Preager Blackmore Limited, Eastbourne, Sussex
Printed and bound in the Netherlands by: Royal Smeets Offset bv, Weert

10 9 8 7 6 5 4 3 2 1

First edition

CONTENTS

FOREWORD

CHURCHYARDS ARE AMONG THE MOST POWERFUL symbols of shelter in our culture. Since the time of their establishment they have been sanctuaries for the living as well as for the dead. When Thomas Gray sat in the gathering shadows of St Giles's at Stoke Poges in Buckinghamshire and began his 'Elegy Written in a Country Church Yard', he captured this atmosphere of quiet and security in a poem that was to become one of the best known and most touching works in English verse. It is a bitter-sweet piece, a hymn to human frailty and to the sacrifices of the rural poor. Yet the lasting impression it leaves is of the continuity and resilience of life: an owl calls from the ivy, a beetle drones, cattle drift slowly past the elms – all glimpsed exactly as they might have been generations before. Life goes on. In the end, violets blooming over a gravestone and a robin singing in a winter yew are messages of hope to believer and non-believer alike.

I am not a very religious person, but time and again, when I have been tired or anxious, or just plain lost, I have found myself drawn to these green refuges and in some way restored. The memories are very strong: a March afternoon and my first truly wild daffodils glinting in a Herefordshire churchyard – a light at the end of a long winter tunnel of illness and trouble; another March day, the first of spring, at St Filii de Eglosros in Cornwall, with a barn owl floating over the head of the churchwarden as he mowed the grass and wild garlic; and then in Suffolk, listening to a night-long duet between two nightingales in the dense scrub in Wenhaston churchyard '. . .the self-same song that found a path / Through the sad heart of Ruth . . .' Keats, like Gray, understood what nature has to tell us about the continuity of life.

Small wonder if in a landscape that is relentlessly squeezing out our opportunities for these healing, first-hand contacts with nature, churchyards are beginning to be regarded as literal and urgently needed sanctuaries. The vast congregation of wild plants and creatures which have found a home in them, and which are so vividly documented in this book, often have simply nowhere else to go. Some – the tombstone lichens, the mistletoe in the limes, the old-fashioned roses run wild – have been there for centuries and are memorials every bit as historic as the church itself.

Yet their continued existence cannot be taken for granted. Our growing concern for them is comparatively new, and it is only slowly establishing its importance against other claims on the worldly territory of the Church. At present, churchyards are regarded principally as resting places for the dead, where a respectful, sombre tidiness, clipped of the excesses of nature, ought to prevail. That is an understandable feeling, but in the light of our growing sense of the interdependence of all life, a more hospitable attitude towards the rest of natural creation might perhaps be an apter Christian response.

As it happens, ideas for reconciling these different views are flourishing. Many involve the resumption of practices which were common when churchyards were partly looked on as the church's 'outside room' and expected to play their part in the intricate community affairs of the parish. I treasure a glimpse a few years ago of a revival of the whole cycle of cloth-making. It was at Worstead in Norfolk, birthplace of one of England's most famous fabrics. Sheep grazed in the churchyard, spinning wheels and looms were at work in the aisles, and the finished cloth was used for renewing the hassocks.

I hope the eloquent arguments in this book will hasten this process of reconciliation, for the challenge of ensuring that churchyards serve the diverse needs of a whole community – and that includes the needs of its wild creatures – is a microcosm of the environmental challenges that face us all. And it is a challenge, moreover, in which the spiritual significance of nature is for once given its rightful place.

RICHARD MABEY

The church of St Mary and St Michael, in Great Urswick, Cumbria, with its fine Scots pine.

7

AUTHOR'S NOTE AND ACKNOWLEDGEMENTS

A NEW ROLE FOR CHURCHYARDS HAS emerged over the last decade – that of nature conservation. There are more than twenty thousand churchyards set around churches and chapels of various denominations in England and Wales. Church and chapel yards vary in size from a pocket handkerchief lawn to several acres, but it has been calculated that the average extent works out, approximately, at about an acre. Taken altogether this represents a sizeable area of land which has survived untouched by either urban development or intensive agriculture, and as such, churchyards have assumed an importance not only for the people of the parish but for its wildlife also. This book looks at the natural history of churchyards and how it can be supported, in the context of their social and community functions.

Much of the research for this book originated with the Women's Institute, whose members noted plants, animals, boundaries, habitats of various kinds, and churchyard ceremonies all over England and Wales during the course of no less than fourteen hundred individual churchyard surveys. Similarly, a number of other organizations – the Botanical Society of the British Isles, the Lichen Society, the county Bat Groups, the British Butterfly Conservation Society, the British Trust for Ornithology – have focused their attention on churchyards and carried out survey work of their own. I have drawn on the work of these specialist groups, generously made available to me to complement my own personal observations.

The idea for this book was not my own, but was originated several years ago by the late John Talbot White in collaboration with Sue Parish (now Manager of WI Books); I am very grateful to Sue for her responsiveness and encouragement during a very full year of travelling, research and writing, in which she made every effort to lighten the load for me. When she brought me into the project, she had already organized the extensive churchyard survey made through the Women's Institute's network of volunteers.

It was only after the sad death of John White in 1983 that I was asked whether I would look at the survey with a view to writing the book. The paragraph which begins my book would, if things had been different, have been the opening to his.

In the writing of this book, I have been advised, criticised and helped most generously by many people involved in different ways with churchyards. My deepest thanks to Arthur Chater, Botanical Recorder for Cardiganshire, who has surveyed all hundred and one churchyards in that region, for his guidance and encouragement and for setting such a high standard of clear-headedness and style in his own work. As one of my dearest friends, Richard Mabey was by far the most ruthless in shaking many misconceptions and structural and stylistic weaknesses out of my first draft.

Mary Briggs of the Botanical Society of the British Isles not only introduced me to those people in the forefront of churchyard research but kept me supplied tirelessly with notes and observations on the subject. I am indebted to Phil Richardson for introducing me to bat-watching in churchyards and to Jack Laundon for his help with the lichens. My thanks go also to David Glue of the British Trust for Ornithology for his observations on churchyard birds. I am grateful to all of these for corrections and comments on various drafts of the book, and especially to Philip Oswald of the Nature Conservancy Council who read and corrected the revised typescript. Credit must be given also to Veronica Watkins who so quickly and efficiently turned indecipherable pages into fair copy.

I am a devoted admirer of Francis Simpson's *Flora of Suffolk* and it was a great pleasure to discuss with him his researches in churchyards which have extended over many years. I was almost sidetracked for good into the fascinations of churchyard archaeology by acquaintance with Dr Warwick Rodwell, who kindly sent me proofs of his book *Our Christian Heritage* and directed me to the CBA research report on churches and churchyards.

I shall remember this period, in which I visited over two hundred churchyards, with particular affection, especially those occasions when I was initiated by other churchyard devotees into knowledge of plants and animals new to me. I am grateful to Dr Francis Rose for the crash course in lichen identification in a beautiful Hampshire churchyard, to Dr Chris Hitch for perambulating Leiston churchyard in Suffolk with me on a similar quest, and to Joy Fildes who sought out several new species on my home ground at Wigginton. I recall with great pleasure a foray into Cambridgeshire churchyards with the ex-warden and Director of Studies at Flatford Field Centre, F.J. Bingley MBE, who led some pioneer churchyard survey work. Another memorable occasion was the July day spent with Dr

Soldier beetles congregating and mating on
flowerheads in July in the grounds of the
redundant church, at Corpusty, Norfolk.
(Life size).

10

Frank Perring of the Royal Society for Nature Conservation, Angela Walker of the Northamptonshire Trust for Nature Conservation and the County Recorder for Botany, Mrs Gill Gent, when they judged the county churchyard competition. I am always glad to visit Ted Ellis, who is, on this subject as on so many others, enthusiastic and widely knowledgeable, and who readily supplied me with a list of topical and literary references.

There were many others who enriched my understanding of the subject through conversation and correspondence. Among these were George Barker, author of the booklet *Wildlife Conservation in the Care of Churches and Churchyards* published in 1972, an early landmark in churchyard conservation; Rev Canon Henry Stapleton, whose edition of the *Churchyard Handbook* was an important milestone; Eva Crackles who investigated herb-planting in churchyards; Dr Alan Leslie who made a study of the goldilocks buttercup with reference to churchyard populations; and Alison Rutherford who has cast new light on ivies. I received generous help from many County Recorders for botany, and both clergymen and laypeople wrote to me about churchyard customs and traditions. I am sorry there was too much correspondence to acknowledge everyone here individually. For helpful guidance in the reference library of the Council for the Care of Churches I am grateful to the librarian David Williams and to the assistant librarian Janet Seeley.

Working alongside Clare Roberts has been both a pleasure and an inspiration. She herself would like to thank Rosemary, Bryan and Simon Roberts for their invaluable help and encouragement. On behalf of Sue Parish, I would like to mention the work of Joy Potter and Richard Findon on the WI questionnaires and to thank them. Thanks are due also to John Murray for John Betjeman's 'Sunday Afternoon Service in St Enodoc Church, Cornwall' and 'Wantage Bells' collected in *Church Poems*, first published in 1981 and to Oxford University Press for 'Manchán's Wish' from *Early Irish Lyrics*, translated by Gerard Murphy (1956).

I should not have been able to write this book without the help and support of my husband John who took on even more than usual of the domestic organization and gave up all his holidays to care for the children while I was away or in seclusion at my desk. A word too for Barbara and Ronald Kilpatrick who were always there to help when needed and for Alice and Howarth who accompanied me on many churchyard visits.

HISTORY
and
HERITAGE

The churchyard, God's acre, is one of the most enduring features of the landscape. Together with the church it forms the physical as well as the spiritual centre of the community. It is the most sacred and usually the most ancient enclosure in the parish. Some churchyards may be even older than the church itself, having their roots in pre-Christian ceremony. The memorials, public and private, are a tangible link between the inhabitants today and their forebears. The churchyard is the centre of communal worship and celebration, the site of the most important occasions of life, baptism, marriage and burial.

John Talbot White

THERE IS SOMETHING WHICH DRAWS PEOPLE, non-churchgoers as well as religious folk, to churchyards. They have a quality that is quite out of the ordinary. A kind of peace exists within them, whether they are set in wild isolation or in the centre of a town or village. Many churchyards are places which have been held sacred for hundreds, sometimes thousands of years, and I do not think it fanciful to believe that outdoor places quite as much as buildings can convey a sense of antiquity and sanctity.

The sense that a churchyard may have an existence that is beyond time and the everyday world is sometimes very strong. The writing of this book began at such a place. Winter evening was beginning to close in as I drove along the causeway between wide ploughed fields to the church of Tilbury-juxta-Clare in Essex. The little circular churchyard was like a bushy island, and the setting sun outlined the shapes of the medieval church and the tall limes of the boundary hedge with their dark nests of mistletoe.

The flora bore testimony to long, continuous care. At the entrance, there was a glossy, dark green mass of periwinkle, 'joy of the ground', the herb which 'hath an excellent value to stench bleeding at the nose in Christians if it be made into a garland and hung about the neck'. There were clumps of gladdon, which is often found in churchyards, the swordlike leaves a rich evergreen, the pods opened to reveal neat lines of

The flowers of stinking hellebore attract bees on a cool March day. (Life size).

Stinking hellebore in bud, in late January at St Margaret's, Tilbury-juxta-Clare, Essex.

14

brilliant orange seeds. Beside a gravestone near the south porch grew stinking hellebore, with strange, pale green flowers edged in purple. It is native to Essex, but has been planted, bird-sown or seeded itself in churchyards there and in neighbouring counties. Near the hellebore, tall briars arched around the gravestones. By the boundary hedge snowdrops were just beginning to appear, the flowerheads like white-tipped spears, preparing to open in February as the flower of Candlemas. The first small leaves of primroses and cowslips were emerging in the grass on and around the graves, and mallows had started into growth beneath the elegant curves of the ivy, both sheltered by the wall of the church tower.

Startled wrens flew out of the masonry and into thick clumps of hazel as I passed by. There was hazel also, together with field maple and blackthorn, in the hedge which topped the low bank of the boundary enclosing the church. Two century-old limes flanked the entrance to the churchyard. Their rough, ivy-covered trunks bristled with an abundant growth of suckers from the base, and mistletoe hung high in the branches. In the failing light, lichens made soft shapes of grey and orange-brown on the gravestones. I could hear ducks quacking in the distance and, when I turned to leave, a large kestrel, her long, sharp-edged wings curved back for landing, was briefly silhouetted against the silky winter sky before vanishing into the shadow of the tower.

There are churchyards as rich as this to be found all over the British Isles. They provide almost every kind of habitat from seashore and rocky coast to chalk grassland, heath and deep woodland. Once, they simply reflected the abundant wildlife in the countryside around them. Nowadays they are all too often little islands of riches set in land so intensively used for agriculture, urban development or afforestation that its traditional fauna and flora have been driven out. In the face of increasing pressure on the chalk grasslands, it is perhaps significant that the three plants which go by the vernacular name of 'sanctuary' in some counties – centaury, yellow-wort and red bartsia – all flowers of the chalk, have found refuge in churchyards.

In some parts of Britain, the name for the churchyard itself was 'sanctuary', and until the sixteenth century any fugitive (unless charged with sacrilege or treason) could claim sanctuary on entering its consecrated ground. Nowadays it is wildlife, rather than human-kind, that needs

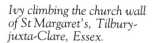

Ivy climbing the church wall of St Margaret's, Tilbury-juxta-Clare, Essex.

The church at St Margaret's,
Tilbury-juxta-Clare, Essex,
from the east.

the refuge of the churchyard. Inside these sheltered confines live flowering plants (wild, naturalized and cultivated), lichens and fungi, and a wide range of animal life: gravestone invertebrates less than a millimetre long, large insects such as dor beetles; glow-worms; butterflies, moths and bees; frogs, toads, snakes, lizards and slow-worms; birds of many kinds; a host of small mammals such as moles, shrews and voles; bats, and even some larger mammals, hares and rabbits, stoats and weasels, foxes and badgers.

Although my principal concern was natural history, I could not help but be struck during the course of my travels by the human activity in churchyards. Whether there was a footpath across the churchyard or not, there were often people walking there. On even the most bitter of winter days, there might be someone tending a grave, clipping a hedge or mowing. In a chapelyard at Capel Rhiwbws, Dyfed, people in adjoining houses draped their washing over the gravestones to dry. Occasionally, a group of children melted into the boundary hedge or a verger came to pin something up in the porch. The church porch is a good barometer of the place of church and churchyard in parish life. Apart from the official diocesan and electoral notices, there are announcements of events in the church and parish, rotas for flower arranging, sometimes a brief history of the church. At St Peter's, Mildenhall, in Suffolk there is a notice explaining the association between the village name and the plant 'meld', now usually called fat hen, which is believed to have grown locally since neolithic times.

The churchyard has a special meaning for the people of a parish – for those who go to church, walk in procession on Palm Sunday, sing carols at Christmas and who are christened, married and eventually buried there. It also means a great deal to others who do none of these things, but who

Welsh poppies (leaves illustrated
above) thriving in the churchyard at St
Margaret's, Binsey, in Oxfordshire, in
July. They are not native this far east,
but naturalize readily from grave
plantings or nearby gardens.

19

simply care about the place where they live. It has always been the local people who look after the churchyard, doing maintenance work such as weeding, and minor repairs. By the seventeenth century it had become the practice in some places for churchwardens to make local landowners responsible for keeping the churchyard boundary walls and fences in good repair. At Cowfold in Sussex the fence was maintained by eighty-one parishioners – their initials can be found carved into some of the palings – and at Chiddingley in the same county fifty-six parishioners looked after varying stretches of fencing, allocated according to their means. Churchwardens' accounts, as far back as medieval times, show that, even then, people were concerned about the way the churchyard was kept, and they would complain and, as a final resort, even take legal action if they thought it was being misused.

Generally speaking, the presence of wild flora and fauna in the churchyard interferes little or not at all with human requirements, although in recent years new techniques of mowing and weed control have started to be applied in churchyards, and conflict has begun to arise. The old-fashioned churchyards are the most hospitable to wildlife and, in truth, to many of their human visitors too.

It is no paradox that churchyards support a thriving fauna and flora. In Christian tradition, as well as in the natural world, there is always life in the midst of death, and churchyards are not morbid places. Benefactors, private and public, often give benches to the churchyard and it is pleasant to sit among the flowers and the warm lichen colours of the gravestones on a sunny day. There, one can observe a friendly interaction between people and nature. The chiming of bells or the muffled sounds of the organ mingle with birdsong and the busy sound of insects or the squeak of a shrew. Although many churchyards provide a home for plants and animals which are regionally and sometimes nationally rare, it would be a shame if they were regarded simply as nature reserves; they are more than that.

St John the Baptist, in Ysbyty Cynfyn, Dyfed.

In these consecrated surroundings it is both possible and desirable for civilization and wildlife to exist in harmony. The churchyard may be a quiet place for reflection, a burial ground and a home and shelter for a wide range of animals and plants. Many of the problems with maintenance experienced by incumbents arise because they try to make the churchyard over-tidy. The flowery meadow of cowslips, fritillaries, orchids and other flowers beloved of people in medieval times, was both beautiful and fertile, and this is a better model for the churchyard than a bowling green. At the other extreme, the ground may be so neglected that coarse, rank vegetation smothers the lichens and small flowers and obscures the graves. The ideal of minimal and judicious management can benefit both the vegetation and the creatures that live in it, so that those who enter the churchyard, whether visitor, churchgoer or mourner, can feel comfortable. It is all the more important nowadays, when so many churches' doors are kept locked except during services, for the churchyard to be a pleasant and meditative place.

Places full of wild flowers and birds, real and miraculous, are associated with the early Christian Church, and the history of the first British saints is touched with details and attitudes towards nature that we associate with earlier religions. According to legend, St Nonna, mother of the patron saint of Wales, finding herself caught in a violent storm, took shelter within a circle of stones. There she found blue sky, sunshine and the song of birds, while the storm continued to rage outside. Soon afterwards, she bore her son, St David, and the place within the stones (believed to have been a stone circle dedicated to the earth and its plenty), at Llannon in Dyfed, became a Christian chapel and chapelyard.

There were many saints who sought places in remote country to live and pray, and chose for company birds and animals rather than men. Almost every representation of St Cuthbert portrays his love for the wildlife of the Farne Islands, and it took the king and some of the most devout men of the northern kingdom to persuade him to exchange his hermit cell in the wilderness for a bishopric. In the account written by the Venerable Bede, Cuthbert wept when they 'eventually drew him from his beloved retreat' and pined so greatly that he returned after two years. St Guthlac, another seventh-century saint, gave up wealth and title for a life of Christian humility and self-denial. He chose for his home the wildest and most

It is still widely held that these two upright stones (and three others) built into the church wall of St John the Baptist, at Ysbyty Cynfyn, Dyfed, were once part of a pre-Christian stone circle – although modern scholars have cast doubts on the subject.

isolated place he could find, a small island in the fens. Ancient spirits haunted him there, not surprisingly, since it appears to have been the sacred place of an earlier people:

> There was on the island a certain great burial ground built over the earth . . . On one side of the burial mound there was dug a great well of water. Over this the blessed Guthlac built himself a house.

This remote retreat became Crowland Abbey, the north part of which is now a parish church. It is hard to believe that it was once an island. Even the strange triangular bridge nearby in the town, built in the fourteenth century to span two streams, now stretches over dry land. In fact, there is hardly any of the original wetland habitat left in Lincolnshire, and none of the wilderness St Guthlac inhabited, though there is wildness in the scream of the swifts as they sweep through the Norman arch of the ruined Abbey just above the place where the saint's cell used to be. There is still a feeling

A magnificent yew dominates the churchyard of St Nicholas, Asthall, Oxfordshire.

22

for plants in the parish, tamed perhaps but still strong, for the Crowland Abbey flower festival has become famous.

The fact that St Guthlac's chosen home at Crowland lay over a site previously venerated by an earlier people is by no means exceptional. There are many examples of churches and chapels built on or close to the holy places of older religions. In 1529, Thomas More gave expression to what seems to have been a long-held tradition of continuity of worship, writing that 'it is clear that God wishes to be worshipped in particular places'. Pope Gregory the Great certainly believed so, and in a letter to Abbot Melitus who was shortly to join St Augustine in England, observed that people would 'continue to frequent the same sacred places' even if the altar there was dedicated to a new god. When Gregory also recommended that the ancient sites and temples of the Britons be appropriated rather than destroyed, he seems to have been acknowledging a tolerance which was already operating. Archaeological evidence, like some folk legends, suggests that the transition from earlier forms of worship, Roman or

British, to Christianity was in many cases peaceful, though there were notable outbreaks of persecution. Work on the temple of Mithras in Queen Victoria Street in London has shown that the building was methodically turned to Christian use after a ceremonial burial of the trappings of the old gods. At Lullingstone in Kent, the private pagan shrine of the villa was converted for Christian worship in about AD 350, and other instances of conversion of this kind occurred in Roman Britain. Evidence from that period found in the city of Bath suggests that a supplicant might invoke the Christian and a pagan god in a single entreaty.

Archaeological excavation has traced the continuity of use of some churchyards back to prehistory. In the case of Crowland, the site was an ancient burial mound; other churchyards are set on early places of worship, burial grounds or within prehistoric hilltop enclosures. At Winwick in Cheshire, a church and churchyard lie over a Bronze Age barrow, and burial urns indicating the presence of barrows of the same period have been found in several other churchyards. An Iron Age burial was discovered in St Martin's churchyard at Wharram Percy in North Yorkshire. Among the most striking examples of churches which are set within ancient earthworks are St Mary's at Breedon-on-the-Hill, in Leicestershire, where the original monastery was founded inside an Iron Age hill fort, and the ruined church at Knowlton in Dorset, which stands dramatically at the centre of a Bronze Age henge monument.

Little is known of the religions which preceded Christianity in Britain but it is generally accepted that the Celtic peoples venerated places of exceptional natural beauty, such as hilltops, groves of trees, springs and rivers. It could be argued that churches and churchyards inherited not only the physical sites but a tradition of seeking out places of special beauty and atmosphere.

Celtic poetry is imbued with this strong respect for the natural world. Indeed, for guidance on the sensitive conservation of holy ground we might look to the Celtic ideal in which love of God is expressed in love of nature. This idea is epitomized in a tenth-century poem of unknown authorship, written about the saint, Manchán of Liath, in southern Ireland, three centuries earlier.

Manchán's Wish

I wish, O son of the living God, eternal ancient King, for a hidden little hut in the wilderness that it might be my dwelling,

All-grey shallow water beside it, a clear pool to wash away sins through the grace of the Holy Spirit,

A beautiful wood close by, surrounding it on every side, for the nurture of many-voiced birds, for shelter to hide them,

A southern aspect for warmth, a little stream across its glebe, choice land of abundant bounty which would be good for every plant,

A few young men of sense, we shall tell their number, humble and obedient to pray the King:

Four threes, three fours, (to suit every need), two sixes in the church, both north and south;

Six couples in addition to myself ever praying to the King who makes the sun shine;

A lovely church decked with linen, a dwelling for God from heaven, bright lights, then, above the pure white scriptures,

One house to go to for tending the body, without meditation of evil.

This is the husbandry which I would undertake and openly choose genuine fragrant leeks, hens, speckled salmon, bees, —

Raiment and food enough for me from the King whose fame is fair, to be seated for a time, and to pray to God in some place.

[*translation: Gerard Murphy*]

The Great Celtic Cross in St Brynach's churchyard, Nevern, Dyfed, which dates from the tenth or eleventh century. Legend says that on April 7 (the patron's day) every year, a cuckoo perches on the cross.

There are no clear facts about how early churchyards were established. Ecclesiastical authorities seem to have advocated burial of Christians within the precincts of the church from at least the time of Gregory the Great, who believed that churchgoers who passed by graves on their way into church would then remember the dead in their prayers. The parish system (or something approximating very closely to it) was established in England and Wales as early as the tenth century, and it was the ordinary Christians of the parish who were buried in the churchyards. Clergy and important personages were interred in the church itself.

Saxon landowners were encouraged to build churches on their land and complied to such an extent that almost certainly most English churches in rural areas came into existence during the late Saxon period. In the latter half of the tenth century, there was also inducement to freehold landowners to establish churchyards, for if a church was given a burial ground, it became entitled to a third of the tithes, which were otherwise due to the minster which administered the district. It is interesting to note that as the Church became increasingly powerful and its ownership of land more extensive, the spirit of this law was reversed. Henry III's Statutes of Mortmain, dating from 1279, forbade individuals to give land to the Church, though this law seems not always to have been obeyed. By the reign of George III it was again legal to donate land to the Church; up to five acres could be given for the provision of a churchyard, glebe or residence for the incumbent.

Although the Welsh king Hywel Dda prescribed an area of one acre in 943, churchyards appear always to have differed widely in shape and size. The name 'God's Acre' is Teutonic in origin and seems not to have been mentioned in England until references in the early seventeenth century specifically to German churchyards. The German *Gottesacker* and Dutch *Godsakker* were terms not primarily concerned with churchyard area. The meaning was more accurately 'God's seed field' in which the bodies of the faithful — the 'seed' — are the potential harvest of the Resurrection. The basis of this idea seems to be the evocative words of St Paul's First Epistle to the Corinthians (chapter 15):

Oxford ragwort on the churchyard wall of St Peter-in-the-East, Oxford, seen in mid-July. (The Church is now used as the library of St Edmund Hall).

How are the dead raised? . . .

There is one glory of the sun, and another
glory of the moon, and another glory of the
stars: for one star differeth from another
star in glory.

So also is the resurrection of the dead. It is
sown in corruption; it is raised in incorruption.

It is sown in dishonour; it is raised in
glory: it is sown in weakness; it is
raised in power:

It is sown a natural body; it is raised
a spiritual body.

One can only guess at what the early churchyards looked like and what
plant life they supported. It is almost certain that most of them were
enclosed. The 'yard' of churchyard derives, like the word 'garden' and
'garth' (still used to refer to churchyards in Scotland and the north of
England) from the Old English word *geard*, which means an enclosed space.
It is thought that the cemeteries of monastic foundations were the model for
parish churchyards, and monasteries generally had several kinds of yard in
which plants were grown.

      One of the earliest depictions of monastery building and land
configuration is the eighth-century plan of St Gall. This is not the actual
plan for the St Gall foundation, a Benedictine house near Lake Constance,
but is thought to be a theoretical representation of ideas current at the time.
In the grounds are a cloister garden, a physic garden and a kitchen garden.
The cemetery, enclosed by walls and hedges, contains fruit trees and
shrubs, but no other plants.

      In addition to their other garden-enclosures, abbeys and
monasteries had one or more highly cultivated gardens under the care of the
sacristan. These '*gardini Sacristi*' provided most of the very large quantity of
flowers and greenery required to decorate the church and to make garlands

Common centaury, the
sanctuary flower, in bloom
in a Suffolk churchyard in
June. (Life size).

or floral wreaths for the clergy on feast days and major religious festivals. Larger churches and well-endowed chapels possessed similar gardens, which remained separate from the churchyard proper. Henry VI bequeathed land for such a garden to the chapel of Eton College 'for to sett in certain trees and flowers, behovable and convenient for the service of the same church'. Churchwardens' accounts list some of the plants which were used, such as box and willow-palm on Palm Sunday, garlands of roses and woodruff for Corpus Christi, roses on St Martin's Day, birch at Midsummer, and holly and ivy at Christmas.

Church decoration became illegal after the Reformation and, although there is considerable evidence that the new plain orthodoxy of service was often ignored (people do not lightly give up their accustomed modes of worship), it was then impossible to keep up elaborate and costly church gardens. Some were sold or fell into dereliction; others, particularly those adjacent to the churchyard, may have been absorbed. Poorer churches and small ones which would not have boasted gardens must have carried on much as usual, probably growing a small variety of flowers within the churchyard. The tended beds of churchyards may possibly be distantly related to those old church gardens.

In the past, the traditional practice of maintaining the churchyard in much the same way as a meadow, by grazing or infrequent mowing, kept the plants and animals in healthy community. However, relatively few people now know or can remember the beauty and fertility of an ancient meadow. Increasingly, the model for a churchyard is that of a suburban garden, scrupulously neat and close-mown. It is both difficult to keep up in a large area like a churchyard and damaging to the wildlife community. The wide range of plants and the animals which depend on them cannot survive in such a churchyard.

We know from a variety of sources that churchyards in the past suffered mismanagement. Unsuitable animals such as pigs, cattle or horses were kept in some; others were overgrazed and the flora depleted, while yet others were left to become impenetrable wildernesses. The state of the churchyard became a perennial cause for complaint among parishioners. Sometimes crops were grown in the churchyard. It is said that an eighteenth-century rector was rebuked by his archdeacon for growing turnips in the churchyard. He hoped to see no such thing when he came

A traditional stone stile built into the wall gives entry to the churchyard, St Mary and St Michael, Great Urswick, Cumbria.

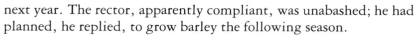

next year. The rector, apparently compliant, was unabashed; he had
planned, he replied, to grow barley the following season.

Up until the last few decades, a churchyard which had been ill-
treated could recover itself. Grasses and wild flowers would grow again,
replenished by seed from the meadows and waysides surrounding the
churchyard. This is no longer the case; in fact, in some counties the
churchyard is the last reserve for wildlife in a parish. A churchyard may
have its origins in prehistory, but its importance as a place for quiet
reflection and the appreciation of the beauty and diversity of nature may
extend far into the future.

It is impossible to look at churchyards today without
acknowledging the debt to the past. What makes a churchyard's small
compass so interesting in terms of its fauna and flora is largely the diversity
of habitat there. This is not a condition brought about by natural causes.
The items of which a naturalist takes special account in a churchyard – the
boundary walls and hedges, the mature trees, the quality of the grassy
spaces, the memorials – have not arrived there accidentally: they are the
result of a long interaction between human and natural history.

It is nearly always easy to locate a churchyard without difficulty;
the familiar tower or spire signals its presence to us now, just as it has to
people since medieval times. The bird species which inhabit these lofty
places seem to be remarkably similar, too. From the early sixteenth century,
there are scattered mentions in churchwardens' accounts from all over the
country of jackdaws, owls, pigeons and starlings. Then as now, birds seem
to have been tolerated in the churchyard and church fabric, but not inside
the church. Measures taken against birds were occasionally violent, but
more often they simply entailed the preventative stopping-up of crevices,
holes and gaps in walls and roofs. At Bradeston in Norfolk, the parishioners
seem to have made an equivalent in net of the modern 'bird-door', for their
accounts list a payment for 'Twynne for ye nette at ye church dore'.

Yews are the tree species most associated with churchyards and it
can be convincingly argued that certain churchyard yews may be the oldest
living things in Britain. However, many other tree species are associated

*Goldfinches eating the seeds of
creeping thistle in a Gloucestershire
churchyard.*

30

with churchyards. There is a most interesting reference to the churchyard elms of St Edmund, Sarum, which must have been mature trees in 1644, since the accounts note that six of them were felled and the rest lopped. The wood was sold to help provide the cost of repairs to the church and its south windows. It is evident that new elms were planted, for in 1650–51 there was a payment for watering 'the young trees' during the summer; they did not all thrive, for there was a resolution in the winter of 1693 to plant 'Elm trees in the room of those that are dead, and as many more as the C.W. [churchwardens] shall think convenient', whereupon sixteen more elms and three sycamores were supplied, planted and tended by a certain 'William Baker gardener'.

Avenues of fastigiate yews such as this one leading to the town church of St Giles, Oxford, are a common sight in churchyards. Sadly, people seem to have given up planting the traditional common yew and have turned to this stumpy, upswept form.

31

It seems likely, however, that before the eighteenth century, many, if not most, of the churchyard trees were brought in as young saplings from local woodland, rather than purchased. This seems to have happened on the borders of West Suffolk in the late seventeenth and early eighteenth centuries. In the churchyards of Groton and Lindsey and by the lane to Great Waldringfield church, all of which are in the vicinity of the ancient limewoods of this region, the woodland specialist, Dr Oliver Rackham, has identified old lime trees of indigenous genotypes. Almost certainly in these parishes, the churchwardens of old made their choice from the most plentiful and striking trees in the wild: the small-leaved lime, a species that is dense and shapely in maturity, burred and bristly in venerable old age.

There is much still to be uncovered about the history of tree-planting in churchyards. From the evidence that we have, the eighteenth century seems to have been a period of considerable enterprise in churchyards, as it was in parkland and great gardens, and the nineteenth century saw not only nationwide work on the 'restoration' of church fabric but also extensive planting. The archaeologist Dr Warwick Rodwell has

outlined a convincing theory that the churchyard elms at Rivenhall in Essex were planted by the landscape gardener, Humphrey Repton, when he was landscaping Rivenhall Park in 1791. While remodelling the church in 1838–39, Repton's son added a formal arrangement of yews, cedars, cypresses and holm oaks. Most of the eighteenth-century elm planting has been wiped out by Dutch elm disease, leaving skeletons or (as at Kedington, Suffolk) great gaps along the boundaries. The healthy elms I saw in West Yorkshire were a sad reminder of how beautiful they had once been elsewhere.

Cedars were a very popular churchyard tree throughout the nineteenth century. In a revealing series of illustrations hanging in the church of St George at Saham Toney in Norfolk, you can see that in 1779 there was a scrupulously neat churchyard with no trees. An illustration dating from 1820 shows a tomb beside an elm, and the latest, dated 1893, has several new trees – cedars, yews and some other conifers. Several of these trees, including the cedars and yews, are still to be seen in the churchyard. At Much Dewchurch, a few miles south of Hereford, there is a large stump around and on which grow spreading honeysuckle, ivy-leaved toadflax, and a few failing roses. I was told that it was a larch stump, and it was only by chance that I discovered that this old tree had in fact been another of the old cedars, felled because they were past their prime, or casting too much shade. The verger kindly showed me round the church, where I happened to see the church banner, which has embroidered on it in silk a beautiful and accurate view of the church and churchyard showing the unmistakable spreading branches of a Lebanon cedar in the place of the old stump.

A pair of parent wrens, seen at St John the Baptist, Fifield, Oxfordshire, in late July.

The big trees of the churchyard are usually yew, lime, beech and horse chestnut, sometimes planted in avenues from the lych-gate to the south porch, or ranged on the boundary to provide a leafy shelterbelt. Large trees were often planted in groups of twelve to represent the apostles. At Acton in Suffolk the lane sloping up to the church is flanked on either side by an impressive avenue of no less than forty-three limes, believed to be about a hundred years old and said to have been planted during the 1885 restoration scheme. Along the path to the church at East Tuddenham in Norfolk, twenty common lime trees, probably planted in about 1810, at the time when the lych-gate was erected, form a shady avenue in striking contrast to the open brightness of the churchyard.

This living lych-gate of yew at St Margaret's, Warnham in Sussex, is over a hundred years old. Twenty years ago, it was even larger, but because it overhung the pavement, it was clipped back by the vicar to its present shape.

33

Scanty elderberries in a churchyard hedge in Dorset, at the beginning of October. The missing ones have almost certainly been eaten by birds, who take full advantage of this early autumn feast. (Life size).

34

The plantings of the last two hundred years have included a number of exotic conifers. Besides cedars, Wellingtonia and even monkey puzzles were popular with the Victorians. Today the choice is more likely to include the ubiquitous Lawson's cypress, which even an admirer of conifers, Alan Mitchell, calls 'the commonest and most gloomy conifer throughout these islands'. It is exceedingly tough and produces an astounding variety of different forms, all equally robust. The presence of these and other conifers provide breeding places for little birds and are particularly important for coal tits and goldcrests.

It is generally agreed that, by the Middle Ages, most churchyards were enclosed by a definite wall, hedge or bank. Archaeological work has shown that these boundaries often changed shape over the years, but nevertheless many of the hedges and walls surrounding churchyards are of great age. Ancient hedges usually contain a large number of species. Field maple, holly, crab apple, rose, elder and hazel are often found, together with the more conventional hawthorn and blackthorn. Some hedgerow planting has a local distribution, such as the cherry plum in north-west Hertfordshire or the Duke of Argyll's tea plant in Suffolk. Oak, ash, beech and elm are among the larger species that are also found in hedges, mainly clipped into the hedge, but occasionally left to grow to maturity. Large trees are most often to be found at the main entrance to the churchyard, on either side of the gate.

Mature trees of churchyard and hedge provide effective shelter for birds, mammals and insects, particularly in areas where woods and hedges are otherwise scarce. They are of especial benefit to birds which may feed, roost and nest in them. In Edlesborough churchyard in Buckinghamshire, I counted twenty nests in the trees and shrubs. Churches in prominent positions provide navigational landmarks and stopping places for some species (spotted flycatchers, for instance) on migration. By contrast, there are butterflies, some of the hairstreaks for example, which depend on a single tree species and which may live out their entire life cycle in and around one large churchyard tree.

The fragrant pink-white beauty of crab apple blossom graces a churchyard boundary hedge at Snead, Powys, in mid-May. (Life size).

35

The other main type of boundary, the churchyard wall, also repays thorough investigation both as a historical artefact and for its natural history. It is not unusual for stone walls to contain carved blocks from earlier buildings, which can sometimes be dated back as far as Roman times. At Heysham in Lancashire, a complete Anglo-Saxon doorway from the church has been rebuilt into the wall.

Old stone churchyard walls are especially important for wildlife in areas where there is little or no local stone. In Suffolk and Cambridgeshire most of the county records for certain ferns refer to specimens growing on church and churchyard walls. Some of these fern observations have a long history. Black spleenwort, which is a common plant in fern-rich counties but rare in Cambridgeshire, was seen on the walls of Ditton and Hildersham by the eminent naturalist, John Ray, and recorded in the Second Appendix to his *Cambridge Catalogue* published in 1685. Another clergyman-botanist, Richard Relhan, also recorded it at these two churches in 1785. In Babington's *Flora of Cambridgeshire*, which was published in 1860 at the height of a period of intense enthusiasm for ferns, nearly all of an increased number of references to black spleenwort are from church and churchyard sites. Twentieth-century observers report that it seems no longer to grow in the two original sites, but have discovered three other church locations for it in Cambridgeshire.

There is usually a thriving assembly of flowering plants on churchyard walls, of which some are of historical note. The 'wild' yellow wallflower, possibly introduced with imported Caen stone in Norman times, survives mainly on church and castle walls and church towers. The plants growing on the abbey ruins at Bury St Edmunds appear to be identical to the wild species. One of only a handful of sites for the now-extinct umbellate chickweed was within Norwich cathedral precincts, while the rare spotted hawkweed, originally observed at Norwich, is now found on the walls of some churches in the surrounding countryside. A more common plant of church grounds is the Oxford ragwort, which spread from the botanical garden to a college wall and thence, in the nineteenth century, along railway lines throughout the country to colonize waste places, town gardens, and churchyard and other walls. The process of colonization continues: I have seen both pink and purple varieties of aubrieta, presumably escaped from neighbouring

A blackcap's nest in brambles by the churchyard hedge of St Mary's at Glemsfold in Suffolk.

St MARGARETS WELL

S. MARGARETÆ FONTEM
RECIBVS S. FRIDESWIDÆ VT FERTVR CONCE?
INQVINATVM DV OBRVTVMQVE
IN VSVM REVOCAVIT
?T J. PROVT ÆD⁻ XTI ALVMNVS VICARIVS?
A.S. MDCCCLXXIV

gardens, spilling over churchyard walls. It is a pretty, if to some eyes rather
suburban, sight, and welcome to brimstone butterflies which feed
enthusiastically on the flowers.

Churchyard memorials are interesting territory for the naturalist
as well as the historian. Self-sown trees often grow from tombs and grave-
beds. At Selborne in Hampshire, such growth is turned to advantage.
Sycamores emerging from all sides of the top slab of a chest tomb form a
leafy screen, which is apparently pruned back to a discreet bushy rectangle
each winter. In many churchyards, neat little grave plantings of box have

*The holy well at St Margaret's, Binsey,
Oxfordshire, which provided Saint Frideswide
and her followers with fresh water. It is believed
to have curative powers for eye ailments. The
area around the well provides a damp habitat for
ferns such as the hartstongue and polypody.
Above it, Solomon's seal mingles with the foliage
of Japanese anemone.*

37

grown into great billowing bushes which completely engulf the stones, providing year-round shelter for birds and other animals. In the small and secluded churchyard at Strethall in Essex, a haven for birds, I stood by a tall box tree and watched a woodpigeon on her nest in July, incubating yet another pair of eggs when the youngsters of most other species were already fledged and flying.

Churchyard memorial stone is, above all, a habitat for those insubstantial but beautiful and long-lived plants: the lichens. Some country churchyards support over a hundred different species, which glow orange, buttercup yellow, blue-green and grey against the stone. There are good historical, conservationist and scientific reasons for keeping churchyard gravestones in place. The lichens which grow on gravestones are attractive to look at, frequently of regional interest and sometimes rare. If the stones are moved, the lichens are almost invariably destroyed. Because they are extremely sensitive to pollution, lichens have been used in recent years to monitor levels of sulphur dioxide in the air and are now providing information on the range and intensity of acid rain. They may also in the future be used to determine the extent of agricultural spray drift. In fact, the lichen flora of churchyards provides a uniquely stable and comparable measure of the state of the atmosphere.

Nineteenth-century literature contains many appreciative references to churchyards. It seems to have been widely accepted that the presence of plants and animals contributed greatly to their attractiveness. When the vicar in Wordsworth's 'The Excursion' tells the sad story of Ellen, he and the poet sit in a pleasant spot in the churchyard:

A long stone-seat, fixed in the Churchyard wall;
Part shaded by cool sycamore and part
Offering a sunny resting-place.

Francis Kilvert made many observations later in the century about the people and animals frequenting churchyards and took evident pleasure in their flora. At Langley Burrell in Wiltshire early on the first Sunday in May 1871, he wrote in his diary:

A hot air balloon, seen drifting over
the churchyard of St Mary, Braemore,
in Hampshire, in mid-June. The air
was full of swifts, which were feeding
their young in nests under the eaves of
this ancient Saxon church, where the
horseshoe bat has also been seen.

Dandelions, ribwort plantain and dog rose growing at the base of the church wall, St Margaret's, Cley next the Sea, Norfolk, in late August. Roses both wild and cultivated grow plentifully in churchyards, providing beauty and scent in summer and haws for the birds in winter. In Cheshire, the dog rose is known as brid briar (bird-briar).

I went into the churchyard under the feathering larch which sweeps over the gate. The ivy-grown old church with its noble tower stood beautiful and silent among the elms with its graves at its feet. Everything was still. No one was about or moving and the only sound was the singing of birds. The place was all in a charm of singing, full of peace and quiet sunshine. It seemed to be given up to the birds and their morning hymns. It was the bird church, the church among the birds. I wandered round the church amongst the dewy grass-grown graves and picturesque ivy and moss hung tombstones. Round one grave grew a bed of primroses. Upon another tall cowslips hung their heads.

In Bredwardine churchyard, a few years later, Kilvert wrote: 'some of the graves were white as snow with snowdrops', taking especial pleasure in these first flowers of spring, which now as then are arguably at their finest in churchyards.

Kilvert admired and appreciated nature and loved the familiar plants. Not for him the preoccupation of a modern botanist identifying, say, one of the many tricky species of *Hieracium* (hawkweed) nor was he, as Wordsworth put it, 'One that would peep and botanize / Upon his mother's grave.' (Though Wordsworth could have done with a botanist at his own graveside, for it was planned, so the story goes, that the lesser celandine, his favourite plant, should be carved on his tomb; but the plant which appears on his gravestone is not the lesser but the greater celandine, a plant quite different in appearance).

We have reason to be grateful to those erudite clergymen who extended the boundaries of our knowledge in every branch of natural history from the sixteenth century onwards. Almost any page of any county flora contains an example of the contribution made by such clergymen of international fame or of minor local repute. Even those who, like John Ray, worked on a large conceptual scale and who travelled widely not only in Britain but in the rest of Europe, kept an eye on the natural history of the churchyard. In *The Flora of Suffolk* we find small scabious (now rather rare but still found in churchyards) first recorded in Suffolk by the Revd Sir John Cullum in 1773, and a scarce introduced plant, birthwort, observed in the grounds of the abbey at Bury St Edmunds in the late nineteenth century by the Revd William Hind. One of the most interesting of the botanist-clergy

The closed buds are yellow-green, shaded pink-lilac.

Small black beetles crawling over the flowers.

Field scabious, flourishing in the churchyard of St Michael's in Idbury, Oxfordshire, where the grass is cut only three times a year. These flowers were painted in late July. (Life size).

was the Revd Professor John Henslow, who in 1837 stepped aside from a brilliant academic career as Professor of Botany at Cambridge to become rector of one of the most backward parishes in Suffolk. In the course of numerous reforms undertaken at Hitcham, he began to teach botany to the village children. Doubtless he took the children into the churchyard to show them the plants. Hitcham churchyard today is well-mown and contains many lawn plants such as daisy and slender speedwell, but some attractive meadow species still manage to survive – scabious, dog daisy and lesser burnet saxifrage, and the yellow flower spikes of common agrimony, which is also known as church-steeple. If you are lucky, I was told, you may see a common lizard sunning itself on a gravestone.

Henslow would have known about the difficulties of keeping a large churchyard in an orderly condition and been interested too in conserving its flora. It is clear that some difficulties encountered by present-day incumbents are not new. An ancient legend describes St Patrick watching a woman pulling nettles in the churchyard to make broth, and in churchwardens' accounts from the fifteenth century there are payments for 'weding within the Churche yerde' and 'cuttyng downe of the Netylles and Wedes'. Similarly the nineteenth-century accounts of the parish of Hook (now in Humberside) show a fairly considerable outlay on nettle pulling and, towards the end of the century, for mowing the churchyard.

The problems of reaching an acceptable standard of orderliness remain much the same today, but there is now a wider choice of ways to deal with them. In some churchyards people continue with the old methods. Hay is still made and, occasionally, sold in a few churchyards, and grazing is coming back into fashion. I was told of a churchyard where the vegetation is clipped from the awkward spots close to headstones and between graves by hand, using a pair of sheep-shears. There are a surprising number of churchyards in which an area of ground is deliberately kept as a small nature reserve. At the other extreme, I have seen churchyards covered by the barest fuzz of grass, mown every week, even during drought conditions. Weed-killers, rotary mowers and grass strimmers should be considered only with extreme caution, for they all too easily become the dominating factor in churchyard maintenance. On their account, graves are flattened, gravestones removed and, in their wake, little natural life remains. The celebrated horticulturist J.C. Loudon wrote early in the nineteenth century: 'Churchyards and cemeteries are scenes not only calculated to improve the morals and the taste, and by their botanical riches to cultivate the intellect, but they serve as historical records.' It would be a tragedy if the practices of the late twentieth century were to destroy the rich nature of 'God's Acre'.

Leaves in opposite pairs.

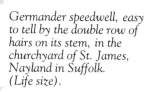

Germander speedwell, easy to tell by the double row of hairs on its stem, in the churchyard of St. James, Nayland in Suffolk. (Life size).

43

CHURCHYARD FAMILIARS

Wall flowers are bright in their beds
            And their scent all pervading,
Withered are primroses heads
            And the hyacinth fading
        But flowers by the score
        Multitudes more
Weed flowers and seed flowers and mead flowers our
        paths are invading.

John Betjeman: *Wantage Bells*

THERE ARE CHURCHYARDS AND CHAPELYARDS the length and breadth of England and Wales, in every imaginable setting: high on hills and isolated tors, on moors, in woods, farmland and river valleys, and on all kinds of soil from chalk or limestone to heavily acid conditions and even on solid rock – there is one churchyard in Wales where graves are not dug but blasted with dynamite. Each of these different environments has its own recognizably different flora and fauna. Is it feasible therefore, to think in terms of the plants and animals typical of churchyards? I believe that it is: in a sense churchyards can be regarded as special environments in themselves. Because they have developed a distinctive identity built around certain predictable elements they tend to have more in common with each other than with the land surrounding them. There are certain regional differences, but the overall picture is remarkably consistent.

The churchyards of England and Wales are predominantly grassy even in towns (unlike those on the continent, which are often paved, concreted over or gravelled) and those churchyards which have not been over-mown, or treated with weed-killer or fertilizer, exhibit the rich flora and fauna of unimproved grassland. Within a comparatively small area churchyards may contain an unusually large number of different habitats. The grass in less frequented spots may be cut or grazed only rarely during the year, giving a meadow-like habitat; verges and sometimes wide expanses of grass are often mown hard and frequently, like a garden lawn. Other places may be more or less left to themselves, forming patches of scrub. Paths, walls and boundaries support the flora of wayside and hedgerow. The walls of the church, and memorial stones of various kinds of elaboration harbour plants, insects, small mammals and birds. In or near many churchyards there is water providing an additional marshy or riverside habitat. There may be the typical flora of the woodland from which a churchyard was originally claimed and finally, there is a rich introduced flora ranging from tiny grave plants to large specimens of indigenous and exotic trees.

The variety and number of animals are determined by the size and nature of territory each requires. A churchyard which has an above-average diversity of habitats contains a quite remarkable amount of animal life. Even in an ordinary parish churchyard there is a surprising number of birds and mammals, both resident and visiting, a wide range of insects, and a higher-than-average representation of reptile and invertebrate life.

Two-spot ladybird on forget-me-not (life size).

Ancient meadowland which supports a richly diverse flora is a habitat which is fast disappearing. A few sites have been designated national or local Conservation Trust nature reserves, but most have already been turned into 'improved pasture', which instead of being left to renew itself is ploughed, fertilized and sown with a restricted range of grasses. Nowhere was the difference between the old and the new style of managing grassland more striking than at Morwenstow in Cornwall, where St Morwenna's churchyard stands adjacent to 'improved pasture'. The churchyard, while extremely pretty, is no richer in species than many another in Cornwall. In May, when I made my visit, it was colourful with the last of the daffodils, lesser celandine, primroses, pignut, yarrow, forget-me-not, lesser dog violet, red campion and many other flowers in bloom, while over the wall there was none of these, not a violet, not even a daisy in sight.

All over England and Wales the sites which meadow wild flowers colonize today are hedgebanks, strips of land by rivers and the few remaining 'meadows of delight'.

Forget-me-nots of many kinds are to be found in churchyards. This one (life size), growing on a grave in early May at St Mary the Virgin in Martlesham, Suffolk, seems to be a garden variety of the wood forget-me-not.

47

Meadow flowers and grasses in Stoke-by-Nayland churchyard, Suffolk. In mid-June, the ox-eye or dog daisies are a dazzling white against the green grass and grey tombs. Common sorrel, ribwort plantain and hawkweed are also to be seen here among crested dog's tail grass, and meadow grass, foxtail and Holcus species.

There are now very few meadows which we can enjoy as Shakespeare did,
but there are countless churchyards which contain a wide range
of meadow flowers:

> When daisies pied and violets blue
> And lady-smocks all silver white
> And cuckoo-buds of yellow hue
> Do paint the meadows with delight
> The cuckoo then, on every tree,
> Mocks married men; for thus sings he
>   Cuckoo,

[*Love's Labour's Lost*]

May-time daisies,
St Mary,
Wareham, Dorset.

49

Shakespeare's 'daisies pied' were not a special variety: in the seventeenth century 'pied' simply denoted contrast. Shakespeare appreciated the beauty in everyday things, especially the daisy with its delicate drama of colours—the white, crimson-tipped outer florets set around the golden centre. When a survey of churchyards carried out in the county of Suffolk was put on computer, there was only one plant common to them all. One might have expected this to be the daisy, but it seems that this species, which is essentially a plant of grazed grassland and latterly of lawns, has not found a place in the very overgrown churchyards. In fact, the ribwort plantain was the only plant which was found everywhere.

The 'violets blue' of Shakespeare's song are the deliciously scented sweet violets which abound in churchyards (though less in the north and far south-west and not at all in central Wales). Some of the sweet violets in churchyards have larger flowers than usual, which may indicate that they are a garden sort which has become naturalized or cross-bred with the wild species. There is also a recognized hybrid which is altogether a more vigorous plant, with larger leaves as well as flowers. The colour of the flowers is generally in the blue-lilac-purple spectrum, but a common variant is white with a purplish spur. The most widespread and common violet of England and Wales is the common dog violet, though it is not so prevalent in churchyards as outside them, possibly because it seems to favour woodland sites. It was no surprise to find the biggest patches in partly-wooded churchyards or under large boundary trees. The effect of a purple pool of colour is quite arresting, as the flowers present themselves more openly than the sweet violet (the traditional 'shy violet').

The petals of the 'lady-smock' or cuckoo flower shade from a deep pink to Shakespeare's silver white. I was impressed by both their prevalence and persistence. Almost all the churchyards I visited in the spring had a few of these delicate and attractive plants. Some colonies were surviving frequent and regular mowing, but the plants were smaller and less numerous and evidently suffering under this treatment. I know of one instance of complete extinction where a group of about a dozen

Sweet violets growing at the base of the church wall, Holy Trinity, Boxted, Suffolk, in late April. (Life size).

'Cuckoo-spit' – foam produced by leafhopper larvae (right).

Sepals turn from yellow-green to ochre with pink-brown tips.

Flowers are palest when first open, becoming deeper lilac, and with veining more pronounced.

Lady's smock (cuckoo flower), one of the prettiest and most characteristic churchyard plants, at Holy Trinity, Boxted, Suffolk, in April. (Life size).

plants was mowed every week from February to late autumn for three years. During the dry weather of the spring of 1984 even the grass succumbed. The only plant that remained green was the diminutive mouse-ear hawkweed, its silvery-haired rosettes of leaves pressed close to the ground lower even than the low set of the mower.

Dialect dictionaries and country glossaries agree that Shakespeare's 'cuckoo-bud' is the bulbous buttercup. It is early-flowering and comes into bloom along with the lady's smock. It too is found in almost every churchyard. Even in Devon and Cornwall and in Wales where this species is less common, it occurs in well over half the churchyards and chapelyards surveyed. In Suffolk, the County Recorder for botany has gone so

A species-rich piece of turf: snowdrops with primrose, barren strawberry, celandine and dandelion leaves at All Saints churchyard, Over Worton, Oxfordshire, in late February. (Life size).

far as to make a special mention of churchyards as a particular habitat for this buttercup, as he does also for another spring-flowering kind, the goldilocks, which blooms soon after the bulbous buttercup. In churchyards as elsewhere, the goldilocks buttercup is generally the less common of the two though it is possibly under-recorded. This wiry plant with its inconspicuous, rather short-lived flowers (often missing several petals) is certainly worth looking for in churchyards, especially in slightly shaded areas under trees where it seems to grow especially well. In Cambridgeshire churchyards I saw the best examples of this species that I have ever come across and have since learned that distinct local forms occur in certain churchyards (though banished from the country around them).

Many of the characteristic plants of meadows, including some of the rarer species, can be found in church and chapel yards. One of the prettiest, and one which I had not expected to see so often, is meadow saxifrage. It seems to be able to cope with a variety of churchyard

52

conditions. I have seen tall plants growing up among high grasses and dog daisies in Oxfordshire, and surviving several years of close mowing at Kedington in Suffolk where, though it does not flower, the leaves appear every year by the side of the main path to the church. Though it looks so delicate with its flat rosette of leaves and its soft greeny-white flowers, meadow saxifrage seems to be able to survive an occasional dose of herbicide. The stronghold of meadow saxifrage is East Anglia, but there are churchyard records of it from many counties from as far north as Yorkshire, to the far south-west, where it is believed to be introduced. In Wales it is found only inland, in the mid-south and in a few places in north Wales and Anglesey. It would be interesting to know how many of the sites on record for this plant are churchyards.

The cowslip is perhaps the best known meadow flower and its religious associations have earned it the country name, St Peter's keys. The legend is that St Peter once dropped the keys of heaven and the first cowslips grew up where they fell. (Old-fashioned keys, St Peter's emblem, resemble cowslips rather more than modern ones.) These flowers have a very wide distribution in churchyards, (though they do not occur in those which are very overgrown) and they are subject to many interesting colour variations. I have twice seen in churchyards the rare deep crimson cowslip with a golden throat which cottage gardeners call Devon Red, but there is a range of colour from the golden yellow of the typical plant to a deep apricot with various throat markings. The churchyard of St John the Baptist in the centre of the village of Hartwell in Northamptonshire, keeps its grass well-groomed, but the gardener obviously takes care to avoid mowing groups of wild flowers such as lady's smocks and primroses and most conspicuously, a group of delightful cowslips which were red, pale pink, rich orange and buttery yellow. Such colour variations are thought to be the result of a cross-breeding between the cowslip and the garden polyanthus.

One of the best meadow habitats I have ever seen is at the church of Little Tew, Oxfordshire. At midsummer, the front and one side of the churchyard are tidily mown, though still fairly rich in plants. A corn dolly, symbol of the earth's fertility, hanging on the west wall in the church, clearly presides over the remainder of the churchyard. There I found a flowery paradise, dominated by waist-high dog daisies with meadow saxifrage, red clover, lesser trefoil, and meadow vetchling flourishing in

Startled blackbird in the ivy, at St John the Evangelist, Little Tew, Oxfordshire, in February.

53

Celandines growing in the grass
between gravestones at Cilgwyn,
Dyfed. (Life size).

Weevil
(life size).

The flowers open in the
sunlight, and close in the shade
or at night. The lower side of the
petals is green-tinged.

The glossy yellow
pales almost to silver
as the flowers age.

Millipede
(life size).

among them. Above their level, plants such as horehound and foxglove, naturalized lilies, great willowherb and purple-black columbines made taller contours. Two spicily scented sweetbriars arched gracefully over the high chest tombs, and the boundary hedge and the trees just beyond were full of birds – chaffinches, a blackbird and a song thrush singing to the background murmur of a woodpigeon.

The plant diversity in meadow churchyards in its turn supports a variety of other creatures. My explorations have often disturbed mallards grazing and searching out insects and other invertebrates in the grass. Where churches were originally manorial foundations, the nearby manor house has often become a farm, and ducks and geese enter the churchyard from that or a neighbouring farmyard. At Chesham in Buckinghamshire, ducks fly to the church from ornamental water gardens about a quarter of a mile away, but in some cases, such as at Kedington, it is not at all clear where they come from. Like the wild ducks who also visit churchyards they recognize a good feeding ground.

Ducks purposefully crossing the High Street in Bishop's Castle in Shropshire to graze in the churchyard of St John the Baptist.

I was pleased to find that churchyards also provide both food and occasional nesting places for the grey partridge; at Berrington in Shropshire, a pair made their nest on a game-keeper's grave. The grey partridge is a native bird that has been declining in numbers for several years. Current agricultural practices, such as stubble-burning and autumn ploughing, are a threat to this species, but the application of herbicides and pesticides which kill or poison its food has been particularly destructive. Churchyard surveys record partridges nesting in various parts of England (for their distribution is widespread, if in places very thin), but it was not until July, late in the season, that I came across a whole family of partridges feeding in a churchyard. They were at Westfield in Norfolk, where turtle doves crooned in the trees, and another frequenter of rural churchyards, the yellowhammer, was in full song.

Sometimes, while I sat on a gravestone making notes, I could hear the high notes of a shrew, and a rabbit once came out to feed about three feet away from where I sat. During my explorations, I was continually surprising wild rabbits, which would bound off into the undergrowth or out of the churchyard. At Hauxton, south of Cambridge, where the River Cam winds through pollarded willows just below the lovely, tile-roofed church, a brown and white domestic rabbit, which was clearly in the habit of visiting from a nearby garden, noted my arrival in the churchyard without much concern. Some people become extremely agitated about rabbits in tidy churchyards, largely in vain, because it is virtually impossible to keep rabbits out. I was told of a churchwarden in Shropshire who waged constant war on the rabbit population to the end of his life. Nevertheless, the rabbits outlasted him and have even been seen hopping about over his grave. He might perhaps have welcomed some assistance from some of the rabbits' natural predators, weasels, a whole family of whom were discovered living in a churchyard shed at Silecroft in Cumbria.

These rabbits were sitting among the graves at St Margaret's, Binsey, Oxfordshire.

I only once saw a hare in a churchyard, and that scudded off out of sight in an instant. However, surveys show that hares regularly visit churchyards throughout rural England and Wales. Hedgehogs are frequently observed visiting or living in churchyards, where they find a plentiful supply of slugs, beetles, caterpillars, and other creatures. Moles, which thrive best in permanent pasture, find an almost ideal habitat in churchyards.

There are a few reports of foxes having made their earths inside churchyards, (cemeteries, which are usually larger, appear to be preferred). However, churchyards, both urban and rural, are patronized by foxes as feeding grounds. In tall grass, they find their favourite prey, the field vole, distinguished by its chestnut back, from the greyish bank vole – more an animal of scrub and hedges, and also very acceptable food for a fox. Churchyards also provide foxes with rabbits, wood mice and worms and, in hard times, moles and shrews.

Badgers, like rural foxes, are susceptible to disturbance by human beings and will move their set if bothered, but there are several records of badgers inhabiting country churchyards which have plenty of cover and where there is little human activity. They are omnivorous and eat a wider diversity of foods than a fox, but the single most important item of diet is the earthworm, though small mammals, frogs, grubs, beetles, nuts, clovers and grasses all form part of their fare. It is not unusual for churchyards to contain all these and so they are often regular foraging places for badgers. Well-worn paths may be seen criss-crossing the churchyards that they frequent.

Bank vole, found dead in a churchyard ditch, Suffolk.

Many species of butterfly are to be found in good numbers, especially where there are flowering shrubs and meadow flowers, and where the grass is not cut too short by rotary mowing machines which destroy the eggs and caterpillars. I was visiting churchyards when I saw my first brimstone of the year (the earliest butterfly) and I was pleased to find at my local church (where there are abundant flowering shrubs, wild flowers, and tall grasses) many other species, some of which I would normally travel some distance to see. As well as harbouring burnet moths in late summer, the knapweed is a favourite with marbled white butterflies. Once, I found a perfect chestnut-brown small skipper sunning itself on a bramble, its wings tipped up in the typical pose of that species. The hedge brown (or gatekeeper), wall brown, meadow brown and speckled wood were all nearby. Most of the blues frequent churchyards, though they are less common than the gaily-coloured small tortoiseshell and peacock, which often hibernate in churches and memorials, or in the churchyard trees.

In a typical meadow community, there is a balance of wild flowers and grasses. If a meadow remains ungrazed or unmown, its character changes, and larger plants, such as cow parsley, hogweed, shrubs and young

trees take over. When cow parsley comes into flower all around a church, it makes a breathtaking sea of lacy white. Two cow parsley churchyards stand out in my mind, one surrounding the pretty flint and tile church at Great Waldringfield in Suffolk, wonderfully unruly, and the other at Church Enstone in Oxfordshire.

In searching for a way to describe such luxuriantly overgrown churchyards, I recalled that vernacular names for wild plants include many with the prefix 'dog'—as in dog daisy, the wild ox-eye—simply indicating a larger version of the normative type. In this sense, Great Waldringfield might be termed a 'dog churchyard'. It is surrounded by large trees, well-grown common limes and horse chestnuts, which hold a thriving rookery of fifty nests or more, and the April air is full of cawing. There are sycamores with flaking bark and large shining, blush-pink buds, and tangles of overgrown forsythia. In and around the mists of tall cow parsley I found nettles, rough grasses, foxgloves, red dead-nettle, and bright naturalized double daffodils with thick, sturdy stems.

At Church Enstone, a path runs the whole length of the churchyard from a far gate. On the right, a jungle of cow parsley grows very high under the yew, ash and lime trees. Here and there a headstone is visible, but it is impossible to make a way through the undergrowth without falling over concealed kerbstones or into a ditch. Most of the smaller meadow species have disappeared but more robust plants, such as a great purple patch of dame's violet and some yellow foxglove (presumably spread from a grave-planting), were blooming healthily when I visited the churchyard. I should add, perhaps, that the parishioners may enter the churchyard by an altogether more decorous approach, where two brilliant laburnums frame the lych-gate and a rose twines up from a mat of garden *Helxine* (baby's tears) by the church porch.

As summer comes, cow parsley gives way to hogweed as the dominant plant, and there are tall patches of columbine and hemp agrimony. It is easy to see why botanists rather disapprove of churchyards such as these, in which the interesting small plants representative of the flora of ancient grassland will have been lost. Overgrown churchyards correspond more to a scrub habitat, which has its own benefits for wildlife and is usually well-populated by birds and mammals.

Six-spot burnet moth, sketched at St Andrews, Rufus Castle, Portland, Dorset. (Life size).

58

St Peter's herb (cowslips), at the
beginning of May, St Margaret's,
Tilbury-juxta-Clare, Essex.
(Life size).

59

Hedges, shrubs and self-seeded trees are usually luxuriant in overgrown churchyards, and provide shelter and food for birds. The robin and the wren, 'God's cock and hen' in the old rhyme, are two of the most familiar of the churchyard birds. It is unusual to enter a churchyard without disturbing at least one wren. Reclusive by nature, wrens will rocket out of view immediately into whatever cover is handy, while robins, bolder in their behaviour, will flutter in full view from one perch to another,

Robins at St Giles,
Hampton Gay,
Oxfordshire, in January.

adopting that characteristic, quizzical attitude quite as readily on top of a headstone as on the traditional garden spade. They will also make their nests more publicly than other birds. I was told of one that continually nested (unsuccessfully) beneath a leaning gravestone, while a pair at Ashill in Norfolk made their nest in a flower arrangement in the church porch.

A tree frequently planted in churchyards, the common lime, is well known for the wealth of suckers that grow around the lower trunk. If they are not clipped, the trees produce a lush screen of foliage over a dense, tangled frame of twigs, the ideal home for wrens. There was a splendidly unclipped lime beside the impressive parish church of St John the Baptist at Cirencester. Like most town churchyards, this one was municipally maintained, but it was very far from that point of shorn monotony reached by the tidiest parks and churchyards. Several other large trees apart from the great lime were leafy from top to base, and although the mowing was evidently regular and frequent, there were patches which had not been over-tended. Despite ugly signs of weed-killer here and there, an imaginative mix of *laissez-faire* and planting made this a most agreeable green place in the middle of the town.

Wrens also use thick ivy as cover for their nests, principally on boundary walls, since increasingly those responsible for the maintenance and insurance of parish churches refuse to countenance ivy on towers or church walls and insist on its being torn down. Whether opposition to ivy on buildings proceeds from superstition or reason is a matter of debate in many a parish. Blackbirds, song thrushes and finches are attracted to dense ivy as a nesting place, a fact that is also appreciated by many a churchyard cat. Blackbirds are so open in their behaviour, it would be a dull place where you failed to see one, dipping a crocus-coloured beak into the church compost heap, searching for insects in the grass, scuffling in the dark recesses of low trees and shrubs, or singing lustily from a tree.

The churchyard song thrush usually chooses the tallest trees from which to deliver the loud, sweet repetitions of its song. Our local church celebrated Ascension Day in 1984 with a John Dunstable sung mass. It was a blissfully warm, still May evening, and the west door was thrown open, letting in the sunset and allowing the notes of a song thrush to mingle with the plainsong.

A common sight in almost any churchyard, a song thrush using the kerbstone of a grave as its 'anvil' for breaking snails.

Pied wagtails skipping across mown lawns and enjoying puddles on the paths are among those species I encountered over and again in churchyards. Spotted flycatchers use the headstones of graves as places from which to dart after insects. They seem to be birds for which people form a special affection—many churchyard observers mentioned them. Starlings are nearly always to be found nesting in niches in church masonry, often in the towers. They will also try to nest inside the church if they can.

Jackdaws often nest in churches and appear to be particularly attracted to square towers. They also use the high features of church architecture from which to spy out the land for food. There is a Norwich weather adage: 'When three daws are seen on St Peter's/Then we're sure to have bad weather'. The crow family figures in folklore mainly as a symbol of doom, but I know of only one saying of this kind attached to the jackdaw and since it is a sociable creature, it is unlikely that many fatalities follow the sighting of a solitary jackdaw, said to presage death.

The homely sparrow is the inspiration for Bede's haunting image of the transience of human life — as it flies from whence who knows into the great hall, and departs again who knows where. This chirpy associate of humankind is to be found only in well frequented places. As one would expect, sparrows are readily to be found in town centres or in the bustle of a village, but where churches are remote or rarely used they have left or failed to arrive. Perhaps the presence or absence of these little birds, which followed Montgomery and the Eighth Army into the desert on campaign, but which soon abandon a farmhouse left empty, ought to form part of the calculation as to whether or not a church should be made redundant!

Ivy is a good plant for wildlife all the year round, particularly for birds. The importance of dense ivy as a safe wind-proof roost for thrushes and finches is often overlooked, and its abundant winter berries provide fare that is appreciated by the occasional overwintering blackcaps and, more commonly, by finches and thrushes (including winter migrants such as bramblings, redwings, and fieldfares).

Snowdrops and aconites under the giant sycamore at St Peter's, Steeple Aston, Oxfordshire, in February. This churchyard, with its wooded surroundings, is a good place to see birds such as jays. The sycamore itself, more than sixty-six feet high, is taller than the church tower, and its girth is about twenty-three feet.

63

Churchyards with abundant shrubs, wild flowers and grasses are full of seeds and berries in late autumn and winter and a boon to birds. Summer migrants frequent churchyards along with the resident population. The warbler I came across most frequently was the willow warbler and often heard the silvery falling cadences of this species among the foliage of some tree or high hawthorn hedge. Rambling hedges or large wildernesses of bramble, hawthorn and elder provide good nesting places for whitethroats and other warblers. Dunnocks sing from hedges both high and low, and in spring it seems that there is a cuckoo within earshot of almost every country churchyard.

Stout boundary hedges attract finches. It is not unusual to hear the half-lazy, half-urgent call of the greenfinch (a great colonizer of churchyards) or the breezy down-scale song of the chaffinch. If they are bounded by hedges, even the sprucest churchyards have their birds. At Cardinham in Cornwall, the neat grounds of the Methodist Church rise to a closely mown grass bank with a hedge, where I watched nesting chaffinches feeding on some dandelion heads that had managed to bolt up and seed between mowings.

Several species of trees seed themselves—principally ash, sycamore, elder and holly, although I have also seen plenty of rowan, oak and yew, but the seedlings rarely make full growth. Rowan and yew seem to fail of their own accord after about a year's growth. Ash and sycamore are often cut to ground level as saplings. They subsequently form several trunks and emerge as a dense coppice tree. Ash specimens of this kind form a very shapely and attractive ornament to the churchyard. They are often left to grow for several years before being cut again and where there is room, they are sometimes allowed to attain considerable size. These coppice trees make good cover for finches and wrens.

Where a mower is steered around a tree or sapling, other plants take advantage of the respite and form a thick island of vegetation. Woody nightshade, a low grower when left to itself in the shade of churchyard trees and not very significant in hedges, seems to come into its own when scrambling eight or nine feet up hollies—often in association with brambles, which it leaves behind in its climb. Red campion, white bryony and stitchwort will grow round the edge of the island, often out of a huge cushion of flowering bramble, and yarrow will reach its full flowering

Dunnock (hedge sparrow) searching for food on a gravel path at St Andrew's in Sherborne St John, Hampshire, in February.

height. Similar vegetation occurs where mowing ends on the margin of some churchyards, and here in the rough turf you quite commonly come across white comfrey. Common and Russian comfrey are also recorded from churchyards, but it is the white which is the characteristic species, perhaps because it prefers slightly drier conditions.

Two or three tree species will sometimes entwine with each other. At Tring Baptist Church in Hertfordshire, elder, ash, sycamore, yew and ivy grow together in an extraordinary patchwork of foliage. Only two miles away on a summer day, at St Bartholomew's, Wigginton, I picked a very sweet red gooseberry from a bush growing inside a holly which was itself closely intertwined with an ash. Elder and gooseberry are both adept at making use of any suitable habitat: I have seen elders growing out of a fork in a churchyard sycamore and a gooseberry out of a poplar. There were far more members of the currant family than I had expected to find, but while one frequently encounters small gooseberry bushes flowering and fruiting on graves, blackcurrants are a little less common. I have even come upon a few feral red currants. Currant plants in churchyards are undoubtedly sown by birds. The seeds germinate in crevices where they have either been left when birds have wiped their beaks after feasting in nearby farms or gardens, or where they have been deposited in birds' droppings.

At the other end of the scale from the scrubby wilderness is the 'lawn' or, in extreme cases, 'bowling-green' churchyard. In general, there is at least a small area, usually on either side of the path from the lych-gate to the porch, which is kept well shorn. Some entire churchyards are like this, but they are so far in the minority. Not surprisingly, lawn-like conditions give rise to the flora associated with garden lawns, but in some cases the incidence of certain species is remarkable. The pretty little slender speedwell which forms mats of delicate blue, is known to have been increasing in lawn habitats, but nowhere more so, it seems, than in churchyards. I saw it almost everywhere and received letters from botanists throughout England and Wales remarking on its colonizing vigour. Another plant which is really rather rare, but seems to occur fairly often in churchyards is

Turf with moss and willowherb seedlings all bound up together at All Saints, Fulham, London, in February. (Life size).

keeled cornsalad, an inconspicuous annual with forked branches, rather narrow leaves arranged in pairs on opposite sides of the stem, and a head of tiny mauve flowers. It tends to grow in the lee of headstones or by walls, just out of reach of the mower.

Most lawn plants are perennials and hug the ground in a rosette of leaves, like the daisy, which thrives in grass that is closely mown. Yarrow manages to survive, flowering as and when it can—its dark, feathery leaves are usually to be found even in a close-cut sward. Mouse-ear hawkweed is familiar not only on closely mown lawns and banks but also on the raised mounds of graves, a micro-habitat in themselves. Field wood-rush is also common here. A small plant with narrow leaves lightly fringed with long hairs, it brings forth its tiny clusters of nut-brown flowers as early as March. The handsome downy, greyish-green rosette of wide leaves belonging to the hoary plantain is easy to spot in short grass from the earliest months of the year. If it has a rest from mowing, it comes into flower from May to August with the palest of pink blooms, very showy for a plantain; in fact, in St Andrew's churchyard at Great Rollright, Oxfordshire the brush-like flower was so dense that I mistook it from a distance for a small, pale orchid.

Burnet saxifrage can sometimes be discerned among the grasses, looking like a rather darker, coarser version of the salad burnet. This plant lies low until late summer, when it puts up its flowering stem with great speed. In meadow conditions, it will grow to a height of over three feet but I have several times found its white umbrella heads of flowers on stems only five or six inches high, dotted all over flat-mown grass.

Some of the most familiar plants of churchyards are those inherited from woodland. Churchyards such as Milland St Luke's in the middle of Woolmer Forest in Hampshire or St Michael, Penkival, on the slope of a gloriously wooded Cornish valley, are relatively few, but many of our churchyards were originally carved out of woods and forests. Now, even in places where the village has become a town and the countryside has receded, the churchyard may retain a relic woodland flora.

One of the most common and evocative woodland plants is the bluebell. Just as in bluebell woods, the flowers can make a glimmering blue mist amongst the green of the grasses and their own leaves. But things are not as simple as they seem. If some plants look different from the others, close inspection may reveal them to be not the native woodland bluebell but

One of the nicest, as well as one of the commonest of churchyard plants: hoary plantain, in June at St Mary's, North Aston, Oxfordshire. (Life size).

66

Wood sorrel growing in a bank by a chapel at Cilgwyn, Dyfed, in May. (Life size).

Petals are white with delicate pink veining.

Flowers have cream stamens with pinhead anthers.

There is a yellow triangular nectary guide on each petal.

The leaves are hairy.

67

the so-called Spanish bluebell, a closely related garden species. In the native bluebell the anthers are cream-coloured and the tips of the slender bells arch back. The Spanish bluebell looks more robust, has broader leaves, and the individual flowers have wider bells and blue anthers. Hybrids, which are frequently white or pink, may show almost any combination of these features. They and the Spanish bluebell are very common in churchyards, probably introduced by visitors planting bulbs from a home garden on a grave.

One of the prettiest flowers of ancient woodland, the wood anemone, does not occur as frequently or in such plenty as the invasive bluebell. Wood anemones generally grow in situations which still resemble a woodland habitat, under trees and in association with other woodland plants. There is always a pleasure in finding its starry white flowers with that subliminal flush of pink. The woodland plant most delicate of all in appearance however, is the wood sorrel, which also continues to haunt churchyards. Low-growing, it makes small soft, pale, clover-shaped leaves, from among which rise white flowers exquisitely veined with lilac.

Lesser celandines are a common sight in most churchyards and very welcome in the bleak early months of the year. My records suggest that they tend to come into flower rather earlier than is usual elsewhere, possibly because conditions are often both sheltered and sunny. However, there are also deeply shaded spots, and I have a note for 1984, recording a Hertfordshire celandine in flower in June. The County Recorder for south-east Yorkshire has noted the slightly less common sub-species *bulbifera* (recognizable from the little bulbils at the base of the leaves, and generally narrower petals) growing in several churchyards when it was not found on waysides in the surrounding country. It would be interesting to know if this variant is to be found in churchyards elsewhere.

*The grey-green leaves of lady's
mantle from a lower part of the
stem.*

68

Primroses are plants of both woods and hedgebanks and they thrive in a very large proportion of churchyards in England and Wales. These populations are of mixed descent. Where they grow among a variety of other woodland plants, they are clearly part of the forest origins of the churchyard. However, they are well-loved plants, which have long been planted on graves. The plantings are sometimes of garden provenance, sometimes taken from local wild populations.

The primrose family naturally produces odd forms or 'sports'. I have occasionally found flowers of unusual colours growing far away from gardens and in situations where hybridization with garden primulas seems unlikely. The garden writer and botanist, John Parkinson, writing in 1629, described no less than twenty-one forms of primrose (including cowslips and oxlips), 'all of which kinds' he remarks 'have been found wilde'. New wild forms are still occurring. In 1982, Bressingham Gardens nursery put on the market a delightful, pale pink double primrose which had been discovered in the wild. I have been very struck by the frequent occurrence of a pretty primrose, pinkish in colour, looking as if the palest of plum-coloured washes had been added to its original yellow. In other

Lady's mantle, one of the many species named after the Virgin Mary, flowering at St James, Piccadilly, in London, in July. This is a plant which readily seeds itself.

A single flower (life size).

69

The colour is not a true pink, but a primrose yellow, suffused with pink.

The churchyard 'pink' primrose, at St Margaret's, Tilbury-juxta-Clare, Essex, in April. (Life size).

respects the plants are the same as the normal form. I found this washed pink primrose, which I have come to think of as the 'churchyard primrose', among almost every primrose population of any size, and in many places where there were no garden polyanthus apparent to create colour hybrids. Other primrose/polyanthus hybrids occur in a variety of colours, usually with a slightly less delicate petal texture. Another form of primrose which I have found several times in churchyards is the rather ungainly form known as variety *caulescens*, in which the flowers grow not from single stems rising from the root but in an umbel of short stems which spring from a single point at the top of a single stout stem. Each sub-stem bears a flower which is just like that of the normal primrose.

There are two rather discreet plants which give a clear indication that the area in which they are growing was originally woodland. The dark green serrated leaves arranged in opposite pairs up the stem of dog's mercury are most easily spotted in February and March, and the plant comes early into spikes of small greenish flowers. Moschatel, or town hall clock, flowers in April and May. Its name comes from the inconspicuous but pretty flower head which presents four almost square 'clock-face' flowers with a fifth flower facing upwards.

Churchyards are the best places to go in the late winter for a glimpse of the first flowers of the year. Only a few weeks after Christmas, the first snowdrops start to appear, closely followed by winter aconites and then lesser celandines and daffodils. The snowdrop, thought to be native in parts of Wales and western England and possibly elsewhere, has been so widely introduced that it would be impossible to identify an aboriginal population without a record of the floral history of a churchyard. It readily becomes naturalized in churchyard conditions and there are many splendid churchyards where both single and double varieties spread over large areas under trees and between the graves. Along with parkland, the churchyard is an important habitat for the winter aconite, which may grow among snowdrops or alone in a brilliant yellow mass. Winter aconites can be difficult to raise, but seem to find churchyard conditions most favourable. I have seen a dozen or so aconites planted on graves double in numbers within only a year or two and spread outside the kerbstones.

Aconites, painted from the large population beneath trees in the church boundary, Drayton Beauchamp, Buckinghamshire, in late February. (Three-quarters life size).

One of the most common naturalized plants is the daffodil, which makes a spectacular spring show in many churchyards. The wild species is smaller and more delicate than any of the garden varieties and, to my mind, much prettier. I have seen and heard of churchyards in several counties where the daffodils seem to be an original wild population, and in Norfolk most of the wild daffodils appear to be found in churchyards. However, daffodils – Lent lilies, as they are still called in some counties – have always been popular flowers, and wild ones were certainly planted on graves in the past. This would account for the cases where daffodils that are to all appearances wild grow in situations in which one would not normally expect to find the wild species. Adding extra diversity, large naturalized populations of garden varieties (some of them interesting old-fashioned kinds) often grow in churchyards. They are fairly robust and persist in less than ideal conditions. A few most exotic garden daffodils, their trumpets a mass of yellow frill, made an odd sight among the wild flowers at Great Waldringfield.

Several of the plant species which are traditionally grown on graves readily become naturalized and spread. Sometimes it takes no more than a bunch of flowers or a wreath laid on a grave to establish a new species in a churchyard. This is the case with flowers like garden lady's mantle and honesty, and may explain the occurrence of some rather rare plants outside their normal habitat or area of distribution. Honesty, which produces the silvery seed pods that find their way into so many church flower arrangements, has become a familiar sight. Occasionally the rare, white honesty, which is fragrant, may have been planted on graves, but the white-flowered kind in churchyards is usually a white form of the common species. At Hawridge churchyard in Buckinghamshire, there is a very odd honesty which has untidy-looking bi-coloured petals (not leaves, as is more usual) splashed with white.

Lungwort is another fairly widespread introduction. This herb may occur in the taller vegetation of churchyard margins, by walls or on graves. The variety most commonly grown has broad leaves with whitish blotches on them, which earned it names such as Virgin Mary's milkdrops and Mary's tears. The way in which the flowers change from pink to blue, both colours (and shades in between) being displayed at the same time, has given rise to a number of biblical composite names such as Josephs and

Lungwort blooms (life size) at St Mary's, Ovington in Essex, in early May. The leaves have light green blotches on a slightly darker green background, and the calyces are covered with dark purple pimples and bristly transparent hairs.

Marys, Children of Israel, Adam and Eve, and Abraham, Isaac and Jacob. Lungwort is also known as Jerusalem cowslip, Bedlam (Bethlehem) cowslip and Good Friday plant (from the time of year it comes into flower). Another member of the borage family which is widely naturalized and more common than lungwort in churchyards is green alkanet, a tall blue-flowered plant with the typical bristly hairs of all borages.

Churchyards reflect the diversity of wild flora which grows in the countryside around them, and this applies to naturalized as well as native species. Winter heliotrope and three-cornered leek are found abundantly in churchyards in Devon and Cornwall, and the drooping star of Bethlehem has even acquired the local name of 'Bodney lily' in the churchyard at Bodney in west Norfolk. In the north of England, the delicately lacy sweet cicely is plentiful around places of human habitation and is believed to be an escape from cultivation. In some churchyards in the Yorkshire Dales it is as abundant as cow parsley in the southern counties.

Cottage garden plants are enjoying renewed interest among gardeners, but they have never been out of fashion in churchyards. Many species planted on graves are brought from local gardens and the introduced plants of the churchyard may be as representative of the domestic flora of the parish as the wild flowers are of the surrounding countryside. Many of them are native wild plants that grow truly wild only in restricted locations or conditions, but have been widely grown in gardens and churchyards. Common Solomon's seal, with its arch of wing-like leaves and creamy flower bells, is a plant of southern woodlands, but it is well established and widespread as an introduction. It shares its churchyard habitat with a hybrid that is the most common garden form. Solomon's seal has had biblical associations since at least the first century AD. Its root is supposed to resemble the seal of Solomon, the magic pentacle which was supposed to point to the five wounds of Christ. It has an alternative English name, 'ladder to heaven' and it is often planted upon graves. In favourable conditions it can spread to form a most attractive small forest of foliage, which arises suddenly as if from nowhere in spring.

Moschatel (or 'town hall clock') is also Good Friday plant, because its greeny blooms appear early in spring about Easter-time.

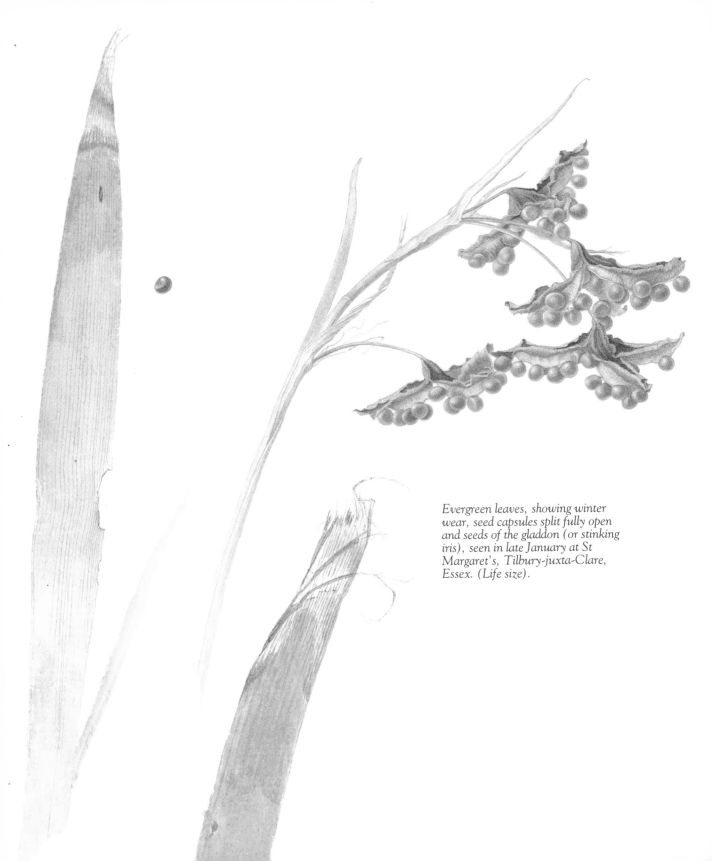

Evergreen leaves, showing winter wear, seed capsules split fully open and seeds of the gladdon (or stinking iris), seen in late January at St Margaret's, Tilbury-juxta-Clare, Essex. (Life size).

During the winter months the bright green spear-shaped leaves and bright orange-red seeds of gladdon, a native iris, are a welcome sight in many churchyards in the south and midland counties. Sometimes the seed-heads are used in flower arrangements for church or graves and the plant's very frequent occurrence must be partly due to this, but I suspect that it is encouraged and perhaps planted in churchyards, as are a number of other evergreen species, their foliage a symbol of life amid death.

Rock may seen an inhospitable habitat, but there are a number of species, both wild and naturalized, which readily colonize the stone habitats that are so plentiful in churchyards if not in the surrounding country. The common houseleek thrives on paved or concreted graves and also on the roofs of porches and lych-gates. It is frequently planted, since it is supposed to bring good luck and give protection against lightning—an important consideration with buildings as high as churches. Another common grave-plant is the large yellow stonecrop whose bright flowerheads make umbrellas above the dense mat of fleshy leaves. A number of the saxifrages, in particular London pride, are also common on graves. Some garden plants such as aubrieta and snapdragons seem to persist on walls long after the original plantings on the ground have been ousted by more strongly growing species. Ivy-leaved toadflax has spread to walls all over Britain since its introduction in the seventeenth century and is now very plentiful.

Several of our familiar native wild flowers are to be found growing on and in the shelter of walls; indeed some of them grow so thickly that the structure beneath can hardly be seen at all. Pellitory-of-the-wall, as its name would suggest, is very common in this situation. George Crabbe makes a mention of it in an early poem:

> Owls and ravens haunt the buildings,
> Sending gloomy dread to all;
> Yellow moss the summit yielding,
> Pellitory decks the wall.

Navelwort, or wall penny-wort, is a typical wall species in the west. Hedgerow plants, such as stitchwort (called Sunday whites in one Devon village) frequently colonize walls, and plantains, sowthistles of all three types and barren strawberry find footholds everywhere.

Ivy-leaved toadflax from the wall of Braemore churchyard, Hampshire. (Life size).

75

Most importantly, churchyard walls are a habitat for ferns, especially in the drier, more easterly counties, where they are generally scarce. The walls of a church, too, are a good habitat, especially near leaking drainpipes and on steps leading down to the crypt or basement, places where there is damp and shade. One of the most familiar and easily recognizable ferns is the common polypody, which also grows on the tiled roofs of churches and lych-gates. Hartstongue fern, with its glossy tongue-like leaves, is another widespread species. The tall neat fronds of male fern grow handsomely at the base of the wall or in damp corners on the north sides of churches. Good specimens will wave triumphantly out of the mower's reach in the narrow gaps between chest tombs. Similar in size, but slightly less common in churchyards is the lady fern, which prefers an acid soil. It has long fronds—with a characteristic droop at the tips—making a large, graceful crown of green.

Three most attractive wall ferns of the genus *Asplenium* make themselves very much at home on church and churchyard walls. Black spleenwort grows in dense, glossy-green tufts. It has about fifteen pairs of leaflets, themselves divided into toothed lobes, decreasing in size towards the tip of each main stem, which is usually curved. The related wall rue grows in more irregular leafy tufts, which look like a scruffier, darker green version of its namesake, rue. Maidenhair spleenwort, like the true maidenhair fern, is altogether more delicate; its forty or so pairs of simple leaflets grow, more or less equal in size, from a thin glossy black stem, and the plant looks like a very large bright green spider. The fronds of the rusty-back fern grow in small, rather stiff clumps, the leaflets slightly cupped and covered with rusty-brown scales on the underside. This plant is mainly associated with the western parts of England and Wales.

Trees possibly do more than any other plants to create the atmosphere of a churchyard. Without them, churchyards are almost invariably bleak and windswept—small plains without any points of reference. Fortunately, only relatively few are like this and many of our churchyards resemble wooded islands set in pasture or arable land, providing shelter and shade.

Yews are the archetypal churchyard tree. They are native in Britain only on well-drained chalk or limestone which indicates that most of the churchyard trees must have been deliberately planted. They are

Male fern, just beginning to unfurl in a chapelyard in Cilgwyn, Dyfed, in spring. (Life size).

76

Herb Robert and hartstongue fern in a grave in St Brynach's churchyard, Nevern, Dyfed. Hartstongue fern quite often colonizes graves in shaded places.

77

present in greater numbers in the west of Britain and also found in Breton churchyards which would suggest a strong Celtic connection. Although it is difficult to age them precisely, some of the churchyard yews are undoubtedly of very great antiquity.

Interestingly the custom of planting yews in holy places is still continued, whatever the reason may have been in the past. The common yew is a protective tree both physically and symbolically: its dense bulk shields the church from wind and weather; in folk belief it gives protection from evil. The yew is also the symbol of immortality and resurrection. There are many medieval references to the decking of churches with yew on Easter Sunday. Even today, it is regarded as a rather special tree. I was quite startled to see in Selborne church during Lent, a very simply fashioned cross of rough-hewn yew branches, placed high before the altar. Outside was the famous ancient churchyard yew, surrounded by a circular bench seat. This tree had the added distinction of supporting two species of lichen—lichens are rather rare on the shiny, flaking bark of yews.

The Windrush Valley from Swinbrook churchyard in late July, with house martins gathering over the churchyard. The pale, dried-up grasses in front of the wall almost hide the gravestones. Pollard willows show the course of the Windrush.

79

Yews were commonly planted by the lych-gate and in some places the priest traditionally met coffins at the yew tree. The records of the parish clerks at Clyst Hydon in Devon contain several references to the planting of yews on graves between 1777 and 1814. At Wateringbury in Kent an epitaph draws attention to a yew tree planted on a grave there in 1597 by a certain Thomas Hood. (This tree measured eleven feet and four inches in girth in 1982).

Most yews planted today are the fastigiate form known as the Irish yew, a natural sport found on the limestone cliffs of County Fermanagh, propagated, and widely distributed. It is a compact tree, used for avenues and small spaces, but continued familiarity with it has not made me like it. I prefer the height, the great tip-tilted branches and the wide skirts of the old yews. The British Trust for Ornithology has records for mistle thrush, greenfinch, chaffinch, linnet, goldcrest and coal tit nesting in yews. They and other observers agree that the fastigiate yew is the more favoured by birds.

Also associated with churchyards are the holly and the rowan. Both are holy trees, with reputed powers of protection against evil; the red berries both trees produce were believed to be particularly effective in this respect. In some places coffins were fashioned out of rowan wood. Like yew, both trees will self-seed and foot-high seedlings of any of these three species are a fairly common sight in churchyards, although holly seedlings seem to be the only ones that are allowed to grow on. I have seen countless small hollies between two and six or seven feet high, but never a rowan or yew at that intermediate stage.

If I had to choose only one plant genus to demonstrate the diversity of churchyard habitats it would be *Geranium*—the cranesbills (not to be confused with the bedding geraniums of gardeners which are classified botanically as *Pelargonium*). There are cranesbills of one kind or another in almost every churchyard habitat. The most widespread is the pink-flowered herb Robert. It can be found beside paths, growing on or at the foot of walls, in banks and shady places and occasionally in the grass sward, and may be in flower from late March right through until October. One of the most cheerful sights of winter is the rosette of filigree leaves, often flame-red at this season, against the dull granite chippings it is now the fashion to spread over graves.

Swifts flying around the church tower, Charlbury, Oxfordshire. They are feeding on the winged insects carried aloft in the updraught.

One of the most attractive species of the churchyard, the meadow cranesbill, grows among the taller grasses in late summer. A typical plant of rough grass verges and field margins (and one which had been adopted into gardens), its wild distribution lies in a wide band down the centre of England, penetrating into the south-east of Wales. It is clearly native in some churchyards, such as St Michael's at Dulas in Herefordshire, and it has been planted in a number of others, in Suffolk, for example. *Gratia Dei* seems to have been a popular name in the sixteenth century, and I can think of no more joyful plant to express thankfulness than this one, with its graceful profusion of sky-blue summer flowers.

Other native *geranium* species to be seen among the churchyard grasses and on overgrown graves include cut-leaved, dove's-foot and small-flowered cranesbills, all with fairly small mid-pink flowers. The handsome purplish-red bloody cranesbill makes shapely hummocks over graves in many West Yorkshire churchyards. As it is native to that region and has been taken into gardens, churchyard plants may be of mixed provenance. At Gayton in Northamptonshire, where bloody cranesbill does not grow in the wild, well-established naturalized plants have long been on record.

A few non-native cranesbills are fairly frequent in churchyards. I saw French cranesbill with its deep pink, veined flowers in a tangle of grasses at Dulas, and it was reported in a number of the churchyard surveys. So, occasionally, was the pencilled cranesbill, an introduced species with pale pink or white flowers lined with dark pink-violet veins. By far the commonest of the introductions, however, is dusky cranesbill with its dramatic, black-purple petals that curve back, away from a contrasting pale centre. The garden name of this plant is 'mourning widow' which might have some connection with its frequency as a grave plant. It grows very handsomely in two London churchyards—St James's, Piccadilly, and St Stephen's in South Kensington. It seems to be most at home in a gardened environment, though there are records of plants that have become naturalized in churchyards in several counties, indicating that it can survive a certain amount of competition from native plants.

One of the prettiest of the cranesbills, and one which illustrates the ambiguous status of some of the churchyard plants, is shining cranesbill.

It has small clear-pink flowers, shining stems, and green
leaves which have a pink tinge to them. Shining cranesbill
is native to many parts of Britain but somewhat patchy in its distribution.
Generally speaking, it is to be found in shady hedgerows among
rocks and on old walls. It also occurs in a number of churchyards. My
records for it include four from churchyards on Exmoor, two from Rutland,
one from Suffolk, one from Lincolnshire and eight from Cardiganshire
(where it was rare fifty years ago), and I have also seen it in North Yorkshire.
However, in the north-west of Yorkshire, where one would expect
it to be wild, the plant I saw was in a stone container by the side of the
porch entrance. I do not know whether it was bird-sown or had been planted
there. In Suffolk, shining cranesbill plants may be native or introduced. It is
not a common flower in that county though it is locally abundant in some
places. At Holton-le-Moor in Lincolnshire, it is known that the
vicar introduced shining cranesbill to the churchyard from Matlock,
Derbyshire, in 1880. Remarkably, the plant still survives there.

*Meadow cranesbill, in early July at
Asthall churchyard, Oxfordshire (life
size), showing buds, flowers and
'crane's-bill' fruits.*

83

SANCTUARY
and
SURVIVAL

*. . . I stood one evening at the little gate at
Brockenhurst churchyard, and counted between me and
the church twenty gravestones stained with the red alga
{Trentipohlia}, showing a richness and variety of
colouring never seen before, the result of so much wet
weather. For this alga, which plays so important a
part in nature's softening and beautifying effect on
man's work . . . is still in essence a water-plant: the
sun and dry wind burn its life out and darken it to the
colour of ironstone, so that to anyone who may notice the
dark stain it seems a colour of the stone itself; but when
rain falls the colour freshens and brightens as if the old
grey stone has miraculously been made to live.*

W. H. Hudson: *Hampshire Days*

THERE IS A STORY WRITTEN BY the twelfth-century monk, Reginald of Durham, which describes how, on the feast of St Cuthbert, a nobleman was hunting in the border country of Lothian when he chased a fine stag to one of the churches dedicated to St Cuthbert. Crowds of people were celebrating the feast, playing games and dancing in the churchyard. The weary stag had just enough strength to jump the churchyard wall and, as if it knew it was in sanctuary, fled no further, but walked quietly to the church porch and lay down. Neither the hounds nor the huntsmen made any move to enter the churchyard and the people at the festival marvelled, says Reginald, at the way St Cuthbert, who had so loved animals during his life, extended his protection to them after his death. Nobody questioned the right of the stag to sanctuary.

Sadly, the story does not end there. A boy was induced to drive the stag out of sanctuary and, once outside the churchyard, it was set upon and killed. Then, as now, there was a difference between ideals and reality in the protection of wildlife. Five out of the six species of deer that occur in the wild in Britain have been observed in churchyards. In common with a number of other creatures, they find churchyards are welcome but not necessarily vital feeding grounds. However, there are some plants and animals for which the churchyard habitat is of crucial importance and that do in a real sense require sanctuary there.

The importance of churchyards is recognized and well-documented in some counties. The Norfolk Naturalists' Trust's Conservation Scheme has shown that, in Norfolk at least, seven plants (pignut, burnet saxifrage, cowslip, ox-eye daisy, meadow saxifrage, sorrel, and lady's bedstraw) are largely dependent on churchyards. In Ceredigion in Wales, churchyards are the main habitat for hedge bedstraw, yellow oat-grass, quaking grass and green-winged orchid.

Some of the many forms of wildlife under threat in Britain, while not confined to churchyards, can find refuge there. The little fern called adder's tongue, a plant of ancient meadows, is an example to be found in a number of churchyards. Among small mammals, the harvest mouse and the water shrew both find churchyards a useful habitat and the red squirrel, now a rare animal, has been observed feeding in those in remote places. Reptiles and amphibians are everywhere becoming scarcer, but snakes and lizards

Common blue butterflies on the delicate, short-lived flowers of pale flax, at St Andrew's, Rufus Castle, Portland, Dorset. (Life size).

find in churchyards plenty of places in which to live, breed and hibernate. They are occasionally seen basking on the warm stone of graves. Frogs, newts and toads are all to be found, and it is important to preserve their churchyard niche when their other countryside habitats are fast being drained and destroyed. The same applies to butterflies and moths, some of which can find everything needed for the completion of their whole life-cycle in a sensitively managed churchyard. The purple hairstreak butterfly, for instance, can find all it requires in life in and around an oak, even in a small churchyard.

A few national rarities such as yarrow broomrape and tall thrift make exciting additions to the churchyard flora, but equally as interesting are the numerous regional rarities which are to be found in many counties. Churchyards provide habitats that are not otherwise available for a considerable range of plants. The most easterly site for navelwort or wall pennywort is the churchyard wall at Litchborough in Northamptonshire. In Kent, churchyards are almost the only places in which to find the *Asplenium* group of ferns; the same is true in Sussex for rusty-back fern and bladder fern. More than half the British species of lichen grow on stone, but since lowland Britain contains almost no natural outcrops of rock, churchyards provide the only significant areas of old permanent stonework upon which they can grow. This is why churchyards are so important as lichen sanctuaries: essentially because they provide a habitat for those lichens that require a stone base on which to grow. It is not, however, a simple provision; there are infinite subtleties. Church and churchyard walls and memorials are often the most ancient stones in a parish, and the lichens which have colonized them are likewise among the most ancient specimens in the country of these long-lived plants. The church walls themselves have often been modified or cleaned and the lichens disturbed, so church wall lichens are rarely as old as the church itself. Nevertheless they often include species not found on memorials.

Churches are usually built on an east-west axis, and so their walls face more or less due north, south, east and west, and each aspect has its own type of lichen flora. Similarly, the various materials of which churches are built each support a characteristic range of lichens. The lintel and sill stones are often different from the main body of the church, which may be built of stone, flint or bricks. Mortar and concrete, too, provide a site for lichens, as do roofs. Finally, there are memorial stones in a variety of materials—limestone, marble, sandstone, slate and granite—facing in different directions, some in the sun, some shaded. Many types of lichens find homes in the long vertical faces of headstones, the horizontal expanses of chest tombs, and in the crannies of carvings, some of them enriched by the droppings of perching birds.

The lichens which grow on a calcareous substrate such as limestone and marble (when eventually it has weathered) are rather different from those colonizing acid stone. There is generally some variation in the materials used for memorials and headstones, even in parishes where local stone predominates. A lichen survey carried out in the limestone Vale of Glamorgan showed that the fashion for sandstone on graves, which was especially prevalent during the nineteenth century, provided acid-loving lichens with sites that they would not otherwise have found in the area.

Many churchyards are exceptionally rich in lichens. The churchyard at Trotton in West Sussex contains about a hundred species, and forty to fifty are often recorded. The greatest number has been found at Mickleham in Surrey, where no less than one hundred and fifty species were identified on stones and trees in the churchyard.

The fact that there are a number of lichens which are impossibly difficult for the beginner to recognize has kept many people from even attempting to identify members of this interesting and often very beautiful group of plants. Nevertheless many of the species found in churchyards are so distinct in appearance, that with only a little knowledge one can make an informed guess. It is well worth investing in a hand lens (a magnification of ten is adequate) to see the tiny intricacies of these plants more vividly. Sometimes, minute insects can be seen moving, living and feeding on the folds and lobes of the lichens. It is easy to become totally absorbed in the tiny details, as I was one sunny spring morning, when working with a hand lens on a chest-tomb that was particularly rich in lichens, until brought back to the world by the attentions of a churchyard cat which joined me on the tomb, biting and butting for further affection.

Caloplaca flavescens is one of the most eye-catching lichens (which still goes by its old name *C. heppiana* in many field guides). It is a deep, rich orange with the lobes of its margin slightly domed. A near relative *Caloplaca aurantia* is paler and more yellow in colour, with flat, spreading marginal lobes that hug the stone. Both are limestone species, commonly found on the sunny side of headstones. Very old plants may have rosettes several inches across. As the plants age they often die back at the centre, making a circle or semi-circle of orange. In Selborne churchyard, the older gravestones are lit by a mass of such small sunsets. There the colour of the *Caloplaca* is smudged with the cloudy white of the species *Verrucaria hochstetteri*, finely dotted with tiny black fruiting bodies.

On the tops of limestone graves, and sometimes on the older sandstone, where bird droppings have had a nutrifying effect over a long period, grow the nitrogen-hungry lichens. *Physcia caesia* has a very neat bluish-grey rosette and off-white powdery encrustations on the lobes. Very similar, but darker, with a more greenish tinge is *Phaeophyscia orbicularis*, which turns bright green or in some cases, green-brown, when wetted. Another common and distinctive grey species is *Physcia adscendens*, whose marginal lobes are raised and hooded at the tip and bear obvious bristles.

Two species which not only grow on the tops of headstones but also provide bright splashes of orange on stone or brick walls are *Xanthoria parietina* and *X. calcicola* (formerly called *X. aureola*). They are quite alike except that *X. calcicola* has small, crusty, rod-like outgrowths that are absent in *X. parietina*, and fewer of the flat fruiting discs. The lobes of both are more leaf-like than those of the *Caloplaca* species, and there is a simple distinction that removes any doubt: if you can lift the margin of the lichen easily with a finger-nail, it is *Xanthoria*; if the margin is tightly fixed to the stone, it is *Caloplaca*.

This common, greyish-white lichen, Buellia canescens, turns greenish when wet. Painted at West Liss churchyard, Hampshire. (Life size).

Parmelia mougeotii, *a small delicate, yellow-grey lichen, found on sandstone tombs and church walls. (Life size).*

89

Xanthoria parietina, a lichen common on gravestones used as bird perches, and quite resistant to air pollution.

Some lichens may be seen in urban churchyards—certainly those in country towns. In fact in London two-thirds of the lichen flora occurs in old churchyards. But the state of health of lichen flora is related very closely to the quality of the air: the standard test for air pollution is the presence or absence of certain lichens, since different species are quantifiably more or less sensitive to sulphur dioxide. In polluted churchyards where old gravestones once bore a thriving lichen growth, some of the species have managed to survive, though not to expand or form new plants. *Caloplaca flavescens* is still to be found on memorials dating from the eighteenth century in a few London churchyards, though it is absent from most of the big cemeteries established in the nineteenth century. The powdery lichens are commonly found in urban surroundings. *Psilolechia lucidia* coats the damp parts of gravestones and walls with a luminous green sheet, and with its liking for damp, often grows inside the incised lines of a name or epitaph, picking out the words in lichen green. *Lepraria incana*, which grows in a loose soft, blue-grey powdery crust, is to be found only on walls and gravestones in dry shady places, as it is unusual in its inability to grow in direct sunlight or rain.

Lecanora conizaeoides is a lichen which positively thrives in polluted conditions. Discovered as late as 1860 and now common all over eastern England, this species is easy to recognize with its grey-green scurfy crust and pale green fruiting bodies with greyish margins. The lichenologist, Francis Rose, describes the fruiting bodies of the *Lecanora* genus and a few other lichens as 'jam tarts' of different kinds, which is of great assistance in distinguishing one species from another. *Lecanora*

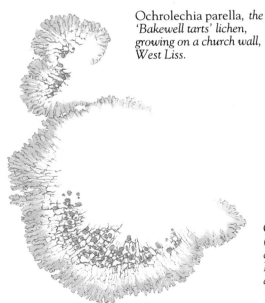

Ochrolechia parella, *the 'Bakewell tarts' lichen, growing on a church wall, West Liss.*

Lecanora atra, *showing the large, distinctive 'blackcurrant jam tarts'.*

Caploplaca flavescens (heppiana) (left), *the orange star lichen. The centre of this one, at West Liss in Hampshire, had disappeared, leaving an arc of orange.*

conizaeoides has 'pale green jam tarts', while those of *L. campestris* are 'milk-chocolate brown tarts'; *L. atra* has large but slightly distorted 'blackcurrant tarts', and *Ochrolechia parella* has 'large pale grey sugar-dusted Bakewell tarts' which almost cover gravestones in many places.

The 'honey tarts' of the slightly scruffy Lecanora dispersa. *(Life size).*

The small lichen *Candelariella vitellina* forms an irregular mustard-coloured crust, usually on the top of sandstone memorials or churchyard walls because it requires an acid substrate that is enriched with nitrogen. It is unusual in that it can survive in both polluted and unpolluted conditions and is common in churchyards, though sometimes overlooked because of its insignificant appearance. The yellow dye extracted from this lichen was used to colour the candles used in churches.

The moss, Pohlia nutans *(below), growing on a tree stump in Wales in April. (Life size).*

The lichen Cladonia fimbriata *(above), growing on a Welsh wall. (Life size).*

There are several lichens which have a special connection with churchyards: *Caloplaca teicholyta*, white with a neat rosette, and *Candelariella medians* which resembles a scruffy golden-yellow *Caloplaca flavescens* (whereas *C. teicholyta* looks like a white version of it) seem to be more common there than elsewhere. The frond-like strands of *Ramalina lacera* are associated with the walls of ruined churches in the east of England. The ten or so known sites for the lichen *Lecanactis hemisphaerica* are mostly on ancient plaster-coated church walls, themselves rare, thanks to the Victorian passion for exposing walls, even ones which were originally designed to carry plaster. Another lichen, *Dirina massiliensis* f. *sorediata*, is native only on shaded cliffs in the north and west of Britain, but it has spread to churchyards and been observed in grey powdery sheets on hundreds of north-facing church walls in many parts.

It is rather more difficult to become acquainted with lichens than birds, or wild flowers, principally because there is no comparable range of field guides available. However, they are certainly one of the most important forms of wildlife that the churchyard shelters and there are many specialities of great interest in store for those who become competent lichen observers. The south-west holds such riches as *Ramalina, Evernia* and *Usnea* lichens, exotic in appearance with long branches, fronds and spidery hairs. In Norfolk the greenish *Haematomma ochroleucum* (so named because its fruiting bodies resemble bloodstains) and *Opegrapha saxatilis* are frequently discovered on north-facing church walls. Another *Opegrapha* is one of the few lichens that manages to grow on the acid, flaking bark of yew trees: *Opegrapha prosodea* is grey with spore-producing organs that look like small mouse droppings.

Occasionally lichen species are found growing an unexpectedly long way from their normal haunts. For instance, there is an attractive species which looks like a green map outlined and subdivided with black lines, called *Rhizocarpon geographicum*, which likes uplands and acid rock. I have seen it only high up on mountain boulders. How then does it come to be found in Monknash and St Bride's Major in Welsh lowland limestone country, or more perplexingly on a church roof in Norfolk? In the last case, the roof was of slate, and it has been suggested that the lichen may have survived, against all odds, from origins in an upland slate quarry.

A Ramalina *species of lichen, growing with* Lecanora *on the west wall of Meline church, Dyfed. (Life size).*

Not only the gravestones, but the graves and grave-mounds themselves provide an interesting micro-habitat for fauna and flora. Close-grazed or mown grave-mounds in chalky regions provide a habitat for attractive low-growing plants such as squinancywort, thymes and milkworts. Inside the kerbstones, grasses sometimes escape clipping, and larger kinds common in churchyards such as red fescue, tufted hair grass or its attractive cousin, wavy hair grass, can grow to their clumpy, mature form, and manage to flower and seed. Sometimes there are rarer grasses, such as the broad-leaved meadow grass, introduced in the eighteenth century and thriving in churchyards such as Lurgishall in West Sussex, Llangurig in Powys, and some others. The calcereous nature of many churchyards enables attractive chalk-loving species, such as quaking grass and yellow oat grass, to become established.

A filigree leaf of the moss Thuidium tamariscinum, growing on damp ground in a shady corner.

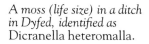

A moss (life size) in a ditch in Dyfed, identified as Dicranella heteromalla.

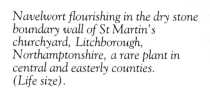

Navelwort flourishing in the dry stone boundary wall of St Martin's churchyard, Litchborough, Northamptonshire, a rare plant in central and easterly counties. (Life size).

93

Admirers of butterflies in the churchyard often forget that these beautiful creatures need a place to lay their eggs, and that the caterpillars need to feed, grow and pupate. Long grass in churchyards harbours many butterfly species in these stages of their life cycle. It also shelters some of the larger insects such as grasshoppers. I have seen dozens of meadow grasshoppers elbowing for space on the kerbs of a grave full of long grass.

Long grasses, on or beside graves, also provide shelter for the slow-worm, a species of lizard which was once very common in grassland, heaths and hedgebanks but now notably less so, having suffered, along with so many other creatures, from the destruction of its habitat. It is still, however, the most common reptile in Britain and the most regularly seen in churchyards. It does not bask in the sun as often as other reptiles, and is more often to be found beneath a flat sun-warmed stone or inside thick vegetation. Slow-worms have been known to survive for over fifty years, but they are by nature as by name, slow-moving creatures, and the speed and violence of rotary blades has dramatically reduced their numbers in churchyards.

Meadow grasshoppers in the churchyard of St Michael and All Angels, Cuxton, Kent, in early July, and common sorrel flowers whose arrow-shaped leaves taste like green apples. (Life size).

94

Coastal churchyards are probably the best in which to discover reptiles and amphibians, of which combined there are only twelve species native to Britain and a few introductions. I have been informed of numerous sightings of adders, common lizards and grass snakes sunning themselves on gravestones. Churchyards which have a damp area within them make a good habitat for frogs and common toads. Newts are also occasionally reported, not only the commonest British species, the smooth newt, but also crested and palmate newts.

Many native wild plants, though rare, occur in churchyards more frequently than might normally be expected and it is extremely difficult to discriminate between survivors of the native flora and planted specimens. I am fairly certain from the way in which it was growing that the double lady's smock growing in Bugbrooke churchyard in Northamptonshire had occurred naturally, but I could not give an opinion on the dozen or so others of which I was notified. This is a species which quite frequently throws up these delightful double-flowered forms in the wild. I have never seen or heard of the double lesser celandine in the wild, but it is a treasured cottage garden plant, and I believe originated as a natural 'sport'. There is only a single reported churchyard occurrence for this and for another intriguing 'flore pleno' form, the double wood anemone. A blue variant of the wood anemone is mentioned by the influential Victorian gardener William Robinson, and I recently found a description of it in a gardening handbook where it is named as 'Robinsoniana', but I have never seen it growing. The 'blue anemones' recorded in the churchyard surveys have so far turned out to be *Anemone apenina* and *Anemone blanda*, introduced garden species which have become naturalized from grave plantings.

Periwinkles (both lesser and greater) are frequently introduced to churchyards, and at St Mary's, Grendon, in Northamptonshire, there is an attractive double form of the lesser periwinkle with sky-blue flowers which I believe is the 'Azurea Flore Pleno'. The original 'Bowles' periwinkle with big deep blue flowers was actually found on a grave by the celebrated gardener Edward Bowles.

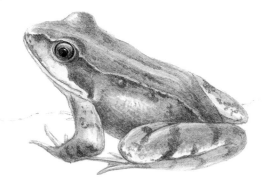

Common frog, no longer so common, in Syleham churchyard, Suffolk, which is by the River Waveney.

95

The double meadow saxifrage in the churchyard of St Nicholas, Worth, Sussex. The double flowers (drawn life size) are shaggy, and have pure white petals, flushed green-yellow at the centre.

96

The double meadow saxifrage, which was originally taken into cottage gardens from the wild, grows in very appealing abundance in the beautiful churchyard of St Nicholas at Worth in West Sussex. This is said to be the plant referred to in the nursery rhyme as 'pretty maids all in a row'. Some of the parishioners in Worth have attempted to grow it in their gardens, but it is believed to root only in the churchyard and so far at least, it seems none of them has met with any success.

I have been told that another old-fashioned double flower, the double soapwort, is to be found in the churchyard at Sutton in Suffolk and I have come across it myself, by chance, at St Michael's, Penbryn, in Ceredigion, Dyfed. This delightful churchyard overlooks woods, hills and sea cliffs, and when I visited it on a summer evening it was so still that I could hear the swish of the waves on the rocks far below. The churchyard was pleasantly overgrown, though it had been grazed (possibly by the sheep in the adjacent pasture), and rich in flowers. The carmine-pink double soapwort made a massive bouquet that completely filled one grave and was beginning to spread into the turf around it.

There was also at Penbryn the white form of the musk mallow, a plant which is found occasionally in the wild, sometimes in gardens and often in churchyards, although usually not in places where one might expect it to have been planted. As it grows well from seed, plants may perhaps have originated in grave bouquets, or arisen from earlier grave plantings that had disappeared. This interesting churchyard also held two kinds of toadflax—the pretty yellow sort, common and widespread, often found on graves and churchyard walls, and also pale toadflax, which is tall, with flowers a delicate lilac striped with darker purple, a native but not at all common plant.

The incidence of some of the scarcer native wild plants in churchyards can be a conundrum. It is not unlikely that snakeshead fritillaries might grow wild in churchyards. Old meadows which were incorporated into churchyards in order to extend their area during the nineteenth century might well have included fritillaries among their flora. They are, however, also treasured garden plants and out of the dozen fritillary churchyards I have been told about, at least one, at Lyndon in the Rutland district of Leicestershire, contains a known introduction. I have come to think that a blurring of origins is not a very serious matter.

Clustered leaves of double meadow saxifrage, growing low down in the moss-covered ground.

Snakeshead fritillaries at their best in early May in a Shropshire churchyard (life size). These were part of a sizable community which had been carefully mown around by those responsible for churchyard maintenance.

98

Snakeshead fritillaries are notoriously difficult to establish in gardens and are rare as wild plants. Where they have been successfully established in churchyards (and fritillaries have appeared at Lyndon every year since 1976), I believe that we should cherish them as much as the colonies we have in the wild. The phrase 'in the wild' requires a certain freedom of interpretation in the case of snakeshead fritillaries. These plants need to be kept in the manner to which they have been accustomed—the regime of the traditional water meadow—and are very vulnerable to changes in management. Nowadays, it entails a deliberate conservation strategy to keep in existence plants which thrived under an older system of agriculture. Places where fritillaries grow in any quantity are carefully managed by national or county conservation bodies.

The yellow star of Bethlehem which grows and seems to thrive in Kedington churchyard in Suffolk is another similar puzzle. I have always seen wild specimens of this plant growing by rivers, but at Kedington it is found, not by the river which runs along one side of the churchyard, but on higher ground. This species is said also to grow in damp pastures, but it is known only in three other sites in Suffolk (one, a small colony, has not flowered since 1937). It is a demure plant with a short flowering season. The yellow flowers do not appear every year, and the narrow leaves are often overlooked. It is not a plant one would expect to find planted in a churchyard, but possibly a botanically-minded vicar decided to experiment, or a parishioner heard of a colony that was about to be destroyed and re-planted it. The question remains open but meanwhile the healthy little colony continues to thrive.

In the churchyard at Scalby in North Yorkshire, there is rare native species called coralroot bittercress. I received word of it from a botanist who lives nearby and described the colony as a fine group of plants. That it is apparently well established is most surprising, since the species is a southern one, specific in its habitat and more or less confined to the Weald and the Chiltern Hills. No one has any idea how it came to be at Scalby.

Orchids are plants very vulnerable to any disturbance of their habitat or changes in its management. The overall population of orchids in Britain has declined dramatically over the past ten years, mainly because of changes in farming practice and land use. It is therefore cheering to find that about fifty surveys reported the presence of one or more species. The surprisingly large range of Orchid species recorded includes the greater butterfly orchid (Dyfed), the bird's nest orchid (Cumbria), and bee, heath-spotted, and southern marsh orchids at a number of sites. Some churchyards contain the orchids which are also to be found in the countryside around. In Jersey, autumn lady's tresses are present in almost every churchyard although they are rare on the mainland. The stately dark spikes of the early purple orchid are to be found both inside and outside churchyards in counties such as Devon and Sussex, as are twayblades and the bright pink triangles of pyramidal orchids in Suffolk. Common spotted orchids, which have a wide distribution, were also noted from churchyards in many counties (except those in the south-west, where they are less common).

In some counties, changes in land use have turned churchyards into a last refuge for certain species, such as the man orchid in Suffolk, where it is now very rare. In Surrey, the green-winged orchid is found in only a few localities, one of which is a cemetery, another a churchyard. This is an orchid which seems to be associated with churchyards in certain areas. I have seen specimens growing in several Sussex churchyards, surviving punishing mowing regimes. At Danehill, the mower had gone over just before the young spikes appeared and consequently the only plant species to be seen on the flat turf was the green-winged orchid. About a hundred small flowering spikes looked rather lost in their bare surroundings. There are also churchyard records from Hampshire and Suffolk, and I suspect that further research will show green-winged orchids to be present in churchyards in several other counties. They are a plant of meadows and pastures, a typical churchyard habitat. I heard a thrilling tale about this species which concerned a chapelyard in Ceredigion where green-winged orchids are not common. One spring when the regular mowing was interrupted, a host of a thousand or more green-winged orchids rose up out of the grass.

A robust green-winged orchid (life-size) in close-cropped grass in a Sussex churchyard. In meadow-like conditions, they can grow to more than twice this size. The flowers are purple with green-striped 'wings'.

101

One of the most interesting of the nationally rare plant species to survive in churchyards is the purple or yarrow broomrape, which comes up regularly in one of the coastal churchyards in north Norfolk. This broomrape is parasitic on the roots of yarrow, one of the commonest and most widespread churchyard plants. Also on record in churchyards are the fumitory, *Fumaria occidentalis*, which is found only in Cornwall, and its relative *Fumaria purpurea*, a plant which grows only in artificial habitats, and is endemic to Britain and Ireland.

Perhaps the most famous churchyard speciality is tall thrift, which grows not on sea coasts but inland, in dry lowland grass. It is taller than the common thrift and now survives in Britain only in a few meadows in the Ancaster valley (now a nature reserve) and in the extension to the churchyard of St Martin's at Ancaster, which is managed with conscientious respect for this rare species.

It is certain that as churchyards become more studied, several other nationally rare plants will be recorded. Apart from lichens, there are not many rare or threatened species which depend heavily upon churchyards, although a number of regionally scarce plants do. All plants have their own natural range, modified by the conditions of soil, habitat and climate, but they will sometimes grow 'out of bounds' in a favourable habitat. Some of the most characteristic churchyard species are rare in some parts of England and Wales, and in these localities are found only in churchyards. Hedge bedstraw and quaking grass, for example, generally scarce in the Ceredigion region of Dyfed, grow in some churchyards there. Similarly, in Jersey, so rich in flora that is rare on mainland Britain, hoary plantain is scarce, and churchyards are the most likely places to find it. The lichen *Candelariella medians*, though seen as a typical indicator of a lichen-rich churchyard in the south-east and eastern midlands, has its only known mid-Wales locality on the church door step at Llowes in Powys.

The bat population in Britain has been on the decline for many years, and despite the protection which is afforded in theory by the Wildlife and Countryside Act (1981), the analyzed figures of the Institute of Terrestrial Ecology's bat population survey, which began in 1978, show a continued decrease in numbers. There are great gaps in our knowledge of how bats live, but one of the main problems is undoubtedly the destruction of their

A handsome early purple orchid (life size), flowering in a Dyfed churchyard—one of the best sights of spring. The rector of this parish had actively resisted attempts to level the churchyard. The monstrous-looking black weevils are also painted life size.

habitat—there are now fewer places where bats can feed, roost, breed or hibernate. Among the remaining sites, churches and churchyards are crucial in terms of bat conservation. Bats have been seen in two-thirds of the Northamptonshire churches that are under observation by the county's Bat Group, and some of the most interesting bat roosts watched by the Durham Bat Group are in or near churches.

The emergence of the county Bat Group represents an exciting recent development in conservation. Bats are extremely difficult to observe, despite the fact that they live in close conjunction with human beings, often in artificial sites such as houses and churches, and our knowledge of them is scant. They are creatures of the twilight and night, both periods when human perception is at its least efficient. We cannot see them, most of us cannot hear them, and all of our senses are sleepy when those of bats are sharpest. However, Bat Groups are initiating a systematic observation of bats all over England, Wales and Scotland, sharing information and encouraging innovation in methods of study. Many half-truths once accepted as fact are being replaced by real information, and new questions are being formulated about bat behaviour.

A device which has helped observers to overcome some of the physical difficulties of bat watching is a 'bat detector' that makes audible the high-frequency echo-location calls made by flying bats. Groups are still learning to interpret the varied pips and squeaks from the little hand-held machine. Observers need to strain all their own senses, but working with the machine certainly does help in locating areas of bat activity and in identifying certain species, possibly high overhead, which might otherwise go entirely unnoticed. I would advise anyone interesting in seeing bats and who wishes to observe them locally, to go out first with a local Bat Group.

On my first outing in search of bats, I went with a group to a churchyard in the north of Buckinghamshire. The evening was still and warm. Pipistrelle bats were already flitting around between the church and the high trees of the churchyard when I arrived. Pipistrelles have a very characteristic flight, darting and fluttery, like that of a house martin. They

*An evening sky filled with bat-wings
over St Nicholas's churchyard,
Brockenhurst, Hampshire.*

are the most common British bats and the species most likely to be seen in churchyards. They roost socially, squeezed together in quite small crevices —in the Buckinghamshire churchyard, some had been seen tucked behind a false pillar in a high, west-facing statue niche, but they prefer a roof space just above the eaves, under hanging tiles or sometimes down behind the lead flashing where a church has been rebuilt and extended, between chancel and nave, for example.

Contrary to popular belief, belfries are not good places to find bats. They are far too full of dust and cobwebs; bats prefer a clean roosting place, and the sound of the bells would be intolerable for them. Church porches are another matter, although research in Northamptonshire suggests that bats avoid porches that are in use by birds. Out of two hundred and eighty-five porches surveyed by the Northamptonshire Bat Group, seventy-five were found to be occupied by pipistrelles, two by Natterer's bats, two by Daubenton's, two by long-eared bats and six by species so far unidentified. The bats usually roost between the underboarding and the roofing material, and most commonly used the part of the porch roof next to the church wall, which they reach by squeezing between the wall and roof timbers. Porches with plastered or stone ceilings are rarely used as roosts, since the bats are not able to find a point of entry into the roof space. Many church porches now have wire mesh gates to prevent birds—and bats—from entering. A sign on one church door in Northumberland is explicit: 'Please keep door shut and so help to keep out bats.' Nevertheless, nine Northamptonshire church porches equipped with wire mesh doors had confirmed bat roosts in them. It is always worth examining porches, even ones which at first appear unpropitious. Bats may use them as a way into the church, squeezing in above the church door, where there is often a gap—small scratch marks will show where they cling and scramble through. In the porch, a sharp-eyed observer may find bat droppings which resemble those of mice, but are dryer and more crumbly and have no smell. An expert in bat identification can tell different species from each other, on the evidence of their droppings.

Scarlet tiger moth (life size). Not widely distributed in Britain, this is a rare sight both in and outside churchyards—though it has been seen in several gardens around Oxford.

The presence of relatively fresh droppings indicates that a roost is in current use. We discovered new droppings from long-eared bats during my Buckinghamshire foray although we saw no long-eared bats at all that night. However, the moon was bright, and it is known that some insects, possibly including the noctuid moths which are among the long-eared bats' favourite prey, fly very high on moonlit nights. There were certainly records of long-eared bats on the site, but if they were flying high or deep within the tree canopy, we would not have been aware of them, since they do not register on a bat detector. Their huge, sensitive ears enable the bats to fix a position on the tiniest imaginable sounds, too high, not only for the human ear, but for the electronic ear too.

Just before dark, we saw a small bat clearly silhouetted against the sky, flying unwaveringly straight and quite slowly above our heads. It was a bat of the *Myotis* genus, and the visual evidence of its size, broadish wings and steady flight pattern, as well as its echo-location calls, confirmed that it was a Daubenton's bat. This species is to be found near still or slow-moving water, as it feeds by skimming insects such as caddis fly from the surface. It roosts, sometimes in churches, but also in large trees, such as willows, which may overhang the water. The attraction of this particular churchyard was the tributary of the Great Ouse bounding the southern

Insects (apart from butterflies) are an often overlooked component of the churchyard fauna. The random selection opposite represents only a small fraction observed in June and July. They are all drawn life size except the large striated capsid bug.

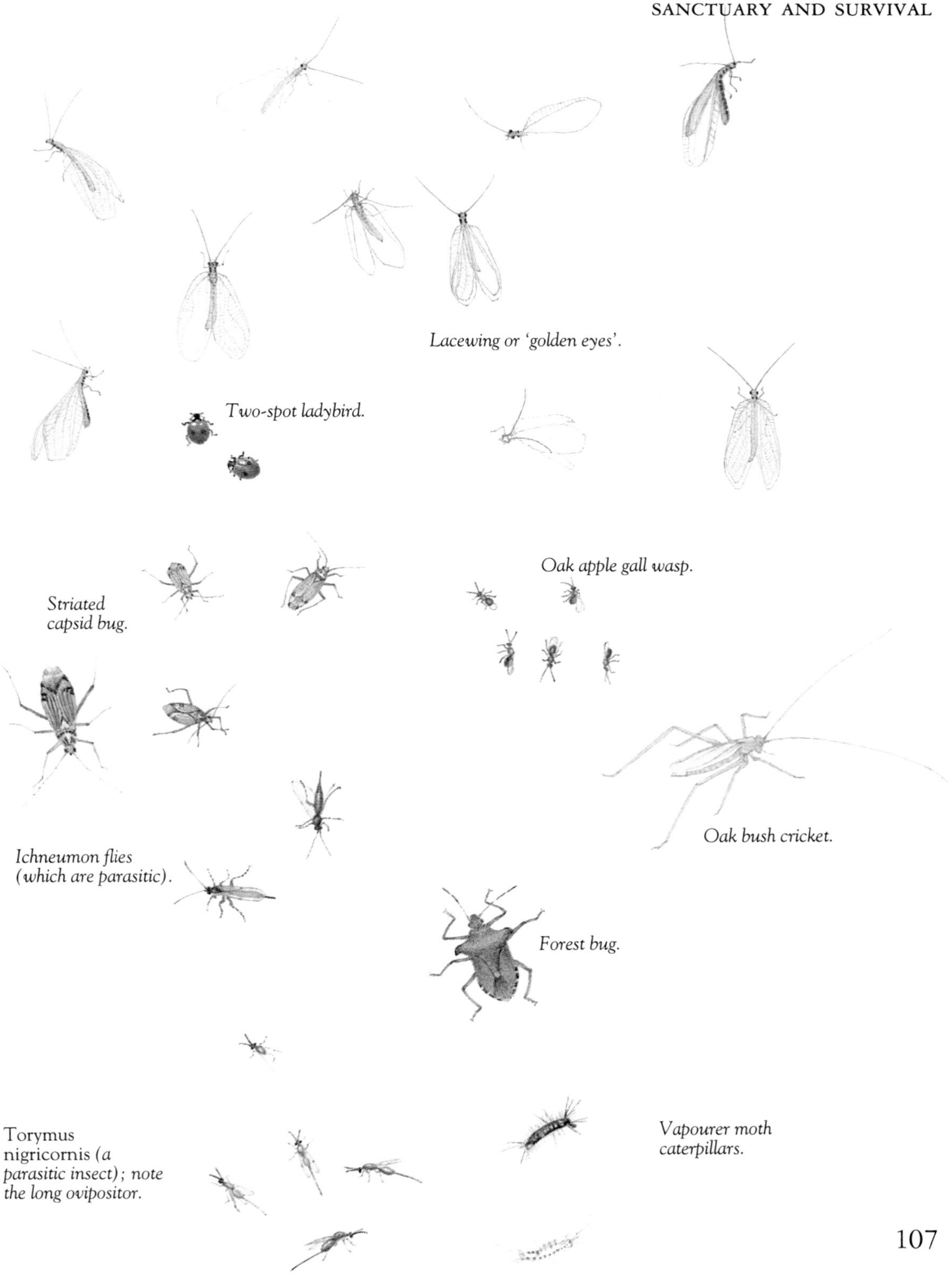

Lacewing or 'golden eyes'.

Two-spot ladybird.

Oak apple gall wasp.

Striated
capsid bug.

Oak bush cricket.

Ichneumon flies
(which are parasitic).

Forest bug.

Torymus
nigricornis (a
parasitic insect); note
the long ovipositor.

Vapourer moth
caterpillars.

107

edge. Later, when it was much darker, the Daubenton's sound came up again on the bat detector, as did that of another *Myotis* genus, the Natterer's bat, which we did not even glimpse.

As it grew late, we became aware of spasms of activity on the detector. They came and went too quickly to get a fix on them, but as we circled the church several times we caught the flash of a bat-wing in the moonlight and finally traced the apparent centre of activity to the south-east end of the chancel. Several times a bat flew close to our heads, and we eventually realized that there were two. A low-beam torch enabled us to examine the chancel wall just below the roof, where the small shape of a whiskered bat landed momentarily before darting off again. After a number of brief landings, the bat paused for a final moment, before disappearing swiftly into a crevice in the masonry beneath the end of the beam.

With its wings folded, the bat looked very tiny on the wide stone expanse of the church wall and, indeed, the whiskered bat is the smallest of the *Myotis* bats. A mature adult is only two inches in head and body length, although the wingspan can extend to about ten inches. This species is believed to inhabit English and Welsh counties northwards to Yorkshire, but it has recently been positively identified further north in a Northumberland church and vicarage. Whiskered bats use both buildings and trees for summer roosts and for hibernation. Natterer's bats will also use both but prefer very ancient churches which have become dilapidated enough to provide access through larger holes and gaps. They also show a preference for very mature trees, especially churchyard yews. Long-eared bats have a similar need for space, and will be found only in churches which have good-sized gaps in the fabric of the roof. They will colonize aisle roofs, if there is a generous space between roof and underboarding. The greater horseshoe bat, only occasionally found in churchyards, is restricted in distribution to south Wales and the south-west of England. This species is very sensitive to disturbance and chooses isolated, barely used or redundant churches. Almost opposite in its life-style and preferences is the noctule bat, which normally roosts and hibernates in trees, appearing less bothered by the presence of human beings in the vicinity. The noctule is sometimes found in suburban churchyards where there are large trees.

Acanthus (above and left), flourishing in the gardens of the churchyard of St James's, Piccadilly. There are several ferns and wild flowers in this churchyard, even though it is in the centre of London.

The desirability of a churchyard as a habitat for bats is influenced both by its vegetation and by the architecture of the church. Plant cover which provides plenty of insects, at least a few large trees, and a church built of soft stone such as limestone, rather than granite or other hard materials, make a generally favourable habitat, though each species has its own preferences. From a bat's point of view the peaks of church architecture are those periods, such as the Middle Ages, which produced a high level of elaborate stonework—pillars, arches, statues, niches, and other decoration. Tall trees and high hedges in the churchyard provide shelter as well as still pockets of air in which insects congregate. Insects are also drawn to a light by a lych-gate often left on throughout the night. Ivy attracts insects, particularly in early autumn, and young bats may feed around the ivy on large trees and churchyard walls, using its recesses as a temporary roost. Even in winter, bats frequent churchyards though the churches themselves show little sign of use. Some species use churchyard trees (especially hollow ones) for hibernation, and I have heard of their resting inside chest tombs during the early stages. There are a great many known reasons why churchyards are important to bats, and no doubt others will come to light as more is discovered about the life history of these little creatures.

Church porches are used for roosting and nesting by birds as well as bats (though apparently not at the same time) and many of the common churchyard species, such as house sparrows, blackbirds and starlings, readily colonize their beams and crevices. There are also numerous records of tawny and little owls, woodpigeons, and blue tits. Roofed lych-gates provide similar shelter. Swallows are often to be seen feeding in and over churchyards. Sometimes they breed there, though never in more than ones or twos, since even the porch and lych-gate combined offer little space for swallows, which are not strongly colonial. However, their nests are very much appreciated by other birds in following years. I was told of a porch in Dyfed where house martins took over the structures built by swallows and I have also heard of blackbirds building their nests on top of a kind of lid, which they made using the old swallows' nest as a bracket. Most exciting of all was a sight that I encountered on two occasions in Norfolk, where swallows' nests at the apex of a church doorway sheltered by a porch had been subsequently taken over by what I came to consider one of the most

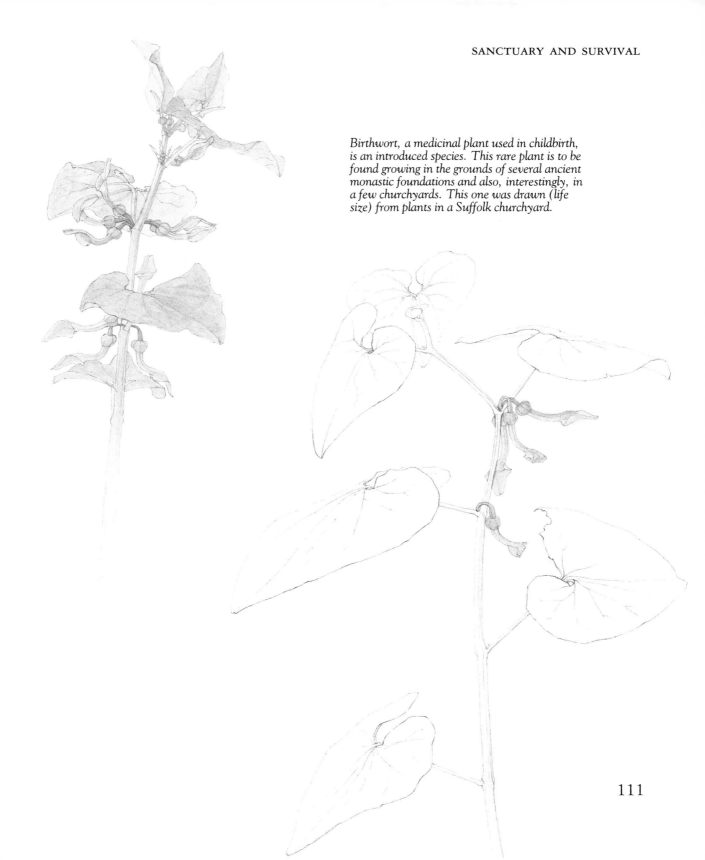

Birthwort, a medicinal plant used in childbirth, is an introduced species. This rare plant is to be found growing in the grounds of several ancient monastic foundations and also, interestingly, in a few churchyards. This one was drawn (life size) from plants in a Suffolk churchyard.

111

characteristic churchyard birds, the spotted flycatcher. When I saw the first nest, the young had flown. The parents flitted around the churchyard, alighting on gravestones and executing complicated aerobatic figures as they caught insects which they took back to the fledglings waiting in the yew and pine trees. At South Pickenham I stopped, drawn to the attractive round tower rather than by any expectation of wildlife in a well-gardened churchyard. As I approached the porch I was greeted by the excited chirruping of nestlings which was hushed into silence only by stern calls from a parent flycatcher agitatedly perched on a nearby gravestone, its beak full of insects. But I caught a glimpse of a tiny feathered head peeping out of the nest in anticipation of its feed before they all subsided into the depths of their nest. This one, like the other, was a refurbished swallows' nest, built at the apex of the arch above the church door.

To birds and many other living creatures, mature trees represent more than a landscape feature: they are home and feeding place. However, big trees everywhere are being cut down faster than younger specimens are coming to maturity. Planting policies which ignore native species do

Rookery just outside the boundary of St. Bartholomew's, Warleggan, Cornwall, in mid-April, said to be the largest in the region. A Somerset name for the rook is 'church parson'.

nothing to help the situation. Churchyards, along with parks, both private and public, are becoming more important as habitat for those birds and other wild creatures that select tall trees as roosts, nesting sites or feeding places. Even with the large-scale disappearance of the elm, a tree popularly planted in the eighteenth and nineteenth centuries and splendidly full-grown in many churchyards until the ravages of Dutch elm disease, churchyards are still rich in fine, large trees, both native and exotic. Such mature trees provide a refuge for a number of bird species that are finding times increasingly hard.

The birds which have suffered most from the absence of elms are those familiar inhabitants of churchyards, the rooks. I was very pleased to hear their loud cawing in a good number of churchyards that I visited. There were rookeries in the churchyards themselves and often in adjacent gardens and parks. These birds have proved themselves adaptable since the disappearance of their favourite nesting places in the strong branches of elms. I have seen a rookery of up to fifty nests in horse chestnuts, another of about twenty in sycamores, and smaller colonies in beeches, willows, holm oaks and Monterey pines. The rook population of Britain has been declining for the last twenty-five years (that is since before the latest attack of Dutch elm disease), and tending towards smaller colonies. The days when hundreds of nests in a colony were commonplace are long past. It remains to be seen whether the rooks' breeding success in the alternative tree species is comparable with that provided by high, safe vantage points in the elms out of the way of most predators. Some of the new nesting sites—pollard willows for instance—are astonishingly low down for this species.

Although the provisions of the Wildlife and Countryside Act still allow for rooks to be shot all the year round by persons authorized by landowners to do so, they seem to live unharmed in churchyards and their environs. At Warleggan, a Cornish churchyard with a rookery adjacent to it, a local man remembered a time when the rooks were shot and seemed glad that this no longer occurred. Rooks have ecclesiastical associations: a Shropshire folk tale says that rooks do no work on Ascension Day, but sit quietly and reverently in the trees, and in the same county, according to the nineteenth-century expert on bird lore, the Revd Charles Swainson, it was thought that if you failed to honour Easter Sunday by wearing some new garment the rooks would 'spoil your clothes'.

Tall, old trees also offer shelter to woodpeckers, and all three species that breed in Britain are seen in churchyards. Once, when I stopped on impulse to investigate an agreeably overgrown town churchyard on the main road at Stourbridge, only ten miles or so from the centre of Birmingham, I disturbed a green woodpecker which had been unconcernedly catching ants on the grassy path, despite heavy traffic nearby. Making loud yaffle noises, it flew up into a large ash which stood between the churchyard and the adjacent school. I was again startled by that hard, laughing cry when another, very large and fine green woodpecker flew across my path as I was making my way up the drive to an out-of-the-way church in the Smethcott area, south of Shrewsbury. Then, only a few moments later, a buzzard flew across, so close that I could see every detail. I saw several buzzards floating over the churchyards in Shropshire and Wales, wings uptilted in typical languid manner. I have not seen them, but buzzards may well hunt in remote churchyards for larger insects, voles, mice and rabbits.

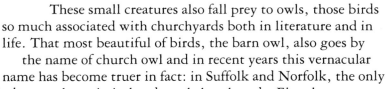

These small creatures also fall prey to owls, those birds so much associated with churchyards both in literature and in life. That most beautiful of birds, the barn owl, also goes by the name of church owl and in recent years this vernacular name has become truer in fact: in Suffolk and Norfolk, the only safe havens for barn owls are in isolated rural churchyards. Elsewhere too, changes in agricultural practice have reduced both food supply and nest sites, believed to be the main limiting factors on the barn owl population, which has now been declining for many years. In quiet rural churchyards there is a supply of food, and spires, towers and old trees with hollow places in which to roost and breed.

Tawny owls, larger birds which vastly outnumber barn owls, also nest in churchyards, principally in large trees in which there are holes, or in the disused nests of other large birds, and also in church towers. They take the same food as barn owls, including the odd sparrow plucked from a roost in ivy or elsewhere, but they tend to rely for a greater proportion of their diet upon earthworms and other invertebrates.

The best times to look out for the barn owl are at dusk or dawn, when it makes a splendid sight, beating like some wonderful ghost along a line of large churchyard trees. It is as well to be prepared for the strange unearthly shriek, which can be frightening in any surroundings, and not for those suffering from weak nerves or a romantic imagination. Anyone who cares about wildlife, however, will feel privileged to see this haunting bird. Tawny owls are much more readily heard and seen. I have listened to them hunting in and about my local churchyard until the early hours.

If you are lucky, you may see other crepuscular birds in certain parts of the country. At Minstead, in the New Forest, the hobbies which breed nearby come in over the churchyard trees or church buildings in swift aerobatic chase of small birds or the moths which also form part of their diet. To the same churchyard occasionally comes one of the most mysterious of all birds, the nightjar, a twilight creature strange enough even for Sir Arthur Conan Doyle, who is buried there. Its evening song, a low, continuous churring, carries for miles over the still forest after dusk, but it is not usually until the light has faded that the nightjar flies in search of noctuid moths and other large insects.

A spotted flycatcher, with a beakful of insects, uses a gravestone as a perch in St. Margaret's churchyard, Binsey, Oxfordshire, in early August. The green woodpecker (above) was sketched in St Mary's churchyard, Speen, Berkshire, in August.

115

In Devon, the black redstart has been seen in churchyards. Still a rare breeding bird in England, it is associated more with industrial rather than ecclesiastical architecture but it may be attracted by high ledges in ruinous churches. There are records of successful breeding in London churchyards and cemeteries. Another rare breeding bird, the crossbill, a colourful finch with a characteristic crossed-over bill in which the tips of the mandibles overlap, has been seen feeding in the large conifers of churchyards in East Anglia, but so far as is known has not yet made its nest in one. Spring (and in some years, autumn) may bring rare vagrants into churchyards. Several hoopoes have been recorded in southern counties, and a golden oriole rested briefly in the churchyard at Balcombe in Sussex.

Churchyards with an ample supply of berries are a focal point for a good many winter migrant birds, including some which are by no means common. Hardy churchyard observers who are prepared to visit during the winter as well as the summer have reported waxwings, which particularly enjoy rose-hips as well as haws and mistletoe, ivy and cotoneaster berries. During one winter, a nutcracker was seen in a Surrey churchyard.

Churchyards are used by almost every kind of bird which is to be seen in Britain—migrants, common resident species, even birds of specialist habitats, such as herons, seabirds, and waders. While churchyards cannot be considered crucial to their existence, there is no doubt that they are of significant benefit to a wide number of birds. Similarly for plants: a small proportion only of the total number of churchyards has received full botanical surveys, but even so, most of the plants on the British list have been found within them. Mammals from red squirrels to red deer, invertebrates from rather rare, pale, woodlice that inhabit the dark regions beneath grave urns, to the flamboyant dragonflies and humming-bird hawk moths, are seen in churchyards. There is hardly such a thing as a churchyard which is wholly devoid of interest to a naturalist, although sadly, less interesting, over-gardened ones have increased over the past few years.

A pair of kestrels nested in the church spire of St John the Evangelist, the Polish Roman Catholic Church in Putney, London, in early July. The family, including the two young, could be seen perching on the parapet together in the afternoons and evenings.

However, this trend does seem to have caused a reaction in
many people, specialist and non-specialist alike, who care about
churchyards. Shaved and scraped, they offend against the deeply held
belief in churchyards as a kind of semi-natural haven. In times of past
peril they offered safety, and people of the early Middle Ages fled to
churchyards with their stock. The churchyard is also the place where the
people of the parish install items of local, historical interest. At the
church in Ivinghoe in Buckinghamshire, there is a great hook which was
used to tear down the thatch from blazing buildings; coastal churchyards
sometimes contain anchors or figure-heads, and many have village stocks re-
erected in them. In Stanhope, once a thriving mining community in west
Durham, a giant fossilized tree stump, thought to be over two hundred and
fifty million years old, was removed to the churchyard where it now serves
as a monument to the industrial past of this small town.

Conservation is second nature in churchyards, and in many places it already extends as much to the wildlife as to the ancient fabric of the church and the historical artefacts. Nature conservation in churchyards is a relatively new concept but it is one which most parishioners readily accept, probably because it fits so well with the traditional image. There is a considerable threat to wildlife all over Britain, much of it official and, as such, beyond local control. One is encouraged to think that the growing awareness of the role churchyards can play in conservation will mean that in many more places, plants and animals will find in them, a true sanctuary.

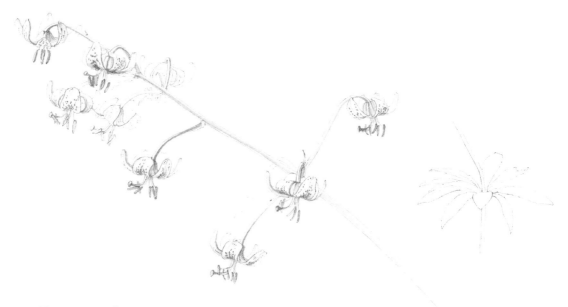

Martagon lily growing in the churchyard of St Mary, Ovington, Essex, in June. Other exotic lilies which have been recorded in churchyards are the tiger lily, Lilium pyrenaicum, Lilium regale, *and the Madonna lily which, because of its white purity, is the plant especially associated with the Virgin Mary and appears in countless paintings of her.*

CELEBRATION
and
CEREMONY

O all ye Works of the Lord, bless ye the Lord: praise
        him, and magnify him for ever . . .
O ye Sun and Moon, bless ye the Lord: praise him, and
        magnify him for ever . . .
O ye Showers and Dew, bless ye the Lord:
O ye Winter and Summer, bless ye the Lord:
O ye Dews and Frosts, bless ye the Lord:
O ye Lightnings and Clouds, bless ye the Lord:
O let the Earth bless the Lord; yea, let it praise him,
        and magnify him for ever.
O all ye Green Things upon the Earth, bless ye the
        Lord:
O ye Wells, bless ye the Lord:
O all ye Fowls of the Air, bless ye the Lord:
O ye Servants of the Lord, bless ye the Lord: praise him
        and magnify him for ever.

From the Benedicte

A PARISH CHURCHYARD IS NOT MERELY a piece of land surrounding the church. Even if it is not used as a burial ground it provides a place for remembrance, thanksgiving, and sometimes recreation. An awareness of its natural history often comes to people as an unexpected insight during some other activity. I was interested to find that it was not so much the isolated and neglected churchyards which were especially rich in wildlife, but often those which were the centre of a greater-than-average amount of parish activity in a town or village.

A wide range of secular events, as well as those connected with the church, takes place in churchyards. There may be craft fairs, flower festivals, strawberries-and-cream teas, markets, fêtes and even sports. There are nationally famous events such as the York mystery plays, and occasions such as local centenaries and anniversaries, which are important only to individual parishes. The celebration of baptism and marriage may include a procession or other traditional ritual in the churchyard, as the sombre ceremony of burial always does.

The calendar of the church itself has two great landmarks, Christmas and Easter, but numerous other minor and local occasions are traditionally observed in many parishes. A considerable proportion of all these churchyard events relate in some way to nature as does one of the best attended services of the church year, harvest festival. It is no accident that one of the most popular and well-known hymns is 'All things bright and beautiful'. A great deal of religious imagery draws on 'all creatures great and small'/'each tiny flower that opens, each little bird that sings'.

Churchgoers cannot fail to be aware of the links between religion and the natural world when the service of Morning Prayer (in all its forms) includes the poetry of the canticle, Benedicite, which is itself based on a more ancient hymn of praise, Psalm 148, with its splendid invocation of wild things and places.

The year in which this book was written was one in which the York mystery plays were performed. As in the fourteenth century, the performance still takes place out of doors in late June (around the feast of Corpus Christi) every fourth year. It no longer moves around the city, but is enacted in the ruins of St Mary's Abbey and its churchyard. The 1984 production brought

Ivy leaves (above) with the elongated central lobe typical of the common ivy, in St Mary's churchyard, Lower Heyford, Oxfordshire, in February. Holly leaves and berries (right), at All Saints, Fulham, London.

122

to the fore the authentic, unpolished voice of the original plays. It began, as the midsummer sun began to drop in the sky, with three plays concerning the creation of the world and all living things. Open-air theatre always has a special quality. When most of us spend the main part of our lives indoors, being out under the sky, in circumstances which are themselves memorable, gives us a heightened awareness of the world about us. We hear the evening song of birds; bats flit by as darkness falls; there is the constant accompaniment of wind and leaves, and the minute peripheral rustles and squeakings of night. After seeing the York plays, a friend of mine retained the memory of an additional drama — the shrieking and display of the peacocks. On another occasion, the barefoot apostles of one play only narrowly avoided a family of hedgehogs on a night-time excursion.

In the parish context, there are still places where local mystery plays and pageants are performed on a much smaller scale, regularly or on special anniversaries. At the church of St Nicholas in East Dereham, Norfolk, the play commemorates the miraculous event said to have occurred in a time of great famine in the seventh century, when deer came out of the forest in answer to Saint Withburga's prayer to the Virgin Mary. Their milk saved the starving people of the village. In 974, a rather discreditable plot resulted in the removal of Saint Withburga's body from East Dereham to the Cathedral at Ely, but a well with healing powers sprang up where her shrine had been.

As part of the anniversary service that I attended at East Dereham, the congregation walked in procession, singing, into the churchyard, where the holy well had been dressed with flowers and flower pictures depicting Saint Withburga and the Dereham deer. Planted around with honeysuckle, roses and herbs, the well was still brimming, even in a year of drought. House martins and swifts wheeled and fluttered above the churchyard. The light of the setting sun illuminated every separate feather of a sparrow's tail as it set down on a gravestone, and highlighted the robes of the priest and bishop as they bent to scoop up water from the holy well.

Flowers and greenery are still very much associated with church festivals, as they were in the past. Some of them are the traditional plants of the churchyard—holly, ivy, primroses, for example—others have become churchyard plants because they have been used in church decoration and seeded themselves when they were discarded: not only the garden form of gladdon called 'citrina', honesty, and lady's mantle, but more unusual species, such as *Kohlrauschia saxifraga*, which has a flower rather like a pink, and has been reported from two churchyards.

The plants most associated with Christmas are holly, ivy, and mistletoe, all of which grow in churchyards, though mistletoe, a plant sacred to the Druids, was never adopted into the Christian imagery and is rarely admitted into church. Holly, which figured in the celebration of the Roman feast of the Saturnalia, also has pagan associations, but is now so firmly established in the Christian tradition that it is referred to as 'Christmas' (though this name applies only to holly used as church decoration). In folk song and custom it is associated with the male principle, ivy with the female, a dichotomy exemplified in a fifteenth-century carol:

Holly and his mery men
They daunsen and they sing;
Ivy and her maidens
They wepen and they wring.

In the more modern Christmas carol 'The Holly and the Ivy', the holly provides the main theme and ivy is relegated to the refrain.

One of the principal church festivals celebrated by a procession before a service inside the church, is Palm Sunday. Since the true date palm of the Holy Land grows in Britain only as an introduced alien in the south-west (where it has been planted in a number of churchyards) the Church adopted other English plants to take the role of the palm fronds which were waved and strewn in the path of Christ on His triumphal entry into Jerusalem. The plant most often used is goat willow or sallow, also named pussy willow because of the soft furry catkins which appear in early spring; at this time, it is often called palm or palm willow. Yew is another plant which is sometimes carried on Palm Sunday and, in some northern counties, it, too, goes by the name of palm.

The Palm Sunday celebration is an elaborate presentation in some parishes. At Kirklington in North Yorkshire, the biblical scene is acted out by children in costume and the procession is led by a child on a donkey. Despite the capriciousness of early spring weather such pageantry is not exceptional, (though in one place the donkey proved too intractable and was dropped from the cast) but a more simple affair is more often the rule. At Kedington in Suffolk, the whole congregation assembles at a hut near the vicarage for a short sermon, then walks, singing, in procession along the road and through the churchyard into the church. Some people bring their 'palm' with them but, for those who do not, the vicar leaves a bucketful of willow palm at the start of the route and suggests that anyone who wishes might pull a branch from the vicarage garden or the churchyard as they pass, in the manner of the original Palm Sunday procession.

It used to be the custom in Wales to call Palm Sunday *Sul y Blodau* or Flowering Sunday. On that day, the graves were cleaned, trimmed and decorated with flowers and greenery. It seems that in earlier times, graves might have been dressed in this way on several occasions throughout the year. An account from Glamorgan mentions Easter, Whitsuntide and Christmas. It was perhaps a way of including the dead in the celebrations. However, by the end of the nineteenth century, the custom seems to have generally been confined to Palm Sunday. It still goes on in parts of Wales, but, although it has been recorded in the past in some Gloucestershire and Staffordshire villages, it never seems to have become widespread in England.

Umbels of ivy berries make decorative patterns on the churchyard wall, St Mary's, Lower Heyford, Oxfordshire. Once believed to ward off evil from domestic animals, ivy provides physical protection and food for a great number of wild creatures, from bats, birds and butterflies, to snails and small invertebrates.

125

A widely-observed activity is the making of 'Easter Gardens' during the days following Palm Sunday. They can be large, elaborate representations or homely, table-top scenes, but the elements always include the garden of Gethsemane, a hill topped by three crosses, and the tomb of Christ. They are made by local children out of moss, ferns, primroses and other decorative plants, which in many cases are picked from the churchyard or local woods.

It is interesting to see how churchyard ceremonies are hardly ever simple re-enactments of the past. They are adapted to suit the present-day needs and interests of parishioners. At Kedington, and in some other places, the old tradition of the Easter Hare who brings eggs has been revived in a Christian context. Easter eggs are hidden all over the churchyard, and after the Easter Sunday service the children in the congregation hunt for them.

Hymns and a Litany sung in procession through churchyard or fields, combined penitence with a supplication for God's blessing at Rogation tide (the week in which Ascension Day falls on the Thursday forty days after Easter Sunday). The official 'beating of the bounds' frequently took place at the same time. This practice reinforced in the collective parish memory the exact extent of the parish and is still observed in some places. At the church of St John the Baptist at Bisley in Surrey, a full beating of the bounds was made in 1983 to commemorate the seven-hundredth anniversary of the installation of the first rector of the church. Parishioners were spared from being dropped in streams and made to climb trees or stiles (as sometimes happened in the past), but they were 'bumped' against thirty-four local boundary landmarks. The ceremony took a whole day, beginning and ending in the churchyard.

Where the custom is preserved today, beating the bounds generally takes place only once every few years, and in a somewhat abbreviated form, though it usually begins or ends with a church service. A Rogation Sunday practice carried out in a group of four parishes near the Kent coast gives new meaning to an old custom. In the course of a walk over six-and-a-half miles, beginning after Holy Communion at St Oswald's, Paddlesworth, the participants go to St Mary and Ethelburga at Lyminge for Matins, to Postlin for Evensong and, finally, to Standford, where the day ends with Compline. Not all the parishioners walk the whole route, but the event is well supported even in bad weather and serves to draw the four parishes, each proud of its separate history and identity, into closer co-operation and friendship.

A prayer for God's blessing on the crops and natural bounty of a parish is still made in some places. At Lythe in North Yorkshire, the congregation walk singing to the fields and the sea. At Worth in Sussex, the vicar of St Nicholas leads the congregation up a lane and around the churchyard to ask for God's blessing on hedges, fields, crops and farm stock—a local farmer obligingly ensures that there are cows in a nearby meadow. If one is to judge from the churchyard and lane at Worth, brimming with wild flowers, ferns, birds and small animals, this is a method of churchyard management which should be taken up elsewhere!

Some country towns and villages persisted in their use of rushes or hay as a covering for church floors until the last century. The rushes, donated from every part of the parish, were renewed with great ceremony in late summer. A correspondent in Humberside described his grandfather's memory of the general excitement when the great rush cart, a hay wain piled high with rushes, rumbled through each village.

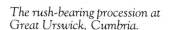

The rush-bearing procession at Great Urswick, Cumbria.

127

Although there is no longer any need for such floor-covering, the rush-bearing ceremony is still observed in several English parishes. The two most famous rush festivals take place in Ambleside and Grasmere in Cumbria. In both cases, the rushes are carried in procession to the church where they are strewn and a service is held. A number of smaller parishes also observe the custom. At Barrowden in Leicestershire, the rushes are cut from church land on St Peter's Eve (June 28) and left to lie a week in the church. At the village of Great Urswick in Cumbria, rushes which grow around the tarn at the centre of the village are cut annually for the ceremony which is held on the church's patronal feast day at Michaelmas (September 29). The procession to the church is headed by a rush-bearing banner, and a traditional sheet, embroidered with rushes, is carried by four girls. Bystanders along the route place offerings for the church in the sheet. All the children carry flowers which they take out into the churchyard after the service, placing them on the oldest graves to show that the dead have not been forgotten.

At Glenfield in Leicestershire, new-mown hay is laid in the church in early July. In the church of St Peter and St Paul at Wingrave in Buckinghamshire, morris dancers or local children strew new-mown hay in commemoration of the bequest of a field to the church by a young woman who lost her way in the dark and was guided to safety by the sound of the church bells. At first, hay for the church was cut from the field, then the revenue from renting it out was used to buy floor-covering such as carpets and hassocks. The field was recently sold and the income put towards

The display of clipped yews in St Mary's churchyard, Painswick, Gloucestershire, consists of ninety-nine well-tended fastigiate trees.

maintaining the church floors. The celebration is now observed with hay donated by local farmers. (It used to be cut from the churchyard, too, but the grass is now mown too frequently to allow for hay-making.) At this time of year, Wingrave church and churchyard are the scene of special services, a fête, and surrounding the church with pennies—fifty pounds worth—in an atmosphere of holiday and general festivity.

Ringing the church with pennies (also carried out at Sutton in Cambridgeshire) seems to be a modern adaptation of the old 'clypping' ceremony, in which parishioners clypp (or clasp) the church, joining hands and walking round the building three times in a symbolic embrace. The meaning of clypping is sometimes misunderstood because the best known instance of it is at Painswick in Gloucestershire, also famous for its ninety-nine fastigiate yews, to which the clypping is mistakenly believed to refer. However, the service continues in many counties from Yorkshire (Guisley) to Cornwall (Helston), and it is being revived at Hastings in East Sussex and at Radley in Berkshire, where the clypping is followed by a sermon in the churchyard.

In medieval times, a considerable amount of money was raised for the church through public entertainment such as plays, dancing and fairs in the churchyard. These events were usually organized and often partly subsidized by the church. Churchwardens' accounts, rich sources of information, list items ranging from the erection of seating for a play, to fitting out morris dancers, and paying a child to dance the hobby horse.

Unnoticed for most of the year, the orb spider claims attention in the dewy days of autumn when its beautiful webs, spangled with droplets, sparkle from bushes and hedges.

Honeysuckle in St Brynach's churchyard,
Nevern, Dyfed, in mid-July. In some parts of
Britain, it was attributed with the power to fend
off evil from animals. (Life size).

There are signs that some churchyards are being reclaimed for a more general kind of community use. The Women's Institute survey disclosed a variety of parish events: church fêtes, fairs, sales of home produce, and—in the case of one woman who sits in the church porch selling bundles of lavender gathered from the churchyard of St Margaret's, at Cley next the Sea in Norfolk—churchyard produce.

Major churchyard events usually take place in late summer, when mowing and trampling of the ground do no harm to the flora. On the contrary, it probably benefits. A well-attended late season fête has the same excellent effect as the practice of running cattle in a meadow; it keeps down the undergrowth and aids the dispersal of seeds—yellow rattle will not drop its seeds fully, unless subjected to this kind of treatment. At Roberttown in West Yorkshire, games held as part of the church fair take place on the north side of the churchyard where there are no graves. The widespread superstition that the north side of the churchyard was the province of the devil seems to have arisen during the Middle Ages. At St Michael the Archangel, Kirkby Malham, in North Yorkshire and St Nicholas, Worth, in West Sussex, the prejudice was strong enough to have caused the making of a 'devil's door' in the north wall of the church. The door was left open during a christening so that the devil could escape readily to his own plot. The Saxons appear to have been untouched by such fears—the best Saxon archaeological finds have been from excavations in the northern parts of churchyards, where the early graves have not been disturbed by later burials. Even today, the shaded northern plot is often the last to be filled and is still in many cases devoid of graves.

Prolonged relief from soil disturbance in parts of the churchyard may be signalled by the presence of plants, such as orchids, which are particularly vulnerable to change. They are less likely to be found in areas used for burial where the ground may have been turned over to a depth of six feet or more several times through the centuries. Some grave-diggers restore the turf when they have filled in a grave, thus conserving all but the deep-rooted plants, but usually at least some of the soil gets inverted, in which case the less fertile soil from deeper down has to be recolonized and the result is likely to be a sward that is less rich than the original.

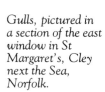

Gulls, pictured in a section of the east window in St Margaret's, Cley next the Sea, Norfolk.

A Suffolk church mouse (house mouse to zoologists).

131

Lavender which grows (along with rue and rosemary) in the churchyard of St Margaret's, Cley next the Sea, Norfolk, is gathered (below right), made into bunches and offered for sale in the church porch.

The imagery of flowers is close to the heart of Christian liturgy. The burial service contains the idea that the life of a man or woman 'cometh up and is cut down like a flower'. Inherent in this, is the idea of resurrection. The dead will rise again as the wild flower on the grave reappears in springtime. Perhaps this is why flowers are so important in graveyard ritual and care, and why so many of us feel that the churchyard is a place for grasses and flowers.

The floral event that has caught the public imagination more than any other in recent years is the flower festival, which now has a firm place in many a parish calendar. Some flower festivals are publicized nationally. Held in the church and sometimes also in the churchyard, they give scope to the imagination for the expression of a renewed interest in flowers and, particularly, in flower arranging. In many cases, a flower festival is accompanied by other events such as concerts, as at Westleton in Suffolk, where the floral display consists entirely of wild flowers. At Needingworth in Cambridgeshire, the flower festival takes place at the same time as the well-dressing, and in other places it may be accompanied by craft stalls or tea for the visitors.

During my churchyard researches, I occasionally attended church festivals and special services, which stand out in my mind both as enjoyable and rather moving events. I had many agreeable and informative chance conversations with clergymen, vergers, churchwardens, gardeners, parishioners and other visitors, but it was when I was on my own among the plants, animals and gravestones, that I was most aware of the peaceful and comforting atmosphere which distinguishes churchyards from other places. I was therefore genuinely surprised when several people expressed the view that researching in churchyards was a morbid activity. In such pleasant surroundings it was easy to forget that churchyards also have a grim image, represented for example, in the terrifying scene which opens *Great Expectations* (thought to be based on Cooling churchyard in Kent), or the dour London churchyard which provides the background to the quarrel between Lizzie Hesketh and Bradley Headstone, or in innumerable horror stories. Such associations are part of our conception of churchyards, though by no means a dominant one; even in Bram Stoker's *Dracula*, it is acknowledged that 'the nicest spot in Whitby' is the parish churchyard which overlooks the bay, where 'there are walks, with seats beside them . . . and people go and sit there all day long looking at the beautiful view and enjoying the breeze.' Perhaps the most important feature about churchyards is that in them, one encounters death within a context of living things. For most people there is solace to be found in nature, and in the thought that the gravestones of those known and unknown to us have the society of birds and butterflies, lichens and wild flowers.

A dunnock built its nest behind this statue of St Andrew above the church door in Weybread, Suffolk.

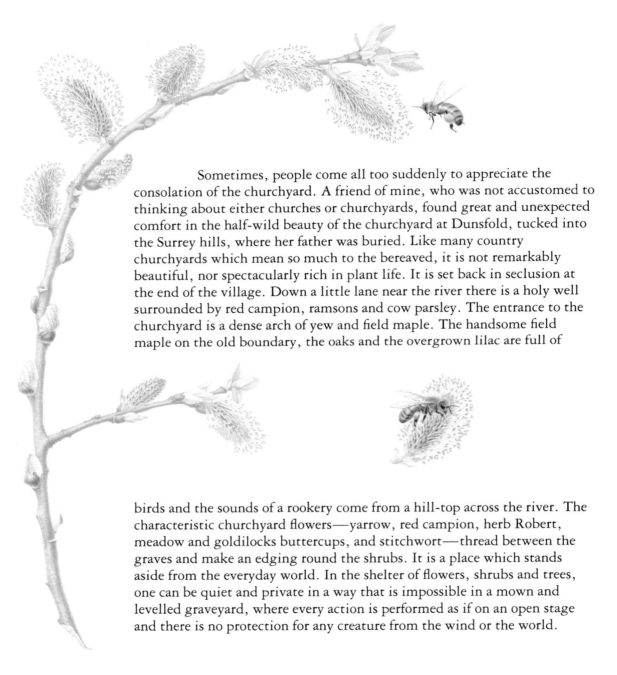

Sometimes, people come all too suddenly to appreciate the consolation of the churchyard. A friend of mine, who was not accustomed to thinking about either churches or churchyards, found great and unexpected comfort in the half-wild beauty of the churchyard at Dunsfold, tucked into the Surrey hills, where her father was buried. Like many country churchyards which mean so much to the bereaved, it is not remarkably beautiful, nor spectacularly rich in plant life. It is set back in seclusion at the end of the village. Down a little lane near the river there is a holy well surrounded by red campion, ramsons and cow parsley. The entrance to the churchyard is a dense arch of yew and field maple. The handsome field maple on the old boundary, the oaks and the overgrown lilac are full of

birds and the sounds of a rookery come from a hill-top across the river. The characteristic churchyard flowers—yarrow, red campion, herb Robert, meadow and goldilocks buttercups, and stitchwort—thread between the graves and make an edging round the shrubs. It is a place which stands aside from the everyday world. In the shelter of flowers, shrubs and trees, one can be quiet and private in a way that is impossible in a mown and levelled graveyard, where every action is performed as if on an open stage and there is no protection for any creature from the wind or the world.

Pussy willows like these seen in St Meubred's churchyard in Cardinham, Cornwall, in March, are carried in place of palms on Palm Sunday in many parishes.

The nineteenth-century poet and botanist John Leicester Warren,
Lord de Tabley, was neither the first nor the last to gain strength in
bereavement from the beauty of a churchyard and its wild plants and birds.
He wrote in 'The Churchyard on the Sands':

> The grey gull flaps the written stones,
> The ox-birds chase the tide;
> And near that narrow field of bones
> Great ships at anchor ride
>
> A church of silent weathered looks
> A breezy reddish tower,
> A yard whose mounded resting-nooks
> Are tinged with sorrel flower

He notes the succession of churchyard flowers and birds:

> Let snowdrops early in the year
> Droop o'er her silent breast;
> And bid the later cowslip rear
> The amber of its crest.
>
> Come hither linnets tufted-red,
> Drift by, O wailing tern;
> Set pure vale lilies at her head,
> At her feet lady fern.
>
> Grow samphire on the tidal brink,
> Wave pansies of the shore
> To whisper how alone I think
> Of her for evermore.
>
> Bring blue sea-hollies thorny, keen,
> Long lavender in flower;
> Grey wormwood like a hoary queen
> Staunch mullein like a tower.

Swallows congregate over St Mary's churchyard, Swinbrook, Oxfordshire.

Old-fashioned churchyards are, by their nature, places of seclusion and shelter not only for the bereaved but for any visitor. Such surroundings, old tombs and headstones, sheltered by overgrown box or yew, make a good place to resolve troubled thoughts or simply to sit quietly.

Even when it was customary for people of status to be buried inside the church, there were those who chose the churchyard for their eventual resting place. In a letter written to Matthew Smith in 1750, Edmund Burke wrote that he 'would rather sleep in the southern corner of a little country churchyard than in the tomb of the Capulets'. (This seems to have been a rhetorical desire, however, for he was buried inside the parish church at Beaconsfield, apparently according to his own wish.) Another who expressed his desire to be buried out of doors, though as a clergyman he would have been entitled to intramural burial, was the metaphysical poet Henry Vaughan, whose grave is at the foot of a yew tree in Llansantffraed churchyard, overlooking the River Usk, which provided the inspiration for so much of his poetry. Nicholas Ferrar, the seventeenth-century religious aesthete, was precise in his instructions that he should be buried seven feet from the west door of the church at Little Gidding in Cambridgeshire, where his tomb can still be seen. It is now situated a little further from the church, which has been foreshortened since Ferrar's death, probably during the Restoration. The path by the pigsty mentioned by T.S. Eliot in *Four Quartets* has recently been re-routed and the sty itself converted, but the small churchyard, despite being kept monotonously neat, is still a pleasant place, full of bird-song from the hedge and sycamore thicket which surrounds it. Caradoc Evans, known for his Anglo-Welsh short stories, wrote the inscription for his own grave at Horeb Chapel, New Cross, in Ceredigion. His stone, dated 1945, reads: 'Bury me lightly so that the small rain may reach my face and the fluttering of the butterfly shall not escape my ear.' The chapelyard is still flowery and full of butterflies.

It is evident that well before the time of Thomas Gray, churchyards were regarded as beautiful and exceptional places, but it was the 'Elegy Written in a Country Church Yard' which not only incorporated those sensibilities of the past, but provided an image of them, so powerful that it has coloured our perception to this day. Above all, this poem firmly established a sense of the churchyard as a special kind of English landscape. It certainly had an influence on the idea of what a churchyard should look like, confirming their rural qualities. This ideal of the country churchyard is still, more than two centuries after the poem was published, the most important factor in our attitude to them.

Gray himself spent much of his later life studying botany and achieved some eminence in the subject. The 'Elegy' does not burst at the seams with natural history as became the fashion in a later period; his ideals were conciseness and perspicuity. Although some of the elements in the 'Elegy'—'the ivy-mantled tower', moping owl, and rugged elms, were familiar poetic territory in the eighteenth century, one has the impression that the stock imagery conformed to his observations, not the other way about. Other details: the lowing herd and the ploughman, the cock crow, the beetle's droning flight and the twittering swallow, summon the scene recognizably, even now.

In the original version of the 'Elegy' (and printed in some of the first editions) were four more lines, of naturalistic detail, just before the Epitaph. Gray apparently decided to omit them later, on the grounds that they made too long a parenthesis at this place in the poem.

> There scatter'd oft, the earliest of the year,
> By hands unseen are show'r of violets found;
> The redbreast loves to build and warble there,
> And little footsteps lightly print the ground.

Haymaking in progress (left) in August in St Nicholas's churchyard, Oakley, Suffolk.

137

Gray foresaw that the 'Elegy' would be a success; he drew attention, in a letter, to how popular Edward Young's 'Night Thoughts' and Hervey's 'Meditations on Tombs' had been just before his own poem was published. Gray could not have known, however, how profoundly people would take the 'Elegy' to their hearts. It has been taught to generations of schoolchildren, some at least of whom were told, unequivocally, that it was the best poem in the English language. Even today, people who know no other poetry can recite Gray's 'Elegy'.

Many poets since Gray have written about churchyards. Their work is in the English pastoral tradition, poems which see the churchyard as enshrining the best country idylls, shelter and peace. 'The winds were still' wrote Shelley—a notable atheist—of Lechlade churchyard, 'or the dry church tower grass,/Knows not their gentle motions as they pass.' Wordsworth describing a 'Churchyard among the mountains' in 'The Excursion' also looked at it as a special kind of grassland:

> Green is the Churchyard, beautiful and green
> Ridge rising gently by the side of ridge,
> A heaving surface, almost wholly free
> From interruption of sepulchral stones,
> And mantled o'er with aboriginal turf
> And everlasting flowers.

The Woolverstone Church rose, a wonderfully scented old hybrid perpetual which was rediscovered growing in Woolverstone churchyard in Suffolk, on a bush thought to be more than a hundred years old.

138

The parson-poet and botanist Andrew Young wrote lovingly of the little east Suffolk church at Friston, and how in Church Field 'the scented orchis/ Shoots from the grass in rosy spire . . .'

Sir John Betjeman was, more than any other, the poet of English churches and churchyards. In a light-hearted poem about St Enodoc in Trebetherick, north Cornwall, where now he is buried, he wrote of going to this most extraordinary ancient church with its strange uneven spire, which stands just clear of the sand that once buried it.

> Come on! come on! This hillock hides the spire,
> Now that one and now none. As winds about
> The burnished path through lady's finger, thyme
> And bright varieties of saxifrage,
> So grows the tinny tenor faint or loud
> And all things draw towards St. Enodoc
>
> . . . . Hover-flies remain
> More than a moment on a ragwort bunch,
> And people's passing shadows don't disturb
> Red Admirals basking with their wings apart.

As the clergyman addresses the congregation inside the church:

> "Dearly beloved . . ." and a bumble-bee
> Zooms itself free into the churchyard sun
> And so my thoughts this happy Sabbathtide.

['*Sunday Afternoon Service in St. Enodoc Church, Cornwall*']

The interests of churchgoers, mourners and naturalists need not be at odds. The church sits within an island of natural life, and there is a sense of its presence at St Enodoc as thoughts wander with the bee, or, on another occasion, in the church of St Nicholas at East Dereham, when the great west doors open to the red-gold sun of midsummer evening and to the background of the quiet Norfolk landscape veiled in haze.

This rose (above) was planted on the grave of Edward Fitzgerald in St Michael's churchyard in Boulge, Suffolk, in 1893. It had been raised in Kew Gardens from seed brought by William Simpson, artist-traveller, from the grave of Omar Khayyam at Naishapur, and planted by admirers of Fitzgerald in the name of the Omar Khayyam Club.

139

In almost every aspect of the furnishing and decoration of the church one can find reflections of the natural life outside. Sometimes they are explicit and local, as at the church of St Petrock at Lydford in Devon, where the Revd G.S. Thorpe was inspired, it is said, during a thunderstorm, to take the Benedicite as the theme for carvings on the pew ends. There we find fine representations of the animals and plants to be found in a Devon churchyard and the surrounding countryside: a thrush with snails, a sparrow on its nest, a woodpecker, daffodils, violets, foxgloves, wood anemones and ferns. There is oak foliage with acorns, a field maple, and a beech tree with a squirrel in it. There is even an adder.

Similarly, at the church of St Mary at Swaffham Prior, Cambridgeshire, there is a large window of pale, watery blue and green stained glass representing the Benedicite. The water lily, sagittaria and bullrush are plainly recognizable, as is their marshland habitat which is one of the last fen sites—Wicken Fen, a property of the National Trust since early last century, and now a nature reserve.

Topiary bird of golden yew, at St Margaret's, Alstone, Gloucestershire.

The natural life of the churchyard and beyond finds expression in the fabric and ornamentation of the church, as it has in the liturgy itself. On the outside of churches, animals and flowers are represented in the stonework, often most memorably as gargoyles. Many of the creatures depicted in gargoyles are fantastic and nightmarish, but others, such as the hare and hound on the church at Kilpeck in Herefordshire, are realistically portrayed.

Some fine, naturalistic weathervanes swing in the wind above parish churches. Most are cockerels, but variations include a fine salmon at Upper Framilode on the Severn, to the south-west of Gloucester and, with equal local relevance, a mallard in flight on the timber bell tower overlooking Walland Marsh, just below Romney Marsh, where the wild duck are as integral to the landscape now as they were in the late eightenth century when the weathervane was made. But nature is not to be outdone. Both cormorant and shag have been observed perching on the weathercock of Norwich Cathedral spire.

Exterior church carvings from St Mary's, Speen, Berkshire (above) and St Mary's, Brome, Suffolk. The cat-faced gargoyle (top left), also on Brome church, provides an unusual site for a bird's nest.

Owls are a favourite subject among the carvings to be found on misericords because, it is said, of the prophecy in Isaiah (chapter 12. v21) that when Babylon is destroyed, its houses will be tenanted by 'doleful creatures; and owls shall dwell there' (though some translations obscurely substitute ostriches for owls). Just as certain saints are brought in to illustrate a local point, Isaiah may well provide a useful route by which to introduce familiar birds of the churchyard and country into church decoration. Other misericord subjects are oak woods with pigs rooting for acorns, fox and hounds, hare and hounds, and roses. At the church of Edlesborough in Buckinghamshire, rightly esteemed for its wood carving and set in one of my favourite churchyards, the misericords depict not only owls but also the very much more unusual subject of bats.

Ivy berries mature from yellow-green to green-black. They are a favourite with overwintering blackcaps.

The naturalistic stone carvings at the chapter house at Southwell Minster in Nottinghamshire are justly famous. There, thirteenth-century masons coaxed the stone of the capitals and vaulted roof into a tumble of foliage 'which is as luxuriant as the undergrowth of a hedgerow in May when subjected to wind and rain', as E.H. Crossley, a connoisseur of church craftsmanship, described it. The plants are so naturalistically depicted, and with such skill, that one can identify holly and ivy, hawthorn with berries,

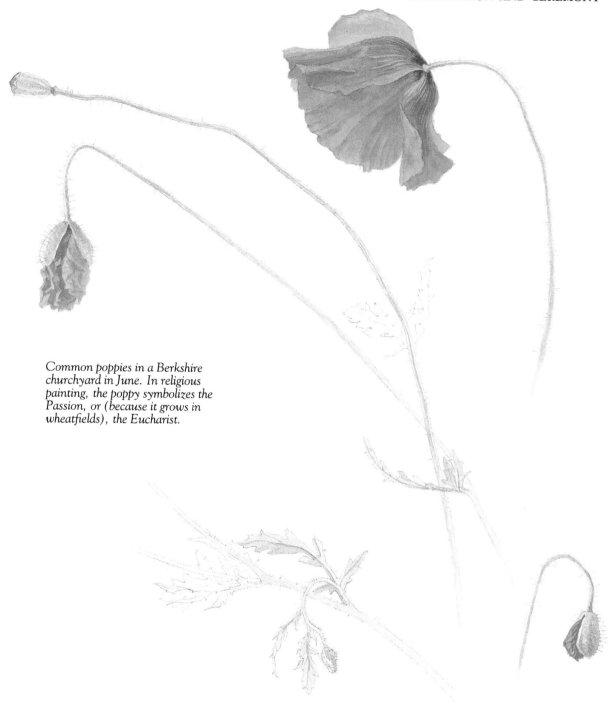

*Common poppies in a Berkshire
churchyard in June. In religious
painting, the poppy symbolizes the
Passion, or (because it grows in
wheatfields), the Eucharist.*

and both the native English species of oak. There is also, I believe, sycamore, one of only two such early church carvings that I know—the other is at Christchurch Cathedral, Oxford. The sycamore's wide-lobed leaf and paired seeds, joined in a narrow angle, are quite distinct from those of the field maple, which is also to be seen at Southwell. The field maple has smaller leaves with more rounded lobes, the angle of its seeds being so wide as to set them almost in a straight line. The Southwell carvings also depict other plants of the countryside, and indeed of the churchyard: buttercups, white bryony, hops, vines and roses. Professor Nikolaus Pevsner, whose masterly description of *The Leaves of Southwell* has brought these beautiful carvings a wider appreciation, remarks that the roses are a double form and not, as most of the other foliage, a wild variety that might be expected in the hedgerow. I note, in passing, that I have seen many double roses of this kind in churchyards. Whether they were there in the thirteenth century, it is impossible to say, but the most popular medieval poem of all, *The Romaunt of the Rose* (by Guillaume de Lorris and Jean le Meung) was written not long after the leaves were carved. The rose figures in monastery gardens and was used for garlands in church processions. For Pevsner, the leaves of Southwell represent an artistic achievement that is firmly rooted in the context of freer and more imaginative religious and philosophical attitudes which developed in the early thirteenth century and reflected an increased awareness of nature itself.

> Could these leaves of the English countryside, with all their freshness, move us so deeply if they were not carved in that spirit which filled the saints and poets and thinkers of the thirteenth century, the spirit of religious respect for the loveliness of created nature?

> [*Sir Nikolaus Pevsner: The Leaves of Southwell*]

A great deal of that feeling for nature is still manifest in parish churches. It no longer shows itself in great works of building. The religious energy for building and rebuilding churches is no longer there and perhaps, in any case, we have grown to love our old churches too much to want to change them. What is remarkable, in an age whose interpretative models of the world are almost entirely mechanistic, is the way in which natural images

A coal tit, a bird associated with churchyard yews and false-cypresses, at St Andrew's, Winston, Suffolk.

144

continue to prevail in church decoration. Flowers and animals feature in items bought or made professionally, such as stained glass, carpets and woodwork. They are even more common in things made for the church by parishioners themselves: the tapestry hassocks, banners, beautiful flower-embroidered altar cloths, even a rug before the altar at Long Compton in Warwickshire, composed of panels depicting wild and garden flowers.

Sometimes the plants of an individual churchyard are mirrored inside the church. At St Peter's, Theberton, in Suffolk, a modern wrought iron communion rail with ivy foliage in the decoration echoes the luxuriant growth of ivy over the tombs outside. The choir stall beyond has carved oak foliage and acorns, in harmony with an overgrown part of the churchyard behind the church which is almost an oak thicket. Memorials inside the church, which tend to be grander than those outside, are generally restricted to classical subjects, and naturalistic detail is mainly confined to cornucopia spilling over with fruit, flowers and ears of grain (reflecting a rich life), willows (for grief) and formal garlands.

A common garden snail half-hidden by ivy on the church wall, at Cilgwyn Dyfed, in July. (Life size).

Common reeds (Phragmites) are picked from the tarn in the village of Great Urswick, Cumbria, to be carried by the Rush Queen in procession during the annual rush-bearing ceremony.

These subjects also appear on the gravestones and memorials in the churchyard, which have a wider range both of the choice of theme and in the quality of the workmanship than interior carvings. The early nineteenth-century work in particular shows a freedom and creativity of expression in gravestones which feature well-observed animals such as sheep or pheasants, occasionally butterflies (signifying the soul), and individual plants including honeysuckle, bryony, roses and ears of wheat. Some gravestones depict cut flowers, roses, violets or lilies, or blooms with severed stems, which signify early death. Later in the century, grave-carving became more conventional; the imagery and its style of execution were standardized—ivy, lilies, forget-me-nots and doves monopolized the gravestones. However, in the context of a country churchyard, even

quite ordinary gravestones standing among wild flowers and trees have their charm. In the isolated churchyard at Drayton Beauchamp in Buckinghamshire, a plain grave is transformed in appearance by a dense velvety pool of dark green lesser celandine leaves growing within the rectangle of the kerbstones. The only nearby building is the rectory where the botanist Henry Harpur Crewe once lived. There is no trace now of his famous pink snowdrops but there are places which are white with the more familiar kind. Beneath a bank by the boundary of the churchyard, there is a grave all overgrown with ivy, single and double snowdrops and winter aconites. The ivy on the ground perfectly sets off the brightness of the flowers, and two or three strands climb up the stone grave cross, their starry leaves mingling with those of the stone-carved ivy.

147

COMMUNITY
and
CONSERVATION

He passes down the churchyard track
         On his way to toll the bell;
And stops, and looks at the graves around,
And notes each finished and greening mound
         Complacently,
         As their shaper he,
   And one who can do it well . . .

Thomas Hardy: *The Sexton at Longpuddle*

THE PARISH CHURCH IS USUALLY THE main landmark of a village and, despite urban development, an important feature in the town landscape. Old churches and churchyards have for a long time been a focus for students of history and architecture. More recently, archaeologists and naturalists have begun to devote serious attention to them. It is easy however, for scholars and enthusiasts to concentrate on details of their subject and to forget that the churchyard still has a practical function, and a role to play in the community life of the district. Any ideas about wildlife conservation need to take into account the feelings and needs of the people of the parish or they are probably impossible to put into practice. If directions for churchyard management come from the outside they can readily stir up resentment, and it is all too easy for an adviser to trespass unwittingly on private feelings about particular parts of a churchyard.

Churchyards develop their own internal logic. Pathways are made or disappear depending on which parts are used for burial. Tragedy, inevitably bound into the history of every churchyard, reveals itself in the paths trodden by the bereaved. There is a new path through tall wild flowers and grasses in a Hertfordshire churchyard that I know well, which was worn by the constant visits of the bereaved parents to the grave of their young child. After a few months, the parishioner responsible for the churchyard grass adopted the track into his regular round of mowing, bringing it into the semi-formal network of pathways, and providing a route for other mourners and visitors to a previously inaccessible part of the churchyard.

The wildlife of the churchyard adapts to the changing patterns of use. The grass around new graves is, by common consent, usually kept short, but that surrounding older, less visited ones, may gradually be mowed less frequently. The area in which the oldest graves are located is probably the quietest and least disturbed and often shelters high numbers of birds, small mammals and insects in well-grown shrubs and taller grass.

There does not need to be a defined management policy for a churchyard to be well cared for. In many parishes, the feeling for nature conservation, if not explicit, is evident in the care with which the churchyard is looked after. Sometimes it is a special contact with living things which has created an awareness of the wildlife of the churchyard and a desire to conserve it. Such a revelation occurred at a spring wedding in a Northamptonshire village. No-one present could have failed to take

Flat-backed millipede (left) with detail of body segments, and centipede (below). (Both life size).

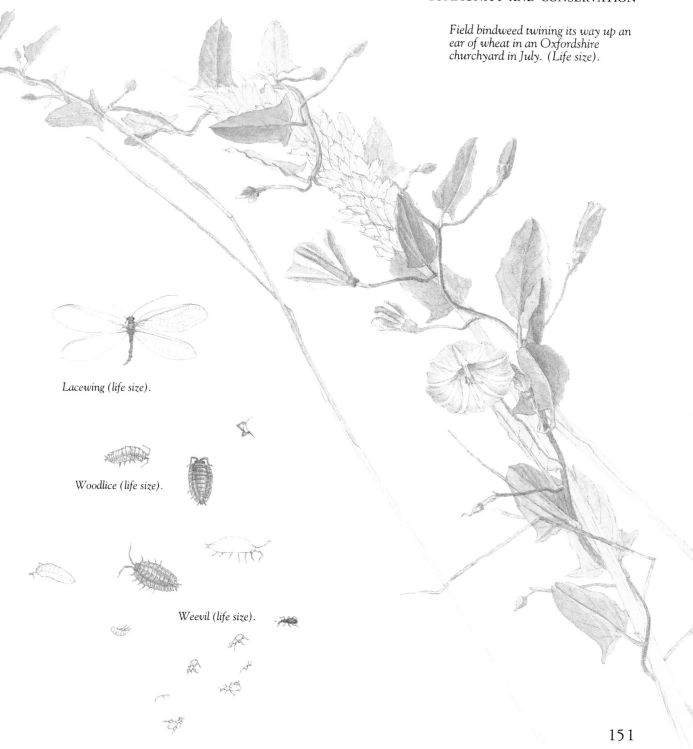

Field bindweed twining its way up an ear of wheat in an Oxfordshire churchyard in July. (Life size).

Lacewing (life size).

Woodlice (life size).

Weevil (life size).

pleasure in the harmonious picture of the bride and bridesmaids in their chosen colour scheme of blue and pale yellow seen among bluebells and primroses. It is still talked about, and photographs are shown to visitors. Should there be any scheme to close-mow that particular churchyard, there will be many voices of dissent.

A positive attitude towards conservation is likely to arise when there is an intimate and sustained experience of a churchyard and the wildlife in it. An excellent example of happy co-existence between humans and wildlife is to be found in the churchyard in Ripponden in West Yorkshire. The local playgroup uses an open space in the churchyard for its activities when the weather is good. On a May morning when I was there, the young children were all out on miniature bikes and cars, in their little playground on the west side of the church, while the churchyard gardener began to cut back the high sweet cicely and long grass nearby, and a dipper flew swiftly along the river which formed one boundary to disappear into a culvert in the bank, where, doubtless, it had its nest. There was also a grey wagtail on the river, flashing bright yellow as it bobbed about. All along the riverside sweet cicely was in flower, but on the opposite side of the churchyard, rhododendron and massed bluebells were dominant, and the pretty pink purslane speckled the bank. Nearer to the church, the shorter grass was full of daisies. Sweet woodruff and some London pride had spread from the graves to colonize the grass round about them. Tall, elegant fern fronds between the graves swayed in the breeze. At the very least, those small children would learn that churchyards are beautiful, peaceful places. It is likely that incidentally, they were also learning quite a lot about nature.

There are many schools, originally church foundations, built beside churches with independent access to the churchyard. Some have their own gate, but the welcoming churchyard of St John the Baptist in Glastonbury also has a special paved path leading from the school across the churchyard to the church. Adults, as well as children, come to this churchyard in summer to have a packed lunch or simply to sit in the sun enjoying the scent of the wallflowers. The Victorians used to make

English partridge seen under the hedge in Holy Trinity churchyard, Boxted, Suffolk, in April.

an outing of a picnic in a churchyard, but nowadays this habit seems to be confined to churchyards in town centres, although there is a parish picnic at St Peter's, Tadley, in Hampshire on the Sunday before St Peter's Day.

Children make unofficial use of the churchyard too and I often came across small groups of them playing among the shrubs and gravestones. One churchyard naturalist confided in an unguarded moment that children are a good indicator species—where they choose to play, the churchyard is likely to be rich in wildlife. Not everyone would agree: a vicar in West Yorkshire recently made a special plea to his parishioners not to allow their children to play in the churchyard. Yet, surely, children are more likely to grow to appreciate and respect the churchyard by being in it than from being kept out?

A considerable degree of practical conservation is inspired from within the parish. The results may not be as extensive as a naturalist might wish, but such care usually has the advantage of being sustained over a long period. Churchyards have to fulfil so many expectations that it would be foolish for anyone to try to establish a kind of model to which they should all conform. Indeed, if churchyards were all turned into standardized nature reserves, we should lose a lot of the excitement and unpredictable variety which occurs in places where human activity and wildlife are in close proximity. We should also lose the results of churchyard grave-planting, which has been continuous over centuries and displays itself in the diversity of naturalized flora and unusual trees.

Oxford ragwort flowers and full and empty seed heads, seen in June (life size). Note that the bracts on the flowerheads are all black-tipped.

153

Yet there are dangers in being too sanguine. When we assume that the churchyards muddle along all right, we would do well to remember that the churchyard at Kettlewell in North Yorkshire used to have lady's slipper orchid (for which there is now only one known site in Britain), and that within living memory there were natterjack toads in Norfolk churchyards. It is also true that careless repointing and restoration have obliterated many historic and botanically important sites for ferns. On the other hand, one should not underestimate the problems encountered in seeing that the churchyard is maintained at all. Many incumbents of rural 'group practice' churches are at their wit's end, when faced with the apparently boundless fecundity of a country churchyard.

Unfortunately the methods used to restore order are often too drastic and destructive. Though I have often heard it categorized as such, these actions are rarely deliberate vandalism, rather that people fail to consider wildlife because they associate it with an unkempt, overgrown environment, not at all suitable for a consecrated burial ground.

It cannot be emphasized enough that wildlife conservation in a churchyard does not mean a churchyard wilderness. Indeed, an overgrown habitat is inimical to many of the characteristic churchyard species. Not a great deal of labour is required to maintain a churchyard which is neat but which shows a concern for its natural life and which is a rewarding place by any standards. It need not necessarily be one that contains great rarities, but simply one in which a naturally beautiful setting is cared for with sensitivity for the landscape, and the plants and animals within it. There are still many such churchyards to show us example.

At Sourton in Devon, the churchyard backs onto a disused railway line which in its working days carried the seeds of pink purslane up to the boundary hedge of the churchyard, where it has outlived the railway. Jackdaws nest in the tower, goldfinches use the pollard sycamores as singing posts, and a willow warbler trills from a tall hawthorn up the hill. Further into the south-west, the church of St Symphorian sits at the heart of the Cornish village of Veryan, with a holy well opposite the gates. In the sheltered mildness of the churchyard grow high beeches, with ramsons lush beneath, and masses of three-cornered leek (which looks slightly like a white bluebell from a distance). There is a rookery in the pine trees, and the camellias lining the path to the church porch flourish in this gentle climate.

Pale flax, a wild plant found in many coastal churchyards, here growing in the chancel of a ruined church, high on the cliffs at Rufus Castle, Portland, Dorset, in June. (Life size).

Field forget-me-not, growing with the flax in St Andrew's, Rufus Castle (life size). This is the most common of the churchyard forget-me-nots.

155

Any visitor, botanist or not, could spend happy hours enjoying the glorious limestone flora of the Dales in churchyards such as St Mary's, Kettlewell-cum-Starbotton, and a dozen others, or in great, meandering, home counties churchyards glowing with bluebells and wood anemones, such as that of St Peter and Paul at Great Missenden in Buckinghamshire.

In certain churchyards, an exceptional quality of care is immediately obvious. Those who think that a churchyard rich in wildlife must be a scruffy place should visit Littleham in Devon where, down a wooded lane in the valley of the River Yeo, lies the church of St Swithun's. I visited it on May Day in a sunny spring, and it was an experience I shall not forget. Full of flowers, trees and birds, it recalled the garden of the dream in Chaucer's *The Romance of the Rose*. There were all the plants I had come to expect in a good traditional churchyard: bluebells, red campion, primroses, the churchyard pink primrose, speedwells, stitchwort and lady's smock. In taller patches of vegetation, hemp agrimony was coming up along with columbines, cow parsley and foxgloves. There were ramsons, dog's mercury, woodrush, and the clear blue of bugle flowers. The churchyard itself was everything anyone could desire, sheltered and beautifully situated, with several benches where people could sit and enjoy the scene and the singing birds. On either side of the main path to the south porch and around the new graves, the grass was neatly mown, but the way in which the parishioners had managed the rest of this churchyard was extremely interesting. They had worked out, in their own way, a method recommended by professional naturalists for churchyard conservation. Instead of mowing everything flat every few weeks, they kept close-mown only grassy paths which wound their way within the taller grass of the rest of the churchyard which was cut once or twice annually. In the north-east corner, this slightly longer grass was spectacularly laced with the pink-purple of early purple orchids. I counted no less than sixty spikes in flower around the path and even in some of the graves—a healthy colony with every likelihood of continuing to be so, it seems.

The practical work in this churchyard is done by a few parishioners who have divided up the large area between them, each taking responsibility for her or his part. One of their number is a woman who is also something of a botanist, and a painter. Her sketch-book, containing paintings of all the plants she has seen in the churchyard, is kept in the

Deadly nightshade growing from the base of a chest tomb in St Cross churchyard, Holywell, Oxford. All parts of the plant contain extremely poisonous alkaloids, and one name for the shiny black fruits is 'devil's cherries'.

157

Wild strawberries growing from crevices in the wall of Cilgwyn church, Dyfed, in July. (Life size). The plants have colonized a huge area of wall, and are frequently visited by birds, which eat the fruits.

church in a hewn-out chest, dating from the tenth century, recently found and restored. This book shows the visitor all the plants which appear throughout the year. I would not otherwise have guessed the presence of centaury and betony, two summer-flowering plants not likely to catch the eye earlier in the year.

Another churchyard which demonstrated in every aspect clear concern for its wildlife was St Michael and All Angels at Bugbrooke in Northamptonshire. Hung on one of the great trees near the main path is a small plaque on which is written a quatrain from 'God's Acre' by Longfellow:

I like that ancient Saxon phrase which calls
The burial ground God's Acre! It is just;
It consecrates each grave within its walls
And breathes a benison o'er the sleeping dust.

159

There are fine, mature lime trees, rooks in the tall beeches, cuckoos calling, lesser celandines and a large patch of lungwort, violets, bluebells, and even one or two delightful, orchid-like double lady's smocks. Near a shrub-lined boundary, I found primroses and wood anemones. A little river skirts the other side. I was told that a small area is to be set aside as a nature reserve

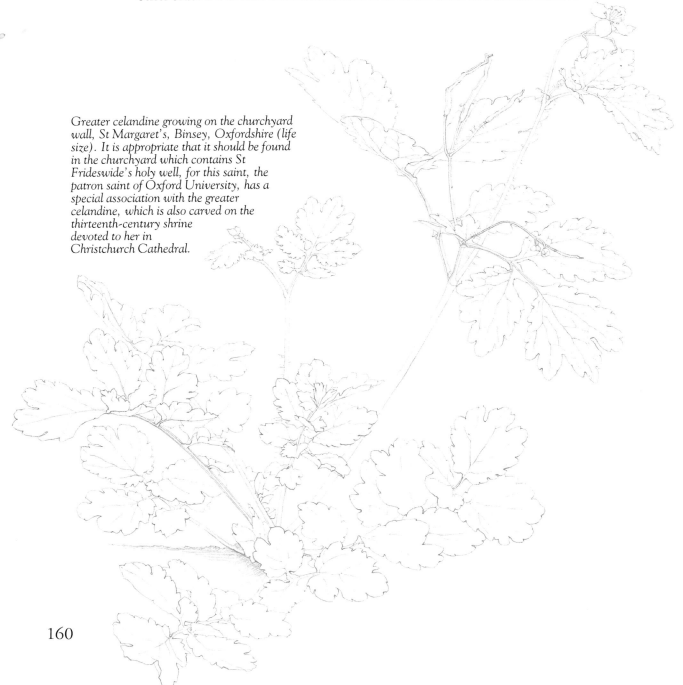

Greater celandine growing on the churchyard wall, St Margaret's, Binsey, Oxfordshire (life size). It is appropriate that it should be found in the churchyard which contains St Frideswide's holy well, for this saint, the patron saint of Oxford University, has a special association with the greater celandine, which is also carved on the thirteenth-century shrine devoted to her in Christchurch Cathedral.

160

when the churchyard is extended, but in fact, the churchyard as a whole is an excellent nature reserve, though a small wild tangle of taller grass would be welcome. In the belfry one reads the melancholy old couplet, 'I to the church the living call, and to the grave do summon all', a prospect mollified by the nature of this churchyard, and made to seem a not altogether undesirable proposition.

I had been alerted by the Women's Institute churchyard survey to expect something out of the ordinary at both Littleham and Bugbrooke, but my expectations for the churchyard at Bibury in Gloucestershire were extremely depressed. I had been very much put off by Alec Clifton-Taylor's description: 'perhaps the most enchanting churchyard in England . . . There is a wide expanse of faultlessly mown lawn and a few standard roses which look exactly right . . . the efforts of a good gardener have doubled our pleasure.' It sounded like a wildlife desert.

However, when I went there, I found it not as artificial as I had feared. There are mop-topped rose trees, but the putti on the beautiful limestone tombs smile down over orange-gold lichens. The lawns are very extensive, but growing on the walls of church and churchyard are many vivid patches of hartstongue fern, and in their immediate shelter, bushy green alkanet, deep blue germander speedwell and towering pillars of dark mullein. Nearby, under the trees grow feverfew and herb Bennet, the blessed plant (also known as wood avens), woody nightshade and lady's mantle, foxgloves, herb Robert and burdock—all in a not very large and rather too well-kept churchyard. Even the Alice-in-Wonderland roses were not quite as they seemed. Some of the regimented line had died and the ones planted to take their places had been muddled, so that the red-white alternation had gone awry. (However, there were no distraught footmen attempting to paint the white roses red.)

Greater celandine leaves are a soft grey-green.

A shrivelled seed pod.

Flowers are like tiny poppies.

161

The man who does the gardening in this churchyard and has done so for eight years, told me he had never given much thought to the churchyard as a place of wildlife—but that, nevertheless, he disliked weed-killers and simply cut the grass around graves. He volunteered, too, that he always mowed around wild flowers. It pleased him to hear the song of the birds and he had seen kingfishers flying over the churchyard. An ardent botanist, birdwatcher or entomologist would no doubt be dissatisfied, but in the context of the Cotswolds, where every house and tidy garden is a picturesque showpiece, this churchyard was managed, I thought, in a remarkably humane way.

When people say that they mow around wild flowers, they usually mean the well-loved flowers of meadow, wayside and woodland such as cowslips, primroses, foxgloves, ramsons or bluebells. People take a natural delight in these plants; one finds small islands of bloom in even the tidiest of town churchyards. Though cutting back after flowering may be hasty, not allowing the plants time to make seed, it is extremely unusual for anyone to mow such flowers in bloom. In only one of all my churchyard explorations have I seen it, and I feel sure that the soggy disagreeable mess of grass and mashed daffodil must have given rise to enough adverse comment in the parish for it not to occur again. However, protection does not usually extend to inconspicuous, less well-known wild flowers. An unusual hawkweed, for instance, which might be of considerable botanical interest, would very likely be seen simply as a dandelion-like weed.

A difficulty which faces churchyard conservation at present is that often neither the incumbent nor anyone in the parochial church council is aware of what they have in their churchyard, nor what methods of management are open to them. Even when botanists have made a full survey of the churchyard, the local people may be entirely unaware, not only of the results, but that it has been done at all. When they are given such information, the response is characteristically one of interest and concern. In a churchyard in Morden, Surrey, gravestone clearance was halted and some of the best stones were saved after a lichenologist contacted the vicar and pointed out how rich in species some of the memorials were. Members of one Durham church changed their attitude towards bats on learning something about them from a local Bat Group representative and finding they were giving harbour to a whiskered bat, rare so far north.

Honeysuckle berries in a Suffolk churchyard at the end of July. (Life size).

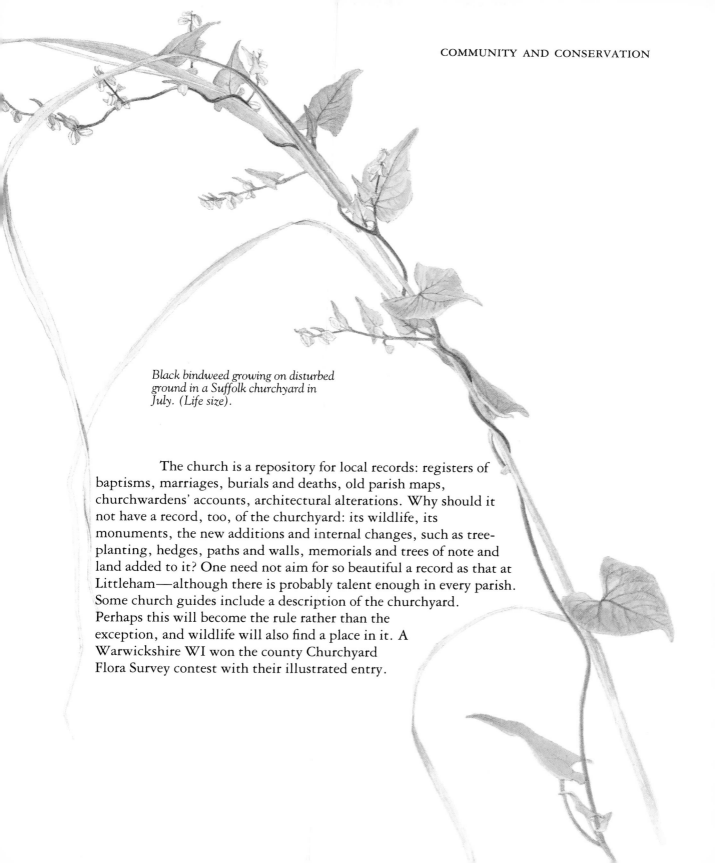

*Black bindweed growing on disturbed
ground in a Suffolk churchyard in
July. (Life size).*

The church is a repository for local records: registers of
baptisms, marriages, burials and deaths, old parish maps,
churchwardens' accounts, architectural alterations. Why should it
not have a record, too, of the churchyard: its wildlife, its
monuments, the new additions and internal changes, such as tree-
planting, hedges, paths and walls, memorials and trees of note and
land added to it? One need not aim for so beautiful a record as that at
Littleham—although there is probably talent enough in every parish.
Some church guides include a description of the churchyard.
Perhaps this will become the rule rather than the
exception, and wildlife will also find a place in it. A
Warwickshire WI won the county Churchyard
Flora Survey contest with their illustrated entry.

Identifying the particular composition of wildlife in any one churchyard helps in its way to ensure that it is cared for and that the individual nature of that churchyard is preserved. Each has its own particular character and it would be so much better to have maintenance which is sensitive to this, and to the needs and resources of the parish, than the present trend towards bland, close-shaved mediocrity and uniformity.

While the parishioners quite reasonably expect a trim, well-kept churchyard, there are only a very few, if any, who are actually able to help with the practical maintenance. It is not surprising that the parochial church councils—who are locally responsible for churchyard upkeep—are influenced by horticultural marketing, which plays heavily on labour-saving claims, and they turn gratefully to rotary mowers, strimmers and chemical weed-killers in an effort to fulfil their task. They, and those who actually carry out the work, sincerely believe that in making the churchyard garden-like they are doing their best for it. It is readily assumed, as a parish magazine from mid-Wales put it, that a 'churchyard which has flowerbeds and a closely clipped lawn with tidy gravestones' is an indication of a healthy and vital parish life. In this context, it is not cleanliness that is regarded as next to godliness, but tidiness. Anything which seems remotely scruffy is removed; gravestones are scraped bare of their lichens and weed-killers assiduously applied around their bases, ivy is ripped from walls, and every week during the growing season, the whine of grass-cutting machinery fills the air. The result of all this activity resembles the aristocratic churchyard described by Thomas Hardy in *A Pair of Blue Eyes*:

Here the grass was carefully tended, and formed virtually a part of the manor-house lawn; flowers and shrubs being planted indiscriminately over both, whilst the few graves visible were mathematically exact in shape and smoothness, appearing in the day-time like chins newly shaven. There was no wall, the division between God's Acre and Lord Luxellian's being marked only by a few square stones . . .

Ironically, churchyards maintained to these standards are still labour-intensive when compared with more traditional ones. However, in the nineteenth century only someone of Lord Luxellian's wealth could afford the

Common toad under tree roots in the redundant churchyard, Corpusty, Norfolk, in May.

One of several wood mice seen running about in the long grass and herb Bennet leaves, over graves in St Nicholas's churchyard, Asthall, Oxfordshire.

exercise, whereas the existence of modern horticultural equipment has brought it within the aspirations of any parish which is able to raise the capital outlay. The question is, of course, whether such highly gardened churchyards are desirable. The idea that the churchyard is a reflection on the community can perhaps be used as an argument against this kind of churchyard and in support of conservation. The seminar organized by The Prince of Wales' Committee in 1982 on the subject of churchyards and chapelyards in Wales concluded that projects which resulted in the destruction of wildlife habitats and the removal or breaking up of gravestones created a churchyard which was 'as much an adverse comment as one overgrown with scrub'.

For the parish itself, the benefits of a shaved and shorn churchyard are dubious—in terms of the practicalities, let alone the aesthetics. Those who diligently try to keep an acre or more as fastidiously tidy as their own gardens create an enormous amount of work for themselves, and for their successors, if such can be found. Gardens demand continuous care and if this is interrupted by reason of illness, death or people moving away, the lawn will not regain its former wild flowers, but will become overgrown with invasive and unsightly species such as nettles, dock and ground elder. I met a churchwarden almost in despair over a churchyard frontage which had grown rank in less than three months, while the churchyard mower had been away for repairs. The rear of the churchyard which was given less frequent attention was pleasant with the sound of bees and grasshoppers. Several different grasses were in flower and in among them the yellows of meadow vetchling, bird's-foot trefoil, and buttercups gleamed brightly; hogweed, the tallest of all the coarse-meadow flowers, grew in sturdy clumps, its off-white saucers soaking in the afternoon sun.

In many of the WI surveys there was a sense of ambivalence towards manicured churchyards, caught in the phrase of an East Sussex member who wrote that her parish churchyard was too well-kept for wild flowers to grow. There was certainly an awareness of the relationship between the kind of management practised and wildlife. A survey from Devon noted bleakly that since the acquisition of a new strimmer and brush-cutter, there had been no voles, frogs, or toads, grass snakes or lizards seen in the churchyard. Slow-worms are another creature very vulnerable to the speed and violence of strimmers and rotary mowers. An additional disadvantage of these machines is that they do not collect the mowings; left to rot, these look untidy and return to the soil nutrients which begin to change the meadow balance of the land in the same way that applying fertilizer does, encouraging a few species at the expense of diversity.

However, the impression given by the surveys was by no means entirely dismal. In some places, an awareness of wildlife had led to practical conservation measures being taken. Several churchyards deliberately set aside an area of long grass to provide a habitat for butterflies and grasshoppers. Many surveys mentioned the butterflies which frequent the churchyard: the yellow brimstone, the subtler tones of the meadow, wall and hedge browns, the colourful small tortoiseshell and peacock, the dramatic comma and the dainty blues. It seemed, however, that although they were very much welcomed, the butterflies' needs in terms of food plants and egg-laying sites were hardly appreciated at all. There were exceptions, such as West Runton churchyard in Norfolk, where sorrel plants are retained as food

Bumble bee on birdsfoot trefoil (above), and small pearl-bordered fritillary (right).

Birdsfoot trefoil visited by bumble bees at All Saints, Monk Sherborne, Hampshire, in early July. (Life size).

for the small copper butterfly. As the churchyard survey of butterflies, underway in Norfolk and Lincolnshire, progresses, the situation should improve.

Birds are given special consideration in some churchyards. In Bugbrooke and many other places, there are nestboxes on the trees. Several surveys mentioned the pride in having a resident owl, especially if it was a barn owl. This is the only bird whose presence is tolerated inside the church; the vicar of St Trinity's, Crockham Hill in Kent claimed he could hear their owl snoring through his sermons. Swifts, swallows and house martins are usually welcome on the outer fabric of the church, and at Caister-on-Sea in Norfolk, where the swallows nest in the porch, the church cleaners solved the problem of their droppings with an improvised dirt tray of newspaper weighted down with sand, which is regularly replaced.

Bats are less popular than birds, though interest in them is increasing. Those who are responsible for cleaning the church tend to dislike roosting colonies because both brass and wood are stained by their urine. Placing drapes in vulnerable spots keeps the problem at bay, but I wish every success to the church helper who is experimenting in the hope of finding a protective polish which will solve the problem.

The greatest threat to the traditional churchyard is not a new one. Thomas Hardy wrote 'The Levelled Churchyard' in 1882:

O Passenger, pray list and catch
    Our sighs and piteous groans,
Half stifled in this jumbled patch
    Of wrenched memorial stones!

We late-lamented, resting here,
    Are mixed to human jam,
And each to each exclaims in fear,
    "I know not which I am!"

The wicked people have annexed
    The verses on the good;
A roaring drunkard sports the text
    Teetotal Tommy should!

Where we are huddled none can trace,
    And if our names remain,
They pave some path or porch or place
    Where we have never lain!

Here's not a modest maiden elf
    But dreads the final Trumpet,
Lest half of her should rise herself,
    And half some sturdy strumpet!

From restorations of Thy fane,
    From smoothings of Thy sward,
From zealous Churchmen's pick and plane
    Deliver us O Lord! Amen!

[fane = temple]

The business of totally clearing the churchyard—of gravestones, kerbs, even the grave mounds, has accelerated with the increased investment in modern mowing machinery. One thing these mowing machines cannot do is to cut close to graves with headstones or kerbs. Some mowers of churchyards simply steer around the graves, leaving tufts of long grass, ferns and wild flowers to be dealt with, or not, as those who tend the graves see fit. From a practical point of view (and a naturalist's) this seems a comfortable compromise, but in many churchyards an even flat turf is desired throughout, and nothing less will do. When the headstones go, so does the shelter they provide. When the ground is flattened, the small micro-habitat of the grave mound becomes a uniform part of the lawn.

The headstones themselves are generally dragged away to be stacked in a pile, or leant against the church wall. Sometimes they are used for paving, which quickly wears away the inscriptions, making investigation very difficult for local historians. Headstones are an important aid to the historian in the traditional churchyard, especially in Wales, where parish records were not generally kept until 1812. One of the few ways the historian can guess at the social relationships and the status of families and individuals in past centuries is to examine the juxtapositions of the grave memorials in the church and chapel yards. Some parishes re-site their headstones in neat lines elsewhere in the churchyard, but this is only slightly preferable to the other alternatives, since the original relationships between graves are lost—as may be the lichen growth of centuries.

A conservation conflict—ivy can shade lichens out of existence and hide epitaphs, but it provides a recess for snails and other creatures. These gravestones are in St Clement's churchyard, Oxford.

169

In any consideration of the management of what may be a very large acreage of grass in a churchyard, it would obviously be absurd to preach against any and all use of motor mowers. While the symbolic figure of Death with his long scythe may habitually walk the poetic churchyard, helpful volunteers who have the skill of this implement and are prepared to put it to use in cutting the churchyard sward are few and far between. Motor mowers are easy to use and when brought into action at sensible intervals help to keep churchyards both trim, and healthy for wildlife.

The scythe is used when the grass is high in late June or July, and the cut can be gathered in for hay. I was notified of only one churchyard, at All Saints, Smallbridge, Devon, where a scythe was still regularly used to cut a part of it, but in several others the churchyard grass was cut for hay. I visited Dulas in Herefordshire, where the churchyard of St Michael contains a rich combination of ancient meadow plants—delicious hay for some lucky beasts. At Grundisburgh in Suffolk, an additional piece of land acquired for the churchyard as burial ground (but not yet used) was also cut for hay. At Morton-cum-Grafton in North Yorkshire, hay-making took place within living memory, and at Wingrave in Buckinghamshire, hay from the churchyard used to be used in the rush-strewing ceremony. Haymaking seems to be well into decline in the present day, but perhaps with renewed interest in old forms of management a change in direction may occur. Certainly, there are few more satisfying sights than watching the tall grasses in an ancient meadow fall silently to the rhythmic beat of the scythe.

Meadow cranesbill at Asthall
churchyard, Oxfordshire, in late July
(life size). The fruits explode,
dispersing the seeds well away from the
parent plant.

The other well-established method of dealing with grass and awkward undergrowth in a churchyard is to graze it, and this is a method which seems to be gaining popularity. In my travels, I have seen goats and small groups of sheep, and heard of other grazing animals: donkeys in Yorkshire, a heifer belonging to the vicar of a Norfolk church, ponies in the New Forest, even mallards, and churchyard geese. There is also a host of unauthorized grazers, principally rabbits, but also hares and deer.

Churchyard grazing is an ancient practice. For centuries, there have been factions to support it while others fought against it. Traditionally, parishioners have the right to burial in the churchyard, but the incumbent has the grazing rights or herbage. He could also, if he so wished, let out his grazing rights to others and now, as in the past, this seems acceptable unless the right is seriously abused. Archdeacon Hale's *Precedents and Proceedings illustrative of the Discipline of the Church of England* cites two extreme examples which came before the ecclesiastical courts of the sixteenth century. The first was a complaint from the parishioners of a certain Ardeby, who accused the parson and the vicar of letting the churchyard 'to them that usethe it wythe vile bestes', (probably pigs, which are unwelcome because they rootle as well as graze). A case was brought a few years later, against the rector of Langdon Hull, who was summoned to explain to the court why he had allowed sheep to be folded inside the church. He successfully defended himself by proving that this had been the only means of saving the animals when a heavy and unexpected fall of snow had endangered their lives, and that they had in any case been there for only 'two workinge dayes'. There are mildly approving recommendations for judicious grazing in several church handbooks dating from the nineteenth century to the present day.

Billy goats resting and browsing holly in St Martin's churchyard, Litchborough, Northamptonshire; by ancient tradition, the rector has the right to keep four goats or six sheep in this churchyard.

In order to protect graves from being trampled and soiled by grazing animals, it is thought that parishioners once pegged out new graves with brambles or willows. George Crabbe describes 'humble graves, with wickers bound' in his poem 'Sir Eustace Grey' and the practice receives fuller elaboration in the quatrain from John Gay's 'Dirge':

With wicker rods we fenc'd her Tomb around,
To ward from Man and Beast the hallow's ground:
Lest her new Grave the Parson's Cattle raze,
For both his Horse and Cow the church Yard graze.

There is a clause in the will of a parishioner at Braughing in Hertfordshire, in 1696, which enjoined that his grave be annually 'brambled'. Another famous example is the pre-Raphaelite painting by Arthur Hughes, *Home from the Sea*, which shows sheep in the churchyard, and the young boy's prostrate form echoed in the shape of a simple construction of withies over the grave behind him. It has always struck me that the frail constructions in this picture would be no match for a sheep; Thomas Hardy's 'tight mounds bounded by sticks, which shout imprisonment' has a truer ring. The wealthy would purchase from a huge choice of cast iron surrounds, custom-made for the grave plot, which made a more effective barrier.

Sheep may safely graze nowadays in many churchyards, even the famous Ingworth and Blickling pedigree flock of black mountain sheep, prized for their fine dense wool, and whose fame reaches far beyond their Norfolk home. Grazing is widespread but, I believe, accepted as the principal means of grass control only in parts of Wales. It seems to have been more common in the past, when churchyard sheep were sometimes

Sheep grazing in the shade of a yew tree in a fenced-off area of St Mary's churchyard, Speen, Berkshire, on a bright August day.

owned by the incumbent or jointly by the parish. At Hannington in
Hampshire, sheep were penned in the churchyard before they were sheared,
and in the porch of Holy Trinity church at Balsham in Cambridgeshire,
there are holes for hurdles which excluded sheep from the church.
Nowadays, sheep are allowed to range unconfined in some churchyards,
though this mainly occurs where there are no recent graves. In churchyards
where burials still take place, the modern methods of limiting the animals
are to erect a large-mesh wire fence pinned to posts or electric fencing.

Even a traditional method of grass control, such as sheep-
grazing, should be permitted with a certain amount of caution. Sheep have
been called 'mowers on four legs' and the comparison is apt. The
overgrazing which occurs when there are too many sheep for the area, or

when they are grazed continuously, is as damaging as excessive mowing. Dividing a large churchyard into plots and moving the sheep around from one to another through the spring and summer may be an answer. Another solution is to let them graze only at controlled intervals, giving the plants a chance to flower and seed themselves.

It is unfortunate that, while it is reasonably simple to keep a traditional churchyard in good order, once the original ground flora has been reduced, it takes a degree of commitment and hard work to restore it to a reasonably healthy condition. Some of the plants will not be seen there again, unless they are brought in and planted. Some botanists strongly object to replenishing the churchyard with plants, but where there is a sensible plan and adequate care with the choice of species and the planting, it can achieve remarkable results.

A major difficulty in advancing the idea of churchyard conservation has been the struggle against an element of popular opinion. For the 'Best Kept Churchyard' competitions of the nineteen-seventies and early nineteen-eighties, interpret simply 'tidiest churchyard'. Even in 1984 the village of Scothern in Lincolnshire which, having entered for the 'Best Kept Village' competition, was marked down by the judges for 'an untidy corner in their churchyard'. The corner in question was an area which had deliberately been left untouched as a conservation area to encourage butterflies and birds. However, following contact made by the local officer of the British Butterfly Conservation Society with The Council for the Preservation of Rural England, there may be recommendations about conservation initiatives. Although the Best Kept Village competition is held under the auspices of the Council for the Protection of Rural England, each county has its own separate organization and the criteria are not standardized. In some counties conservation is already a consideration. The village of Staplefield, which has twice won the Sussex title, was awarded points for the care it took of its churchyard orchids.

On a national level the care of churchyards has been a matter of concern to the Church in Wales, which is the only body at present seeking to exercise control over the graveyards for which it has responsibility (this leaves aside those managed by chapels and local authorites). The 1982 seminar of the Prince of Wales' Committee (a registered charity concerned

Carved stone butterfly and snail (above and below) on a tomb in St Brynach's churchyard, Nevern, Dyfed, together with a real common garden snail (right).

with the Welsh environment) was held specifically 'to discuss the increasing number of ill-advised projects taking place in burial places, particularly in churchyards and chapelyards throughout Wales'. Regarding the removal of gravestones it recognizes that 'churchyards are important for archaeological, aesthetic and ecological reasons, and their character should be retained for future generations'. The main findings and conclusions of the seminar are summarized well in a five-page leaflet published in 1984 and which gives ideas and guidelines for the upkeep of graveyards.

By far the most enterprising practical churchyard scheme is that initiated by the Northamptonshire Naturalists' Trust in collaboration with the county's Rural Community Council. They offer advice to any parochial church council in their region on how to manage a churchyard with respect for wildlife. They also run a churchyard competition and measure the entrants, not in terms of tidiness (though neatness is a consideration), but in terms of conservation and richness of wildlife. The judges' comments also include suggestions for improvement. When I visited the first winners of this competition (begun in 1983) at Woodford on the hillside above the River Nene, it was clear that many of the suggestions had been taken to

heart. As suggested, the grass mowings had been raked up, grass paths through the churchyard were close-mown and clearly defined, and the policy of maintaining medium length and, in unobtrusive corners, long grass had been continued. It is a most attractive churchyard, neat, but full of tremendously healthy and varied wild flowers, grave plantings, introduced and native trees. Birdsong seemed to come from almost every tree and the warm, delicious, resiny scent of the balsam poplar planted by the entrance lingered in the air.

Litchborough churchyard, which earned the Northamptonshire prize in the year this book was written, was exceptional, even to its walls. On them grows common polypody, herb Robert, germander speedwell, ivy-leaved toadflax and several other plants, the most interesting of which is navelwort, a rare occurrence so far east. A devil which is half goat is a common characterization of Old Nick, but nothing could have been further from this than the serene and handsome white goats tethered firmly to gravestones in this churchyard. They peer gently around to observe anyone entering the churchyard and then return to the business of consuming all the vegetation within reach. A map in the church porch shows how the churchyard has been divided into eight sections which are managed on a rotational basis. The area grazed by goats this year will be allowed in the next to grow to high grass for hay. The grass on either side of the path to the church is always kept close-mown and a far corner is left mostly untouched for the benefit of butterflies and grasshoppers. There are high hedges and plenty of well-grown trees and shrubs. The plants in this churchyard are a particular pleasure to the eye, in form as well as colour. Not having been continually chopped back, they have developed their own shapes. There are roses which really ramble, towering foxgloves and a good bushy patch of comfrey. An ex-grave plant, the willow-leaved bellflower, with flowers of deepest blue, was managing to flower bravely in the turf. On and around the church walls alone, there are twenty species of flowering plants and ferns: plants as varied as mullein and the small, dense cushions of pearlwort, made up of bright green thread-like stems and tiny leaves (which offered a chance for keen botanists to compare two species—annual and procumbent pearlwort). The ivy makes patterns along the wall behind spiny-leaved teasel and the delicate foliage of columbine, and chickweed sprawls bright green on the ground.

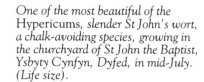

One of the most beautiful of the Hypericums, *slender St John's wort, a chalk-avoiding species, growing in the churchyard of St John the Baptist, Ysbyty Cynfyn, Dyfed, in mid-July. (Life size).*

There are plants of the woodland, meadow, hedgerow, lawn and of rock and garden habitats, all looked after with evident care and understanding. Non-flowering plants such as liverworts, mosses and lichens also made a good showing, and a dead stump, covered in ivy, had been left to provide a habitat for saphrophytes.

The moving spirit behind this remarkable churchyard is a rare individual who combines a sense of what is appropriate for a churchyard with a strong appreciation of natural history. The result is almost ideal: a churchyard in the centre of the village which is as attractive to people as it is to wildlife. When I arrived at Litchborough in the hard glare of the summer's afternoon, the lightly shaded entrance to the churchyard beckoned an invitation I could never have resisted. In *Nature in Downland* over eighty years ago, W.H. Hudson wrote of how 'often during a long walk over the downs in hot weather' he thought of the church and churchyard 'as of a shaded fountain in a parched desert'. So they still seem to many of us.

Common toadflax (life size), a familiar of churchyards and hedgerows, at Cley next the Sea, Norfolk, in late August.

APPENDIX I

EVERY CHURCHYARD HAS ITS OWN individual character and interest—it usually takes several visits to appreciate fully what each holds. These two surveys, from mid-Wales and Derbyshire, illustrate the kind of picture which emerges from close observation and research in the churchyards concerned.

EGLWYS NEWYDD (HAFOD) CHURCHYARD, DYFED
Arthur Chater

Arthur Chater works in the Botany Department of the British Museum (Natural History). He is also Recorder for the botanical vice-county of Cardiganshire and has for many years had a keen interest in churchyards and their conservation. He has published both on the natural history of churchyards and on the subject of gravestones.

EGLWYS NEWYDD IS NOT BY ANY means the richest in species of the hundred churchyards in the Ceredigion district of Dyfed, or the most varied in habitat—nor are the rarest plants contained within it, but it perfectly represents the balance between nature and human activity that makes a good churchyard such a delight. It is still as George Eyre Evans, a local historian, described it in 1903 'a veritable "God's Acre",—calm, restful, picturesque, and well-kept'.

The second highest churchyard in Ceredigion, it is situated on a steep south-east facing slope in the Ystwyth valley. The first church on the site was built in 1620 to serve both the local lead mining community and the Herbert family at the mansion of Hafod Ychtryd in the valley. Thomas Johnes, a later owner of Hafod, had the church rebuilt in 1803. The Forestry Commission now owns much of the Hafod estate and their conifer plantations now enclose the churchyard on three sides.

Many of the plants and animals found in this churchyard are tokens of its earlier history. Two large pedunculate oaks flanking the path to the church, together with three others

beyond the church, must have been among the five million trees, half of them oaks, that Thomas Johnnes planted on his estate about 1800. Few are now left standing. One oak has been so severely lopped that it is little more than a bristly trunk—but a haven for birds and innumerable insects. Winter moths swarm on its trunk and twigs on frosty December nights. Around the church are six yews, the three largest measuring about 410cm in girth. Yews of this size are usually well over 300 years old and one can assume these were planted when the church was founded. Two of them are fused together at the base, giving the appearance of a great forked trunk.

The grassland is varied and surprisingly undisturbed, although there are graves all over the churchyard. Above the entrance path it is heathy, with ling, blaeberry and heath bedstraw among the fescue and sweet vernal grass—and there are no fewer than five different ferns. The clumps of lady and male fern which unfurl their new fronds so quickly after having been cut, are one of the chief delights. The slope below the path is damper and the vegetation consists of tall herbs such as meadow sweet, sorrel and pignut, a relic of the unimproved meadows that are now so hard to find in this neighbourhood. Shaded by yews and the crowded conifers which surround the churchyard, the level damp turf to the south-west of the chancel contains the plants of a damp woodland clearing: lady's smock, wood sorrel, marsh thistle and yellow pimpernel. (Is this a relic of a plant community dating from before the development of the churchyard?) Further south-west there is rich heath flora, harebell, wavy hair-grass, tuberous bitter vetch, heath bedstraw and wood sage—similar to that on the few remaining rocky ungrazed slopes elsewhere in this valley.

Many of the graves are covered with sandy gravel from the nearby lead mines, so toxic that only certain kinds of plant can survive. A resistant form of bent grass grows on some and one of them used to have a resistant form of sea campion which developed on the polluted spoil heaps of the mines from plants which spread up the rivers from the coast to these beach-like habitats, and was brought into the churchyard with the gravel. Other graves have on them comparatively unpolluted river gravel, and these are carpeted with the upright whitish lichen *Cladonia furcata*. Hedge bedstraw grows in the turf of one grave—a lime-loving plant, inexplicably frequent in the predominantly acid churchyards in Ceredigion, and very rare outside them. The naturalized flora includes Welsh poppy, snowdrops, creeping jenny, fox-and-cubs and wild daffodils.

The old dry stone walls are densely covered with mosses and lichens. Tussocks of wood meadow grass, smooth meadow grass and polypody fern grow from the vertically set coping stones. On the walls and elsewhere in the churchyard is a conspicuous yellow hawkweed *Hieracium grandidens*, a rare introduced species known only in Ceredigion from this churchyard and nearby walls.

Most of the headstones are made from local grit-stone or shale or North Wales slate, and there are others of Forest of Dean stone and sandstone. All are well populated with lichens, except for memorials of granite whose polished surfaces are devoid of any life. Marble can look out of keeping amongst vernacular stone, but being limestone, it can have biological compensations. One particular marble headstone is pleasantly disguised by a film of greenish algae which I observed one night being grazed by a total of 19 brown-lipped snails *Cepaea nemoralis* (which in this churchyard are pure yellow, lacking the usual brown or black bands), two tree slugs *Limax marginatus* and no fewer than 84 specimens of a species of woodlouse *Philoscia muscorum*. Two of another species *Oniscus asellus* were feeding on the bird droppings on top of the stone, and at its base were 24 individuals of the tiny chrysalis snail *Lauria cylindracea* which are abundant in this churchyard. The common garden snail *Helix aspersa* is also present. The best way to observe such creatures is to go out on a damp, mild night with a torch and to shine it on the headstones.

The larger animals of the churchyard are more difficult to spot, but at night, I have seen a polecat crossing a path, a palmate newt on the rim of a yellow brick grave enclosure, a frog, a hedgehog and voles. The birds treat this graveyard as if it were a clearing in the forest. There are goldcrests in the yews, nuthatches on the oaks and buzzards and ravens overhead.

A high-walled memorial enclosure to Thomas Johnes and his family is filled to overflowing by a great rhododendron which in early June is an incandescent mass of crimson flowers. Across the path is the grave of the last squire of Hafod, T. J. Waddingham (died 1938), who left to the church the acre of land to the north-east, which was officially incorporated into the churchyard in 1978. Laboriously cleared of its oak woodland and subsequent growth of scrub, this part was sprayed with *asulam* to clear the bracken. This killed the bracken and appeared to do little harm to the rest of the vegetation, and revealed a vast population of bluebells, a relic from the old woodland, and a glorious sight in late May (everything is later than usual at this altitude). Scrub has again formed on the slope above the bluebells: hazel, birch, a thicket of brambles and wild raspberries, sycamore saplings and even a sweet chestnut. Bracken is re-invading from both above and below but is not yet a serious problem.

Eglwys Newydd churchyard has benefitted from a job creation scheme. Paths were improved, leaning gravestones straightened and the place brought up to scratch without harm to its natural vegetation, but such schemes usually happen only once, and the regular maintenance often stretches the resources of the parish to the utmost. In some years the grass has been cut once only, but in 1983 five sheep were given the run of the churchyard with very satisfactory results. Constant grazing, though, would of course make the churchyard as dull and poor in species as the nearby sheepwalks above the forest. As it is there are about 120 species of flowering plants and ferns in this churchyard, and thanks to the way it has been tended it is one of the most beautiful and interesting sites in the valley.

ST OSWALD'S PARISH CHURCH, ASHBOURNE, DERBYSHIRE
K. M. Hollick

Miss Kathleen Hollick has lived for many years in an old house next to the churchyard in the market town of Ashbourne in Derbyshire. Her late father established plants in it, and she has given advice on its management, especially with regard to grass-cutting. At present, West Derbyshire Council is responsible for the maintenance, and carries it out very satisfactorily—waiting until plants such as daffodils die back before cutting, for instance. Miss Hollick is Recorder for the botanical vice-county of Derbyshire.

THE AVENUE OF LIMES was planted early 19th century and pleached. Mostly common lime, a few small-leaved and there were some large-leaved. The row on the north side of the vicar's walk is being felled by the local council—being roadside and about at the end of their lives.

The church has a 'weeping' chancel, that is crooked. The daffodils were planted by the late Dr H.H. Hollick over the period 1910–40. He also in the 1930s planted the bluebells—including many Spanish bluebell (*Endymion hispanicus*) in blue, pink and white (and hydrids with common bluebell *Endymion non-scriptus* are present in plenty). The snowdrops he planted also at this time, have all done well. The most numerous daffodil is the cultivar 'Emperor'; and 'Cervantes'. 'Victoria' and an old bi-colour are also present. ('White Lady', 'Lucifer', 'Conspicuous' and 'Tresserve' are also present.) *Narcissus poeticus ornatus*, a cultivar of poet's narcissus and *ornatus recurvus* ('Old Pheasant's eye') grow to the north of the church, a few *N. asturiensis* (a very small species) occur east of the chancel by the path, and there are wild daffodils (*N. pseudo-narcissus*) in the south section.

Some blue anemones (*Anemone appenina*) were planted by the late Mr Peveril Turnbull early this century, and did well for many years, though they are declining now. Dr Hollick planted dog daisies in the 1940s and these have thrived and multiplied to make a splendid sight, especially in the east section where bulbous buttercup and meadow clover are also excellent. There is often an odd clump of harebells growing in the church walls on the south side and they are also to be found in the close-mown grass south of the chancel.

Some years ago there was a good colony of quaking grass north-west of Spalden's almhouses—gone now unfortunately. When the great Cambridge botanist John Ray visited Ashbourne in 1670, he recorded hairy rock-cress (*Arabis hirsuta*) on the church walls—none observed in living memory.

Other good meadow flowers include hogweed, pignut, goat's beard, greater burnet saxifrage. There was much sweet violet in the shade of the cedar of Lebanon before it lost nearly all of its branches in the heavy snows of 1940—now all gone—though the remains of the cedar are still there: planted c.1840. Some nice wood anemone to the north of the nave. Mosses present include *Thuidium tamariscinum*, *Tortula muralis* and *Brachythecium rutabulum*.

APPENDIX II

A SELECTION OF PLANTS WITH RELIGIOUS NAMES AND ASSOCIATIONS.

Abraham, Isaac and Jacob	Comfrey and lungwort are both given this name because they have flowers of different colours (ranging from pink to blue) on the same plant.
Adam and Eve	Lungwort (as above Abraham, Isaac and Jacob) and also early purple orchid, spotted orchid, lords and ladies (possibly because of double tubers but more likely because of different flower colours either on the same plant or within a colony).
Angel's eyes	Germander speedwell, because the flowers are as blue as the sky.
Apostles	Star of Bethlehem.
Archangel	Yellow archangel and, less commonly, red deadnettle.
Bats-in-the-belfry	Nettle-leaved bellflower, possibly because of the way the flowers are clustered on the branches up the stem.
Blessed thistle	Milk thistle, more commonly (Our) Lady's thistle (see below).
Cain and Abel	Early purple orchid and marsh orchids (see Adam and Eve). Pluralized—columbines.
Candlemas bells	Snowdrops because of their time of flowering in February. (Candlemas is 2nd February.)
Candlemas caps	Wood anemone, for the same reason as above.
Christians	Bullace, the wild plum tree, used to describe the fruits.
Christmas tree, Christmas, Christ's thorn	Holly, always regarded as a powerful plant and adopted into Christianity from pagan origins.
Christ's ladder	Common centaury.
Church broom	Teasel, because the shape of the flowerhead resembled the broom used to sweep high places.
Church steeples	Agrimony, because of the form of the flower spike.
Churchwort	Pennyroyal, possibly strewn in churches where its sweet scent and flea repellant properties would be appreciated.
Easter bell, Easter flower	Greater stitchwort, because of the time of flowering.
Easter Ledger, Easter ledges, Easter mangiant, Easter mentgions, Easter hedges	Bistort, used in Easter ledger pudding, apparently still eaten in the Lake District, said to aid conception. It begins to bloom in June, later than Easter, so Geoffrey Grigson (in *The Englishman's Flora*) is probably right in believing Easter ledger to be a corruption of *Aristolochia*, birthwort, which also aided conception and delivery.

183

Easter lily, Easter rose	Daffodil, because of the time of flowering. Primrose is also called Easter rose in Somerset.
Eve's cushion	Mossy saxifrage.
Eve's tears	Snowdrop.
God Almighty's bread and cheese	Wood sorrel, from the edible leaves.
God Almighty's flowers, God Almighty's thumb and finger	Bird's-foot trefoil from the trefoil leaf and the finger-like pod.
God's eye	Germander speedwell (see angel's eyes above).
God's finger and thumbs	Fumitory, perhaps from the elongated shape of the flowers.
God's grace	Field wood-rush.
God's meat	Hawthorn, from the young edible leaves.
God's stinking tree	Elder was supposed to have been used for the cross.
Gratia dei, Grace of God	Meadow cranesbill.
Good Friday flower	Townhall clock (moschatel), from the time of flowering.
Good Friday plant	Lungwort, a plant with many religious associations, in flower at this time.
Herb Bennet	In French *herbe de Saint-Benoît*, also 'the blessed herb' in Somerset. The root has a sweet, spicy scent and this fragrance was supposed to repel evil.
Herb Robert	*Herba Sancti Ruperti* or *Herba Roberti* in mediaeval Latin, a plant dedicated to St Robert (St Robert of Salzburg?) but also associated with the magic of Robin Goodfellow.
Holy grass	*Hierochloë odorata*, a rare aromatic grass.
Holy herb	Vervain, believed to be very powerful against devils and demons of disease.
Holy innocents	Hawthorn.
Holy water sprinkle	Horsetails, from the old holy water brush which resembled these plants.
Keys of heaven	Cowslip—from the resemblance of the flowers to old-fashioned keys.
Ladder to heaven	Solomon's seal (see page 73).
Lady Mary's tears, Virgin Mary's milkdrops	Lungwort, the leaves of which are spotted white, traditionally where the drops of Mary's milk fell on them.
Lady's bedstraw	There are many plants prefixed 'lady's' denoting a plant dedicated to Our Lady. She has been given a whole range of domestic accoutrements represented by plants e.g. comb, cloak, mantle, cushion, glove, hatpins etc. The commonest churchyard plants only are mentioned here, among which ranks lady's bedstraw, a very familiar plant of churchyards almost everywhere in England and Wales.

Lady's cowslip	Yellow star of Bethlehem.
Lady's mantle	Native and garden *Alchemilla*.
Lady's smock	The Christian aspect of a plant whose other associations are with cuckoos and springtime loving and promiscuity. Our Lady's smock (the garment) was one of the relics which St Helena found in the cave at Bethlehem.
Lady's thistle	Milk thistle, from the white veins on the leaves caused when the Virgin's milk splashed on to them.
Lady's tresses	So called because the stem with flowers winding up the autumn lady's tresses resembles a braid of hair.
Lent lily, Lent cups, Lents, Lent pitchers, Lenty lily	Wild daffodil, because of the time of flowering.
Marybuds	Mary names are associated with the Virgin Mary. Marybuds is used for several species of buttercup and for marsh marigolds, also called Marybout, and Mary's gold.
Mourning widow	Dusky cranesbill.
Parson-in-his smock, Parson-in-the-pulpit, Parson pillycods, Priest-in-the-pulpit, Priesties, Priest's pintle	Lords and ladies, names associated with the extraordinary cowled spathe.
Parson's nose	Green-winged orchid.
Priest's pintle	Early purple orchid, a venereal herb with strong sexual associations; this name corresponds to the French *testicule de prêtre*. This plant also has holy names such as Gethsemane and Cross flower, its flowers supposed to have been splashed by Christ's blood as he hung on the Cross.
St Candida's eyes	Periwinkle called thus in Dorset (see text).
St John's wort	There are a number of plants named after saints, sometimes because the flowering season is around the time of the saint's feast-day (as is the case with St John's wort, *Hypericum perforatum*).
St Peter's herb, St Peter's keys	Cowslip, from the flowers which resemble a bunch of keys, the badge of St Peter. Legend says that when he dropped the keys, cowslips sprang up from the ground.
Sanctuary	Common centaury, probably a corruption of the *Centaurium* of its scientific name. Also yellow centaury, *Blackstonia perfoliata* and red bartsia.
Star of Bethlehem	Each flower is like a white star, bringing to mind the star which led the three wise men to Bethlehem. Greater stitchwort is also known by this name and as twinkle-star.
Sunday whites	Greater stitchwort in Devon.

185

Tree of heaven	*Ailanthus altissima*, altissima means very tall which explains the common name.
Trinity flower	Heartsease or wild pansy of which William Bullein wrote 'Three faces in one hodde (hood). . . *herba Trinitatis*'.
Virgin Mary	Used for lungwort and hemp agrimony. Also a prefix in many vernacular names (see 'Lady' names).
Whit Sunday	Wild daffodil, still blooming at this time if Whit is early. Similarly wood sorrel, is a Whitsun flower, and guelder rose is also known as Whitsuntide bosses in the cultivated form. Whitsuntide gilloflower is the double lady's smock in Gloucestershire.
Widow wail, Weeping widow	Snakeshead fritillary, possibly because its flowerheads hang as if in grief and perhaps for the dark colour of the pink ones; dark flowered plants were frequently given 'widow' names.

APPENDIX III

GENERAL BIBLIOGRAPHY

The Church in British Archaeology Morris, Richard (CBA Research Report No 47, London 1983)

Church Poems Betjeman, John, illustrated by John Piper (John Murray, London 1981 Pan Books 1982)

The Churchyards Handbook Stapleton, Revd Henry & Burman, Peter (CIO Publishing, London 1976)

Collins Pocket Guide to English Parish Churches Betjeman, John (ed.) (Collins, London 1968)

English Churchyard Memorials Burgess, Frederick (SPCK, London 1979)

Graves and Graveyards Lindley, Kenneth (Routledge & Kegan Paul, London 1972)

Our Christian Heritage Rodwell, Warwick & Bentley, James (George Philip, London 1984)

FIELD GUIDES

The Birds of Britain and Europe Heinzel, H., Fitter, R., and Parslow, J. (Collins 1974)

Collins Guide to Mushrooms and Toadstools Lange, M. and Hora, B. (Collins 1965)

The Complete Handbook of Garden Plants Wright, Michael (Michael Joseph/Rainbird 1984)

Ferns, Mosses and Lichens of Britain and Northern and Central Europe Jahns, Hans Martin (Collins 1983)

A Field Guide to the Butterflies of Britain and Europe Higgins, L. G. and Riley N. D. (Collins 1975)

A Field Guide to the Insects of Britain and Northern Europe Chinery, Michael (Collins 1973)

A Field Guide to the Reptiles and Amphibians of Britain and Europe Arnold, E. N., Burton K. A. and Ovenden, D. W. (Collins 1978)

Grasses Hubbard, C. E. (Penguin 1968)

The Handbook of Mammals Corbet, G. B. and Southern, H. N. (Blackwell 1977)

Lichens, An Illustrated Guide Dobson, Frank (The Richmond Publishing Co., Orchard Road, Richmond, Surrey, 1981).

The Moths of the British Isles (2 vols) South, Richard (Warne 1961)

The New Field Guide to Fungi Scothill, Eric and Fairhurst, Alan (Michael Joseph 1978)

The Observer's Book of Lichens Alvin, K. L. (and Rose, F.) (Warne 1977)

The Oxford Book of Flowerless Plants Brightman, F. H. (Oxford University Press 1966)

The Oxford Book of Insects Burton, John (Oxford University Press 1973)

The Oxford Book of Invertebrates Nichols, David and Cooke, John (Oxford University Press 1971)

Towns and Gardens Owen, Denis (Hodder & Stoughton 1978)
The Trees of Britain and Northern Europe Mitchell, Alan and Wilkinson, John (Collins 1982)
The Wild Flower Key Rose, Francis (Warne 1981)

APPENDIX IV

WILDLIFE AND CHURCHYARD ORGANIZATIONS

Botanical Society of the British Isles
c/o Department of Botany
British Museum (Natural History)
Cromwell Road
London SW7 5BD

British Butterfly Conservation Society
Tudor House
Quorn
Leicestershire LE12 8AD

British Lichen Society
Conservation Officer:
Dr Anthony Fletcher
Leicestershire Museums Service
96 New Walk
Leicester LE1 6DT

British Trust for Ornithology
Beech Grove
Station Road
Tring
Hertfordshire

Council for the Care of Churches
83 London Wall
London EC2M 5NA
(Information on the legal background to churchyard conservation is available from this source.)

Fauna and Flora Preservation Society
Tony Hutson (Bats)
c/o Zoological Society of London
Regents Park
London NW1 4RY

Mammal Society Bat Group
Phil Richardson
10 Bedford Cottages
Great Brington
Northampton NN7 4JE

Nature Conservancy Council
Northminster House
Peterborough PE1 1UA

Royal Society for Nature Conservation
22, The Green
Nettleham
Lincoln LN2 2NR

Royal Society for the Protection of Birds
The Lodge
Sandy
Bedfordshire SG19 2DL

Other specialist societies which might give advice are:
British Bryological Society (mosses and liverworts)
British Herpetological Society (reptiles and amphibia)
British Mycological Society (fungi)
Conchological Society of Great Britain (molluscs)
Royal Entomological Society (insects)
Addresses of the current secretaries for these societies may be obtained by writing to:
British Museum (Natural History),
Cromwell Road,
London SW7 5BD.

APPENDIX V

THE TWENTY COMMONEST CHURCHYARD BIRDS

The British Trust for Ornithology censused twelve English churches and churchyards during 1971–81, and ranked the commonest breeding birds as follows: blackbird, greenfinch, robin, song thrush, house sparrow, blue tit, wren, dunnock, starling, great tit, chaffinch, goldfinch, spotted flycatcher, linnet, goldcrest, bullfinch, mistle thrush, carrion crow, coal tit, and swift.

187

INDEX

Page references in italics indicate illustrations.

Place names are followed by their counties; counties are also indexed separately.

Scientific names (in brackets) have been given for all plant names and for animals wherever there is a possibility of confusion (though not when the scientific name is supplied with the English one in text or caption). Scientific bird names have not been included as birds are generally easy to find in the field guides under the standard names used here throughout.

spp = species (plural)

190

LEIGH-ON-SEA
A HISTORY

Sunrise, Low Tide, Leigh by William Thornbery, 1858-98.

LEIGH-ON-SEA

A HISTORY

Judith Williams

Phillimore

2002

Published by
PHILLIMORE & CO. LTD.
Shopwyke Manor Barn, Chichester, West Sussex

ISBN 1 86077 220 X

Printed and bound in Great Britain by
THE CROMWELL PRESS
Trowbridge, Wiltshire

Dedicated to
John and Christine Selby –
thanks, Mum and Dad

Contents

List of Illustrations

Frontispiece: Sunrise, Low Tide, Leigh by William Thornbery

Acknowledgements

The illustrations in this book are reproduced by kind permission of the following: Derek Barber 3, 5, 20, 23, 27-9, 38, 42, 57, 59-61, 69, 71-2, 75, 79, 81-2, 91-2, 94-5, 97, 105-6, 111, 117-20, 122, 125, 127-8, 131, 136-8, 141; *frontispiece* by kind permission of the Beecroft Art Gallery, copyright Southend Museum Service; Ros Bryant 113; Marjorie Doe 104,116; F.G. Hair & Son 74; Echo Newspapers 9, 13, 19, 103, 145-7, 150; Essex Record Office 32, 52, 70, 100, 139; Kath Hinton for photographs from the Reg Sims collection 16-18, 56, 76-8, 98, 107, 135, 140, 144, 148-9, 152-5; Elizabeth Holland 30, 40, 64, 66, 84-7, 151; Leigh Town Council 157; Janet Purdey for photographs from the Jessie Payne collection 8, 132; Christine Selby 34, 39, 102, 109; John Selby 2, 21; Sue Selby 33, 156; Southend Museums Service 1, 7, 12, 14, 25-6, 31, 37, 43-5, 53-4, 62, 65, 68, 73, 83, 88-90, 93, 101, 108, 110, 115, 121, 123-4, 126, 130, 133-4, 142; Southend-on-Sea Borough Libraries 4, 6, 10, 41, 48-9, 80, 96, 114, 129; West Leigh Junior School 99. All other illustrations are from the author's own collection.

Very great thanks are due to Derek Barber, who not only provided many of the photographs used in this book but also inspired me with his passion for local history.

Similarly, Elizabeth Holland not only provided copies of treasured family photographs but also spent time recounting her memories. Also, thanks to Kath Hinton for allowing me access to the collection of photographs taken by her father, Reg Sims.

Thanks to John Selby for his sketch of Lapwater Hall and for plentiful advice, and to Christine Selby for postcards from the Agnes Blower collection, access to her private library of relevant books, and for proof reading. Equally valuable was the babysitting service she provided, which solved no end of problems for me.

Also to Marjorie Doe for the loan of her fascinating collection of memorabilia, and to Doris Williams for taking the time to share her memories.

Thanks, too, to Ken Crowe of Southend Museum, to the ladies of Southend Record Office, to Clare Hunt of the Beecroft Art Gallery and the staff of Southend Library information department, particularly Susan Gough. Similarly, thanks to Peter Jones of the Salvation Army and to Roy Richards who emailed from Canada with his reminiscences of Leigh Swimming Club. Also, to Graham Dent of the Leigh Sailing Club, Geoff Fulford and Louise Burfoot of Leigh Town Council, Cheryl Woolf and Jenny Davey of West Leigh Junior School, the secretary of the Boyce Hill golf club and to Jane Wheeler for her detective work.

Others who have given their time to pass on knowledge or direct me to information sources include: Andrea Ames, Fr Tim Barnes, Margery Beacham, Carol Carlile, Simon Deacon, PC Steve Dewberry, Fr Robin Eastoe, Pat Elliott, Richard Hair, Robert Hair, Ada and Derek Harniman, Kate Herbert, Sue Hibberd, Karen Holyhead, Cyril Johnson, Rev. Margaret Jones, Janet Kirkpatrick, Bruce Neagus, Carole Pavitt, Gwen Rawlinson, Shirley Rowe, Hilary Shallis, Deborah and Mick Skeels, Mavis Stipple, Ron Whitear, Jim Worsdale, Anne Wray and Ian Yearsley. Thank you all very much.

One

Beginnings

The town of Leigh-on-Sea nestles in a landscape formed over fifty million years ago. At that time, the area that is now south Essex was inundated by the sea and, beneath its deep water, 140 metres of London Clay were laid down, on top of previously deposited chalk. As the sea became shallower, Claygate and Bagshot Beds were in turn deposited over the clay.

Between thirty and ten million years ago, earth movements raised these sediments above sea level and rivers, draining the land, cut down through the deposits creating a system of valleys. These valleys included those of the river Thames and the Prittle Brook, both crucial features in the subsequent development of the town of Leigh. The ice sheets failed to reach south Essex during the Ice Ages, and the region was subject to wind-borne deposits blowing from the flat plain of the North Sea area. Following the retreat of the last Ice Age, about 10,000 years B.C., south Essex was almost entirely covered by forest.

The first evidence of human activity within the boundaries of the current town of Leigh relates to Bronze-Age man, who three thousand years ago was living along the banks of Prittle Brook and in small forest clearings, hunting and gathering in the woodland. Where there was a large enough local population to serve, bronzesmiths set up forges and became part of a bronze-founding centre stretching from Leigh to Shoeburyness. Much of the raw material was scrap metal brought over from France and used to cast tools and weapons such as the socketed axes, gouge and spear-head found in central Leigh in the 1880s. A second hoard, discovered in 1926 buried on the banks of Prittle Brook between Flemming Avenue and Tankerville Drive, included 14 socketed celts (axes), 17 celt blades and numerous fragments of celts, swords and spears.

A thousand years after the Bronze Age the Trinovantes tribe of ancient Britons held all the land from Colchester to the Thames. Romans are known to have walked along the top of Leigh cliffs, perhaps surveying their ships sailing past to Londinium and their salt workings down on the fringes of Canvey Island, since submerged by rising sea levels. They left behind a scattering of coins, later discovered in Churchfield and Shorefield when the area was part of Leigh Hall Farm, and found in gardens in Seaview Road, Beach Avenue and the Broadway as late as the 20th century. Further coins and pottery were discovered on Leigh Park Brickfields (now the site of Belfairs High School), and Roman amphorae were dug up in the mud of Leigh Marsh during the 19th century, but no evidence of Roman buildings has been found in the town.

The Anglo Saxons, who took possession of Essex in A.D. 527-9 and formed the kingdom of East Saxa, made a more permanent settlement on the site. Indeed, the name of the town comes from the Saxon word 'leah' meaning the pasture or the place, and marker trees, ditches and earth banks which they used to define ownership boundaries are still discernible in Belfairs Woods today. In 1892 silver Saxon coins were discovered together with a skeleton in a shallow grave in West Street. Of the coins found (written reports are inconsistent as to the exact number), several were of the date of Alfred the Great (A.D. 871-90), while others were struck by Plegmund, who was Archbishop of Canterbury between A.D. 890 and 914. The Saxons also organised the county into hundreds for administrative purposes, placing Leigh in the Rochford Hundred and part of the Honour of Rayleigh. Leigh Hall paid a hidage rent, a tax payable for every

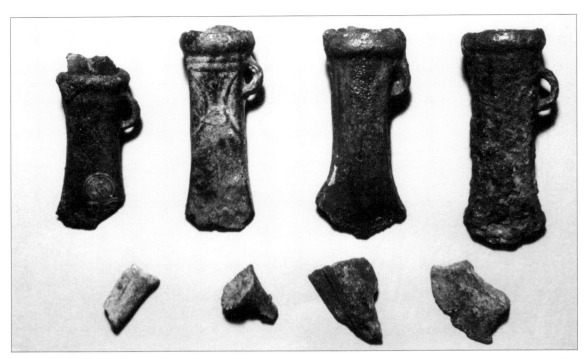

1   These Bronze-Age artefacts were found on the banks of Prittle Brook between Flemming Avenue and Tankerville Drive. Most are axe-heads and tools.

hide of land, to the Honour of Rayleigh, on the feast of John the Baptist at least until the Norman invasion.

Domesday Book, 1086, gives the first written record of Leigh (Legra), showing it as held by one freeman, Ranulf, as a manor with two villeins (villagers), two bordars (cottage dwellers of slightly lower class than the villeins) and pasture for 100 sheep. There was one plough belonging to Ranulf, plus half a plough belonging to the men, probably owned jointly with another parish, hence the half. The survey also lists 'five bordars by the water who do not hold any land'. From the survey, therefore, it may be supposed that, including women and children, the population of Leigh numbered some thirty to forty people in 1086.

Ranulf was probably Ranulph Piperell or Peverell, who also had the care of North Benfleet manor and land at Hockley. He was a knight who had accompanied William the Conqueror from Normandy and had distinguished himself at Hastings. Subsequently the king had conferred several Essex manors and estates on Ranulf, who, in addition, had the dubious honour of being married off to William's mistress, the Saxon noblewoman Ingelrica, when the king had tired of her. The land held by Ranulf at Leigh was held 'in demesne', meaning it belonged directly to King William, and for tenure of the land Ranulf would serve in the king's army when called upon. In turn, the villeins and bordars would work his land.

The survey indicates the manor of Leigh consisted of one hide, an area of roughly 120 acres but varying in size according to the quality of the land. The sheep pasture may well have been marshland, as it was common practice to graze sheep on the marshes. The bordars by the water would have used stop nets or kiddles that would be staked across a channel of the out-going tide to catch fish. The marshes would also have been a rich source of wildfowl. However, as the Domesday survey records no fishery (i.e. a fishing business) at Leigh, A.C. Wright suggests that the bordars were probably the operators or master-mariners of the local carrying trade, rather than fishermen.

At the time of Edward the Confessor, just before the Conquest, Leigh's livestock comprised one rouncey (horse or pack animal), five cows, five calves and 100 sheep. By 1086 the town could boast two rounceys, four cows, five calves and 103 sheep. It was previously worth 40 shillings, but after the Conquest 100 shillings. From its beginnings, then, Leigh was a community split by the geography of the area, the steep cliff cut by the river Thames forming a natural divide between the farming community at the top of the hill and the boat-men down at the water's edge.

Two

Early Development

Between Domesday and 1913 the parish of Leigh stretched from the current boundary with Hadleigh on its western extreme to a line running roughly up Grand Drive, Chalkwell Park Drive and Middlesex Avenue in the east. It ended just to the north of the present Blenheim Chase, on a line joining up with Scrub Lane in Hadleigh. The town's development was greatly influenced by the geography of the area. The dense woodland in the north of the parish was managed for timber supply, while farms developed along the two ridges of the Prittle Brook valley, where the Bagshot Beds and Claygate soils were preferable to the clay in the valley. However, the most rapid development continued to be the river front as, from the five bordars by the water of the Domesday record, a fishing and trading community grew up along the foreshore.

LORDS OF THE MANOR

From Ranulf in 1086, the title of lord of the manor of Leigh passed down through Ralph Gernon to Richard de Southchurch, who is known to have held the manor in 1279. In 1316 it was held by John de Arpeton of Canewdon. John de Arpeton (also known as John Appeton or Dippetone) sold the manor to Robert Rochford (d. 1337), owner of the manor of Rochford, and the two manors were linked together for the next three hundred years.

Edward III (1327-77) retrieved the estates from Sir Thomas Rochford and conferred them upon William de Bohun, Earl of Northampton (d.1360).

2 Effigy of Richard Lord Rich, from his tomb in Felsted church. He was Lord High Chancellor (1547-51) and Speaker of the House of Commons. His main residence was Rochford Hall, where he died in 1567.

3 Leigh Hall was situated half-way between the current Broadway and Pall Mall. Leigh Hall Road now runs just west of where the house stood. This photograph was taken *c.*1890 and shows the south front of the house.

During the tenure of William's son, Humfrey de Bohun (d.1372), the land was tenanted by Lawrence Ware. Subsequently, in 1451, Humfrey de Bohun's widow gave the Leigh manor to James Boteler, her son by her third husband, James, Earl of Ormond. When James Boteler was beheaded for his Lancastrian sympathies, Edward IV gave the manor to his own son-in-law, Thomas Grey, Marquis of Dorset. However, on the accession of Henry VII in 1485, the estates (Rochford and Leigh) were restored to Sir Thomas Boteler, brother of the beheaded James, along with the title, Earl of Ormond.

Through Thomas Boteler's daughter, Margaret, the estates passed to his grandson, Thomas Boleyn (also called Bullen). Thomas Boleyn's daughter Mary became his sole heir when her brother and sister, George and Anne, were beheaded by Henry VIII. During much of Mary's tenure the Leigh estates were held in her name by her second husband William Stafford. From Mary Boleyn's son, Henry Lord Hunsdon, the estates came to Richard Lord Rich in the mid-16th century. Leigh manor remained in the Rich family, the Earls of Warwick, until 1673 when the Rich estates were dispersed.

LEIGH HALL

Nothing is known of the lord of the manor's residence before 1561, when the manor house was rebuilt by Richard Lord Rich. Known as the Mansion House and later as Leigh Hall, the manor was situated a quarter of a mile east of the church, just north of Hall Road (now Leigh Broadway). It was a large building facing south, its massive entrance porch leading through to rooms panelled with Spanish oak. Views from the overhanging upper storey took in Margate church, the Medway and Gravesend, and a foot-path ran directly between Leigh Hall and the rectory.

Besides a garden and orchard, Leigh Hall's grounds included a yard and farm offices to the north of the house, and a pond and stables to the west. By 1577 the lands of Leigh manor were worth £4 0s. 6½d. for rents of assize, and £13 3s. 0d. from the tenants of the manor lands, which included oyster layings on the foreshore, properties in the High Street, Strand Wharf, and Belfairs Farm. There is no evidence that the lords of the manor actually resided at Leigh Hall, and for most of its history the grand residence was tenanted by farmers.

4 Side view of Leigh Hall. Between Domesday and 1400 Leigh appears on maps and in records as Legra, Legha, La Legh, Lega, Leye, Legh by Hadley and Lygh.

THE CHURCH

On the cliff above the fishing village, Leigh church, dedicated to St Clement, the patron saint of mariners, dates from the mid- to late 15th century. It was built on the site of an earlier church, possibly founded by the de Arpeton family, lords of the manor during the 13th century, and the first known priest of the parish was John de Haveringe in 1297.

The nave, north aisle and eighty foot high church tower, the oldest parts of the building, are all of Kentish ragstone, and the tower was visible both from vessels on the river and from the northern extremities of the parish. The porch was built slightly later, about 1500, of Tudor brick-work, and it originally sported castellations. The south aisle did not come into existence until major extension work was carried out in 1872. Before 1600 the church boasted windows depicting the manorial arms of the families of Nevill, Bohun, Ormond, Le Marney, Rainforth, Tyrell, Bourchier,

5 Interior of St Clement's Church. Between 1500 and 1897 the church comprised a nave, small chancel, north aisle, tower and porch only.

Earl of Essex, Lord Rochford and Boleyn, all former lords of the manor.

Notable among the early rectors of St Clement's is William Negus who, in 1585, preferred to be suspended from office rather than wear a surplice. Such was the parishioners' faith that they wrote to the Reverend Negus, begging him to reconsider, for 'we are deprived of our spirituall comfort ... if it continue, it will be our ruin'. The appeal was effective and the suspension was recalled. However, the Reverend Negus fell into further dispute with the bishop and was deprived of the living at St Clement's in 1609.

It was obviously a steep climb to the church for the majority of worshippers, who lived in the cluster of cottages down by the river, but, as well as being visibly prominent, the church was sited to be equally accessible from the river, the scattered farmsteads in the north of the parish and the manor house.

LEIGH STREET

The first dwellings of Leigh's townspeople were wooden shacks which, as the settlement grew,

became crowded together on the narrow strip of level ground between the cliffs and the river Thames. Four footpaths led up the hill to the north, while wharves and slipways gave access to the sea on the south side.

Leigh Street, the passage between the houses, was the only street in the parish, and community life revolved around the market place at the east end of the street, the centrally placed Strand Wharf, and the conduit house. At the conduit house villagers drew their water supply from a reservoir holding 44 hogsheads of water, the only supply of fresh water in the village. The water originated as a spring bubbling out of the cliff in Tile Kiln Meadow, just east of the top of Billet Lane, and was channelled downhill through a series of pipes and small cisterns.

The only direct approach to the village from the west was via a bridleway from Hadleigh, sometimes impassable at high tide, leading to Leigh's town gate set in a protective fence. Immediately inside the fence on the north of the Street was a

6 The *Crooked Billet* is a late 16th-century timber-framed house with a cross-wing at the east end. The back of the building was demolished by the railway company in 1855, soon after which it was refronted in brick; it was altered again in 1937 and re-roofed and extended in 1944.

cottage known as Gilmans-at-the-Pale (i.e. Gilmans by the fence). Its Tudor fireplace and over-hanging upper storey were typical of the buildings during the 16th century, as was Jone Bayliss, the wooden cottage on the opposite side of the street, with its own waterfront and wharf.

Between Gilmans and the *Crooked Billet* pub, which dates from 1500, Billet Lane joined the Street. The lane was so called from the name of the Haddock family home, The Old Billet, built in 1430 on the east of the lane just north of Leigh

Street. Immediately east of the *Crooked Billet* was Osborne House, home of the Salmon family. Opposite the house led a hard walkway, suitable for taking cattle across the creek to Leigh Marsh at low tide. By the 17th century this way was no longer of any use, being submerged beneath mud deposits. Osborne House itself was demolished in 1912.

On the south side of the street, the original *Peter Boat Inn* was built in 1645 and was run by members of the Osborne family for many years. However,

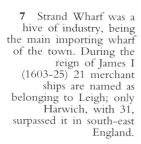

7 Strand Wharf was a hive of industry, being the main importing wharf of the town. During the reign of James I (1603-25) 21 merchant ships are named as belonging to Leigh; only Harwich, with 31, surpassed it in south-east England.

the original building was burnt down in 1892 when the landlord tripped on the stairs and dropped his oil lamp. The inn was rebuilt in brick. Between the *Peter Boat* and the river ran Alley Dock, a narrow cobbled passage. At the western end of Alley Dock a communal toilet overhung the seawall, while at the eastern end were stabled the horses used to pull wagonloads of goods, from the wharves, up the hill for distribution inland. The alley was also the site of an early town gaol, and the cottages and tenements along the alley were among the most poor and squalid dwellings in the town.

The eastern end of Alley Dock emerged at Strand Wharf, a focal point for the village as early as medieval times, principally because it remained in the hands of the lord of the manor and was available for public use, while other landing sites passed into private ownership. The wharf is documented as early as 1255 when Beatrice, daughter of Henry III, tried (unsuccessfully) to elope from Strand Wharf at 'La Lea' with Ralph de Binley. Ralph was accused of killing a foreign merchant on the wharf and was subsequently exiled from England. Later, Beatrice sailed from Leigh to marry her father's choice of suitor in France. The cottages on the wharf belonged to Leigh manor and their ownership was passed down along with the lord's title. When Anne, daughter of Thomas Boleyn, the Lord of Leigh manor, married Henry

VIII, the cottages formed part of her dowry. Soon afterwards, it became the prerogative of the Master of Trinity House, the local guild of pilots, to live on Strand Wharf.

In 1626 a bailiff was appointed to collect tolls at Strand Wharf and a by-law was enforced in 1651 stating that, 'if any vessel or vessels shall come with any commodities to sell at the Strand Key to the inhabitants of the town of Leigh, it shall pay towards the maintaining of the said Key 4d a time for every such vessels that cometh with fish or malt, for vessels that come with coal, 2d a time, under the name of wharfage'. James Steel was appointed as collector of wharfage at this time.

Situated at the head of Strand Wharf was the *Crown Inn*, no doubt frequented by visiting merchants and passengers waiting to embark from the wharf. When, in 1406, Henry IV crossed to Leigh from the Isle of Sheppy, he took refreshment in the *Crown* before continuing his journey to Pleshey. The inn entertained nobility again in 1554 when Frances, cousin of Mary Tudor and mother of Lady Jane Grey, escaped from England via Leigh, spending the night at the *Crown*. Another supporter of Lady Jane Grey, Dr Edwin Sandys, escaped from prison and fled to the coast of Leigh, from where he sailed to France. On Elizabeth I's accession, Dr Sandys returned to England and became Archbishop of York.

8 Juniper's Cottage was originally a wealthy mariner's house, but latterly two shops with tenements above. Joe Juniper displayed fish for sale on a stall in front of his shop.

Further along Leigh Street, an Elizabethan manor house of the type occupied by prosperous mariners was built in 1589. This property was later owned by Thomas Constable, the uncle of the artist John Constable. It became known as Juniper's Cottage at the end of the 19th century, after its then owner, Joe Juniper, and was subsequently divided into two tenements with the ground floor front rooms trading as a fishmonger's and a teashop.

The east end of town was dominated by the market place where, in medieval times, most of the day-to-day trading would have taken place. It was here that an annual fair was held on the second Tuesday of May, although the town was never officially granted a market charter. The market's exact location has never been identified, although it is most likely to have been held in the angle between Leigh Street and Leigh Hill, between the *Kings Head* and the *Bell Inn*, with a manor house, now the *Ship Inn*, at its north-west corner. The *Kings Head* inn was originally built as a public house but was used as a private dwelling between 1671 and 1720. It was rebuilt and opened as an inn again in 1740, under the name of the *Angel*, before reverting to the name *Kings Head* in 1766.

A slipway known as Kings Strand, after the *Kings Head* opposite, marked the east end of the village on the south side of the street. On the north side was the *Bell Inn*, again dating from the Tudor period, and two or three cottages stretching a few yards beyond this to where the level terrace of ground disappeared into the hill.

The only roadway in or out of the fishing settlement wound its way up the hill from the market place to the church. To accommodate horses pulling heavy loads up from the wharves, the road was built on a gentle gradient, rising to the east and then bending sharply north to join Hall Road east of the churchyard. Thus the hill became known as Horse Hill, pedestrians taking the steeper but more direct footpaths rising from Leigh Street to Chess Lane at the brow of the hill. At the top of Horse Hill, one or more of the horses would be uncoupled from the wagon, leaving just one or two to continue down Elm Road to distribute merchandise inland or to London via Hadleigh, Rayleigh and Wickford. At the important road junction of Horse Hill, Hall Road and Elm Road stood the parish church, the

stocks, a jossing block (similar to a whipping post or pillory) and the manorial pound.

CRIME

The use of stocks and a jossing block, where petty criminals could be tethered and ridiculed by other villagers, indicates that the lord of the manor held some powers of punishment. However, serious criminals were probably held in the gaol in Alley Dock before being transferred to Chelmsford to be tried at the Assizes.

To give an example of the wide range of crimes committed in Leigh, Judge Thomas Walmesley and Serjeant John Dodderidge found Judith Saye of Leigh not guilty of stealing a pair of stockings from George Elliott on 13 July 1610. Much more seriously, Richard Jackson, a husbandman of Leigh, came before Judge Robert Houghton and Serjeant Ranulph Crewe on 6 March 1620, indicted for rape. The court heard that on 2 February 1619, at Leigh, he raped Mary Goodladd aged ten years, Rachel Bonner aged 11 years and Liddia Duke aged 11 years. On 10 January 1620, again in Leigh, he raped Elizabeth Dagnett aged 12 years. Jackson was found guilty and hanged.

FISHING

Remote from the agricultural land on the high ground, the river and marshes provided the primary means of support for the riverside community. An inquisition of 1290 for the parish of Leigh notes that John de Benfleet 'had seisin of Sandflete marsh for eight days, taking eight chees of the issue and fishing in the fleet'. The 'chees' would have been the large, round, strong-flavoured sheep's cheeses typical of the marshes, valued by sailors for their keeping qualities on long voyages.

The right of fishing on the marshes was the prerogative of the lords of the manor, and land subject to the overflow of the tide was eagerly sought to lease. In 1551 the inhabitants of Leigh leased the fishery of Hadley Ray from the lord of the manor of Hadleigh, at that time Richard Lord Rich. It was worth £10 a year. The draining or walling of marsh caused much passion as it affected neighbouring marshlands. The owners and lessees of Hadley Ray were obliged to defend their rights legally against other fishermen on several occasions,

9 The *Ship Inn*, built as a mariner's house, became a public house during the 18th century. It was very prominently placed, being at the junction of Church Hill Lane and Leigh Hill.

particularly against others from Leigh who repeatedly claimed the right to dredge and fish in the Ray. In 1554, for example, Lord Rich successfully sued William Gillet for taking mussels. Later litigation is recorded in 1652, 1671, 1724 and even into the 19th century.

The earliest fishing methods, using stop nets and kiddles, were well suited to the area, where nets could be staked across channels of the outgoing tide, catching anything in its path. However, owing to the indiscriminate catch, kiddles were outlawed as early as the 13th century, when King John forbade their use. The population flouted this law and a further by-law was made in 1697 stating that 'no person using the art, mystery or craft of a fisherman shall pitch, set or erect any Riff, Hedge or halfnet upon stakes or otherwise, within the full sea or low water ... being an engine that will utterly destroy small fish'.

The deepwater channel of Leigh Creek, then known as Leigh Road, meant that fishing from Leigh was not dependent on the tides, a definite advantage for the village. Double-ended craft of 12 to 14 feet long and with a two-man crew were typical of Leigh fishing boats from 1540, and became known as 'peter boats', named after Saint Peter, the patron saint of fishermen. These rowed boats had a pointed stern and a wet well in the middle of the boat to keep the catch alive until it was landed. Boats without a wet well would tow a koff, a floating fish box.

The mud flats off Shoeburyness were a favourite fishing ground for the peter boats and were a guaranteed source of sole, turbot, whiting and flounder. Daniel Defoe, writing in 1722, noted that the flats 'are so full of fish that ... the whole shoar is full of small fisher-boats in very great numbers, belonging to the villages and towns on the coast, who come at every tide ...'.

Much of the catch was landed at Strand Wharf, along with provisions bought over from Kent, London and the continent. The main market for Leigh's fishing catch was London, and with inland roadways being in such poor condition the fish were sent up river by sailing boat for sale at Billingsgate. Bad or foggy weather sometimes prevented sailing, so seven large holding pits were constructed on the marshes, their sides of puddled clay standing above the level of the tide and being fed with fresh seawater via pipes. Fish were stored here until they could be conveyed to market or, alternatively, kept for periods when fish stocks were low and they could be sold for a high price. The system was ideal for flat fish, such as plaice or sole, which would burrow into the mud in the bottom of the pits, from where they could be safely retrieved at the fishermen's convenience. These fish pits were still in use at the end of the 19th century.

TRADE

As early as the 14th century Leigh was a flourishing trading port on the Kent – Rayleigh – Chelmsford – Pleshey route, handling, among other cargoes, the licensed corn-barges carrying grain from south-east Essex to Canterbury. By the 15th century it was fulfilling a coastal trading role in an era when land communications were poor. Merchants owned ships at Leigh, which they used for coastal or North Sea routes, cargoes being split at Leigh for inland distribution via the Thames. Sea trade increased to such an extent that a customs officer was appointed to Leigh in 1565, in which year the examiner of customs at Harwich reported, 'Leigh is a very proper town, well-furnished with good mariners, where commonly tall ships do ride, which town is a common and special landing place for butter, all manner of grain and other things'.

Records rarely refer to exported goods, although hay and straw were sent by barge to London to bed and feed the horses so vital to the capital's transport system. A record from 1693 indicates that it was not unusual for two hundred coal ships to be lying at anchor off the Leigh coast. Of the many ships trading between England and the continent that gave Leigh as their place of origin, however, most were owned by London merchants; although Leigh residents were making a living from merchant shipping, it was the London dwellers who were making fortunes. Transport of goods between ships and from ship to shore depended upon Leigh's specialist skilled boatmen: hoymen, lightermen, bargees and wherrymen.

PARISH AFFAIRS

From medieval times parishes were obliged to elect officers for the collection and allocation of communal funds. Parishioners chose two church-wardens annually as legal guardians of all church property with responsibility for the management of income. Under the Poor Laws introduced in Tudor times, all parishes in Essex were further required to make formal provision for poor relief and for the upholding of law and order. The 1555 Highways Act expected every parish to elect two surveyors of the highways to ensure that all householders provided labourers to repair the roads on four appointed days each year.

In Leigh a meeting was convened quarterly to administer these matters. Known as 'vestry meetings', more often than not the gatherings were held in a local inn. For example, in 1783 the vestry meeting took place at the *Waterman's Arms* and in 1785 at the *Queens Head*. At the Easter meeting, two churchwardens were elected, along with one or more overseer of the poor and one or more constable. The appointments were then sent to Rochford for approval by the magistrates. Although the role of churchwarden was considered a privilege, its holder often serving for many years in succession, the other offices were time-consuming and often unrewarding, and officers served for one year only.

The system caused some resentment among the Leigh parishioners: farmers begrudged the poor relief rates, as most of the poor resided in the old town, while the fishermen felt little responsibility for the repair of the roads, most of which were in the north of the parish. As early as 1594, Leigh parishioners were cautioned by magistrates at the Quarter Sessions over the neglect of the Sallom Brook Bridge, where Turner's Lane (now Eastwood Road) crossed the Prittle Brook.

It is hardly surprising that most of Leigh's residents were unconcerned about inland roadways when 'Lee Road', the creek, remained the town's main transport corridor, providing employment for the men and food for their families, and bringing traders to the town. As prosperity increased, support industries built up. Old wills refer to Leigh residents Robert Stevens, butcher (1577), Nicholas Colte, schoolmaster (1587) and Roger Jones, tailor (1592). By the 16th century Leigh was definitely on the way up.

Three

Ships and Seafarers

The heyday of Leigh, the mid-16th to mid-17th centuries, coincided with a period of British history in which shipbuilding and naval supremacy were vital to the country. Henry VIII's policy was to encourage the building of ships that could be used as war vessels and occasionally paid a tonnage allowance to ship builders. Leigh's situation was ideal for a port, with a deep water channel and a harbour sheltered by high ground to the north, and Canvey Island protecting it from the prevailing south-west winds, as well as being within easy reach of both London and the continent.

Leigh's transition from a fishing village and small trading port to a centre for shipping was well underway by 1511 when a fleet was assigned to cruise between Dover and Calais to keep the passage clear for English shipping. Among the vessels undertaking this task was the *Peter* from Leigh, commanded by Adryan Dunkan. The *Peter* carried 13 soldiers, 35 mariners and two gunners. Other Leigh ships employed with this fleet were the *Powle* (35 tons), the *Gabriell & Julyan* (85 tons) and the *Kateryn* (30 tons). In 1522 Leigh was recognised as the main port of south-east Essex.

The increased volume of shipping led to the formation of a guild of pilots who took responsibility for guiding inward coming vessels. A similar guild at Deptford provided pilots for outward bound vessels. The two guilds were united by Henry VIII in a charter dated 1514 and became part of the national organisation, Trinity House. Trinity House was responsible for removing dangerous wrecks, placing buoys and sea marks, and granting licences to seamen. Members of the guild were highly respected in the community and a brass inscription was mounted in St Clement's to the memory of the brothers of Trinity House who 'laboured worthily for the welfare of the mariners'. Notable among the Masters (leaders) of the guild were Leigh men Robert Salmon in 1591, Richard Chester in 1615 who came to Leigh in the 1590s from Hartlepool, and William Goodlad in 1638.

Queen Elizabeth I, continuing her father's precedent, kept close account of the number of men and ships available for service during wartime, and developed the incentive scheme by paying five shillings per ton for new vessels exceeding 100 tons. With deep-water access to its wharves and generations of experience, Leigh was perfectly situated to take full advantage of the scheme and became a hive of industrial activity. In 1594 five ships qualified for Queen Elizabeth's subsidy. In addition, that same year, 686 crowns were paid to John Goodlad, John Bridecake and Richard Harris of Leigh towards the cost of building three ships; 640 crowns were paid to Richard and William Goodlad and Laurence Moores for three ships; and 620 crowns were paid to William Hand, Robert Salmon and John Skinner for three ships. The largest of all the subsidised ships built at Leigh was the *Globe*, of 340 tons, built in 1599.

In 1572 a register was completed by Thomas Colshill, a London surveyor of customs, to the effect that Leigh's fleet included 27 vessels of between 50 and 100 tons, nine of between 20 and 50 tons and four vessels of under 20 tons.

ADVENTURERS

Notable among Leigh's seafarers are those who joined Sir Hugh Willoughby in 1553 when his three small ships called prior to an ill-fated expedition to find a route around the Arctic Circle. Two of the ships became ice-locked and all the crew perished. The third ship reached a Russian port safely. Another adventurer was Andrew Battell, a Leigh mariner captured by the Portuguese and taken to Africa. Battell spent nearly twenty years in the southern hemisphere before returning to his native Leigh where his story was documented by Samuel Purchas, vicar of Eastwood, in his book of explorers published in 1613. However, perhaps the most famous ship to have docked at Leigh is the *Mayflower*, which visited the port in July 1620 to embark passengers and stock supplies before rounding the coast to Plymouth and continuing its journey to the New World.

WAR

With a thriving shipbuilding industry, Leigh increased in importance and its responsibilities increased likewise. When Charles I issued a writ in 1626 that Essex should provide £8,000 towards the defence of the realm, the Rochford Hundred had to raise £308 1s., and in Leigh 85 people were assessed for the tax, the largest number of eligible people in any town in the hundred. Between them, they had to find £25 8s. Only Prittlewell, Canewdon and Rayleigh had to raise more, indicating the relative importance of the parishes.

Leigh was used as an embarkation point for the shipment of troops and during the 17th century thousands of men passed through on their way to the continent. War office documents record that, in 1686, Leigh had seven beds available for visitors and stabling for 15 horses. The high standing of Leigh's shipbuilding reputation was acknowledged during the first of the wars with the Dutch in 1652, when Admiral Blake brought his fleet to Leigh to be refitted following damage in battles off Goodwin Sands. The Admiral's choice of Leigh in preference to the Kent ports of Chatham and Gravesend, influenced by the prevailing winds, was vindicated when the ships subsequently performed magnificently and were victorious in battle.

During the second Dutch war, in 1667, enemy ships led by De Ruyter sailed up the Thames and into the Medway, causing destruction in Kent and at Tilbury before anchoring at Canvey Island. The Essex militia assembled at Leigh and rumours of invasions by the Dutch led to the formation of a land force, similar to the home guard. Samuel Pepys noted in his diary of 17 July 1667: 'My sister Michell

came from Lee to see us; but do tattle so much of the late business of the Dutch coming thither that I am weary of it.'

PRESS GANGS

Strong lads brought up to know the ways of ships and the sea were obviously a valuable commodity to the Royal Navy, and Leigh became a favourite haunt of the press gangs seeking additional crew members for their ships. The gangs usually outnumbered the victims and were backed by the law, and Leigh suffered greatly between 1639 and 1640 when Essex was required to supply over 2,000 men for service in Scotland. Apprentice fishermen were exempt from naval service and it was agreed in 1652 that Leigh hoys might retain two men and one boy free from impressment. Even so, the following year, one thousand men were seized from ships anchored in Leigh Creek.

When a naval guard was established at the mouth of the Thames to deter Dutch invasions the Navy took advantage of passing vessels, dragging men from incoming ships. Merchant ships provided rich pickings of provisions as well as men, resulting in Leigh suffering from loss of income as well as manpower. In the town, press gangs would wait in the churchyard, sharpening their cutlasses on the convenient large tomb of Mary Ellis opposite the church porch, hoping to capture young men coming out of the service. However, a secret passage concealed beneath the flagstones of the church tower was used to hide eligible men until the press gang had gone. With sufficient warning, the men of the town would take to the woods north of Leigh and wait till the press danger has passed. Relatives would creep out in the dead of night to take provisions to those hiding in the woods. When Deputy Admiral Pulley was unable to find 150 crew members at Leigh he wrote that his efforts had been hampered by the local people.

GOLDSPRING THOMPSON AND THE NORE MUTINY

One that didn't get away was Goldspring Thompson, born into a large Leigh family in 1777. He married in his teens and before he was 20 had been press ganged into the Royal Navy. Conditions at sea were harsh. Pay was a pittance, food was abominable and discipline was severe. Goldspring Thompson was serving with the Thames Estuary fleet in 1797 when the crews, encouraged by the success of the Portsmouth fleet, made demands for improved conditions.

When petitions sent to the Admiralty had no effect, the crews seized command of the ships anchored at the Nore, a sandbank at the mouth of the Thames, but still their demands were refused. Richard Parker, elected leader of the mutineers, ordered the fleet to form a line across the estuary and prevent merchant vessels sailing to London. It was at this point that public sympathy turned against the mutineers. The fishermen of Leigh saw an opportunity and went out under cover of darkness to the ships of the Nore and sold food to the sailors. Members of Trinity House also went out from Leigh and sunk marker buoys and beacons in the Channel to hinder any escape attempted by the mutineers.

Goldspring Thompson and another sailor, seeing how badly things were going, escaped from their ship in a small rowing boat, but were spotted and pursued. The two jumped overboard and tried to swim for Leigh but Thompson was carried by the tide onto Canvey Island where he crawled into a wheatfield to hide, eventually escaping to Barking. He did not go back to Leigh until he was sure all danger had passed. Meanwhile, the Nore mutiny had collapsed. Some sailors escaped to France; others were captured, including Richard Parker who was hanged on the yardarm of the Admiral's flagship, the *Sandwich*. Twenty-nine other mutineers were executed and 29 imprisoned.

Impressment laws became obsolete in 1835, by which time Goldspring Thompson had returned to Leigh, where he died in 1875 aged 98, leaving eight sons and daughters, 50 grandchildren and 53 great-grandchildren.

LEIGH MARINERS

Not all Leigh men were reluctant to join the Navy, and the town can boast several prominent sailors among its ancestors. Notable among them was the Haddock family, who lived in Billet Lane from the 14th century and of whom at least nine members were high ranking officers in the Royal Navy. The first recorded member of the family is John Haddock, who held 12 acres of land with one messuage and a marsh in common with partners, for two shillings a

year, before his death in 1327. By the 15th century the family had risen to become people of considerable means and rank, and Captain Richard Haddock, who died in 1453, is commemorated on a plaque in St Clement's Church, together with his wife Christina, seven sons and three daughters. His son John is also commemorated in St Clement's, together with his wife Alice and their 11 children.

Another Richard Haddock, born in 1581, joined the Navy and served James I. He achieved command of a ship but had to retire because of failing eyesight. His son, also named Richard, was born in 1629 and joined the Navy at an early age. In 1653 colonial and commercial competition initiated a war with Holland, and Richard was made captain of the *Portland*. In 1657 he was given command of the frigate *Abragon*, which was part of the fleet patrolling the English Channel, watching for Spanish marauders. His letters to his father from this time are in the British Museum. The war against the Dutch continued until he left the Navy in 1667. For the following five years, Richard traded in the Middle East as a merchant captain. However, when the Dutch attacked the British fleet again, in 1672, Richard rejoined the Navy as captain of the *Royal James*, flagship of the Earl of Sandwich. At the Battle of Sole Bay he was one of the few surviving officers after, wounded in the foot, he leapt into the sea from his burning ship.

In 1674 Captain Haddock faced a court martial on a charge of conveying merchant goods 'on terms of freight for his own benefit'. He was sentenced to six months' imprisonment and ordered to pay all profits to the king. However, the incident appears to have had little affect on his career and in 1675 he was knighted by Charles II for his bravery and received £40 from Parliament in recognition of his service to the Navy. Richard became First Commissioner of the Victualling Office, represented Aldeburgh in Parliament in 1678, and sat as MP for Shoreham in 1685-7. He eventually achieved the rank of Admiral and position of Comptroller of the Navy.

A fighter to the end, at the age of eighty Richard was still campaigning for financial compensation for the loss of his toe during the Sole Bay battle. On 6 February 1715 the body of Sir Richard was brought from London and buried in his own vault in Leigh churchyard, near the east gate. His eldest son, also Richard Haddock, was Comptroller of the Navy from 1734 to 1749, while his youngest son, Nicholas (1685-1746), was notable as the first to board the Spanish galleons during the Battle of Vigo Bay in 1702. He became a captain in his early twenties and was made Commander in Chief at the Nore in 1733. Promoted to Admiral of the Blue in 1744, Nicholas saw much action in the Mediterranean. In appreciation of his services in the protection of trade in the Mediterranean, the Italian merchants in London presented him with a magnificent gold cup. Born in the little cottage at the foot of Billet Lane, Nicholas ended his days on a country estate, Wrotham Place in Kent.

Another member of the family, Captain William Haddock, commanded the *America* against the Dutch in 1653 and was awarded a gold medal by Cromwell for his services. When he retired from the Navy, he purchased some land in Leigh where he settled to live out his life, and was eventually buried in the vault at St Clement's on 17 November 1697.

Other notable naval families from Leigh include the Bonners, who flourished as a maritime family in Leigh for several generations. During the early 16th century they owned a tenement called Salt House with an adjacent dock and quay. A brass memorial, formerly in the church, shows that Mary Bonner of the town bore 11 sons and eight daughters. She died in 1580. The Bundock family were sailors, fishermen and boat builders in the town for generations, beginning with 'John Bundocke, maryner' who died in 1601 aged forty-two. The family owned Gilmans in 1642.

The first recorded member of the Hare family was Captain Thomas Hare, who died in 1572. Captain Steven Hare of Leigh was master of the ship *Mimion*, 1580-1, and master of the *Content*, 1587–8. The Hares continued in Leigh throughout the 17th century and were wealthy enough to own a home with 12 hearths, the largest house in Leigh in 1675 at the time when all hearths were subject to tax.

The Salmon family, concerned mainly with mercantile and maritime life, are first mentioned on an inscribed stone in St Clement's, dated 1472, in commemoration of Robert Salmon, and on a brass for Thomas 'Saman' and his grandson who died on the same day in 1576. There is a black stone on the floor of the north chapel and engraved on a brass plate, 'Here lyeth Robert Salmon who took to his

10 Sir Nicholas Haddock (1685-1746) earned his place in Leigh history as a successful mariner.

11 Monument for Robert Salmon from St Clement's Church.

13   Eden Lodge, originally a mariner's house, served as licensed inn, part of the Lazarus gin distillery, the home of church organist Henry Thompson and the residence of the wife of William Makepeace Thackeray. The name it is remembered by dates from the 1840s when it was owned by the Rev. Robert Eden.

12   Apart from the two cottages far right, which were added at a later date (*c.*1850), this building on Strand Wharf was originally one large mansion, lived in by mariner Richard Chester (d.1632). Some of the rooms were richly panelled in oak, with ornate door furniture. The buildings were all demolished in 1940.

wife Agnes with whom he lived thirty-two years, and had issue by her sixe sonnes and four daughters. Ob. 6 Sept 1591.' This Robert Salmon was Master of Trinity House in 1588. His son, again Robert Salmon and Master of Trinity House in 1617, is featured on a bust inside the church. He was married to Martha Andrews, sister of the Bishop of Winchester, and he died on 18 June 1641 aged seventy-four. One of his sons, also Robert Salmon, was Master of Trinity House in 1641, while another son, Peter, was educated at Eton and Cambridge and became a great 17th-century physician. Altogether the Salmon family lived in Leigh for 300 years.

Richard Chester is remembered as being Master of Trinity House in 1615, at which time he lived in a large weatherboarded house on Strand Wharf. He also owned the property at the foot of Leigh Hill that became known as Eden Lodge. He died in 1632 and is commemorated in St Clement's together with his wife, Elizabeth, four sons and one daughter.

The first mention of the Goodlad family was when 'John Goodlad of Lygh' contributed to a benevolent fund advanced by the inhabitants of the Rochford Hundred in 1523. The Goodlads were among those building ships for Elizabeth I, and Peter Goodlad was drowned off Greenland soon after the whale fishery commenced there in 1641. His relative, Captain William Goodlad, was Chief Commander of the Greenland fleet for 20 years and was serving as Master of Trinity House in 1638, the year that he died. Captain Richard Goodlad, a Brother of Trinity House, died in 1693.

Captain John Rodgers of HMS *Unicorn* distinguished himself by his 'magnanimous conduct' in the engagement with the Dutch in 1672, while Captain John Price was prominent in the navy in Queen Anne's day, and William Brand, also a son of Leigh, commanded the *Revenge* at Trafalgar.

BLACKE HOUSE

Blacke House, an imposing stone-fronted edifice set in four acres of land, was associated with the town's wealthy maritime families for many years. It was built facing east at the north-west corner of the churchyard in 1620 on land formerly belonging to the Hare family. An early owner of the house was Stephen Bonner, a mariner who died there in 1644 and willed the property to his wife. In 1671 Anthony Deane, a prominent naval architect and friend of Samuel Pepys, sold the house to Thomas Printupp, a mariner, for £200. Thomas Printupp and his third wife, Anne, are remembered by a stone they erected in the church in memory of four of their children, two of whom died in 1662 and two in 1667. Elizabeth Stevens sold the house at the end of the 17th century to her daughter Ann and grandson Samuel Whittaker, and it was renamed Leigh House during the 19th century.

THE END OF AN ERA

By the 17th century the shipbuilding industry in Leigh was in decline, mainly due to the silting up of the channel which rendered the port unable to handle the larger vessels. Fishing took over as the dominant industry and fishing smacks became a more common sight in Leigh Creek than warships.

14 Blacke House (later called Leigh House) had two storeys, an attic, a cellar and a north wing added around 1815. This photograph was taken *c*.1926.

Four

Beyond Leigh Village

Beyond Leigh Street woodland continued to dominate the north of the parish. As trees were gradually cleared, so farmsteads were established and expanded on the land above Leigh cliff. There were ten of them in upland Leigh, arranged neatly along the ridges of the north bank of the Thames and the two ridges of the Prittle Brook valley. They were Belfairs Farm, Gowles and Brickhouse Farm in the far north; Leigh Heath, Leigh Park, Lapwater Hall and Elm Farm on the main road between Southend and London, and Chapmanslord, Leigh Hall Farm and Oak Farm overlooking the Thames. The other early farmstead in Leigh was Leigh Marsh Farm, isolated in Leigh Creek. Belton Farm, sometimes called Ellis Farm, did not come into existence until the 19th century, although its name is associated with the family of John Belton who lived in the area in 1488.

Benton, writing in 1867, wrote that coming from Prittlewell the soil 'increases in tenacity towards Leigh', indicating some of the problems Leigh farmers may have found with their soil. It was common practice to fertilise it with copious amounts of seaweed, purchased from the fishermen, and with chalk. Daniel Defoe noted in 1722 that it had been common practice for many years for chalk from Gravesend to be 'fetch'd away by lighters and hoys and carried to all the creeks and ports in the opposite county of Essex … and sold there to country farmers to lay upon their land'.

The majority of the land was turned over to arable farming, with some cow pasture, and corn was grown in sufficient quantities to warrant its export from Strand Wharf to London, along with hay and straw. Timber was also a valuable commodity. More often than not, the farms were owned by absentee landlords and leased to tenant farmers.

BELFAIRS FARM

Belfairs is one of the handful of farmsteads known to date from before 1600. In fact, the earliest recorded date of Belfairs farm in the far north-west of the parish is 1234, when it was part of the holdings of Leigh manor. Sometimes written as Bell Fares or Belfry, the farm may derive its name from Alan Belenfent, employed by the Dean and Chapter of St Paul's to oversee management of its woodland in that area during the middle ages. Alternatively, it may come from the friars subsequently brought in to protect precious timber from thieves, ringing bells to warn of their presence; or even from a house just over the boundary in Eastwood, where a bell mounted on its roof was periodically rung to guide travellers through the woods. The farm comprised over 105 acres and remained in the possession of the lord of Leigh manor throughout its existence.

GOWLES

Also in the extreme north of the parish, Gowles, sometimes written as Gouls or Goulders, dates from 1504 when its fields were just clearings on the fringes of Wakering Wood. P.H. Reaney cites references to 'Bretonheth voc Gowles' in 1504 and to 'Goolles in auncyent tyme called Shoplondeleghe in Leigh' in 1506.

It belonged to Edmund Tyrrell in 1543 and was still in his possession in 1576. The farmhouse was passed by a bridleway – a 'grassy lane of unequal width' according to Benton – leading from Earls Hall in Prittlewell and joining up with Scrub Lane in Hadleigh. The original house burnt down in 1840 when it was in the possession of siblings Charles and Elizabeth Martyn. They sold the property, extending to some 130 acres, to Dr F.E.

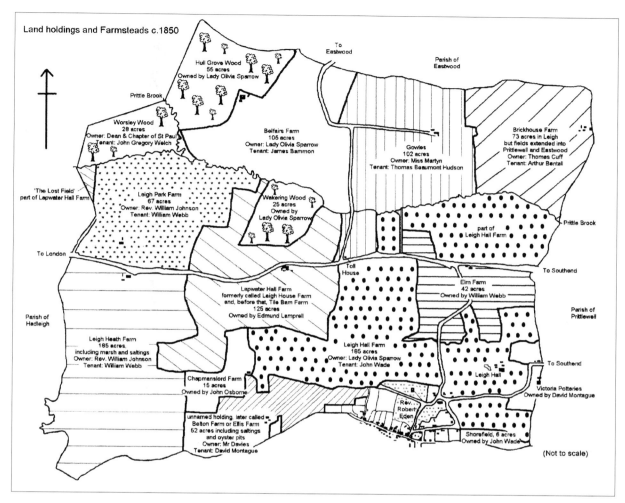

15 Although the owners and tenants named on this map of farmholdings show the situation in 1850, the boundaries of the properties remained relatively unchanged between 1600 and 1900.

Hicks of London in 1849, who built another house on the site in 1851. While the land was let to tenants, Dr Hicks used the residence as a holiday retreat for his family during the autumn months.

BRICKHOUSE FARM

Brickhouse Farm straddled the borders of Leigh, Prittlewell and Eastwood parishes, and had a notch carved in the kitchen mantelpiece where the boundary ran. It originally stretched to 158 acres, of which 73 were in Leigh. The soil was heavy for farming, but included some turnip land. The farm included a field of approximately one acre called

Bell Ropes which, in 1701, was sold to John Addison for £6. In 1712 he sold the field to William Hutton, the churchwarden of Leigh, for 20 shillings plus a weekly allowance.

The earliest known owners of the farm were somewhat unlucky. In 1722 Abraham Caillovel sold the farm to John Lane, who died four years later. It was willed to his nephew, Henry Lane, but Henry died before he was twenty-one and the farm came to his sister, Mary. When Mary herself died unmarried in 1772 the farm passed to her cousin, Arthur Holdsworth. Arthur Holdsworth's grandson sold the farm to Joseph Cuff in 1805 for £3,800 and

16 Brickhouse Farm was situated roughly on the site of the present fire station, facing east onto Eastwood Lane (now Mountdale Gardens). Eastwood Lane followed the route Mountdale Gardens – Westcliff High Schools private road – Eastwood Boulevard – Eastwood Lane South – Chalkwell Hall.

17 Side view of Brickhouse Farm. In 1914 Southend Council acquired 24 acres of Brickhouse land for an isolation hospital to treat tuberculosis. When the project was abandoned in 1931, six acres adjoining Manchester Drive became sports pitches, and an allotment site after the war. The remaining land became the Counties housing estate and Blenheim Park.

his son, Thomas Cuff Adams, eventually sold the farm to Arthur Bentall in 1866, by which time its lands had been extended to 546 acres, one of the largest farms in the area. Bentall purchased the Bell Ropes field for an additional £30, and that money was placed in the hands of the churchwardens for the repair of St Clement's bells. School playing fields in the area still bear Bentall's name.

LEIGH HEATH FARM

Another of the oldest farms in the parish was Leigh Heath Farm, recorded as Le Heth as early as 1534 (P.H. Reaney). This farm's fields, amounting to nearly 200 acres, were situated in the south-western corner of the parish, while its farmhouse was on the main road to Hadleigh, now the corner of London Road and Cottesmore Gardens.

The property included stables, barns and a path, Chaceway Lane, running the length of the property from the London Road due south to the marshes, and in 1556 it was owned by William Harrys,

together with a property called Triggs. The original farmhouse was replaced with a new building sometime during the 18th century, and in 1793 the farm was owned by John Webb, and later by the Johnson family. Reverend William Prior Johnson leased the farm to William Webb and later to Alfred Raynham Archer, a yeoman, for 14 years at an annual rent of £3,150. The property was kept intact and farmed up until the 1920s.

LEIGH PARK FARM

Leigh Park Farm, comprising 67 acres, was bounded by the main road to Hadleigh on the south and Prittle Brook on the north. It was mainly arable and pasture, with a small orchard. It was leased to William Carpenter for 21 years at an annual rent of £340 in 1619, and was owned by the Johnson family, along with Leigh Heath Farm, for about 100 years from the middle of the 18th century. These farms in the west of Leigh were more gravelly than others in the parish.

18 Eastwood Cottage, sometimes called 'Little Hill', dated from *c.*1650 and stood slightly north of Brickhouse Farm. The cottage burned down in the 1950s.

19 Leigh Heath Farm was situated on the London Road where Cottesmore Gardens now joins it. The house faced east.

20   Leigh Park Farm, *c.*1900. The farmhouse still exists as numbers 71 and 73 Olive Avenue.

LAPWATER HALL

Lapwater Hall was originally called Tile Barn Farm, and later Leigh Park House or Leigh House Farm, and comprised 125 acres. Its current name is said to have come about when Gilbert (or Gabriel) Craddock bought the red brick property in 1750 and employed local builders to renovate it. The workers were entitled to three pots of ale a day as

21   This sketch of Lapwater Hall by John Selby was taken from an old etching dating from the 1860s. The hall was a double-fronted house with a magnificent pillared front door embellished with an ornate knocker. A second wing was added in 1844 which included a ballroom.

part of their payment and when they requested more were told to 'lap water' from the pond.

Legend also says that Craddock was the alias of notorious highwayman Cutter Lynch, described in *Macmillan's Magazine*, June 1892, as 'Jerry Lynch, the high-toby gloak'. He rode a horse with no ears, fitting a pair of wax ones to disguise the animal and evade detection. It is said he arrived at Lapwater Hall late one night breathless and wounded by gunshot. When constables arrived at the door he escaped out the back entrance but staggered into the pond where he was found dead next morning.

In 1818, when the property was owned by Anthony Blackborne and occupied by John Spencer, several of its farm buildings fronting onto the main road were destroyed by fire. Plans were drawn up to replace the stables, barns, cowsheds and piggeries. The house later came into the possession of Edmund Lamprell, one of St Clement's churchwardens. He was a tenant for 21 years from 1841 and owner for 20 years.

ELM FARM

Elm Farm has been variously recorded as Adam's Elm, Allen's Elm and Ellen Elm, but since the end of the 19th century generally as Elm Farm. In 1777 Tobias Batty, a victualler, and his wife, Sarah,

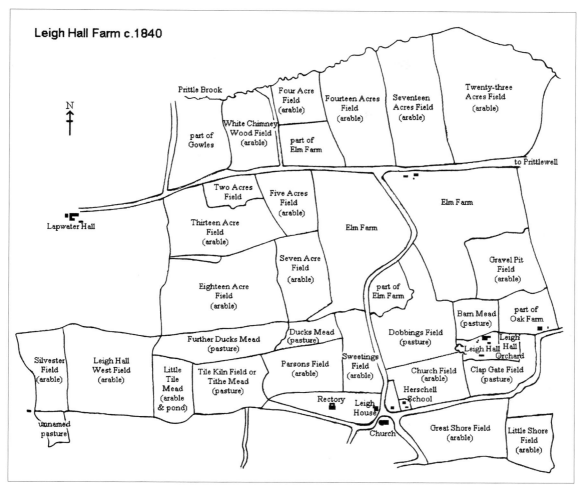

Leigh Hall Farm c.1840

22   Map showing the field names and boundaries of Leigh Hall Farm, *c.*1840.

surrendered 'Ellen Elme', which they were renting for 16 shillings a year, to Joseph Crook, a coach-maker. It was bought by William Webb in 1780 for £800 and was thought to be one of the best farms, consisting of good, useful mixed land with a farm-house called Swiss Cottage. When William died in 1793 the farm passed to his infant son, John, and in 1851 came to John's widow, Elizabeth.

In 1856 the 42-acre farm was put up for auction, and in 1861 Swiss Cottage was replaced with a new, brick-built farmhouse. In January 1881 James Thomas Smith, a wealthy coal merchant, purchased the farm for £2,100. He also purchased Leigh Hall Farm. The Elm ceased to be farmed in 1893.

The elm tree from which it took its name was just west of the farmhouse at the junction of Elm Road and the London Road; it was a massive specimen, believed to date from about 1600. By 1700 the tree measured some thirty feet around but was hollow at the centre, so that twelve men or seven cows could fit inside it at the same time. The tree eventually lost its branches to old age and finally disappeared altogether around 1830.

LEIGH HALL FARM

As with the other farms, Leigh Hall was rented out to tenants. An early tenant of the land was John Pope who came into dispute with other

23 View from Leigh Marsh. In 1806 a 34ft long whale was stranded on Leigh Marsh, and in 1826 another of 46ft was towed from Foulness to Leigh. A third whale was brought to Victoria Wharf in the 1880s, where it was examined by local physician Dr Murie and eventually buried on Leigh Marsh.

residents of Leigh over taking oysters laying on land belonging to Leigh Hall. In 1812 Lady Olivia Sparrow, the lady of the manor, leased the farm to David Harridge for a rent of £360 a year for eight years. The lease provided for Lady Olivia, her family and friends to hunt, shoot, fish, 'or otherwise sport upon' the premises during the tenure. Mr Harridge had to ensure that all the 'boxes, suckers and going gears' of the pump belonging to the house be kept in good repair and that all doors, window frames and other outside wood and ironwork be regularly painted with oil. The rules of good husbandry were to be followed: a quarter part of the arable land was to be planted with wheat or rye, a quarter with barley or oats, an eighth with clover or grass seed, an eighth with beans or peas, and the remaining quarter to lie fallow.

OAK FARM

William Harrys, owner of Leigh Heath Farm, also owned Oak Farm, which had a small Tudor farmhouse just north-east of Leigh Hall, on the Prittlewell border where Leigham Court Drive is now. This farm included woodland and pasture, and should not be confused with Burnt Oak Farm, located at the top of Highcliff Drive in the parish of Prittlewell. The original house dated from the Elizabethan period and a plaque dated 1774 recorded the date of renovations. Oak Farm does not appear on maps or in records after 1850; its lands were most probably swallowed up by the neighbouring Leigh Hall and Burnt Oak farms.

CHAPMANSLORD

Chapmanslord was a small farm of 16 acres on the crest of the hill half a mile west of Leigh. Its name arises from the combination of eight acres of land, which had belonged to a merchant, Andrew Chapman, in 1506, with an adjoining three acres of land and a garden belonging to Mr Lord. The deeds of the farm itself go back to 1718 when the Rev. Clement Hobson of Kent and Edward Butler of Surrey were joint owners. It later came into the possession of William Reynolds, an oyster dredger who died in 1755 and bequeathed £5 to the poor of Leigh, £100 to William Carr of Hawkwell and three guineas to William Johnson of Leigh to buy a mourning ring. The farm itself went to Reynolds' cousin, William Norris.

William Norris sold the farm to David Harridge in August 1761, and it was occupied first by widow Elizabeth Harridge and, in 1778, by David's son, Thomas, a merchant.

It was sold to John Osborne in 1801 and is listed on the 1851 census as Leigh Hill Farm. It remained in the Osborne family until the late 1870s when the house was known as Sylvester's Hole and was primarily accessed from Chess Lane. The farm survived until the beginning of the 20th century when it was sold off for housing development.

LEIGH MARSH FARM

In the 16th century the island that is known today as Leigh Marsh was divided into Haughness Marsh, belonging to Hadleigh manor, and Axfleet Marsh, which belonged to Leigh manor. Situated in Leigh Creek, it was the only farm in the parish where dairy farming dominated and where a large proportion of the farm's produce was from fishing.

In 1613 Axfleet Marsh, some 200 acres, belonged to Thomas Malby of Chalkwell. In 1649 Thomas Malby junior sold the marsh to Lambert Pitcher and John Lagram. They sold it on to Peter Barratt, who sold it to John Stephens. John Stephens was responsible for much of the sea wall around the marsh, and after his period of tenure it is described as comprising 50 acres within the walls and 50 acres of saltings outside the walls. Charles Mason purchased Axfleet Marsh in 1719 and added Haughness Marsh in 1729, forming Leigh Marsh into a single property.

Around 1760, two elm trees were either deliberately planted or self-seeded on Leigh Marsh,

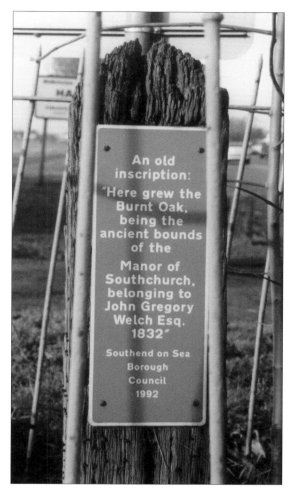

24 The Welch family burnt oak boundary marker. The Welch's woodland ran north from this point, west of the Leigh border, but included woodland in the parish of Leigh north of Leigh Park Farm.

leading to its subsequent name of Two Tree Island. One of the trees fell in 1958, and the second soon afterwards. They had formed a distinctive landmark, there being no other trees or shrubs within a considerable distance.

In the early 1800s the farm was occupied by Thomas Beaumont, and 50 years later was owned and farmed by Stephen Allen as four fields of pasture. There was no farmhouse on the marsh itself, and the farmers lived in Leigh Street. In 1873 it was conveyed to Arthur Bentall for £6,760 and by 1892 was owned by William Foster.

WOODLAND

While the majority of the parish was thus divided between private landowners, the woodland stretching from the north-west corner south to Leigh Heath Farm had been owned by the Dean and Chapter of St Paul's Cathedral since at least 1536. In that year a survey of monkish assets prepared for Henry VIII showed that 80 acres of woodland stretching from Thundersley to Leigh, and including Leigh woodlands Horsley Wood, Hull Grove and Wakering Wood, was owned by the church and was valued at £4.

George Asser of Barling leased the woods in 1695 for a period of 21 years, after which the lease was repeatedly renewed at an annual rent of £25, and the group of woods was handed down through his family, often through the female line as part of a marriage settlement. The family held the title of lord of the manor of Southchurch, so this area of Leigh was accepted as being part of Southchurch Manor. The Dean and Chapter of St Paul's reserved for their own use 'the trees of Oak Ash and Elm which at the time of last felling were of or above 20 years growth, to grow for Timber-Trees'. They also stipulated that 12 young trees were to be left to grow during the term of the lease. This ensured a supply of timber for St Paul's Cathedral. No part of the underwood was to be of more than 15 years' growth, or converted into tillage or any other use without a licence.

When George Asser died his woodland, which straddled the border of Leigh and Hadleigh, passed to his son-in-law, John Davies of Navestock, who later became Reverend John Davies of Southchurch. In 1746 it came to his daughter's husband, Thomas Drew of London, and, in 1795, to his daughter's husband, Thomas White of Cheltenham. In 1797 Thomas White's 18-year-old daughter, Frances Asser White, married John Gregory Welch of Cheltenham, and in turn brought the Leigh woodlands to the marriage, along with properties in Southchurch, Shoebury, Paglesham, Barling, Wakering, Stambridge, Foulness, Rayleigh and Hadleigh. John Gregory Welch erected a plaque on a burnt oak marking the extent of his tenure. Welch and Frances produced 12 offspring and the properties were divided into several parts in marriage settlements for the children. The Leigh woodlands passed to eldest son George Asser White Welch, who lived at Hadleigh House at Victoria House Corner, Hadleigh, and a Richard Hall was appointed as his trustee.

In 1872 the Ecclesiastical Commissioners for England took over the woodland from the Dean and Chapter of St Paul's by virtue of an Act of Parliament, and in 1876 George Asser White Welch and Richard Hall surrendered the leasehold interest to the new owners, ending the family's 180-year tenure.

Five

Poverty and the 18th Century

From the Earls of Warwick, descendants of Richard Lord Rich, Leigh Manor passed down to Henry St John, Henry Viscount Bolingbroke, Francis St John and then his son, also Francis St John.

The high profile of Leigh as a port during the 16th and 17th centuries had encouraged growth in population and the build-up of support industries in the town, for example blacksmiths, wheelwrights and cobblers. However, gradual silting up meant that by the 18th century Leigh Creek could no longer accommodate larger vessels, leading to a sharp decline in the shipbuilding industry and merchant shipping. The associated loss of money coming into the town meant that growth could not be sustained. Founder of Methodism John Wesley summed up the situation on his first visit to Leigh in 1748, when he noted in his diary, 'Here was once a deep open harbour; but the sands have long since blocked it up, and reduced a once flourishing town to a small ruinous village.'

The silting up of Leigh Creek was related to the loss of land from the coast of Chalkwell, east of Leigh. Philip Benton estimated that throughout the 18th century, and into the 19th century, over two yards of land was washed away annually from the cliff, which was about twenty-one feet high. Thus, seven to eight thousand tons of soil was lost to the sea each year. During the early 19th century the footpath and stile connecting Leigh and Chalkwell was completely destroyed on three occasions, entailing the loss of some twelve acres of land.

THE DECLINE OF LEIGH

After Leigh lost its attraction for wealthy merchants and prosperous naval officers the large Tudor houses built two or more centuries earlier were too expensive for the ordinary fishermen to maintain. Some properties lent themselves to use as inns, while others were divided into two or more tenements.

Eden Lodge, for example, sited at the foot of Leigh Hill, became licensed as an inn under several successive names: the *Queens Head*, the *Angel*, and the *Kings Head*, before becoming a gin distillery during the 19th century. Similarly, a manor house close by, formerly owned by Thomas Stephens, opened as the *Ship Inn*, with a licence transferred from an earlier public house, the *George Inn*. When the Haddock family home was sold in 1707 it became a beerhouse known as the *Old Billet*. Gilmans, meanwhile, became divided into three or four tenements. When it was demolished, the licence from the *Old Billet* was transferred to the *Cole Hole*, built *c*.1860 on the Gilmans site.

Numerous public houses catered for the population, and were particularly well used at times when it was too stormy for fishing. Consequently, the town became notorious for the drunkenness and coarseness of its fishermen. Again, it is John Wesley who paints a vivid picture of the destitution of much of the population. In October 1756 he wrote in his diary, 'Where we dined, a poor woman came to the door with two little children; they seemed half starved as well as their mother, who was also shivering with an ague [fever]. She was extremely thankful for a little food …'

In 1773 Richard Chester's former house on Strand Wharf was let to the overseers of the poor for use as the parish workhouse. However, by 1790 it had been divided into three tenements. Soon afterwards, a cottage in Billet Lane became the workhouse and the lane was known colloquially as 'Workhouse Lane'.

The decline in the town was putting strain on the administrators of the rating system, and the loss

25   The *Crooked Billet* with the *Cole Hole* beyond it. The *Cole Hole* was built by William Foster around 1860 on the site of Gilmans. When it lost its licence in the early 1900s it became an engineer's workshop.

of wealthy inhabitants came to the attention of magistrates at Chelmsford as early as 1651. A petition was set before the magistrates indicating that '… the chief inhabitants of the town many of them being dead and others being removed thence, the said Towne is much decayed in its ability, soe that the Strand Key in the said Towne, which is a usuall place for landinge of vessells, is fallen into greate ruine for want of reparacions'.

The court ordered the local constables, Thomas Drake and Robert Sawyer, to levy a charge equally on all inhabitants to pay for the repair of the quay, where commonly landed goods included cherries, mackerel, brandy, cauliflowers, hay, cloves, malt, sprats and herrings. But the following Quarter Sessions heard that only part of the tax had been collected and found that '… several complaints have been made unto this Court

toucheing the neglects of the Inhabitants of Towne of Leigh in payeing the moneys rated upon them towards the repaire of the Strand key there', and that £23 11s. was still outstanding.

Several inhabitants appeared at court and complained that 'the word Towne in the said former orders mentioned should not extend to the Inhabitants of uplands of Leigh'. However, the court found that these inhabitants should be included in the rate and ordered the moneys in arrears to be speedily collected by the constables.

A similar situation occurred in 1661 when a complaint was made to the court by William Willis and John Alburrowe, constables of Leigh, that some inhabitants of the parish refused to pay towards the rate laid out for the repair of bridges, maimed soldiers and charitable uses. Those refusing or neglecting to pay were be sent for and bound over to answer their

26   Billet Lane was once a major thoroughfare, joining Leigh Street between the *Crooked Billet* and the *Cole Hole*. The first roof seen here on the left of the lane is that of the workhouse.

contempt at the next Sessions. Eventually, the collection of a rate from the parishioners for the repair and upkeep of the Strand Wharf died out with the continued difficulty in collection and the fact that amounts received were too small to be worth the administration costs.

Tax collector Eustace Seymor and local constable Richard Kinge encountered difficulty in collecting

Hearth Tax duty from Leigh residents in 1669 when widow Elizabeth Motley not only refused to pay the money but threatened to kill the officers. She was supported by a mob of townspeople, using threatening language against the officers, who eventually left empty-handed.

Many of the problems Leigh encountered over the collection of road taxes were resolved by an

27   Turnpike Cottage stood at the junction of London Road and Turner's Lane (now Eastwood Road). When turnpike trusts were abolished in 1860 it was used as a private residence until 1923, when it was demolished. Around 1900 the Barwell family sold refreshments here, and it was last inhabited by the Nay family, descendants of whom still live in Leigh.

Act of Parliament in 1747, which authorised the Essex Turnpike Trust to implement turnpike arrangements on the main route from Leigh, through Hadleigh and Rayleigh to Shenfield. Tolls were collected at Turner's Corner, with gates across both London Road and Turner's Lane (now Eastwood Road). Turnpike Trusts were abolished in the 1860s and Leigh's turnpike cottage became a private residence.

OYSTER FISHING

The outlook was more promising for the fishermen than for those whose livelihoods had depended on building warships. A Mr Outing threw some tiny oysters out of his boat onto the marsh one day in about 1680. Returning to the same spot some months later, he noticed how the oysters

had grown. Thus, almost by accident, the practice of cultivating oysters along the Leigh marshes began; Mr Outing made his fortune and oysters, mussels and winkles became the staple catch of the Leigh fishermen throughout the 17th and early 18th centuries. It became the practice to collect jelly-like oyster spawn from Jersey or Cancalle Bay in France and bring it back to grow to maturity in the favourable conditions of Leigh Marsh for some seven to eight months.

These 'artificial layings' supplemented the few natural oyster breeding grounds on the Leigh and Hadleigh marshes. Dr Murie, writing in the 19th century, noted that many years before his time 'several old Leigh men managed to eke out a living by picking up, at times, four or five pecks of very saleable native oysters, from small self-reared brood, the whereabouts of which only the men themselves knew'.

Jealousy of the Leigh men's success with oyster layings arose across the river and, in September 1724, Kent fishermen organised a raid of the Leigh oyster beds. A fleet of a hundred smacks from the Kent coast sailed onto Leigh marshes and, with flags flying and guns firing, succeeded in carrying off some 1,000 bushels of oysters. When the case eventually came to court at the Spring Assizes, held at Brentwood, the Kent men claimed the oysters were lying in common waters. However, Lord Chief Baron Gilbert ruled in favour of Leigh, with the Kent men being ordered to pay over £2,000 compensation. By this time the oyster beds had become valuable property and, in 1773, 800 acres of foreshore was being leased for £6,000 a year.

The fishing boats would leave on the early morning tide and anchor at Maplin Sands at the mouth of the Thames estuary, where the men would rake winkles from the sands by hand for four hours until the tide returned. The gradual decline of winkle and oyster fishing was partly due to increased pollution in Leigh Creek. The little peter boats were gradually superseded in the late 17th century by larger pink sterns, with boomless mainsails. These were clinker built and varied in size between two and four tons.

SMUGGLING

Smuggling was a convenient means of making a few extra pounds and, brought about by need rather than greed, was rife in Leigh during the 18th century. However, this was not the stuff of romantic adventures. Smuggling was a serious crime in times when the Crown needed every penny of customs tax to support its armed forces, and was punishable by transportation or even hanging. More often than not it involved hard, dirty work in cold, wet, uncomfortable conditions and capture would lead at least to the confiscation of your boat and thus your means of supporting your family. As fishing was itself an extremely dangerous occupation with a high mortality rate, risking their lives was nothing new for the men of Leigh, and the rewards of a successful smuggling run were high.

When the *Peter Boat* inn was accidentally burnt down in 1892, a secret room with direct access to the waterfront was found in the basement, with evidence of its being used to hide smugglers' contraband. The wooden cottages adjacent to the inn were also victims of the fire and were found to have inter-connecting attics, used for transferring illicit goods between houses to outwit customs officers. From hiding places such as these, contraband would have been carried up the hill and passed on to the highwaymen, gypsies and vagabonds who inhabited the common land of Eastwood and Daws Heath.

In addition, Leigh fishermen could supplement their incomes by 'wrecking'. With thousands of tons of goods passing by in sailing ships, boats and barges on their way to London, opportunities were abundant. Leigh boats would moor at the mouth of the Thames with a lamp alight in their topmasts to lure merchant ships onto the sands. The fishermen could then secure payment for pulling them off again, and also benefit from collecting goods that had been thrown overboard to lighten the ship.

Excise duty had been introduced during the English Civil War to offset the financial cost of conducting it. A wide range of items was subject to this tax and an additional Revenue Tax payable for exports. The first customs officer was appointed at Leigh in 1565 and a customs house built at the head of Strand Wharf in 1738. Here, the officer would supervise the loading and unloading of goods at the wharf, to see that the appropriate duty was paid, and was kept busy in the receipt and storage of seized cargoes of smuggled goods. By 1760 a list of 800 goods on which customs duty was payable had been drawn up and over the subsequent fifty years another 1,300 items were added to the list.

As smuggled goods were sold at significantly lower prices than their legal counterparts, the wealthier inhabitants often connived at the illicit trade. Legend says that George Walter, son of the rector Edward Walter (1808-37), went as far as to become personally involved in local smuggling escapades. Small boats could hide amongst the local oyster dredgers, making covert transfers of contraband almost under the noses of the customs officials. However, successful confiscations by Leigh customs officer Thomas Lee in 1764 included French lace, brocade, silks, cambrics and lawns,

28 This view of the Old Town front demonstrates how the houses abutted the river, allowing smuggled goods to be transferred quickly from ship to land. A.E. Copping recorded that the coastguards' office was 'ominously hung with guns, bayonets, pistols and other facilities for sudden human slaughter'.

leather gloves, silk stockings, pearl beads, crystal stones and watch chains.

In 1768 a smugglers' sloop was stopped off Maldon and sailed around to Leigh where its haul of gin, brandy and tea was taken into the customs house and the boat was burnt as a warning to other aspiring smugglers. A sale of contraband seized from smugglers in 1781 included 680 gallons of gin, 82 of brandy, 47 of rum, 275 quarters of port, 28 of Lisbon, 120 of claret, 33 yards of calico and 'much foreign china'. A sloop and small sailing boat were sold at the same time.

John Loten, the collector of customs in Leigh in 1786, wrote that he knew of ten local vessels employed in illicit traffic between Leigh and

Paglesham. Implicated in the trade were two related families: the Dowsetts of Leigh and the Blyths of Paglesham. John Dowsett was the master of the *Big Jane*, working out of Leigh in a legitimate business carrying cargoes to the continent. *Big Jane* was well armed with at least half a dozen six-pounder brass cannon and customs officers were justified in their suspicions when, on 31 May 1780, the boat was captured by two customs cutters 'after a chase of 11 hours and a smart firing on both sides, in which the lugger (*Big Jane*) had three men wounded and her hull and sails damaged'. The boat was found to be carrying 23 cwt of tea and 252 half ankers (one anker being about eight gallons) of Geneva, brandy and rum. However, the smugglers escaped by taking

29 The white building just left of centre is Pittington House. When the *Diamond* ran aground on Chapman Sands, in 1804, six Leigh boat owners were paid £12 each for helping to re-float her.

to their small boats and rowing across the sandbanks where a cutter could not follow.

The *Leigh Review* of 1783, quoting the Maldon customs officer, indicated the determination of smugglers, referring to them as 'desperate fellows' and noting the increasing practice of working with a larger crew in their cutters than the customs officers dare attack. Customs officers wrote to the Board on 29 January 1792 expressing concern as to the increase in the size and force of smugglers' vessels as well as the number of men and guns: '… in defiance of all law they have the audacity not only to carry on their illicit designs in sight of the revenue cruisers but when they have approached within a certain distance they have actually fired into and threatened to sink them'. In consequence, continued the letter, mariners employed to assist the customs officials have refused to tackle the smugglers, alleging that no provisions were made towards their support if injuries were sustained. An example of compensation at the time was £10 for the loss of a hand or foot and the surgeon's bills paid.

Even into the 19th century, Leigh customs officer J. Baxter declared that he had made seizures every day in July of 1802. Goods confiscated and later sold by customs officials included brandy, rum, sherry, wine, tobacco, tea, coffee, lace and silk.

On more than one occasion, indemnities were offered to smugglers for surrendering and volunteering for the Navy for three years. However, when the war with France ended at Waterloo in 1815, naval ships and men became available to reinforce the customs service and a significant

30   The Methodist Society Class of 1902, taken in New Road as a present for the class leader, Edward Collins.

reduction in smuggling was seen. In that year a new brick-built customs house was erected on the site of the original. However, this was taken over by the railway company in 1856, after which customs officers worked out of the coastguard station at the east end of town.

Leigh was made a coastguard station in 1840 and coastguards joined the front line in the struggle against the smuggling trade, up to six men working from the weatherboarded two-storey coastguard station on Leigh's eastern foreshore. Unlike the majority of Leigh's inhabitants, who had been resident in the town for many generations, coast-guards and customs officers were employed from distant parts of the country to avoid collusion with the indigenous population.

One of the last recorded cases of smuggling in Leigh occurred in 1849, when Charles Cotgrove was in Chelmsford county gaol after wine, spirits and cigars had been found on the *Spray*, a boat he

was in charge of. The owner of the *Spray*, Mr Martin, said the goods had been picked up at sea, 'probably floated out of a wreck', and that it was seized before they had time to declare it. The *Spray* and Mr Martin were released on payment of £250, but Cotgrove was not released – possibly as he had threatened to throw the coastguard overboard.

Despite the decrease in smuggling, customs officials continued to be busy. A letter dated 6 January 1872 from the customs officer at Maldon to the committee of the Privy Council for Trade complained that Leigh fishermen were plundering coal from vessels in the Thames:

> Leigh offers peculiar facilities for such practices. These fishermen come crowding in from the sea on the tide so that the Coast Guard boat cannot board half of them. They moor their vessels at their back doors and as there is no patrol in that locality they may safely discharge into their own houses any plunder or contraband they many possess. ... the remedy for this evil lies with the

31 John Cook's memoirs record that his house was near the Conduit House, whereas this house, known as Cook's Place, was immediately east of the customs house. It is therefore uncertain whether this was actually his home. It had been divided into three tenements and was used as a tearoom by the time it was demolished in 1939.

Coast Guard who to afford the necessary protection should keep a patrol night and day on that part of Leigh occupied by the fishermen ...

Leigh's coastguard station was demolished in 1854. The 1815 customs house building survives as a private residence.

METHODISM

The vibrant Methodist community in Leigh has its roots in the 18th century when John Wesley, founder of the Methodist Church, visited the town. By chance, Leigh fishermen moored at Southampton one night in 1748 had come across John Wesley preaching in the town and persuaded him to visit Leigh. The great man subsequently visited Leigh on at least six occasions between 1748 and 1756, which he recorded in his diary. The townsfolk were impressed by Wesley's teachings

to such an extent that a Methodist society was formed and, in 1811, a chapel was built at the bottom of Billet Lane at the western end of the village. This first chapel was demolished in 1874 by the railway company, and a replacement built in New Road in 1879. This in turn was replaced in 1932 after vibrations from the railway had made the building unstable.

STAGE-COACHES

In the summer of 1791 the London Stage Coach Company began a service departing every Monday, Wednesday and Friday from the *White Horse* in Southchurch via Leigh to the *Blue Boar* at Aldgate, London, and returning every Tuesday, Thursday and Saturday. The journey took some eight hours and a single fare cost around £1, compared with two shillings and sixpence for a hoy covering the

32 John Cook inherited Folly Farm (part of Prittlewell parish until 1913) from his father-in-law and bequeathed it to his daughter, Margaret. The farmhouse, standing between Sandleigh Avenue and Fernleigh Drive, was purchased by Harold George Howard around 1910 and run as a dairy and later a milk float depot. The site was developed for housing in the 1990s.

same distance on the Thames. The *Carlton Hotel* in Leigh Broadway, at one time called the *Kings Head*, was used as a stable and a staging post for the coaches. It received a liquor licence in 1896 and its stables were later of use to the local fire brigade.

THE MOYER FAMILY

Several generations of the Moyer family were benefactors of the parish, the earliest of whom was James Moyer, who bequeathed '£50 to the poor of Lee' and is buried in St Clement's churchyard. Captain Lawrence Moyer of Milton-Shore, Prittlewell, son of James, gave £100 to pay £5 a year for ever to the town of Leigh. His generosity was in commemoration of his deliverance from a shipwreck in 'Leigh Road' [Leigh Creek], his ship being driven onto the sands. The money was to go

to 20 poor seamen's widows, all apart from 20 shillings which was to pay for a sermon to be preached on 6 August each year.

Sir Samuel Moyer erected a free school at the foot of Leigh Hill for instructing children in the principles of Christian religion. When he died, in 1716, he left £20 to the poor of Leigh to be distributed as directed by his wife, and records from 1723 show that Lady Rebecca Moyer was paying £20 annually towards Leigh Charity School. Samuel saw that his father's legacy was honoured and for several years after his death £1 1s. was paid to the minister for the preaching of a sermon, five shillings was paid to the parish clerk for his attendance and the remainder of the £20 was distributed among the poor by the churchwardens. The beneficiaries received between five and seven shillings each, depending on their age. The payments eventually lapsed, were revived for a while by John Cook, but lapsed again after a few years.

DR JOHN COOK

During the 18th century Leigh benefited from the presence of surgeon Dr John Cook and, subsequently, his son, also Dr John Cook, a public-spirited and respected member of the community who acted as local physician for 26 years. The Cook family originally hailed from Pittenween, Scotland, but John jnr was born in Leigh in 1704. At the age of nine he was sent away (by 'his cruel father' so his memoirs say) to Scotland to be educated, eventually taking his degree at Edinburgh University. The family were of considerable means and when John's beloved mother, Elizabeth, died on 1 January 1718, aged 30, she was buried in linen, for which privilege a fine of 50 shillings was given to the poor of Leigh. This was in accordance with the statute then in force for burying in woollen cloth.

Dr Cook jnr returned to Leigh to take over the practice on his father's death in 1726. His first wife, Susannah Heber of Hadleigh, died in childbirth in 1728 and Cook subsequently married Elizabeth, daughter of Lemuel Bradley of London. Elizabeth bore her husband many children, most of whom died young. Their eldest surviving son, John, became a rector, another son, George, was a surgeon in Prittlewell, while a third son, Lemuel, became the next surgeon of Leigh but had no children of his own.

Although a religious Christian, Dr Cook believed in the supernatural and ghostly visitations. He collected books on necromancy and astrology, and regularly contributed to national publications such as the *Gentlemen's Magazine*. His articles included advice on making brandy from potatoes and another expounding the theory that the left eye sees objects larger than the right eye. His house was a large wooden-framed building, one of the tallest in the town and adjacent to the cottage in which he was born. It was here that John Wesley is thought to have stayed on his visits to Leigh. Dr Cook died on 13 June 1777.

Six

Changing the Town Plan

Samuel Prout, a traveller through Essex in 1804, dismissed the town of Leigh in his journal as 'Small and very dirty. Principally inhabited by fishermen'. However, the 19th century saw enormous changes in the town. The population rose from 570 in 1801 to 2,667 by 1901, making Leigh the third largest town in the Rochford Hundred. The shrimping industry took over from the oyster trade, the parish priest and lady of the manor brought about great improvements in sanitation and education, and the railway line cutting through the Old Town sparked the end of the old way of life for people throughout the parish.

LADY OLIVIA SPARROW

During the 18th century the manorial rights had passed through Francis St John's daughter, Mary, to his grandson Sir Robert Bernard (d.1789). Sir Robert Bernard's daughter married Robert Sparrow of Worlingham in Suffolk. When their son, Robert, came into the estates in 1803 he adopted the name of Bernard in honour of his maternal grandfather, becoming Robert Bernard Sparrow. Two years after assuming the lordship of Leigh manor, Robert Bernard Sparrow, by now a brigadier-general, died of a fever while returning to England by ship, aged only 33. He was buried on the island of Tobago and his estates, though entailed to his male descendants, passed to his widow, Olivia, for her lifetime.

The Rt Hon. Lady Olivia Acheson was the eldest daughter of Arthur, 2nd Viscount and 1st Earl of Gosford. She married General Robert Sparrow of Worlingham, Suffolk in 1797 at the age of 22 and was widowed eight years later. Lady Olivia Bernard Sparrow, by all accounts, was a woman of strong convictions who took her responsibilities as lady of

the manor very seriously. She preferred a low church service and apparently fell out and would not worship with the Rev. Robert Eden at the traditionally high church of St Clement's.

Although concerned with the education, health and religious well-being of the people of Leigh and Hadleigh, where she was also lady of the manor, Lady Olivia does not appear on the local census returns. As Leigh Hall was let to a tenant farmer, and Lady Olivia had close connections with Suffolk where she was born and buried, it is impossible to say how much time she actually spent here. However, she was a keen sportswoman who spent time riding and hunting on her Leigh lands. She retained the right to hunt, shoot and fish on Leigh Hall land and, rather than rent out Hull Grove Wood, employed a gamekeeper, Daniel Scratton, to manage it for her. The stables used today by Belfairs Riding School were built by Lady Olivia for her own use. She proved herself a kind and philanthropic landlord until her death in 1863.

WATER SUPPLY

The water supply to the residents of Leigh Street, from the conduit leading down from the spring in Tile Kiln Meadow, was often impeded by weed and debris collecting in the pipework and needed regular maintenance. This, together with a diminished water flow during dry years, resulted in the supply proving inadequate for the growing population. A committee was set up in 1825 and a subscription collected from the parishioners specifically for the maintenance of the conduit. A brick shelter was built around the reservoir in Leigh Street with gates that could be locked by the committee to enable rationing of the water when it was in short supply.

The pipework was repaired in February 1826, and the original lead pipes were replaced with glazed pipes manufactured at the new Phoenix Pottery (later called Victoria Pottery). After the repairs, the water was measured to be flowing at a rate of two gallons per minute. The supply still proving inadequate, a petition was presented to Lady Olivia Sparrow in 1832. Lady Olivia granted the parishioners a piece of ground 14 feet square in the middle of Strand Wharf and Samuel Purkis of Baddow was hired to sink a well. The well was bored to a depth of 25 feet, the total depth from the surface being 284 feet, and the day water was obtained was declared a day of thanksgiving. An iron pump was set up over the well and the north side of its case inscribed with the details of Lady Olivia's gift of the land. On the west face were the names of the committee entrusted with the management of the well, and on the south side was inscribed: 'He clave the hard rocks in the wilderness. He brought waters out of the stoney rock so that it gushed out like the rivers. Psalm lxxvi 16 & 17 verses'.

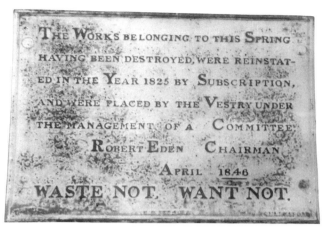

33 Inscription placed above the Conduit House by the Rev. Robert Eden.

34 Lady Olivia's well at the head of Bell Wharf was in daily use until the 1920s, when the drainage and sewerage system was completely overhauled. The cottages on Victoria Wharf in the background of this picture were pulled down in the 1920s.

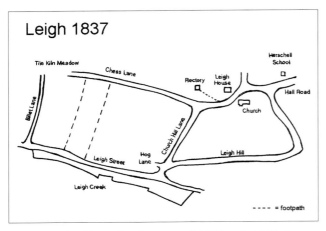

35 These sketch maps of 1837 and 1847 show how Church Hill Lane and Chess Lane were replaced by Church Hill and Rectory Grove. In 1841 half the population was under 16 years of age, 125 men were fishermen, 53 were agricultural labourers, and among the 112 other working men there were sailmakers, victuallers, pottery workers, plumbers, carpenters and bakers.

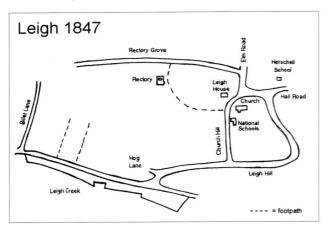

The population continued to increase, and by 1836 the water supply was once again insufficient to meet their needs. Lady Olivia then granted another 14 square feet of ground at the head of Kings Strand (now called Bell Wharf), and another well was bored by Samuel Purkis. The total depth from the surface of this well was 249 feet, including 24 feet dug and bricked. A pump was set up over this second well, within a brick enclosure, and as before, an iron plate recorded Lady Olivia's gift. The two wells were given to the inhabitants subject to a quit-rent of one shilling each per year, with

the churchwardens and overseer of the poor becoming trustees.

Despite the initial enthusiasm, the conduit and wells fell into a state of disrepair and, again, water supplies ran low, particularly in years of drought. The committee devised a system of locking the wells and conduit house at stated hours, and sometimes imposed a charge of one farthing per load of three gallons of water as a means of meeting the repair expenses. Poorer people were allowed to pay less, but the scheme led to litigation, dispute, opposition, dissatisfaction and frequent brawls.

Two inhabitants applied to the County Court and the case against the system was heard at Rochford on 10 February 1858. Consequently a new system of management was agreed whereby the wells and conduit were amalgamated into a single charity. The water committee was discharged and the trustees of Lady Olivia's wells were removed from office. The rector, churchwardens, overseers and four resident inhabitants, rated for at least £10 a year, were constituted trustees. These trustees were given the power of raising sums necessary for the repair of the works and the administration expenses by the sale of water.

Surveys of the water were taken in 1871 by the Rivers Commission Laboratory and analysis showed that water from both wells and the conduit contained certain quantities of sewage contamination. Water from a spring east of the churchyard, which had been supplying both the Lazarus Distillery at Eden Lodge and the newly built National Schools, was declared unfit for domestic use.

THE HERSCHELL SCHOOL
Education was another priority for Lady Olivia, and in December 1834 she opened a school for poor children in Hall Road (now The Broadway), just north-east of the church. She invited the Rev. Ridley Herschell to become the master there, and he was so successful that it became known as the Herschell School, and his residence on Leigh Hill as Herschell House.

Ridley Haim Herschell was born in Poland in 1807 to Jewish parents. He converted to Christianity and was baptised at the age of 23. A zealous missionary, he did not confine himself to the school but took it upon himself to preach to the poor, despite being warned by the rector, Edward Newton Walter, that it was dangerous to go down into the town because of the 'untoward character' of the population. However, Herschell was not deterred and on his first excursion to Leigh Street preached to a congregation of 30, most of whom probably turned up out of curiosity. By the time Herschell left Leigh, less than 18 months later, he was attracting congregations of about 500 people, and 700 people gave one penny each towards a Bible and Prayer Book as a farewell gift. When Reverend Herschell died in Brighton on 14 April 1864, aged 57, 300 people attended his funeral. The school continued under the supervision of Mrs Ridley Herschell.

REVEREND ROBERT EDEN

In 1830 the parish was still dominated by Leigh Street, with Leigh Hill (colloquially called 'Horse Hill') still the only roadway to and from the river. However, four footpaths led from Leigh Street up the hill to Chess Lane (previously called Churche Lane), which was the main path running west from the church. These paths were the main pedestrian routes up the hill. This situation was changed deliberately by the new rector, the Rev. Robert Eden, in 1838 when he decided to improve his residence, the rectory.

Born in 1804, the son of a baronet, Robert Eden came into the Leigh living in 1837. He had inherited a considerable sum of money from a member of his previous parish, Messing, and purchased several properties and fields in south Leigh. Before 1838 the rectory was a white brick structure built in the 1790s by a previous incumbent, the Rev. John Davey Hodge. It was weatherboarded at the back and ends and had a single tiled roof with gabled ends. It stood slightly east of the new rectory and faced south. Designed to accommodate his household, which included a governess for his five children, a footman, coachman, cook, housemaid, lady's maid, nurse and kitchen maid, the new rectory was built of red brick with three storeys plus a cellar and an impressive porch facing east towards the church.

While building the rectory, the Rev. Eden purchased land called Sweetings on the north of the property, increasing the glebe to some six acres.

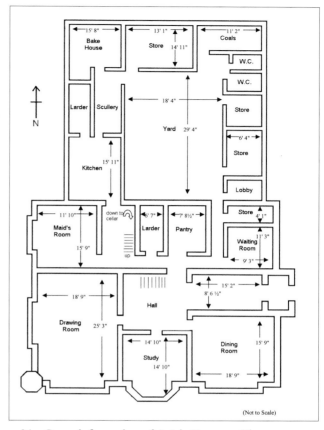

36 Ground floor plan of Leigh Rectory. There were five large bedrooms on the first floor and a further four on the second floor for the servants, but only one bathroom.

The glebe meadow lying between the rectory and Billet Lane was subsequently the venue for many Sunday School picnics and May fairs. Immediately north of the main house were the domestic offices, kitchens and kitchen gardens.

Eden's plan included incorporating Chess Lane into his land, giving him private access between the church and rectory. To replace the right of way, he laid out Rectory Grove on the northern boundary of his property but included a high fence, ensuring the privacy of his own family while denying travellers the view over the estuary. The absorption of Chess Lane into the rectory grounds also blocked access to the four footpaths down to Leigh Street. These included Billet Lane and two more that led up from opposite the *Peter Boat* inn.

37　An annual May Fair was held on the rectory meadow, seen here *c*.1899. Clement's Court flats now stand on this field.

The fourth was Church Hill Lane, leading up from the *Ship Inn*. Church Hill Lane was ten to thirteen feet wide with thick hedges on either side and benches for the old people to rest themselves on; it was 'kept clean' by having cockle shells from Canvey Island strewn on it. The lane had been the subject of dispute a few years earlier when certain residents were accused by others of allowing their pigs to block the way.

It was via Church Hill Lane that those who were to be married approached the church, and those who were to be buried were carried. Obviously, pedestrian access from Leigh Street was needed and so Eden created Little Hill (now called Church Hill), leading directly to the church door. However, this new right of way was steeper than the previous route, and it proved impossible to carry adult corpses up the new path. Thereafter bodies from the Old Town were carried by cart up Leigh Hill and entered the churchyard from the east.

The Rev. Eden did not use his money only for selfish aims, and the townspeople benefited from his generosity. In 1847, for example, at his own expense, he built the National Schools on Church Hill below the church. He retired from Leigh in 1851 and became Bishop of Moray Ross and Caithness in Scotland, where he founded Inverness Cathedral. He died in 1886.

THE NATIONAL SCHOOLS

The St Clement's National Schools were of an Elizabethan style, built of Kentish ragstone to complement the church. The school building was 90 feet long by 82 feet wide and included residences for the curate and master, the total project costing £1,500. Without his personal fortune the priest would never have been able to afford such major works, as tithes due to the rectory in 1846 were only £501 15s. per annum. Out of this the rector had to pay the curate's wages, as well as maintain his house and grounds. He also had to stretch it for

38　W. Thorp & Sons opened their undertaker's business on Leigh Hill in 1838.

the calls made upon him from his population who were, as Benton notes, 'for the most part composed of people frequently necessitous'.

Henry Simpson became the first headmaster of the boys section, while Emma Caroline Ray was headteacher at the girls school. Her husband, Arthur, later became head of the boys school until Christmas 1888 when Arthur Henry Thatcher took over, by which time 59 boys, 47 girls and 60 infants were in regular attendance. Arthur Thatcher became a well-known and much respected member of the community in Leigh. Born one of nine siblings on 8 January 1861, Arthur won a scholarship and spent two years at Culham Training College. He took a post as headteacher at the Cookham Dean, Berkshire church school for two years before joining the Leigh National Schools on a salary of £96 per annum. His brother, Edward, later joined him as assistant master.

The schools continued as the main educational establishment in the town until 1890 when North

39 The National Schools on Church Hill. Sixty-nine per cent of people living in Leigh in 1851 had been born in the village, the highest percentage of people living in their birthplace in the Rochford Hundred.

40 National Schools' boys section, photographed in 1890 as they transferred to Leigh Board School. Arthur Thatcher is standing back left. He became a local councillor and founder member of the Leigh Debating Society, which successfully ran from 31 January 1905 to 12 March 1951.

41 A south aisle was added to St Clement's Church in 1897, but terminated in a lean-to vestry with a corrugated iron roof until the scheme was completed with a Lady Chapel in 1913.

Street School was built. It continued as an infants only school until 13 December 1907 when the infants department opened at North Street. The south wing of the school (the boys section) was pulled down in 1913 owing to unstable land conditions. The remaining north wing was sold to Mr W.G. Beecroft, who converted it into a dwelling house. It was purchased by the church in the 1950s and briefly served as St Clement's rectory before being resold to a private resident in 1980.

ALTERATIONS TO THE CHURCH

Between 1500 and 1872 St Clement's consisted of the nave, north aisle, tower and porch only. It stood in a churchyard of three rods and six perches in area until another plot of land (calculated to be able to contain 200 corpses) was gifted by Lady Olivia as an eastward extension to the churchyard.

During the early 19th century musical accompaniment to the church services was provided by an orchestra standing in the gallery in the bottom of the tower, with violincello, violin, flute and clarinet. Rev. Robert Eden gave the church its first organ

in 1837. In 1838 he embarked upon an extension of the church building that involved the lengthening of the north aisle and the raising of the chancel roof to match the nave. He removed the castellations from the porch and replaced them with a gabled roof. Unfortunately, several historic monuments were removed and destroyed at this time.

In 1872 further alterations were initiated by the Rev. Walker King, rector of St Clement's, involving the extension of the chancel at a cost of £900. The whole of the east wall was taken down and rebuilt 17ft. 6in. further east and a window was put in each of the extended north and south walls. The chancel was raised by two steps and a low stone wall was made to separate the nave from the chancel. This was surmounted by a light wooden screen, said to have been made by the rector's son, Robert, who succeeded him as rector. Three rows of stalls were provided in the new chancel for the choir, two rows for boys and one for the men, with two stalls for the clergy to the west. A new mahogany altar rail was fixed into the wall at each end and supported by wrought-iron

42 Elm Road, *c*.1900. The wall of Leigh House dominates the right of this picture.

stanchions. The floors of the chancel and sanctuary were tiled, with tiling continuing up the sanctuary to a height of six feet.

Murals by George Brewer, a member of a local family, were painted either side of the east window and over the altar was a stone reredos with crocketed gothic arches. A new roof was put on over the old chancel, as well as over the new chancel and sanctuary. Gas was introduced for lighting the church in 1883 and a meter was set in the east wall of the north aisle.

THE POOR

A fisherman's work was hard and dangerous. Rarely did a year pass without some loss of life at sea. In a parish dominated by fishing and agriculture, there were few opportunities for widows and orphans to support themselves and many depended on parish relief. Weekly payments varied from one shilling to three shillings and sixpence, supplemented by coals and clothing when necessary.

A letter from the overseers of Leigh to the Poor Law Commissioners in 1835 requested advice:

Our parish is paying poor rates to an amount of 9 shillings in the pound on a two thirds assessment. We have many widows with from 2 to 8 children and for these we can find no employment nor have we a workhouse to put them in ... . Our great difficulty is the want of a workhouse, the present one being merely a cottage situated in Leigh, the very worst place for such an establishment...

In 1853 a club was formed to help fishermen living within one mile of the *Crooked Billet* in times of sickness. Initially called the United Brethren, it became known as the Billet Club. The club allowed the village policeman to join but must have regretted their decision when the man became ill and became a drain on club funds for quite a few months.

The farms of north Leigh were hit by the agricultural depression and, in the 1860s, Lawrence Davies of Elm Farm wrote a letter recording that he had not made a shilling profit in two years and that the good rector, the Rev. Walker King, had been moved to return some or all of the tithes owed. He hid the note in the rafters of the farmhouse where it was discovered in 1920.

43 Leigh Broadway, *c*.1900, originally just a track between Leigh Hall and the church, developed as a residential street before becoming a shopping parade. The *Carlton Hotel* held a liquor licence since 1896 and advertised a 'fine billiard room and commodious livery and bait stables'.

44 General stores, Eastwood Road North, *c*.1920. The signpost in the distance is the *Woodcutters' Arms* sign, the pub itself on the opposite side of the road, behind the bushes.

45 Leigh Hill was a busy shopping parade in the early 20th century. There continued to be a good deal of heavy horse traffic up Leigh Hill from the wharves where barges would unload.

Despite Lady Olivia's improvements to the water supply, the growing population still suffered with cholera epidemics. Seventeen people died between August and September 1849 and 11 died between August and September 1856. Consequently, a temporary laundry was set up and two laundresses employed, paid for out of the church offertory, and the townsfolk laid drains along Leigh Street down to the creek, at a cost of £84. However, continued overcrowding encouraged the spread of infections and a few years later scarlet fever broke out, resulting in further loss of life.

In times of extreme hardship, such as these, a soup kitchen was opened at Mrs Brewer's cottage on Leigh Hill on Tuesdays, Thursdays and Saturdays when the soup was sold at one shilling ha'penny per quart.

LEIGH COMICALS

The Leigh Comicals was a social club, founded in 1850 with a membership of 150. The club met in the *Peter Boat* public house, and charged a subscription of three shillings and sixpence with a five shilling fine for absenteeism. The first money collected was spent on a tent, cooking utensils, dishes and cutlery. The society then had to increase the subscription rate to meet further expenses and, as a result, membership declined. They did successfully organise at least one feast, though, during which, it is recorded, Frederick Cotgrove was fined five shillings for throwing a hot potato at Tom Plumb. Most of the society records were unfortunately lost when the *Peter Boat* burnt down in 1892.

NICKNAMES

The practice of using nicknames became prevalent among fishermen and their families during the 19th century, examples being 'Ponto', 'Lumpy', 'Bobber', 'Moulder' and 'Ratsy'. With extended families passing the same names down through the generations, many people possessed similar Christian and surnames, and their nicknames were the only way to distinguish between them. In 1851, of a total population of 1,370, there were 68 members of the Cotgrove family in Leigh, 56 Osbornes and 50 Turnidges. There were 122 Williams, 98 Johns, 65 Sarahs and 55 Marys, most of whom were living along Leigh Street.

SHRIMPING

Down by the river, fishing continued to provide the main income of the people throughout the 19th century. Of a total male population of 695 in 1851, 225 men from twelve years old upwards were employed as fishermen.

At the beginning of the 19th century, oysters and winkles were still a lucrative business. John George Baxter, for example, was born in Leigh in 1806 to a large poor family and had a limited education, but he amassed a fortune from the winkle and oyster grounds, later moving to Southwark as a rich man, although he 'generally visited Leigh on Good Friday to attend the annual tea meeting'.

From the 1830s, however, shrimps became a more lucrative catch. By 1872 the oyster and whelk business had been abandoned, shrimps becoming the mainstay of Leigh fishermen's livelihoods. A typical day's shrimping started early, often before sunrise, depending on the time of the tide. As the tide began to rise the fishermen walked across the mud to their skiffs (small boats which took them to where the larger boats were anchored further along the creek). Shrimps were caught in nets trawled behind the boats and kept alive in the wet well of the boat before being brought ashore in baskets to one of the seven or eight boiler houses in the town, such as on Billet Wharf, Baxter's Yard and Strand Wharf. Owning a boiler offered another employment opportunity in the town, and in the 1850s three elderly ladies, Mary Noakes aged 63, Eleanor Frost aged 62 and Mary Frost aged 70, owned boilers and charged the fishermen one penny or a ha'penny to boil one gallon of shrimps in seawater with added coarse salt.

Shrimping grounds varied depending on the seasonal movements of the shrimps. A favourite ground was Blyth Sand, almost opposite Leigh on the Kent shore. However, most catches were made along a line between Margate and Blacktail Spit off Foulness. When shrimps were scarce, some Leigh fishermen sailed forty miles up the Essex coast in May and worked out of Harwich until September.

Occasionally, Leigh boats worked on the south coast, using Shoreham, Sussex as a base, or even as far afield as Holland, Belgium, France and the Channel Islands.

George Emery is credited as being the first Leigh man to install a boiler actually in his boat, and others followed suit, finding it cheaper and time-efficient to arrive ashore with the shrimps already cooked. To accommodate several nets being trawled, boats developed into the larger bawleys, the name 'bawley' being an abbreviation of 'boiler boat'.

With eighty or more vessels engaged in shrimping by 1870, and as many as 100 gallons of shrimp were being caught by one vessel in a single day, 2,000 gallons of shrimp could be sent to London each day, providing a joint income for the Leigh fishermen of some £15,000 a year.

NIGHT CARTS

Cooked shrimps were usually sent to London by boat, but unfavourable weather occasionally necessitated their transport by road. James Cook started a regular overnight road service in 1820, large open carts being stacked high with pads of shrimps. The pads were rectangular lidded baskets which held eight to ten gallons of shrimps each. The loaded carts left Billet Wharf at 6-7p.m., needing four horses to pull them up Leigh Hill. The route went via Wickford and Shenfield, where the horses were changed, and reached Billingsgate at 4-5a.m.

When Mr Cook unfortunately fell and broke his neck, William Hay, landlord of the *Crooked Billet*, bought the business. Hay employed four journeymen to run the business and made additional profits by also carrying passengers. However, the business, along with a rival company run by Abraham Surridge, ceased with the opening of the railway.

LEIGH HOUSE

In 1792 Blacke House, the mansion opposite St Clement's Church, was purchased by John Loten, formerly a lieutenant in the Marines and then collector of HM Customs at Leigh for 33 years. He added several rooms to the house by building a northern wing. Rumours of hauntings in the house date from the discovery, by Loten, of a female skeleton beneath the cellar stairs. In 1800 he enlarged the grounds with the purchase of a piece of land to the south, facing Chess Lane. He planted two cedar trees in the grounds, one of which fell in the storms of 1987 although the other is still standing. He was also responsible for planting ivy on the house and on the church tower.

Loten lived at the house until he died in 1815, aged 63, and the house passed to his son Captain John Loten who was commander of the *Safeguard*, a 32-gun brig in the Quarantine Service. John Loten jnr died in 1827 and was buried with his father in the north-west corner of the churchyard. Leigh House, recorded on the 1851 census as Hill House, was then purchased by David Montague, who was a churchwarden at St Clement's for 31 years. Montague was a wealthy man, owning several fields and properties in the town. He was the owner of a brick and tile yard and Victoria Pottery and advertised as a brickmaker, pot maker, lime-burner, coal dealer and farmer.

Montague renamed the property Leigh House and increased its grounds in 1852 by purchasing land to the north, formerly part of Sweetings belonging to Leigh Hall. He died in 1864 aged 81 and is buried in Leigh churchyard with his wife. Leigh House became the residence of F. Millar QC, and its final owner was Dr William Douglas Watson. The house was pulled down in February 1927 to make way for Broadway West, and its gardens were taken over by Southend Corporation. Its fine chimneys were taken up to Hadleigh on a handcart and can still be seen gracing the roof of a house on the corner of Rectory Road and New Road.

VICTORIA POTTERY

Leigh brickfield, nearly all of which was in the parish of Prittlewell, was owned by Mr Turner and David Montague between 1832 and 1859. The pottery, originally called the Phoenix Pottery, stood at the end of Leigh Broadway, where it curves into Leigh Road, with the brickfields stretching eastwards behind it. Philip Benton writing in the 1860s noted, 'The brick fields … are not an attractive feature and much of the neighbourhood has lost it rural character'.

In its early days the pottery concentrated on the manufacture of bricks and pipes and by 1850 employed 50 men and boys, most of who were not

46 John Loten's grave, inscribed: 'Sacred to the memory of JOHN LOTEN esq many years Collector of HM Customs at this port who departed this life the 6th November 1815 aged 63 years. Also Cap JOHN LOTEN who departed this life the 1st November 1827 aged 38 years'. The adjacent grave is of John Loten jnr's wife, Mary.

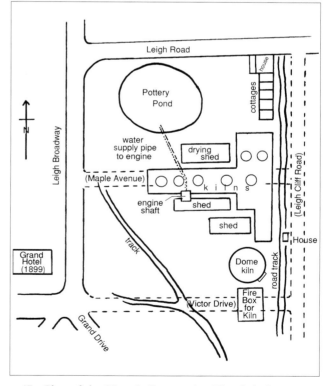

47 Plan of the Victoria Pottery site. The dashed lines indicate where roads were laid across the site after the pottery closed.

48   Victoria Pottery kiln, *c*.1880, viewed from the south-east corner of the site.

49   The Victoria Pottery, *c*.1880, viewed from the south-west corner. In 1851 the pottery employed five potters, a kiln burner, two tile makers and one brickmaker. Most of the pottery workers were born elsewhere, while Leigh's 243 fishermen and 30 agricultural labourers were mostly indigenous.

50 These stoneware flagons and ginger beer bottles are typical of the later products of the Victoria Pottery.

51 Bark texture vase. Vases with high-relief flowers and leaves were also produced.

Leigh natives. Local pockets of clay were exploited for the coarser products while pipe clay was imported via Bell Wharf and Victoria Wharf. In 1860 the potteries were taken over by Gallichan & Co. who developed the output into brown stoneware, making all kinds of bottles and jars for pickling and preserves, together with large quantities of drainpipes for sewerage and agricultural purposes. Much was exported all over the world.

However, the pottery closed down in 1898 and its buildings, including the landmark kiln, were demolished. The fine row of elm trees, which had marked the northern boundary of the property, were cut down and thrown into the pottery pond to make way for the widening of Leigh Road.

THE RAILWAY

Robert Eden and Lady Olivia Sparrow were influential figures in Victorian Leigh, but neither was to have as far-reaching consequences for the town as the laying of the railway in 1854. Built by the Eastern Counties and the London and Blackwell Company, it was originally intended to follow a route up Belton Hills to a station on the site of the present Salvation Army citadel, hence the naming of Station Road. However, it was eventually considered more financially expedient to lay the track straight along the coast, rather than tackle such a steep gradient. The decision was to have a

devastating effect, physically, on the riverside village but also a beneficial effect on health and social integration.

The only route along the coast from Benfleet to Southend was straight though the middle of Leigh and, inevitably, many old buildings were demolished in its path.

One casualty was the Wesleyan chapel, built on the north side of the High Street in 1811. In compensation, the railway company built a new chapel with seating for 300, west of Billet Lane, in 1879. The back of the *Crooked Billet* was removed, and the former *George Inn*, at the time a private house, was completely demolished and a level crossing laid in its place. The original *Smack Inn* was sited partially in the path of the railway and it too was completely demolished and a new *Smack* was built opposite, next to Juniper's Cottage, south of Leigh Street.

When the railway's route necessitated the demolition of the *Bell Inn*, its bricks were used to build up the Kings Strand, which became known as Bell Wharf. Nearby, the *Kings Head* was cut in two by the railway and for a time was shored up on either side, with trains running through the centre, until it too was pulled down to make way for a new booking office. The owner, William Foster, then purchased land in New Road, east of Billet Lane, and built himself a large house with a

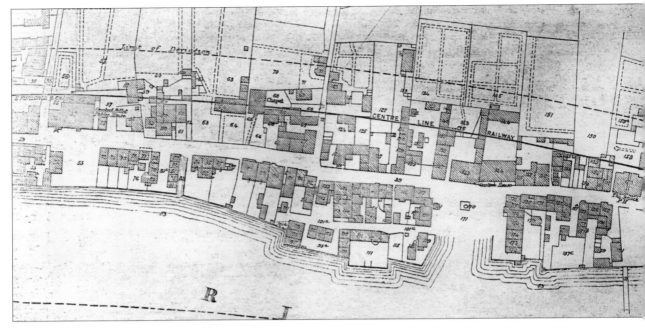

52   Proposed line of railway through the town. This map shows how the railway destroyed many buildings and separated others from their long gardens. It also gives an impression of the size of the town before the railway was laid. New Road now runs approximately where the Limit of Deviation is marked on the map.

terrace facing south which he named Pittington House. Foster was the largest shareholder in the gas works opposite the *Crooked Billet*, and Pittington House became the first in Leigh piped for gas lighting. The house and its extensive grounds were eventually developed for housing.

Other properties demolished as a direct result of the laying of the railway included the coastguard watch house at the extreme east end of the town which made way for goods sidings adjoining the station. Nearby, Mrs Loten's cottage, Match Corner House, was also destroyed. Despite what may now be seen as a loss of 'heritage', many of the cottages destroyed were those described by Benton as 'ancient hovels', and had contributed to the unsanitary conditions in the town.

A level crossing was provided for pedestrians at the foot of Leigh Hill, later supplemented by a footbridge. When the railway eventually opened to traffic in July 1855 the station south of the level crossing catered for trains travelling west to London while a small waiting shed north of the line took passengers to Southend. The first stationmaster was Mr Twist.

The direct line to London avoiding the Tilbury loop opened in 1888, and the 'up' station was rebuilt slightly further east. The building is now used as the Leigh Sailing Club headquarters. A second level crossing was provided where Billet Lane joined Leigh Street immediately west of the *Crooked Billet*. This was closed when the line was electrified.

Local fishermen were among the first to benefit from the railway. In 1855, when carriage by rail first became possible, 467 tons of oysters and over 29 tons of winkles, mussels and shrimps were transported to London. By 1864 the oyster trade had declined but 704 tons of winkles, mussels and shrimps were conveyed. Winkles and whelks were sold by the bushel, while mussels were sold by the sack, each sack weighing 200 lb. Rail transport was more reliable and efficient than either the night carts or sailing boats had been. During the 1860s the railway was also providing employment for 16 men resident in Leigh.

The loss of properties in Leigh Street stimulated housing development up the cliffs, and members of

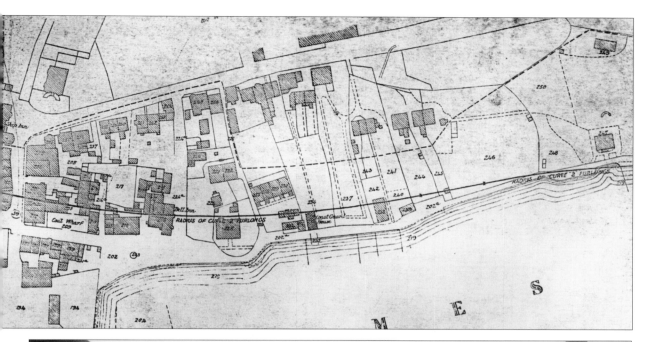

53 High Street, looking west. The original station is on the right and a new *Smack Inn* has been built opposite the site of the first *Smack*, beyond which is Juniper's.

54   There were many objections to the proposed closure of this level crossing in 1886 and again in 1922. The railway company did keep it open for a few years, but by 1930 the crossing had been replaced by a footbridge.

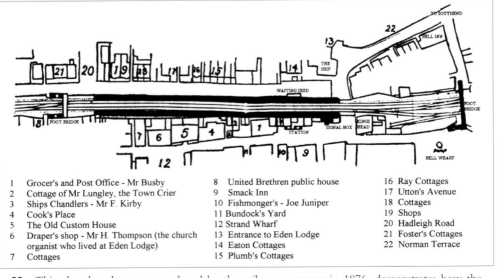

1	Grocer's and Post Office - Mr Busby	8	United Brethren public house	16	Ray Cottages
2	Cottage of Mr Lungley, the Town Crier	9	Smack Inn	17	Utton's Avenue
3	Ships Chandlers - Mr F. Kirby	10	Fishmonger's - Joe Juniper	18	Cottages
4	Cook's Place	11	Bundock's Yard	19	Shops
5	The Old Custom House	12	Strand Wharf	20	Hadleigh Road
6	Draper's shop - Mr H. Thompson (the church	13	Entrance to Eden Lodge	21	Foster's Cottages
	organist who lived at Eden Lodge)	14	Eaton Cottages	22	Norman Terrace
7	Cottages	15	Plumb's Cottages		

55   This plan, based on one produced by the railway company in 1876, demonstrates how the railway platforms fitted between the buildings.

families that lived in Leigh Street for centuries moved north of the railway.

THE END OF THE MANOR OF LEIGH

Lady Olivia Sparrow died on 12 February 1863, aged 88, and was buried at Brampton in Suffolk. Her only son Robert had died in 1818, aged only 19, and her daughter, Millicent, who had married Viscount Mandeville and become the Duchess of Manchester, died in 1848. In 1852 Lady Olivia had agreed with her grandson, William Drogo Montague, the eldest of Millicent's nine children, to disentail the family estates in Essex. Those not disposed of by private contract between then and Lady Olivia's death were sold by auction, including the Herschell School. The remaining manor lands, with 30 tenants producing £42 a year, were sold to Ernest Wild of Middlesex for £1,130, while Leigh Hall, together with 224 acres of farmland, was purchased by Thomas James Smith, a coal merchant of Sun Wharf, Deptford for £8,042.

Soon afterwards the Churchyard family acquired the manorial rights, and Mrs Mary Churchyard sold them, in turn, to William Theobald. On his death early in the 20th century, the manorial rights

56 Fisherman Frederick Cowey and his wife, Margaret, among the first to make their home away from Leigh Street, are pictured here in their living room in West Street.

were acquired by the Southend Corporation. Leigh Hall itself was let to Arthur Bentall and his son Pendrill in 1879. Twenty years later it was sold to timber merchant William Taylor who was responsible for its demolition in 1907. The mansion's balustrade and fine oak panelling from the dining room found a new home across the Atlantic in New England.

57 The road from Eastwood. The north of Leigh remained very rural until the 1930s.

Seven

Leigh Urban District 1897-1913

An Act of Parliament in the mid-1890s replaced parish vestries with parish councils, and Leigh's council was established in 1894 as part of Rochford Rural District. By this time the community living in Leigh Street and Leigh Hill included bakers, grocers, carpenters, drapers, bricklayers and butchers. Three years later, in 1897, Leigh achieved independence when it was designated an Urban District, heralding an era of rapid development and population growth.

URBAN DISTRICT COUNCIL

Leigh Urban District Council, formed on 1 April 1897, adopted a coat of arms sporting a fishing boat and a cockleshell. Frederic W. Senier was elected as Chairman of the Council, J. Meacham

58 This ship and cockleshell motif adopted by Leigh Urban District Council was included in the stained glass windows of the council offices built in 1912.

the Vice-chair and, pending the building of council offices, the council met at the Board School every Tuesday at 8p.m. Inspired by the success and growing wealth of neighbouring Southend, it embarked upon a scheme to make Leigh an attractive resort for trippers and holidaymakers from London. A set of five groynes was constructed on the foreshore in order to form a sandy beach, and a footbridge was built over the railway enabling pedestrians to cross when the level crossing gates were shut. In 1897 the council purchased Bell Wharf for public use, for the sum of £185, and in 1899 took over part of Two Tree Island for a sewage works.

By 1899 development had stretched as far as Woodfield Road to the east, Hadleigh Road to the west, and was beginning to creep north towards the London Road, although the town centre was still considered to be the old village, where Leigh Street was renamed High Street. The town was lighted by gas from the works belonging to Mr S. White, opposite the *Crooked Billet*. The *Essex Review* of 1899 commented of Leigh that 'hundreds of picturesque residences have in the last few years made their appearance on its wooded slopes', and A.R. Hope-Moncrieff wrote of Leigh in 1909, 'Here now spreads a colony of smart new houses and shops flowering out from the root of the old fishing village.'

In 1900 six acres of land were purchased along the seafront for a recreation ground with seats and shelters, now known as Cliff Gardens, and an additional public area was laid out as the Marine Parade Pleasure Ground. The 1908 Leigh-on-Sea official guide indicated that the Leigh Park estate (from Westleigh Avenue east to Leigh Gardens) was being developed 'with a view to meet the growing demands of those who seek the ease and

59 Cliff Parade. Several houses along Cliff Parade offered boarding house accommodation in the early 1900s. The *Cliffs Hotel*, near the corner of Avenue Road, has been replaced by an apartment block.

60 Bell Wharf pictured in July 1923. Southend Corporation workmen are re-laying crane rails, used to assist with unloading ships. Note the railway footbridge in the background, leading to Leigh Hill via a road that is now just a private driveway. The footbridge itself was considered unsafe in 1952 and taken down.

61 Leigh beach, *c*.1910. Fishermen's nets were hung to dry on the sea wall railings. Traditional hemp nets were prevented from rotting by boiling in liquor steeped in oak tree bark, or dipped in tar. With the arrival of the railway, cotton trawl nets were brought in from the West Country.

62 Bathing station. This open-air swimming pool was built by the council to attract day-trippers and an active swimming club was formed. Mixed swimming was allowed, mixed sun-bathing was not. One lady still resident in Leigh recalls how she used to climb over the locked pool gate for a free swim before school.

63 Cliff Gardens. Nightingales were commonly heard in these six acres of gardens, laid out in 1897.

quiet of a country home with ample and pleasant surroundings'. The guide went on to assure potential visitors that 'Leigh is one of the healthiest spots that can be found around the coast', and supported its claim with the comforting statistic that 'only ten cases of infectious diseases occurred during the whole of the year 1907'.

J.W. Liversedge, surveyor to the council, was the architect of new public offices in Elm Road, comprising council chambers with a police station and fire station attached. The foundation stone was laid on 9 August 1911 by the Chairman of the Council and the buildings, which had cost a total of £5,000, were opened for business in 1912. Frederic Senier, who had been the first chairman of the Leigh Ratepayers Association, went on to be Chairman of Leigh Council five times. He later became mayor of Southend (1918-1920) and was knighted in 1924 for public and political services. Arthur D. Larter was the Sergeant-in-Charge of the original police station. Sergeant Larter, described in the press as 'a genial and efficient member of the police force', remained at Leigh until he retired in 1913. The fire station completed the council buildings. Its second floor was used as a rest room,

64 Drinking fountain at Cliff Gardens. The 1908 Leigh-on-Sea *Guide* said of the town '... with its bracing winds from the north sea and the ozone from its beds when the tide recedes, Leigh is preeminently a resort for those who are seeking to restore lost health'.

with a billiard table, while the top floor provided accommodation for the station master and his family.

The agricultural depression at the end of the 19th century had hit Leigh badly, and neither farmers nor landowners could afford to maintain either their businesses or their buildings. Thus, many

65   Marine Parade gardens, looking east. The 1946 *Guide* to Southend intimated that in Leigh 'Residents can sun themselves on the coldest days, fancying themselves on the French Riviera'.

66 Council Offices, *c.*1912. The left-hand section of this building still exists as the police station, and retains the original green tiling and stained glass. Adjoining it is the old police station and fire station, now demolished. Before 1912, Leigh's police force operated from the front room of the inspector's house at 41 Leigh Hall Road.

67 Foundation stone of the council offices. Both Frederic Senier and Stephen Johnson became mayors of Southend.

of the farming estates became available for purchase, enabling the council to encourage residential development. The principal landowners at the beginning of the 20th century were William Foster of Pittington House, Alexander Underwood Higgins of Lapwater Hall, General Booth of the Salvation Army, Mrs Miller of Belfairs Lodge and Frederick Ramuz, proprietor of the Land Company. William Foster, former owner of the *Kings Head*, was by occupation a victualler and coal merchant. He used some of his acquired wealth to purchase land north of the High Street and Leigh Marsh. Alexander Higgins, a surveyor, property speculator and developer, owned Lapwater Hall plus five adjoining fields formerly belonging to Leigh Hall.

THE LAND COMPANY

Frederick Ramuz, originally a London resident, became a major developer in south-east Essex and was mayor of Southend between 1898 and 1900. He was responsible for the first large-scale housing development in Leigh. In 1893 his Land Company purchased 334 acres of the parish, including Leigh Hall Farm, Elm Farm, Gowles and part of the Victoria Pottery. Ramuz laid out roads in a grid pattern and divided the land up into building plots, marketing the area as the 'Leigh Hall Estate'. Building plots were offered to local builders, often via auction sales held in a marquee set up on the estate.

Ramuz obviously had a sense of history as he named Olivia Drive after Lady Olivia Sparrow, Lord Roberts Avenue after her husband and son, the Duke of Manchester Drive after her son-in-law, and Tankerville Drive after her granddaughter's husband, the Earl of Tankerville. Flemming Avenue commemorated Emma Lucy Flemming, who loaned Ramuz £10,000 for the purchase of the estates.

In 1896 Ramuz sold a portion of Clap Gate Fields to Henry Choppin, at that time a licensed victualler living on Leigh Hill, for £400 for a hotel to be built. Deeds show that Ramuz agreed never to build another hotel in the Broadway, London Road or Leigh Road area in his lifetime. The 50-room hotel opened in 1899 as the *Leigh-on-Sea Family and Commercial Hotel* on the corner of Leigh

68 The *Grand Hotel*,1899, was advertised as 'the largest and finest hotel in Leigh, commanding grand sea views, replete with every modern comfort, billiards and lawn tennis'. There was a viewing platform on the roof.

Broadway and Oakleigh Park Drive, and by 1910 had changed its name to the *Grand Hotel*. Henry Choppin also owned the new *Bell Hotel* on Leigh Hill.

The farmhouse at Elm Farm was purchased by Henry King in 1900, who then leased the property to George Mills, a local lime and cement merchant, with an option to purchase the freehold at a later date. Mills obtained a licence to sell wines, beer and spirits on the premises, but he was acting on behalf on Frederick Ramuz, who was providing the finance but apparently wished to conceal his involvement in the scheme. The premises were held in Mills' name until the conversion of the farmhouse into a public house was complete. The

69 The *Elm Hotel*, *c.*1910.

70   Belfairs Lodge, built by Colonel Miller. This photograph was taken *c*.1920.

71   The Broadway, looking east, *c*.1905.

72 Shops in the Broadway, *c*.1905. The junction with Alexandra Road is near the centre of this picture, with Mr Johnson's butchers on the corner.

building opened as the *Elm* public house in the autumn of 1900, at which point Ramuz employed Mills as manager on a salary of £2 per week.

THE SALVATION ARMY

From the 1890s William Booth began to purchase enormous tracts of land in the west of Leigh in his capacity of founder and General of the Salvation Army. Booth had identified neighbouring Hadleigh as an ideal location for the establishment of a farming colony for the rehabilitation of homeless, poor or alcoholic men from the East End of London. Among his purchases was Leigh Park Farm, which the organisation used as a receiving centre for the destitute and homeless men or those sent by various Poor Law authorities who came to work at the farm colony. The land belonging to the farm was turned over to large orchards, growing apples, pears and cherries.

New recruits were given a bath and their clothing was fumigated or, if beyond repair, replaced. For their time at Leigh Park, sparse food and basic bedding were the reward for labour on the farm-land. The men slept in dormitories where reveille

was at 6a.m. and lights out was at 9p.m. They were taught the rudiments of farming and assessed for their commitment to the way of life. As their health improved on this strict but undemanding regime, they were given more physically and mentally challenging tasks until, typically after about three months in Leigh, they were transferred to the main colony at Hadleigh. Leigh residents benefited in particular from milk from the colony's dairy herds, and the colony hospital was under the supervision of a Leigh doctor who visited twice a week. Leigh Park farmhouse still exists as numbers 71 and 73 Olive Avenue, and remnants of its orchards can be seen on Highlands Boulevard.

In 1892 Booth, referred to in the deeds as 'General of the Salvation Army and Director of the Darkest England Scheme', purchased Leigh Marsh Farm and fishery from William Foster. He further purchased Leigh Heath Farm in 1893 from William Stewart Forster and William Cholmeley of Middlesex for £5,500. The land included meadow, arable land, marsh and a small wood, altogether comprising just over 171 acres, and became part of

73 Leigh Broadway from the church tower, *c*.1910. The houses set back on the left are on the site of the Herschell School. The Woolworths building was built on the site soon after this picture was taken.

the land farmed by members of the Hadleigh colony. In June 1900 he acquired three plots of the Leigh Hall estate from William Bolton for £250.

William Booth died on 20 August 1912, when his responsibilities and property passed to his son, William Bramwell Booth.

MRS MILLER

Mrs Miller was the widow of Major Miller who had purchased Belfairs Farm during the 1890s. A keen sportsman, Major Miller had envisioned a sporting estate with hunting, riding and shooting. He stocked the fields with game birds, notably pheasant, for which he imported a diet of large Spanish ants. He then built himself a new residence, Furze Field House, later called Belfairs Lodge.

LEIGH BROADWAY

Apart from the *Carlton Hotel* and Lady Olivia's little school at the west end, the first buildings on Hall Road, the direct route from St Clement's Church to Leigh Hall, were high-class residential dwellings, which began appearing towards the end of the 19th century. The first shop in the road was James Nash's grocery shop, opened on the corner of West Street in the 1880s. As more shops opened up in rapid succession, the road was renamed Leigh Broadway.

74 Grimes the greengrocer was an early trader in Leigh Broadway. These premises now belong to Hair & Sons estate agents.

75   Procession in Leigh
     Broadway, *c.*1905.

TRANSPORT

A tramway from St Clement's to Southend High
Street opened in July 1901, with a single track
laid along Leigh Broadway, Leigh Road and the
London Road. The Southend-on-Sea Light Railway was a 3ft. 6in. electric tramway equipped
with overhead wires, and it cost tuppence to travel
from Leigh to Southend, and one penny for
children. One could also take a horse-drawn
carriage from St Clement's to St James the Less in
Hadleigh in the opposite direction, for the price
of fourpence.

A second tram track was laid in 1910, and by
1914 trams were running approximately every five
minutes from 5a.m. to 9.30p.m. A bus service was
started in June 1914 to run alongside the tram
service and, in the opposite direction, the 'Hadleigh
fourpennies' were superseded by a motor omnibus
service connecting Leigh with Hadleigh and
Rayleigh. The tram company eventually ran three
routes through Southend and Leigh, via Leigh
Road and the London Road, the journey taking
minutes.

76   No.54 tram to Leigh. Trams were painted in
various shades of green. This particular one was
built by Brush in 1921 as an eight-wheel top-
covered car. A bell hanging next to the driver was
rung vigorously to warn pedestrians of the tram's
approach.

77 Annie Overton joined the tram company as a conductor in 1914, aged seventeen. When war broke out she volunteered to be a driver and became the first female tram driver in Britain.

By 1925 trams were running every two minutes from Southend to Leigh and a trolleybus service was started up as a way of modernising the system. The last tram was taken out of service in 1927. Trolleybuses were finally abandoned in 1954, partly owing to rising electricity prices, which rendered them less economical than motor buses, and partly to the inconvenience of overhead wires.

ROBERT STUART KING

When Canon Walker King died in 1892 he was succeeded as rector of St Clement's by his son, Robert Stuart King, who held the living for nearly 58 years. Robert King had been born in Leigh rectory on 4 April 1862 and gained an MA from Hertford College, Oxford. He was ordained by his uncle Edward, the Bishop of Lincoln, and followed his father's love of football, helping to form the Old Rectory Yard and the Leigh Town football clubs. He served as an officer of the council, a member of the Leigh Debating Society, and took an active role in supporting the cause of Leigh against the dominating influence of Southend Corporation. He was known for his wit and humour and was a popular speaker at the annual party held for his parishioners.

78   Leigh Broadway, *c.*1930. Travelling west is tramcar no.38, a 70-seater built by Brush in 1912.

79   London Road at the Elms, *c.*1930.

Church Extension

With the growth in population at the end of the 19th century, a decision was made to add a south aisle to St Clement's with a Lady Chapel at its east end. Most of the medieval south wall was demolished and piers and arches were erected to match those on the north of the nave. However, by the time the south aisle was completed there was no money left for a Lady Chapel and the aisle was dedicated in 1897, terminating with a vestry. Previously, the basement of the tower was used as the vestry.

In 1889 a clock was presented to St Clement's by F.C.J. Millar QC of Leigh House, described as Leigh's chief parishioner. The clock, made by Gillett & Johnston of Croydon, had two convex dials, each five feet in diameter, one pointing south, the other east, in the directions where most of the inhabitants of Leigh resided. It required winding once a week until an electrical system was introduced in 1967.

In 1913 the rector applied to complete the scheme with a Lady Chapel and new vestry,

80   The King family. Robert Stuart King is standing far left. Also in the picture are his father Canon Walker King (standing second from right), mother, uncle, three brothers, three sisters, a brother-in-law and baby nephew.

81 St Clement's Church, 1900. These carriages were the first 'Hadleigh fourpennies', named after the fare from Leigh to Hadleigh. The original east wall of the north aisle is still visible here as the vestries have yet to be built.

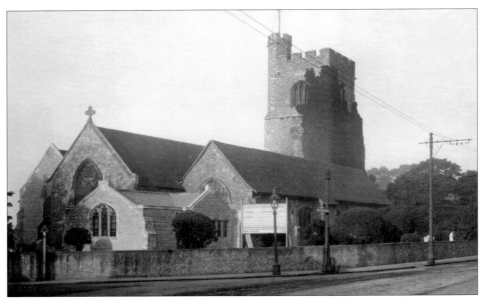

82 St Clement's Church in 1915, now with the vestries in place and the Lady Chapel visible south (left) of the chancel. Note also the tram cables.

83   Rectory Grove, *c.*1910.

designed by Sir Charles Nicholson. The altar of
carved oak was a gift from the Sunday school. A
priest's doorway was destroyed to make way for
the arches between the chancel and Lady Chapel,
but the local authority insisted on an additional exit
at the east end of the church and a further door
was inserted in the south wall. A vestry was constructed outside the ancient east wall of the north
aisle, and a doorway cut into the wall.

At the end of the First World War it was decided
to erect a memorial chapel to be dedicated as the
Chapel of the Resurrection. A staircase was
constructed in the north-east corner leading to a
gallery constructed to house the organ. Part of the
gallery was cantilevered out to make room for the
altar beneath it. The chapel was completed with an
oak screen designed by Sir Charles Nicholson in
the front and to the south.

LEIGH BOARD SCHOOL

By 1888 there was over-crowding at the Herschell
and National Schools and provision of a larger school
was discussed. A school board of five members was
elected by ratepayers on 29 May 1889 comprising

Benjamin Barnard, a grocer and baker, the Rev.
Walker King, St Clement's rector, Robert Johnson,
a fisherman, John Osborne, a builder, and Henry
Churchyard, a ship's chandler. Four sites were
considered for the location of Leigh Board School:
Shorefields at the top of Marine Parade, Dobbins
(sometimes called Dobbings) Field, Sweetings on
the corner of Rectory Grove and Elm Road, and
an area comprising five plots of land owned by a
Mr Latter. At a cost of £150, Dobbins Field, north
east of St Clement's was chosen, although the choice
was criticised at the time as being 'at the very
furthest extremity of Leigh'.

Architect Walter J. Woods, who designed
Southend Pier, was selected to design the school
and the builders were Samuel Darke & Son. Many
residents objected to the school because it would
cause an increase in the rates of one shilling every
six months. The *Southend Standard* of 23 January
1890 reported that '… the ratepayers of Leigh are
unable to unpocket such a sum … The fishermen
could not stand it except after their very best season,
and its influence on the remaining part of the parish
would be to depopulate the recently erected houses

84 Leigh Fire Brigade, *c*.1925.

and prevent any further development for years to come'.

Despite such pessimism, the school eventually opened in North Street on Monday, 29 September 1890 as Leigh Board School. Arthur Thatcher marched up Church Hill with his class of boys from the National Schools to become the first headteacher of the new school. Local papers reporting the opening commented on '… very handsome buildings', intended to accommodate 200 boys and 200 girls. The floors were of wood blocks and around the walls of the rooms was a dado of glazed bricks four and a half feet high. Boys and girls were separated at all times, there being a fence down the centre of the grounds, boys to the east and girls on the west. Emma Ray became the first head of the girls at Leigh Board School, while Miss Annie Young took charge of the infants.

The school accepted all those former pupils, aged between seven and 14, of the Herschell School, which continued as an infant school until 1913. To accommodate the growing number of pupils, a tender of £1,619 was accepted from local builders William Thorpe and Sons to extend the school by the addition of an extra classroom for each of the boys and girls departments, and the new rooms were ready for use in early 1899. By this time Arthur Thatcher had six teachers under him and

267 boys on the books. His salary was £230 p.a., and he remained at the school until his retirement in December 1925.

By 1900 the 269 pupils in the girls department were supervised by seven teachers under the leadership of Miss Mahala J. Read, who received a salary of £164 p.a. Annie Young, head teacher of the infants department, had charge of four teachers and 206 children, and received an annual salary of £120. On 29 September 1903 Essex County Council took control of educational matters under the 1902 Education Act. The School Board was disbanded, and the school became known as Leigh North Street School.

THE FIRE BRIGADE

In 1899 Leigh Ratepayers Association set up a committee to consider forming a fire brigade. On New Year's Day in 1900 the committee announced their decision that the council should purchase fire-fighting equipment and the brigade be financed by public subscription. A sub-committee comprising representatives from the council and the Ratepayers Association came into being on 4 May 1900, and Captain A. Montrie was appointed chairman, with Frederic Senier as Honorary Secretary.

The new fire service employed three officers and 12 men under the leadership of Captain Harold

85 Fire brigade practice, *c.*1925. The building on the left is a temporary façade constructed by the brigade for practice purposes. It was erected in the garden behind Leigh House, courtesy of the owner Dr Douglas Watson.

E. Johnson, and on 10 May 1900 the brigade was fully constituted. The first fire it attended was in Victoria Road, where a wooden house was damaged. Later that year it was agreed that ratepayers should not be asked to finance the brigade and, instead, public fund-raising events were held.

In January 1901 the brigade obtained a manual engine from the Southend brigade for £40 and demonstrated it to the public by pumping jets of water over the roof of St Clement's Church. By the end of January enough money had been raised to purchase uniforms for the men. In January 1903 the Urban District Council assumed responsibility for all fire brigade matters and encouraged the building of a shed adjacent to the Board School to act as a headquarters. However, in 1904 a two-storey brick building was erected on the east side

86 Leigh section of Southend Fire Brigade, *c.*1925.

of West Street incorporating a stone block on the front elevation inscribed with 'LFB 1904 H E JOHNSON CAPTAIN'. Until 1904 calling the brigade out was the job of a call-boy runner. When the new station was built an electric alarm system was introduced, operating from Captain Johnson's private residence. This system endured until 1913 by which time a new fire station was built in Elm Road, adjacent to the new council offices.

With the absorption of Leigh into Southend in 1914, the fire brigade lost its autonomy and became the Leigh section of the Southend brigade. Captain Johnson became the second officer of the Southend brigade under Captain Harvey and these two officers were awarded MBEs for their services during the 1914-18 war. Captain Johnson remained with the brigade until 1940. The fire station in Elm Road

continued to be used until 1968, when a larger station was built in Mountdale Gardens on the site of Brickhouse Farm. The Elm Road station and drill tower were demolished and the site became a car park. The 1904 station still exists in West Street.

BOAT BUILDING

By the end of the 19th century, peter boats and pink sterns had been almost entirely replaced by bawleys, the last peter boat fishing for eels in 1902. Mr Parsons was a well-known boat builder, specialising in bawleys, at the turn of the century. Bundock brothers also built bawleys in their yard at the east end of Leigh Street, between the railway and the sea wall, later relocating to a premises west of the *Smack*. Essex fishing vessels were registered with the letters LO (London), HH (Harwich) or

87   Harbourmaster James Oliver at his office on Bell Wharf, *c.*1921. James Oliver later became stationmaster of the local fire brigade, and lived over the fire station in Elm Road during the war.

88 The original cocklesheds were little more than tiny wooden shacks, with mountains of discarded cockle shells behind them. Leigh is described in *Kelly's Trade Directory* as being '2,331 acres, of which 1,016 are ooze'.

MN (Maldon) depending on where they had been built or originally owned. As Leigh was not a port of registry, most craft built and owned at Leigh were registered LO.

In 1910 a suit of sails for a bawley cost about £380 if ordered direct from Leigh's local sailmaker Francis A. Turnidge, and took about ten days to make. Turnidge was the son of a bawley owner and was apprenticed as a sailmaker at the sail loft on Victoria Wharf in 1894. The owner of the business died in 1900 and Francis took over, running the business until he retired in 1964. In 1919 Leigh Boat Building works was founded, building yachts and fishing boats. Later it became the Estuary Yacht Club.

COCKLES

The *Victoria County History* records that at the turn of the century the boats belonging to Leigh were mostly small and chiefly engaged in taking whitebait and sprats. The value of the united catches in 1907 was estimated at £15,000. However, during the 20th century cockling took over from whitebait, sprats and shrimping as Leigh's main fishery. Cockles would be raked from the exposed seabed for four hours between tides. Short handled rakes were developed for this purpose, and cockling was carried out all year round.

The cockles were loaded into wicker baskets shaped like large buckets. Back at Leigh two loaded baskets would be hooked to short lengths of rope hanging from each end of a wooden yoke carried on the cocklers' shoulders. The baskets were thus carried down a plank from ship to shore. In the early days of the industry, the cockles were laid in Leigh Creek to purge them of impurities for a few days before being taken to the sheds lining the foreshore west of Leigh Street to be boiled in coppers of hot water. However, in the 1890s cockles contaminated with sewage discharge caused a major poisoning scare, and the laying up of cockles was subsequently forbidden; cockles then had to be cooked by steam rather than by boiling. Once steamed, the meat was separated from the shells by sieving. They were sold to passers-by or sent by road or rail for sale in London.

It was not long before the Leigh cockle beds were worked out and the fishermen turned to the beds off Maplin Sands and Southend flats. By 1918 several cockle boats had had 7-9hp auxiliary engines installed, and by 1928 full-powered motor cocklers were being built. At that time, 15 Leigh cockle boats were working five to six days a week all year round. Hand raking was not replaced by mechanical dredging until 1967.

89   Osborne's cockle shed, Billet Wharf, 1915.

LEIGH REGATTA

With the formation of the Urban District, the council wished to encourage the annual Leigh Regatta, which was based on regattas that had been held at Southend for decades previously. Not only did it provide entertainment for locals, but it was seen as a tourist attraction, and the local press reported that on regatta days trains arriving from London were 'seriously over-crowded'. A committee was formed, the members of which occupied a barge moored off Bell Wharf for the duration of the event and acted as judges. Much of the credit for the organisation in the early years was due to Francis Turnidge, the sailmaker, who acted as regatta secretary. Music was supplied by C.F.D. Bundock's band, the members of which received free refreshments for their efforts.

In 1910 £104 3s. 3d. was raised by local subscription, of which £56 15s. was disbursed as prize money, the remainder covering the cost of the event. The programme followed much the same course every year, with rowing, sculling and swimming races, walking the greasy pole and fireworks in the evening. In the sailing classes, the winning bawley and cockle boat received a championship flag for its respective class, presented by Francis Turnidge. The bawley race of 1912 was typical, with £4 and a championship flag for the winner, £3 for second place and £1 for the third and fourth bawley. The course started at Westcliff Crowstone and finished between a Union Jack and the committee barge at Bell Wharf. The prize winners that year were the *Doris*, owned by W. Lucking, the *Vera* owned by A. Kirby, *Nil Desperandum*, owned by W. Oliver, and the *Honor* owned by F.C. Cotgrove.

90 Large crowds were attracted to the annual Leigh Regatta, and trains from London were overcrowded with trippers on regatta days.

The 1912 regatta also saw three races for yachts: under 17ft long, under 25ft long and over 25ft long. Yacht races attracted 32 entrants. Four motor boats started in a handicap race and the Essex Yacht Club had a 17ft one-design class. There was a veteran's sculling race for the over 65s, with a first prize of a new Guernsey and two shillings and sixpence, second prize a Guernsey, third prize half a ton of coal and fourth prize a quarter of a ton of coal. In 1913 the veterans' race attracted five starters, the oldest aged 77.

In the millers versus sweeps event, two men each in a bawley joined by a length of rope from each transom pelted each other with paper bags of soot and chalk. A race for fishermen in thigh boots was run along the foreshore. Climbing the greasy pole was done vertically and ashore and cost one shilling to enter. There was a similar competition for walking a horizontal pole rigged out from the committee boat's side, with a live pig in a cage suspended from the end as a prize. By 1912, the pig had been replaced by a flag,

91 Pleasure boat trip. When Leigh amalgamated with Southend in 1913, the residents of Westcliff living between the Crowstone and the *Gypsy* (the Essex Yacht Club HQ) expressed a wish that that part of the borough be known as Chalkwell Bay.

92 The *Gypsy*, Essex Yacht Club, after which the present bridge over the railway is named.

LEIGH SAILING CLUB

When the West End Sailing Club, which had begun in 1903, was wound up in 1911, some of its members formed the Leigh Sailing Club. Sir Frederic Senier was a founding member and first commodore of the club and a headquarters was set up in a cottage on Strand Wharf. The club was seen as a further attraction to the town and the 1913 official town guide boasted, 'The members of the club are about as keen and capable a set of jolly good fellows and rattling sailormen as you will find anywhere'.

The club later moved to a converted barge, *Veronica*, on the seafront, which in 1938 was replaced by the former topsail schooner *Lady Quirk*. This vessel deteriorated so badly that, after the war, the club met in an upstairs room at the *Crooked Billet* until they found a meeting place in the old railway station, previously occupied by the Essex Yacht Club. The sailing club gradually purchased the freehold of the whole building from the railway company, and continues as an extremely successful club today.

the flag winner claiming his pig back on shore. Second prize was often a duck. The last race for sailing bawleys at Leigh Regatta was 1928. The regatta was abandoned at the start of the Second World War but was re-launched as a fund-raising event in 1973.

93 Elm Road from church tower, *c.*1910. Leigh House dominates the bottom left corner of this picture. Wesley Methodist Church can be seen further down the road on the right. Opposite it was the house of John Osborne, a builder and benefactor of the church. Notice the fields in the background, north of London Road.

WESLEY METHODIST CHURCH

The growth of the residential population above Leigh cliffs prompted the Methodist community to think about providing a second chapel for their congregation. Land in Elm Road was donated by John Osborne, a builder, and in 1900 a hall known as Wesley School-Chapel was built at the rear of the plot. The hall was used as a church while money was raised for a permanent church at the front of the plot. At 3p.m. on 4 May 1904 the door to the new Wesley Methodist Church was opened by Mrs John Osborne and the dedication service was led by the Rev. John H. Goodman of London. During the afternoon a large gathering enjoyed a shrimp tea in Wesley Hall, and that evening a public meeting was held with the mayor

of Southend in the chair. Rev. C. Craggs became the first minister.

On the last day of 1914, a few months after the outbreak of the First World War, John Osborne died. The Wesley Methodist Church leaders minutes read, 'Our indebtedness and that of future generations to Mr Osborne is very great, and we give thanks to God for his noble life and generous spirit'. The Osbornes, who lived in a large house built in the 1880s on the corner of Rectory Grove, gave Wesley Hall, Wesley Manse (1911) and much of the church including the galleries (1912) and organ (1907), and the ground on which all were built. In his will Mr Osborne asked that all monies owed by the church be cleared. A memorial brass on the south wall of the church records his generosity to local Methodism.

94 The *Woodcutter's Arms* became part of Leigh when Eastwood joined the borough in 1913. A beerhouse is known to have existed on this site since at least 1863, when it was owned by James and Hannah Rand. The pub was completely refurbished in the 1920s and again during 1999.

95 Turner's Corner, August 1922. The road bending right is Eastwood Road (then Turner's Lane). Straight ahead is the track to Gowles, which was replaced by Westleigh Grange farm just north of Tankerville Drive about 1900. By 1923 the Gowles track was transformed into Blenheim Chase dual carriageway.

BELFAIRS

The north of the parish remained an area to be avoided by respectable citizens at this time. The north-west corner of Leigh, from Turner's Lane (now Eastwood Road) through Belfairs Woods and stretching across Belfairs Common and Beggars' Bush to Daws Heath and into Eastwood, had been frequented by vagabonds and highwaymen from at least the 1600s. By the end of the 19th century the area comprised an enormous gypsy camp.

Alfred Boynton, a resident of Alley Dock in the old town, was a large man and not one to avoid a fight, but even he was cautious of the gypsies. He occasionally walked from Leigh to Chelmsford but told a friend, 'I took pertic'ler care to go round by Rayleigh to give them gypsies a berth. Talk about rough! They'd knock down their own mother to steal the watch and chain off her back'.

96 Aerial view of south Leigh, *c.*1925. Broadway West has not yet been laid out. The footbridge over the railway is clearly visible.

WEST LEIGH SCHOOL

Residential growth west of the town led to a decision to build another primary school, and West Leigh School was formally opened by the mayor of Southend, Alderman Francis JP, on 13 September 1913 with two departments: infants and mixed juniors. The 278 juniors were accommodated in six rooms, built to accommodate 40 children each, under head teacher Mr E. Hood, a former teacher at North Street, and a staff of six. In view of the number of pupils, on the recommendation of the Education Committee, two additional rooms were furnished at a cost of £62 15s. 6d.

West Leigh infants department had 171 pupils under headteacher Miss A. Durrant and a staff of four teachers. The school buildings were extended in 1927, when the mixed school was separated into boys and girls departments.

A month after West Leigh opened, Leigh amalgamated with Southend.

NOVEMBER 1913

Southend Corporation had first proposed to incorporate Leigh into the Borough of Southend in 1906 but this was successfully opposed by Leigh Council. However, resolve to remain independent waned in the face of rising cost of roads and sanitation, and Leigh's inability to compete with Southend in attracting revenue from trippers, and Leigh officially became part of Southend on 9 November 1913. The last meeting of Leigh Urban District Council was held in 1914, and Southend itself became a County Borough on 1 April 1914.

By the time Leigh finally succumbed to pressure from Southend it had changed from a small community dominated by its traditional fishing industry to a town typified by a residential population living north of Leigh Cliffs. The original village was already being referred to as the 'Old Town'.

Eight

Urban Development: The Growth of Leigh

With the absorption into Southend came boundary changes, and in 1914 Leigh was extended to include that part of Eastwood south of the A127 (at that time just a cart track) and that part of Prittlewell west of Chalkwell Park, bringing the population to around 10,000 people. The council offices, opened only two years previously, were deemed too small and work began on a larger building of a similar style further along Elm Road, now the Leigh Community Centre.

Rail travel was already encouraging London workers to settle in Leigh and make a daily trip up to the city by train. Indeed, Leigh owes much of its continued development to the railway since its growth as a holiday resort was severely impeded by competition from Southend and there was little increase in industry.

97 Eastwood School, Rayleigh Road. When Eastwood amalgamated with Leigh, in 1913, pupils were encouraged to attend either West Leigh or Chalkwell schools to alleviate overcrowding at Eastwood school.

The administration of local schools passed from Essex County Council to Southend Town Council through its education committee, and the Board of Education wrote stating that it was proposed that the Leigh schools should be known as the Southend-on-Sea Leigh-on-Sea Council School and the Southend-on-Sea West Leigh Council School. With regard to the former, the education committee decided to ask to maintain the current name: Leigh North Street Council School.

Throughout the parish, services and public facilities were developed to serve the growing population moving into the residential areas developed by such as Frederick Ramuz. An early benefit of the amalgamation was the laying out of a comprehensive drainage and sewerage system during the 1920s at a cost of £25,000.

LEIGH LIBRARY

Leigh's first library opened in 1919 in the former council offices, now the police station. Then, in April 1926, the council agreed to purchase the rectory and convert it into a library. The east-facing porch was dismantled brick by brick and re-built on the north side to coincide with the opening of a new access road, Broadway West. Internal walls were taken down to make an open-plan library on the ground floor with a separate staff room and ladies' and gentlemen's toilets. On the first floor was a reading room. The library was finally opened on 9 October 1928 by Councillor Arthur Bockett, with a stock of 8,500 books. The gardens were opened to the public in June 1930 under the management of Southend Council Parks Department. Further internal structural alterations were carried out in 1972.

98 Chalkwell school pupils, *c*.1930. The school was built in 1908 in Prittlewell parish, but became part of Leigh in 1913.

99 West Leigh mixed juniors, *c*.1935. The headmaster is Mr Gibbs and the teacher Mrs Rombaut.

100 Ordnance Survey map, 1922. Although the area immediately east and north of St Clement's is quite densely built-up, building elsewhere is patchy. There was hardly any development north of the London Road at this time. There is no Broadway West or Belton Way. The circle west of the High Street is the gasworks.

101 East Broadway, *c.*1910.

102 Broadway, looking west, *c.*1920.

103 Leigh Library, on the day it first opened, 9 October 1928. Anyone visiting the library today enters through what was the original rectory's larder. From 1927 the building now called Watson House was used as the rectory until the old National Schools building was purchased by the Church in the 1950s.

CINEMAS

Between 1910 and 1965 four cinemas opened and closed in Leigh. The Empire Palace cinema opened first on 3 December 1910, to a full house of 400 patrons, eager to see the silent film *The Heads of the World*. The building, situated at the end of Leigh Broadway behind the *Grand Hotel*, was described in the local press as 'very bright and comfortable'. However, it had no ceiling and the iron roof support girders were clearly visible. The front seats, the 'tuppenny forms', were a series of hard benches. Behind these the upholstered seating had narrow backs and, apparently, had been known to tip the whole row onto the people behind because of rotten floorboards.

Film shows were augmented by live vocal performances, the piano being played by Mr Dickenson, occasionally supported by violinists and sometimes a drum. The usherettes wore black dresses with white aprons. In the 1930s the building was refurbished to accommodate 'talkies'. However, with competition by that time from three other cinemas, the Empire showed its last film on 9 December 1937. The building lay vacant for some years before being taken over by a small 'fancy goods' manufacturing firm. It now sells hairdressing supplies.

104   Empire Palace flyer.

105   Dossett's bakery, in the premises built as Henry's Hall.

Almost opposite the Empire was Henry's Hall, opened in 1912 as a theatre. Original plans for a grandiose concert hall with a skating rink were apparently shelved at the last minute. Moving pictures were shown for a short time in the hall, which was on the first floor, but after 1915 live entertainment took precedence. In 1923 the hall was purchased by the Dossett family and converted into a bakery. Today the building is very little changed externally and houses a cleaning supplies firm.

Perhaps the best loved of Leigh's cinemas, and certainly the longest running was the Coliseum, opened in Elm Road in April 1914. The proprietor was Charles Dare and the architect Frank Bowhill. The original auditorium with a barrel ceiling was decorated in gold and red and seated 600 in plush seats. A live orchestra accompanied the silent films.

Towards the end of the 1920s the Coliseum was completely refurbished to accommodate talking pictures. Developments included raising the roof 20 feet and the addition of an upstairs foyer and balcony. Seating provision increased to 1,100 and the colour scheme was changed to old gold with a mottled blue ceiling. However, the new look did not go down well with the general public, and in November 1936 the cinema closed again for further 'improvements', this time under the direction of architect George Coles.

The Coliseum reopened on 26 December and the *Southend Times* reported that it had, like a phoenix from the ashes, 'arisen in all its splendour with only the name as a reminder of the past'. The new interior decorations were elaborate, the seats luxurious and the colour scheme a delicate shade of pink. Innovations included heating and ventilation as well as usherettes attired in trousers and berets. An orchestra was still employed to provide music during the intervals. The manager at this time was Mr V.F. Theobalds and admission prices were sixpence, ninepence or one shilling for a seat in the stalls, and either one and fourpence or one and sixpence in the circle. Local resident Roy Dilley remembers the closing of the curtains being so painfully slow that they had to start closing them several minutes before the end of the film!

On 12 May 1937 every seat at the Coliseum was free during the morning for George VI's

106 Dossett's bakers, 8 The Broadway. Charles Dossett came to Leigh around 1900 and opened his first bakery on the corner of Scarborough Drive. In 1905 the shop moved to the Broadway. There were eventually nine Dossett's shops from Rayleigh to Shoeburyness. The company was wound up in 1983 after the death of Norman Dossett.

Coronation broadcast, and at 8p.m. the King's speech was included in the programme. In 1954 the Coliseum was purchased by the Essoldo group, which continued to run it as a cinema until 22 May 1965. Harry Lamber, Essoldo's general manager, said at the time of the closure, 'Business was very poor. It [the cinema] is just not wanted in the area'. The building was converted into a bingo club, which was successful until the 1980s. After a few years vacant it opened for a disastrous (as far as local residents were concerned) year as a nightclub in 1999, and was finally converted into shops and flats in 2002.

Leigh's fourth cinematic enterprise was the Corona, opened in Leigh Road on 25 October 1929, on the site of the Victoria potteries. The building, costing £23,000, was sponsored by the South East Essex Cinema Syndicate consisting of local councillors and members of the community, and could seat 1,530 in its blue and gold auditorium. The interior plasterwork and murals

107 Howard's Dairies milkman in Manchester Drive.

depicted scenes reflecting the local fishing industry, with fish, crabs, cockles and seagulls. There was an orchestra for several years, but it was supplanted by Mr H. Williams and his two-manual Christie organ, which was still in use until after the Second World War.

Like the Coliseum, the Corona was absorbed into the Essoldo group in 1954. Cinemascope was installed but again economic pressures forced the

108   Coliseum Cinema, Elm Road.

109   Father Leolin Hilditch, first vicar of St Margaret's.

cinema eventually to close, its last showing being on 4 April 1959. The building was used variously by a soft drinks distributor, a specialist car construction company and a DIY shop before being converted into a snooker hall in 1982. During the 1990s the upstairs became a ten-pin bowling alley.

ST MARGARET'S

When Canon Walker King died on St Margaret's Day 1892 his son, Robert Stuart King, who succeeded him as rector, decided that if a mission church was built in the parish it should be dedicated to St Margaret. However, it was not until 1919 that a temporary building was erected approximately on the site of the present church hall on the corner of London Road and Lime Avenue, being central to the built-up area of Leigh. This temporary structure was used daily for 46 years, 12 as a church and 34 as a hall.

St Margaret's remained a mission church within St Clement's parish for six years, during which time it was served by the clergy of St Clement's, Canon King and his curates. When it was granted independence, on 1 January 1925, Father Hilditch was appointed priest-in-charge, his salary paid by the congregation.

A fund for the provision of a permanent church building was begun in 1926, and within three years £2,000 had been raised and architectural plans submitted by Graham Lloyd LRIBA accepted. St Margaret's was formally designated a parish on

111   110 Leigh Park Road was so named as it led to the Leigh Park Estate, west of Westleigh Avenue.

17 May 1929, and on the following St Margaret's day Father Hilditch was licensed as its first vicar.

Building work on the church itself was finally commenced in June 1930 by local builders Flaxman and Sons, and on 26 July the Bishop of Chelmsford laid the foundation stone before an audience of 500 people. The permanent church building was consecrated by the bishop on 7 March 1931, having cost a total of some £8,500, and the temporary building became the church hall. On the same day the Bishop consecrated St Thomas' Church, a wooden structure built in the High Street by Leigh fishermen.

In 1935 Father Hilditch encouraged the purchase of a plot of land in Tattersall Gardens for another church. However, that same year the Conventional District of St Barnabas, Hadleigh was formed and took over that part of St Margaret's lying north of

the London Road and west of Sutherland Boulevard and, after some 40 years, the site in Tattersall Gardens was sold.

A north aisle and Lady Chapel were added to St Margaret's in 1938. Fifteen years after its founding, Robert King, by now Canon King, organised a tent campaign on land in Elmsleigh Drive given by Mr Eric Brewer, and a temporary church of St James were erected on the site. This northern section of the original parish of St Clement's became the parish of St James.

OUR LADY OF LOURDES
Prior to 1910 Catholics living in Leigh were obliged to travel to Shoeburyness to celebrate mass, and it was 1912 before a church was established in Leigh itself, by Fr John O'Neill. The first public mass was celebrated in a house in Leigham Court Drive in

111 This view towards Leigh Heath Farm (which can just be seen in the distance), *c.*1920, was probably taken from the corner of Medway Crescent, which marked the boundary between the eastern half of the Leigh Health Farm estate and the later-developed western half.

SOUTHEND-ON-SEA

THE VALUABLE FREEHOLD BUILDING ESTATE
Known as LEIGH HEATH FARM
Comprising an area of about 53 ½ ACRES
In practically a square block, possessing frontage of over 1,300 feet to the London Road and over
1,000 feet to Thames Drive.
The whole of the Land stands on a high level and commands extensive VIEWS OVER THE THAMES
ESTUARY and is between half a mile and one mile of the new Leigh Station, which, with its approach
roads, is practically completed.

KEMSLEYS

Are instructed to SELL THE ABOVE by AUCTION, at the London Auction Mart, 155, Queen
Victoria Street, London, E.C 4, in October in one Lot.
Particulars and Conditions of Sale may be obtained from Messrs. Ranger, Burton and Frost,
Solicitors, 179 Queen Victoria Street, London, E.C 4; or from the Auctioneers, 154, Bishopsgate,
London, E.C 2, and 33, South Street, Romford.

112 Sale particulars of Leigh Heath Farm.

113 The foundation stone of Highlands Methodist Church was laid on 27 April 1927. This original building is now the church hall.

November 1912, at which time 121 Leigh residents were registered Catholics. The following year the corrugated iron drill hall in Marguerite Drive, built in 1900 for the 20th Company of the Essex Volunteers, was purchased for £625 and dedicated to St Joseph and St Patrick. This hall served as Leigh's Catholic church for over fifteen years.

On 7 October 1924 the foundation stone of a permanent church was laid by the Bishop of Brentwood. The finished building, based on plans drawn up by Sir Charles Nicholson for St Alban's church in Westcliff, was consecrated in August 1929. Dedicated to Our Lady of Lourdes and St Joseph, it was in the Early English style, could seat 600 people, and cost £12,234.

LAND SALES

By the 1920s the Salvation Army project in Hadleigh was no longer seen as viable and William Bramwell Booth began disposing of land at Leigh. In August

114 Aerial view of the Leigh Park Farm estate, *c*.1930. Sutherland Boulevard and Highlands Boulevard are under construction, beyond which are visible the remnants of the Salvation Army's orchards. Leigh Heath farm can be seen in the bottom left-hand corner.

115 Post office and library, Sydney Road, *c*.1930.

TYPE "B"

ELIZABETHAN HOUSES LEIGH·ON·SEA

SEMI-DETACHED HOUSE.

Frontage 28ft. Depth 120ft. to 150ft. approx.

• • •

ACCOMMODATION. Three Bedrooms. Two Reception rooms. Tiled Bathroom. Seperate W.C. Linen Cupboard. Tiled Kitchenette. Tiled Larder and Cloak Cupboard.

FEATURES. Artistic stoves with dual coal and electric fires to choice, in the two main Bedrooms. Special decorations to choice. Built-in Wardrobe Cupboards in the two main Bedrooms. Closed in bath with "Marblexa" panel. Pedestal Lavatory basin, Shaving mirror, Soap dish and other accessories fitted to bathroom. Independent boiler (colour to choice) with hot and cold water supply to kitchenette and bathroom. Auxilary Electric Immersion water heater installed in property. Special built-in dresser and sink cupboards with two draining boards installed in kitchenette. Single panel doors with first class locksets.

SPECIAL FEATURES Lounge hall makes a useful and commanding entrance. Electric shades and fittings to choice.

• • •

Complete with main drainage, gas, electric light and power.

Garage room.   Garage extra if required.

116 From the sale catalogue of Leigh builder A. Wells, who was responsible for many properties on the Highlands estate. The larger houses on the Highlands West estate (Ewan Way, Buxton Avenue, Woodlands Park), which sold for between £1,300 and £1,500, advertised not only a tradesman's entrance but also 'a separate WC for the servants'.

1923 a strip of land on the London Road frontage was sold to the Southend Corporation for road widening purposes. On 30 June 1927 the eastern section, 26.219 acres, of the Leigh Heath Farm estate was sold to the Southend-on-Sea Estates Company for £17,042. However, Booth included clauses in the deeds to ensure that future development should follow his plans for the area. The deed stipulated 'Neither the land hereby conveyed nor any existing or future building theron shall be used for the manufacture, sale or supply of wine, beer, spirits or other intoxicating liquors nor for the purpose of public entertainment'. However, shops 'for occupations, trade or businesses not of a noxious, noisy or offensive character' could be erected on the portion of land fronting London Road. Every house was to be either detached or semi-detached except in Chapman's Close and Thames Close, where they could be in a terrace of four, and those fronting London Road, which could be in blocks or terraces.

The purchasers, the deed continued, could submit plans for the continuation of Marine Parade, with gardens on its south side, to where it adjoined the proposed road marked on the plans as New Arterial Road. The Salvation Army subsequently co-operated by paying half the cost of construction of the new arterial road, which was named Thames Drive. The remaining, western, section of Leigh Heath was put up for sale in 1933, with the same restrictions placed on subsequent development.

The Leigh Park Farm estate was similarly sold and was developed, largely by local builder Mr Walker, between 1920 and 1935 into the Park View estate, later known as the Highlands estate. In 1936 Southend Corporation purchased the Leigh Park brickfields from Mr Brush and extended Highlands Boulevard to join up with the London Road. The

117 Leigh Park grocery stores, *c*.1930. This parade of shops on the London Road between Barnard Road and Herschell Road is under construction.

118 Burnt Oak Farm, one of the many properties once owned by Dr John Cook, was replaced with shops and housing on the Leigh Road-Highcliff Drive corner in the 1930s.

brickfield itself remained largely undeveloped for the next fifteen years. During the 1920s the Coleman estate was developed around Eastwood Road North and Kent Elms Corner. Frederick Ramuz bought Burnt Oak Farm in Leigh Road, Little Folly Farm on the London Road, and part of Chalkwell to form the Cliff Estate.

In 1927 Leigh House was purchased from Dr Douglas Watson and immediately pulled down. A road was driven through the grounds behind the house to join up with Rectory Grove, west of the rectory, by now the new library. This was named Broadway West and, at first, provided only access to the library and a convenient turning place for buses. The first shops opening in Broadway West were Marjorie Simkins' fruiterer's, Edith Clark's confectioner's and Mrs Fanny Coppitter's refreshment bar, along with the Regal Valet Service cleaners. By 1935 Broadway West had developed into a commercial centre with a fishmonger,

119 This section of Eastwood Road North was sometimes called Pickett's Road after Pickett's Farm, just to the north in Eastwood.

120 Coombes Corner. Opposite this post office during the early 20th century was Easley's Nursery, which supplied many of the rose bushes for Chalkwell Park when it was originally laid out in 1926.

121 Victoria Drive, *c.*1915.

122 Woodfield Park Drive, January 1922. Building plots were sold and built upon before the roads were made up. This area was developed by the Land Company from 1896, with plots being sold at auctions for as little as £25 each.

ironmonger, tailor, draper and florist. Among the new stores was clothier Simpson & Barnes, which traded from the same premises until 2000.

The 1930s saw the development of the Elms area, north of the London Road, and the infilling of the Leigh Hall estate. Plans to add 122 houses to the Leigh Housing Estate, similar to housing already built at Kent Avenue, were accepted at a cost of £426 each. In 1933 most of Eastwood became absorbed into Southend as part of the Leigh-on-Sea district. The remaining north-east portion joined Rochford.

THE CHAPMANSLORD ESTATE

After the First World War, fearing that British workers would follow Russia into Bolshevik revolution, the government began a Homes Fit for Heroes campaign, building houses for returning soldiers. Land was purchased from the Chapmanslord farm and an estate comprising Canvey Road, Ray Walk and Ray Close was developed by the Chapmanslord Housing Society Limited in 1920. It was designed on a 'garden city' theme, to be attractive, spacious and with larger than average gardens, but the Homes Fit for Heroes campaign only lasted two years, ending abruptly in 1921.

HOUSEBOATS

From the end of the war, homeless people began to take up residence in houseboats moored to wooden jetties between the cocklesheds and the site of the present Leigh Station. Together they became a floating village. At their peak, between the wars, there were some two hundred floating homes in Leigh and Benfleet creeks. The vessels ranged from converted dinghies to ships' lifeboats

123   The Bungalow Tearooms, Grand Parade, *c*.1915.

124   London Road at Leigh cemetery, 1930s.

125 Jones' Corner, *c.*1930.

and barges with added superstructure. Freshwater was collected from the cocklesheds for a few pence per bucketful and, with no sanitation, any waste was dumped into the estuary.

Dwellings were permanent enough for the postman to call and a general store and a confectionery business were run from the boats. Local tradesmen made regular deliveries of bread, milk and food. The boats were lit by oil lamps and warmed by oil stoves. The Port of London Authority and Southend Council campaigned to remove the houseboats because they were seen as a health hazard, and so

126 Canvey Road, *c.*1920. Note the 'Private Road' sign.

127 Houseboats. The old gas works on Billet Wharf can be seen in the background. Washing lines were a typical feature of the boats, as were cats, kept to deter the rat population.

that part of the promenade could be developed. The last houseboat had gone by the end of the 1950s.

E.K. COLE

One of the few industries starting up in Leigh was that owned by Eric Kirkham Cole, whose original premises to manufacture radios were two rooms in Leigh opened in 1925. The following year he acquired a small purpose-built factory on the London Road, just north-east of the *Elms* public house, and took on a workforce of over fifty employees. The original EKCO two-valve receivers, complete with batteries and headphones, sold for £6 10s.; six were produced each week. In 1930 E.K. Cole Ltd moved to Priory Crescent, Southend where it became the largest producer of radios in the country.

BELFAIRS GOLF COURSE

Leigh Park Golf Club opened just prior to the start of the First World War with a nine-hole course on land formerly belonging to Belfairs Farm but members were dissatisfied both with the golfing conditions and the news that the estate within which the golf club lay was to be compulsorily purchased by Southend Corporation. A letter dated 23 October 1921, addressed to Mr Cooper, Leigh Park Golf Club, Belfairs Farm, suggests plans for members of the Leigh Park committee to view fields at Boyce Hill Farm in South Benfleet as a potential alternative location for their golf club. It was later agreed that the club move to Boyce Hill, leaving the Belfairs estate available for Southend Corporation.

The estate taken on by the Corporation included the stable block built by Lady Olivia Sparrow in the late 19th century, latterly used as an Elim Chapel, and Major Miller's new house, Belfairs Lodge. Various suggestions were put forward as to the estate's use, one of which was a rubbish dump. However, a golf course for the use of 'working men' was decided upon. Belfairs public golf course, designed by Harry Colt of McKenzie, Colt and Allison, was officially opened on Saturday 11 September 1926. A crowd of 400 to 500 people gathered to see Mayor Alderman H. Dowsett take an inaugural shot from the first tee. He admitted golf was not his game when the ball only travelled a few yards, and he was presented with the cleat as a memento. The ceremony continued with an exhibition of golf by two champions and two local professionals.

The course covered some one hundred of the 266 acres of the Belfairs estate, and Mr Colt commented that he never would have embarked on the project had he realised the trouble involved in grubbing up the trees and levelling the furrows. Initially, the cost of an annual season ticket at the

128 Eastwood Road, looking north from Prittle Brook, *c*.1920. It was originally intended that the western side of the road should be left undeveloped to provide a vista for the public.

129 Aerial view of north-west Leigh, *c*.1930. The tennis courts, bottom right, are now Bonchurch Park. The *Woodcutter's Arms* can just be made out centre-top. There has been no development of the Fairway area.

130   The Popular Guest House stood on the site of Cavell Lodge on Blenheim Chase. It gave its name to the Popular Road House next door, now the Old Vienna.

course was three guineas, while a single round could be played for two shillings at a weekend or one shilling and sixpence on a weekday. Such was the demand for the park's facilities that seven bus routes were serving the park during the 1920s and '30s. The course was redeveloped in 1937 when the putting green was laid out and a bandstand erected.

BELFAIRS NATURE RESERVE

Southend Corporation also had plans for Belfairs woods, which were adjacent to the golf course. In 1922 the Ecclesiastical Commissioners sold Great Wood, Dodds Grove, Horsley Wood, a cottage garden and paddocks to James Pratt Harvey, a timber merchant of Heath Farm, Leigh, for £4,500. He in turn sold it to George Homes of London. In 1938 Southend purchased over forty acres of Belfairs Great Wood, in conjunction with Benfleet Urban District Council and Essex County Council. The aim was to create an area of nature reserve and for this purpose £1,000 was raised by voluntary subscription. Southend was one of the first authorities to own a nature reserve and, until 1960, it was the only nature reserve in Essex.

The reserve now covering some 90 acres is one of the best preserved examples of ancient woodland in south-east Essex and is managed using traditional methods to encourage a wide range of plants and animals. Features of the wood include hollows formed during gravel extraction and dug for saw pits, with the more recent addition of bomb craters. Within the nature reserve, several of these hollows have been dammed and now form small ponds for aquatic life. Thirty-seven male and female butterflies were released into the reserve in 1997, and nesting sites for a population of some 60 to 100 common lizards were established in 2001.

LEIGH HORTICULTURAL SOCIETY

On Thursday 4 June 1925 a group of gardeners met in the small hall at Elm Hall in Elm Road to discuss the setting up of a gardening society for the people of Leigh-on-Sea. Mr Cranley Perry of Vernon Road was elected as chairman and subscriptions were set at two shillings and sixpence per member or four shillings for a husband and wife. The meeting proposed to hold two flower shows a year, in July and October. The first president of the society was Sir Frederic Senier and membership increased rapidly.

131 Leigh United Football Club, 1935/6. Several of these players lost their lives in the Second World War.

132 Belton Farm. Navvies working on the railway were billeted here and apparently enjoyed many a good fight with the locals.

133 Chalkwell Station, 1933. Chalkwell was under the Leigh stationmaster for nearly a year until the new Leigh station opened.

During the 1920s and '30s shows were held in Chalkwell Park, with bands, sideshows and dancing displays. The show benches themselves were set up in large marquees, with a smaller tent devoted to an exhibition of produce by unemployed gardeners working under the auspices of Southend Public Welfare Council.

Interest in the society was re-ignited after the war and by the time of its silver jubilee, in 1950,

134 The 'new' Leigh station, 1934. Newspaper sellers waited on Belton Way to catch the passing trade. When trees were felled on Belton Hills for the construction of Belton Way several families of rooks were made homeless.

membership had reached almost one thousand. It was following a flower-arranging demonstration at the society that the Leigh Floral Arrangement Group came into being in January 1955. In October 1985 the Manchester Drive Allotment Society became affiliated, and the society celebrated its 75th anniversary at Chalkwell Park Rooms in June 2000.

RAILWAY STATIONS

Southend Corporation's vision for Leigh as a quiet residential suburb resulted in the development of little industry. Therefore, many of the settlers found employment in London and were dependent on the railway for daily transport to their jobs. To meet the needs of this growing population of commuters, work was begun on a new, larger railway station in February 1933. At the same time

Chalkwell station was built to serve the Ridgeway estate, which had developed after the First World War as a high class dormitory area.

Residents of Leigh Old Town saw the closure of the old Leigh station as disastrous for the fishermen and for business people on Leigh Hill, and a petition of 3,000 signatures, supported by Canon King, was presented to the council in protest against the closure. In addition, residents proposed that a Society for the Preservation of Old Leigh be formed with Canon King as chairman.

135 Steam train passing through Leigh, *c.*1950. Steam trains can have done little for the cleanliness of the air in Leigh, and in 1913 a journalist noted with irony that a platform sign asking passengers to refrain from spitting was heavily begrimed.

136 The appearance of a photographer in the High Street seems to attract more interest from the residents than the flooding. Until 1892, the area that is now the *Peter Boat* car park was the site of four shops, several cottages, a stable and a slaughterhouse.

137 Flooding at Bell and Victoria Wharves in 1921. The tall building on the left, Turnidge's sail-loft, still exists; those behind it on Victoria Wharf do not. The wharf was named after the Victoria Potteries who owned it for several years, although it was subsequently associated for many years with the Tomlin family.

138 Flooding at the *Crooked Billet*. A certain amount of flooding was expected in the Old Town in spring and autumn. However, this high tide on 21 November 1921 was exceptional.

Approach roads to the new station were begun, for which the name Belton Way was adopted. Agreement was made for LMS railway to contribute £20,000 to the construction of the new road, the Salvation Army as the principle landowner would contribute £3,000 and Southend Corporation would meet the remaining costs. Chalkwell station, the smaller of the two, opened within six months, but it was almost a year before the Belton Hills station was completed. Charles Booth & Son, the building contractors, employed 60 to 70 men to work continuously on Leigh station which, owing

139 Ordnance Survey map, 1939. Development south of the London Road is almost uniformly dense, compared with the 1922 map. Broadway West has been cut through and the new station built. The timber yard in Leigh Hall Road is on the site of Leigh Hall.

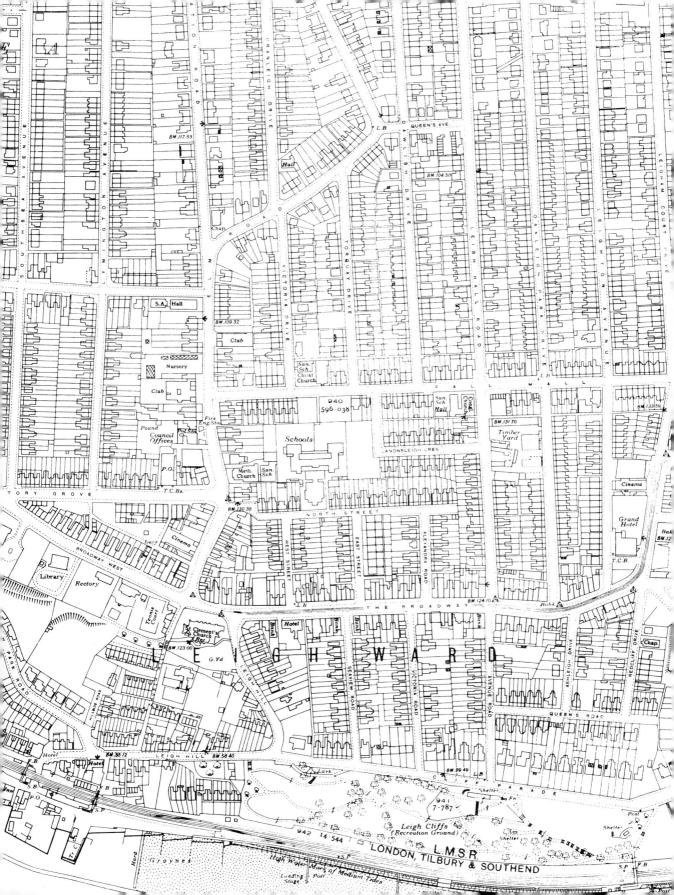

to the wet, clay soil, was built on reinforced concrete piles, driven 35 feet into the ground at 12 feet intervals.

The last train pulled into the old Leigh station just as St Clement's was ringing in the new year on 31 December 1933. The next morning, Monday 1 January 1934, Belton Way was lined with traders eager to catch the passing trade; officials waited at the station to oversee the proceedings and buses carried passengers to it from the church. The first passenger to pass through the gate was Mr H. Anstey of Queen's Road, Hadleigh, one of over 4,000 season ticket holders to use the station that morning. The two entrances, one facing north, the other east, were surmounted by name-plates stating 'Leigh-on-Sea' in chromium, black and green. This colour scheme was followed throughout the station. There were steps and a lift down to the platforms, each 700 feet long, with ten seats on the up platform and eight on the down. The waiting rooms, like the booking hall and offices upstairs, were centrally heated and laid with block flooring.

A bridge had been constructed beside the station for access to the goods yard, which included a large cattle dock, a cockle shed and a space for the storage of coal. An arrangement was made for fishermen's produce to be transported free of charge from the wharves by lorry to the new station.

Although the station was in use from 1 January, an official opening ceremony was held on Thursday 4 January when the Mayor of Southend, Councillor H.E. Frith, met the 12.25p.m. from St Pancras. Sir Josiah Stamp, the President of the LMS railway, was travelling on the train and invited the mayor to declare the station open. Officials and guests then boarded the same train and travelled to Southend for a celebratory lunch at Garon's banqueting suite.

OLD TOWN

The relocation of the station left the original village isolated from the growing community at the top of the hill. Residents, and particularly the traders of Leigh Hill, demanded that New Road be extended to join up with Belton Way so that commuters would be encouraged to travel that way. To complement the new stations, several councillors were pushing for more ambitious 'improvements' to south Leigh, including extending the roadway from Chalkwell Esplanade along the seafront, through Leigh, and across to Canvey Island. The scheme involved a huge carpark on the beach behind Chalkwell station, providing parking for 1,500 vehicles. The foreshore between Chalkwell station and the boundary with Hadleigh would then be developed to include a bowling green, concert area, lido and swimming pool.

With a view to the implementation of these plans, Southend Corporation had begun purchasing property in the old part of town as early as 1930. Purchases included the 400-year-old 'Smugglers Cottage', near the *Peter Boat*, and the old blacksmith's shop on Leigh Hill, occupied by the Jocelyn family for three hundred years. In 1939 number 14 High Street was purchased for £400, while numbers 75 to 78, which included Cook's Place, were purchased for £700. The next year the 17th-century cottages on Strand Wharf were demolished. In 1934 the Corporation purchased the Salvation Army's land south of the railway station, including Two Tree Island and Leigh Marsh, and began negotiation with the railway company for land adjacent to the line.

Alderman Johnson was against excessive development in Leigh and reminded a public meeting of the council's original vision for Leigh: 'keep it quiet, keep it beautiful'. Discussion over the plans was still on-going when the Second World War called a halt to all major development work.

Nine

The War Years

THE FIRST WORLD WAR

Leigh and its neighbour Southend were two of the first towns in the country to experience bombing raids in the First World War. Residents were awoken at 2.45a.m. on Sunday 9 May 1915 by a zeppelin dropping incendiary bombs on housing between Pall Mall and the London Road. The airship continued flying west and dropped further bombs on Marine Parade and the Old Town. At least twelve bombs were aimed directly at the Old Town gas works, opposite the *Crooked Billet*, but all missed.

The zeppelin then turned eastwards, passing over Leigh Broadway and the *Grand Hotel*. Eye-witnesses report that the airship seemed to hover for a long while over Leigh Road. By the time the next bomb dropped in a back garden behind Leigh Road, hundreds of people were out in the street. Steam hooters had been sounded, intended as a warning to residents to seek cover, but the opposite effect was achieved and at the first sound of the hooter people had thronged the street, eager to see the zeppelin. They were nearly hit with shrapnel when a second bomb exploded in the air over Leigh Road, showering the crowd with debris.

Eventually the zeppelin continued eastwards and out of Leigh. No one in Leigh was injured that day, but, as soon as the trams started running at 6a.m. the next day, sightseers flocked to the town to witness the bomb damage. Miss A. Durrant, headmistress of West Leigh School infant section, recorded in the school logbook for 10 May 1915 that many bombs had been dropped on the town during the night. 'Although most of the children were up at 3 o'clock and went through a most terrifying experience, only ten were kept at home during the day', she wrote

proudly. After that the captain of the fire brigade, Harold Johnson, would personally warn North Street school of impending attacks.

The boys department of the school took over vacant land next door to grow vegetables for the war effort, while the girls knitted socks, mufflers and balaclavas for troops throughout the war period. In September 1915 the trustees of Wesley Methodist Church decided that the church hall should be placed at the disposal of soldiers billeted in the town and that no meetings of the church or school should be held in the hall on weekday evenings. However, it closed as a soldiers' club in October owing to the small number of soldiers using it and the expense of gas lighting.

The worst injuries Leigh suffered were on 12 August 1917 when zeppelin bombers damaged properties in Victoria Road and Cliff Parade. On 26 September 1918 the Reverend Lawson of Wesley Methodist church was informed that a battalion of soldiers was to be stationed in the town and the Wesley Hall was opened as a soldiers' institute. Meanwhile, the Empire Palace cinema was open for free shows for soldiers.

On 11 November 1918 at 10.50a.m. the siren sounded its last All Clear, signalling the signing of the Armistice, and the bells of St Clement's were rung. At West Leigh school the hall was quickly decorated with flags and streamers and the children were assembled for a thanksgiving service. As at North Street School, a half-day holiday was proclaimed and the school was dismissed amidst great cheering.

THE SECOND WORLD WAR

Leigh began preparations for war in the summer of 1939, and by 29 July Anderson shelters had

140   The Leigh-on-Sea First World War ambulance.

been constructed around the town. The largest public air-raid shelters were at St Clement's Court (which had been built in 1937 on the former rectory meadow) with space for 300 people, at H. Abbott & Sons, 282 Leigh Road (120 spaces) and the *Old Bell Hotel* on Leigh Hill (150 spaces). Several shops in Leigh Broadway provided shelters for up to fifty people. Public shelter trenches were constructed at Marine Parade near Thames Drive (1,000 spaces), Sutherland Boulevard (60 spaces), Chalkwell Park west side (280 spaces), West Leigh Schools (200 spaces), Chalkwell Hall schools (100 spaces) and at Eastwood schools (150 spaces).

Several ARP shelters suffered after heavy rainfall and, occasionally, the wardens were forced to evacuate to nearby garages. The shelter at Sutherland Boulevard was filled with water for nearly a fortnight in October 1939, much to the delight of local children who used it as a paddling pool.

SHIPBUILDING

Johnson & Jago's became responsible for the building and repair of £2 million-worth of ships between 1939 and 1946, employing 200 workers building small naval and assault craft. The company had been founded in 1932 and in 1936 had taken over two tenancy agreements from the Essex Boat Company, who had been leasing land from the Salvation Army adjacent to the new railway station. In 1940 the yards were turned over to the admiralty. Slipways were laid and thousands of tons of mud were moved to obtain sufficient depth of water for the vessels. At peak of production one 112ft. motor launch was turned out every five and a half weeks, and, by 1946, 70 ships had been built for the war effort. The motor launches built in Leigh took part in mine-laying and sweeping, anti-submarine work, RAF rescues and as hospital carriers. Leigh-built craft took part in the Dieppe and St Nazaire raids, in the North Africa landings and invasion of the Continent, and saw service in the Mediterranean and Greek Islands.

141   Motor launch built by Johnson & Jago.

142   Launching a Johnson & Jago ship.

143 Dunkirk memorial, St Clement's churchyard, erected in 1972.

DUNKIRK

On Thursday 30 May 1940 the Navy at Southend sent word that they wanted small boats with volunteer crews to go to Dunkirk to assist with the evacuation of British soldiers. Volunteers were to be at the pierhead by 8a.m. on Friday morning.

Arthur 'Warfa' Dench, owner of the *Letitia*, and his son, Jim, were the first of the Leigh men to sign up, and they went around Leigh collecting loaves of bread to hand out to the stranded soldiers. Six Leigh cockle boats answered the call and, on 31 May 1940, the *Defender*, *Endeavour*, *Letitia*, *Reliance*, *Renown* and *Resolute* left Leigh around 10a.m. Naval ratings provided drums of fuel, rations and extra deckhands. By 7p.m. that night the boats were under attack from German bombers and, avoiding injury by taking a zig-zag course, reached Dunkirk independently.

Their role was to ferry troops from the beaches out to the larger ships at anchor in deep water. The broad-beamed, flat-bottomed bawleys, designed to be beached at high tide on the sandbanks while the fishermen got out to gather their cockles, were ideal for the shallow waters off Dunkirk. Each boat, around 30ft long by 10ft wide, rescued about 1,000 soldiers with repeated trips from the beach to the ships.

As the *Letitia* started home at 1.15a.m., the *Renown* came up behind and yelled that they had engine trouble, so the *Letitia* threw them a line and began to tow. At about 1.50a.m. the crew of the *Letitia* heard a terrible explosion and a hail of wooden splinters came down on her deck. The *Renown* had hit a mine and was completely destroyed with the loss of all crew. The Leigh boats returned to Ramsgate, and then sailed on to Leigh where their families were waiting on the beach.

Naval Control sent the following letter of appreciation addressed to Sydney Ford of 9 High Street, Leigh, dated 4 June 1940: 'The ready willingness with which seamen from every walk of life came forward to assist their brother seamen of the Royal Navy will not readily be forgotten.' Arthur Dench later recalled the crew of the *Renown*, saying, 'They knew nothing of war. They went to save, not to fight … It was a small tragedy in the great disaster of those days of war, yet great in the hearts of Leigh people.' In 1972 a memorial was erected to these Dunkirk heroes in St Clement's churchyard.

DEFENCES

Following the evacuation from Dunkirk a hectic programme of defence construction was put in hand to fortify all vulnerable stretches of the coast against enemy invasion, and Southend became one of the most heavily defended areas of Essex, an island ringed with concrete barriers, pill boxes, barbed wire and gun emplacements.

144   An estate of prefabricated housing was built between Eastwood Old Road and the A127 during the war to accommodate key workers making parachutes at the Airborne Industrial Estate. These 'temporary structures' were not replaced with permanent housing until the early 1970s.

The geography of Leigh – the Belton Hills and Leigh Cliffs – provided a natural defence at the west of the borough, but east of Chalkwell station a continuous concrete anti-tank barrier was erected stretching as far as Thorpe Bay. Anti-tank road barriers eventually enveloped the town, with no unauthorised traffic being allowed east of Hadleigh. From Eastwood a defensive line ran south to Leigh, with cut-off lengths of steel being dropped into sockets across the roadway to present a hedgehog-like defence. Farm vehicles were used to block the roads between Hadleigh and Leigh.

Concern mounted over the Thames acting as an easy navigational aid on the direct route from Germany to London and sites along the coast were acquired for anti-aircraft emplacements. Nine holes of Belfairs golf course were requisitioned by the military, and at 'TN5 Belfair Farm' technically advanced anti-aircraft weapons, 3.7 inch guns, were sited. The guns were manned by the 82nd Heavy Anti-Aircraft Regiment RA, but the instruments

in the concrete Command Post were under the control of the female ATS. The 82nd had been formed in November 1938 at Barking with two batteries from Barking and one from Leigh. Their headquarters was in Eastwood Road North, opposite the *Woodcutters Arms*, and the men served in North Africa and Italy before returning to Britain.

The Belfairs site developed into a major complex with concrete gun emplacements and a small village of Nissen huts to provide accommodation and service facilities. However, there was a high risk of civilian casualties if V1s were brought down over the town and the battery was later moved out to Foulness Island. Nothing now remains of 'TN5 Belfair Farm', although the pattern of the emplacement sometimes shows up on Belfairs golf course as a shadow on the parched grass in very hot summers.

When Anti-Aircraft Command was disbanded, in 1955, the heavy regiments, including the 82nd,

145 Bomb damage at Pall Mall. Soldiers were billeted in the roads off Pall Mall during the war. Leigh suffered bombing raids throughout 1940-3, the worst in mid-December 1940 when many houses were totally razed to the ground.

merged to form the 459th (Essex) HAA Regiment RA (TA). The light units joined them five years later and the regiment later amalgamated with a London unit to form the 300th (Tower Hamlets) Light Air Defence Regiment RA (TA), with R battery stationed at Leigh. Territorial units were stationed at the Eastwood Road North HQ until the 1990s, when the site was developed for housing.

HOME GUARD

The Belfairs home guard was one of the first in the country to be formed and would practise drill on the hard surface between the bowling greens at Belfairs Park, often before an audience of interested local residents. In July 1941 the Southend Home Guard held an exercise at Leigh. 'German paratroopers' had taken the railway station which was enthusiastically re-captured by the Home Guard, cheered on by spectators gathered on Belton Hills.

COMMUNITY SPIRIT

Wesley Methodist church hall opened as a community centre for the people of Leigh, and the church opened as a social club for HM forces where everything was free, including weekly concerts. Seventy female volunteers ran the club and in the six years from 1940 two and a half million meals were served. Although Father Hilditch had referred to St Margaret's church hall as a 'chronic invalid' as early as 1932, the war prevented its refurbishment and it continued in daily use at the disposal of the community. It became a Church Army canteen for over two years and survived bomb damage. Father Hilditch and his assistant, the Rev J.S. Willard, filled and sewed sandbags, which were piled around the servers' vestry and the boiler house. This was where the congregation would gather if an air raid began during a church service. Our Lady of Lourdes Catholic Church was open from dawn to dusk and during September 1939 received 2,000 communicants.

146 Bomb damage at Westleigh Avenue, 1941. During this raid the Elim Church in Glendale Gardens was destroyed. It was rebuilt and re-opened in 1950, when 400 people gathered at the building to sing hymns and join in prayers.

147 Vardon Drive was nearly completely demolished during a single raid in April 1941, when 18 bungalows were destroyed and a further 25 seriously damaged. A Mrs Spink, her adult son and Mr Fowler, who was the local milkman and an auxiliary fire fighter, were killed.

148   Housing in Manchester Drive and Pavilion Drive was severely damaged on 16 August 1943.

The executive committee of the Leigh Ratepayers Association decided to abandon meetings until the cessation of hostilities. Similarly, the Leigh Debating Society cancelled meetings until further notice. Wesley Church Sunday school outings were cancelled and replaced by indoor parties. Letter deliveries were reduced from four to just three deliveries a day because of reduced trains, lighting restrictions and staff shortages; deliveries were made at 6.45a.m., 9.30a.m. and 4.30p.m.

For the duration of the war, consent was given to use land adjoining the east side of Belton Way East as allotments. Allotments were also cultivated on the open land between Pall Mall and the playground of North Street School, which area is now the school playing field. As in the First World War,

the boys at North Street grew produce for the war effort and, in 1944, won the schools' gardening competition, receiving a silver cup and 40 books. The gardens are now under the swimming pool and junior hall. The council also allocated the major portion of the Manchester Drive Sports Ground for allotments, leaving just three pitches. Similarly, arrangements were made to cultivate land at Treecot Farm for the production of vegetables to supply the municipal institutions. Undeveloped plots in Thames Drive were also cultivated.

LEIGH SCHOOLS AT WAR
On 4 September 1939 the head teachers at West Leigh were informed that the schools would not re-open until shelter trench accommodation was

149 Bomb damage at Pavilion Drive.

150 The British War Relief Society would drive through the town after an air raid dispensing cups of tea from their mobile canteen.

151 Funeral of H.E. Johnson, first captain of Leigh Fire Brigade, *c.*1940. The pallbearers are members of the fire brigade, emerging from Wesley Methodist church. Behind the church's iron railings the notice board advises, 'Trust God and put a cheerful courage on'.

complete. The school re-opened for the juniors on 7 November for alternate morning and afternoon sessions and trench drill became a regular feature of school life. The juniors were taught in the infant classrooms as the junior schoolrooms had been taken over as a first-aid post, while the infants were taught in groups at private houses.

In January 1940 two classes began to be taught at St Margaret's church hall, but it was not ideal as the temperature in the hall was measured at 31 degrees fahrenheit. The logbook noted, 'The children are very cold and wearing overcoats'. Some children were transferred to North Street School, where shelters had been built in the playground, with lessons transferred there whenever the sirens sounded.

Later that year, the threat of bombing raids resulted in a general order for evacuation and, on Sunday 2 June 1940, all Southend schools were evacuated. One hundred pupils from Leigh North Street junior and 79 from the infant department were sent to New Mills in Derbyshire, while West Leigh School was evacuated to Ashbourne Rural District, also in Derbyshire. The children of Chalkwell schools were also evacuated, via two double-decker buses. Leigh North Street closed between July and December 1940 when it re-opened for one session a day under the supervision of Miss D. Nicholls.

Seven classrooms at West Leigh were available for the teaching of the few children remaining in Leigh, under the headship of Mr Morris. The civil defence authorities occupied part of the infant school building, while the health department was occupying three classrooms, a storeroom, staffroom and cloak-room in the junior building. The semi-compulsory evacuation turned Leigh into a ghost town. The congregation at Wesley Methodist church sank from 380 to fewer than 50 members.

The 1944 Education Act became operative in Leigh from 10 April 1945. On this date West Leigh became West Leigh High School, and 145 pupils from North Street who were eleven years old or over were transferred there. Previously, everyone had remained at the same school up to the age of 14 unless they passed the scholarship examination for a place at Westcliff High or Southend High schools.

VICTORY

On Wednesday 9 May 1945, two days after VE day, a thanksgiving service was held at Chalkwell Park, with an informal parade of servicemen. On 6 June 1946 at 10a.m. North Street School held a thanksgiving service followed by a Punch and Judy show. The afternoon saw sports held on the play-ground, followed by a party in each classroom. All those who were drinking at the *Peter Boat* inn that day signed their names on one of the beams to mark the end of the war.

Ten

Post-War Development

The 1946 town guide said of Leigh, 'There is a great purity of air and the prevailing breezes are bracing and invigorating'. It continued, 'Leigh is being more and more recommended by Harley Street physicians and hospital authorities as a place for recuperating tired nerves, strengthening the lungs and generally restoring a broken or debilitated constitution.' That year Southend Corporation revived discussions on the Leigh Improvement Scheme, first mooted in 1913, and approved a plan for implementing the proposals in successive stages.

On 31 July 1947 royal assent was given to the Southend-on-Sea Corporation Act, which empowered the Corporation to reclaim the Leigh Marsh lands, to use part of these lands for the extension of the promenade from Chalkwell to Leigh

Station, and to construct a harbour. The Act included undertakings for the protection of the fishing and boat building industries. Some councillors called for the demolition of the whole of the north side of Leigh High Street to accommodate two additional railway tracks and facilitate the proposed leisure developments. However, no immediate action was taken. In north Leigh development was much less controversial, with infilling of housing between Elmsleigh Drive and Eastwood Road, and along Blenheim Chase during the late 1940s.

1950s DEVELOPMENT

Residential development continued during the 1950s with housing estates built around Bellhouse Road and Orchard Grove, and council housing built south of the A127 at Kent Elms. The Fairway

152 Uncle Tommy Dixon's show was set up on the beach behind Chalkwell station. Free shows were staged during the summer in the late 1940s and early 1950s and members of the public were invited onto the stage to perform.

153 Storm-damaged houseboats, 1953. This picture was taken between Leigh station and the cockle sheds. Belton Farm can just be seen behind the undamaged houseboat.

was developed down to Woodside, and then up from Eastwood Old Road, across Belfairs Common. St Aidan's church hall was built in 1955 and served as both hall and church until the present church building was constructed in 1971. The land was one of seven sites purchased before the war by the Archdeacon of Southend in view of the expanding population. Progress Road was developed into the main industrial area of Leigh, and housing spread into Eastwood. To serve the new housing estates, the Fairway Primary School opened in September 1953, as did Blenheim Chase Primary School, built at a cost of £110,000 to accommodate 560 children.

In 1953 pupils of West Leigh High School were transferred to a new site in Herschell Road, formerly the Leigh Park Brickfields, and occupied adjoining sites as Belfairs High School for Boys and Belfairs High School for Girls. Mr G. Stockdale was appointed as the first headmaster of the boys school while Miss E. Wiseman (later Mrs Perry) became headmistress at the girls school. Nine male and five female teachers were transferred from West Leigh to Belfairs school, which adopted the double-headed eagle as their badge, once the coat of arms of Lady Olivia Sparrow. The schools closed at the end of the summer term 1985 and re-opened in September as the co-educational Belfairs County High School. St Christopher's special school opened in Eastwood Lane (now Mountdale Gardens) in 1954. Carnival Gardens was opened in Eastwood Road North in 1955, with this explanatory plaque: 'This estate was built and maintained by the voluntary efforts of the Southend-on-Sea Carnival Association. Opened 17th May 1955 by HRH Duchess of Kent.'

1953 FLOODS

On the night of Sunday 31 January 1953 exceptionally high tides linked with unfavourable winds caused the worst flooding disaster Essex had seen that century. There was no loss of life at Leigh, as at Jaywick or Canvey Island, but the town suffered damage to property and possessions and severe disruption to daily life for weeks afterwards. A flood warning was given in the early hours and residents of the Old Town moved their belongings to upstairs rooms. Water covered the living rooms to a depth unknown in any previous flood. By daylight the full severity of the situation was realised when nearby Canvey Island was seen to be completely underwater.

Hundreds of Leigh yachtsmen answered a police appeal for dinghies and small motor boats to assist in the rescue operation at Canvey. Many craft were put onto lorries and rushed there. Others were involved in rescuing 160 people cut off at Leigh Beck, the easternmost point. They brought the survivors to Bell Wharf, from where they were taken to a rest centre set up at St Clement's hall. During the rescue operations a second high tide warning was given at midday on Sunday. This tide was lower but, even so, water came up to three feet in homes in Leigh High Street. The electricity supply at the cockle sheds failed and two sewerage workers were stranded on the roof of their hut on Two Tree Island. The railway line was completely under water, and full service was not restored until 19 February.

THE FISHING INDUSTRY

Following the war, with increasing opportunities in London, the importance of the fishing industry as a local employer had continued to decline. In 1951, 52 vessels and 100 men were employed in the fishing industry. By 1952 numbers had fallen to 36 vessels and 80 men. A temporary fillip to the industry was provided in the 1950s by the discovery of whiteweed. This fern was dyed, dried and used for flower decorations and was even sent abroad for decorating coffins. 'We made so much money out of it, we called it Klondyke,' remembered retired fisherman Douglas Emery. Eventually, the whiteweed beds were exhausted. In 1970, 30 fishing vessels were operating from Leigh, employing 63 men.

154 High Street, 1950s. This lady artist is sitting where the entrance to the car park under the bridge is today. The terrace of housing on her left has, of course, been demolished.

1960S DEVELOPMENT

The 1955/6 Town Development Plan included provision for an extension of Chalkwell Esplanade to Leigh station, the road running north of the railway line. However, while carrying out improvements linked to the electrification of the railway, the British Transport Commission contributed to the cost of a large flyover bridge west of the High Street and the new road was redesigned for south of the railway.

The 1960s saw the opening of Kent Elms health centre and library in 1964 and Darlinghurst Primary School in September 1968. On 28 March 1969, Mr A.J. Frame, Her Majesty's Inspector of Fire Services, opened a new fire station on the corner of Mountdale Gardens on the site of Brickhouse Farm. During the 1970s the 'astronauts' estate was

155   View of the Old Town in the 1950s.

built at Eastwood, around a Safeway superstore, with road names such as Neil Armstrong Way and Aldrin Way.

LEIGH IMPROVEMENT SCHEME REVISITED

To reach agreement, finally, upon the Leigh Improvement Scheme, a sub-committee of the Policy and Finance Committee of Southend Council was constituted in July 1972 under the chairmanship of Alderman Alvra Scholfield, to 'examine and report upon matters affecting Old Leigh (including the Road to the West)'.

From the hundreds of letters sent in, the committee received deputations from 19 groups and individuals, including the Leigh Ward Ratepayers Association, the Chamber of Trade, the Southend

156 When Leigh Regatta was revived in 1973 by the local boy scouts, it included traditional events such as the cockle race with wooden yoke and wicker baskets.

West Young Conservatives, the Wesley Young Wives Club and the Leigh Sea Front Action Group. Each was asked whether they would still object to a road to the west through Leigh, even if it were proved essential to the borough or that Southend would stagnate without it. Although the Chamber of Trade expressed some reservations, all individuals and groups said that yes, they would oppose the new road under any circumstances. Therefore, the resulting committee report recommended that the council should abandon the proposed Road to the West scheme, stating '… we are convinced that the damage to the environment by constructing such a road outweighs any other advantage there may be to the Borough'.

A suggested alternative, that Blenheim Chase might be continued westwards through Belfairs Park to the A127, was also deemed 'wholly unacceptable'. Similarly, plans to extend Belfairs Park Drive through the woods to join up with Poors Lane in Hadleigh were abandoned. Proposals to raise the

height of the sea wall throughout the Old Town by an additional six feet were also rejected in favour of a more aesthetic improvement of the walls.

CONSERVATION AREAS

Leigh Hill was designated a conservation area and the Leigh Hill Society was inaugurated on 22 March 1973 as an amenity group to serve the interests of the Leigh Hill Conservation Area and its surroundings. Two years later members of the society amalgamated with the Leigh Sea Front Action Group to form the Leigh Society, dedicated to the preservation of the heritage of Leigh. The aims of the society are to promote a high standard of planning and architecture in Leigh and to secure the preservation, protection, development and improvement of features of historic or public interest.

It was instrumental in bringing about the restoration of the Conduit House by members of the local branch of the Royal Institute of British

157 Mike King, first Chairman of Leigh Town Council, 1996.

Architects to mark European Heritage Year, 1975. The 5ft. 6in. bluestone pillar that had been erected in 1712 to mark the head of the spring was removed from Rectory Grove and placed in the Conduit House enclosure for safe keeping.

Furthermore, the society promoted the award of conservation status to Leigh Old Town, and that part of the town south-east of St Clement's, in honour of its unique historical value. It campaigned vigorously against a proposed seaport on Maplin Sands on the basis of detriment to Leigh's fishing industry and a massive increase in traffic through Leigh. In October 1975 Southend Council voted 37 to seven against the seaport. During the 1970s Two Tree Island, which had been a rubbish tip since 1936, became Leigh National Nature Reserve, of international importance for its wildfowl.

In 1990 the eleven hectares of Belton Hills was recognised as an area of botanical and entomological importance and was designated a local nature reserve. Several rare or threatened species, including small tortoiseshell and orange-tip butterflies, six-spot burnett moths, mallow, field scabious and bithynian vetch, have all been found there.

INTO THE 21ST CENTURY

In 1996 several prominent residents agreed that, despite its growth, Leigh retained an individual identity, distinct from that of Southend, and proposed the formation of a town council. The idea caused much controversy in the town, particularly in view of an increase in rates to finance the proposition. However, the majority was found to be in favour of the move and a town council was elected in June 1996, which now boasts 16 councillors, with Geoff Fulford as Town Clerk.

Leigh looks to a future as a thriving commuter town with a busy shopping centre, but it also looks to the past with the renovation of Plumbs Cottages, the return of the Dunkirk boat the *Endeavour* to Strand Wharf, and the possible reconstruction of Juniper's Cottage. With its own town council and popular annual entertainments such as Leigh Regatta, Music Festival, Folk Festival and Art Trail, Leigh continues to defend fiercely its unique character. The railway line that changed the face of Leigh nearly 150 years ago still plays a major role in the fortunes of the town, the easy commuting distance to London continuing to attract 'those who seek ease and quiet … with ample and pleasant surroundings' (in the words of the 1913 *Town Guide*).

Select Bibliography

Allen, D.H., *Essex Quarter Sessions Order Book 1652-1661* (1974)

Benham, Hervey, *The Smugglers' Century* (1986)

Benton, P., *A History of the Rochford Hundred* (1867)

Bride, H.N., *Old Leigh* (1954)

Bundock, John, *Leigh Parish Church of St Clement* (1978)

Bundock, John F., *Old Leigh: a Pictorial History* (1978)

Copping, A.E., *Gotty and the Guv'nor* (1907)

Dilley, Roy, *The Dream Palaces of Southend* (1982)

Gaynor, Arthur J., *Almost a Century* (1993)

Harley, Robert J., *Southend-on-Sea Tramways* (1994)

Jarvis, Stan, *Smuggling in East Anglia 1700-1840* (1987)

Leather, John, *Smacks and Bawleys* (1991)

Longden, Peter, *Wesley Methodist Circuit 1897-1997* (1997)

Martin, Chris, *The Urban Development of Leigh* (undated, unpublished)

Morant, Rev. P., *The History and Antiquities of the County of Essex, Vol.I, 1763-1768* (1978)

Pewsey, Stephen, *The Book of Southend-on-Sea* (1993)

Pitt-Stanley, Sheila, *Legends of Leigh* (1989)

Reaney, P.H., *The Place Names of Essex* (1935)

Rombaut, John, *The Church of Our Lady of Lourdes and St Joseph* (1997)

Ryan, Pat, *Brick in Essex* (1999)

Sanctuary, Jim, *The Flowering of a Community* (2000)

Selby, Susan, 'Old Leigh' (1980) unpublished

Spooner, B.M. and J.P.B. Bowdrey (eds.), *Hadleigh Great Wood* (1988)

Smith, J.R., *Southend Past* (1979)

Smith, Ken, *Essex Under Arms* (1998)

Willshaw, Barbara, *From Slates to Computers* (1990)

Yearsley, Ian, *A History of Southend* (2001)

Young, John, *Fifty Years at Saint Margaret's Leigh-on-Sea* (1981)

Various issues of *Essex Countryside* magazine, the *Southend Standard* newspaper and of *Leighway*, the magazine of the Leigh Society.

Index

References which relate to illustrations only are given in **bold**.

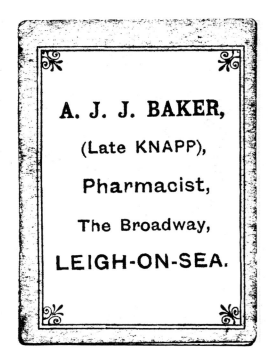